"*Penny moved!*"

"I was standing right here, Dad. You must have moved her hand yourself."

"She moved!" At the edges of Harvey's mouth appeared the beginnings of a smile.

"Dad, she didn't move! It won't help giving me false hope!"

At that moment Mary walked in, carrying what looked like the hospital's entire supply of blankets. Harvey turned and looked his wife in the eye. "Penny moved, Mary."

"She did not move!"

"Don't yell at your father, Hal! He's got to be careful with his heart." She covered Penny, checking and rechecking her hands to gauge her temperature. "Maybe you just didn't see it, Hal. I would think you would be excited at the possibility. Anyway, we ought to go; it's late. We'll be back tomorrow. Hopefully, Penny will be able to greet us. Let's go, Harvey."

For just a moment Harvey looked down and seemed surprised to find himself still clutching his daughter-in-law's hand in both of his own. He put it back at her side with unusual care and reached across the room to take his wife's. Forgetting herself, Mary smiled and accepted it, following him out of the room.

Hal watched them leave, walking down the hall side by side. It wasn't until the elevator had closed behind them that Hal realized what had been so wildly wrong.

He hadn't seen it until he watched from behind as his father kept in perfect step with his mother's long strides. His father's legs were no longer bent.

New York   London   Tokyo   Sydney

*For my husband, Jay,
whose constant love and support made
this dream a reality.*

*Special thanks to my family and friends
for their encouragement,
especially Michele and Eric Pullman
for their technical support.*

I can't thank any of you enough.

Chapter One

Penny wore her ValueBin sweat suit the morning of the day she died. She was jarred awake at five A.M. by the wails of her youngest, Benjamin, who, she thought, was most likely a bat in a former life and had carried over his nocturnal lifestyle into his present state of being. She was certain with each of her three children that whoever had come up with the expression *sleeping like a baby* had never actually spent the night with one. As of late, lullabies sounded less like songs and more like pleading.

In the six months since Benji was born, she could count on one hand the nights she had gotten more than three hours of sleep in a row. So it was no surprise to her that as she reached down to pull on her socks the floor seemed to reach right back up at her. She sat down and let the wooziness pass. The small Cape Cod rocked and swayed. It was bursting at the seams with clothes that needed to be put away and toys that accented every corner. Every day Penny promised herself it would all be cleaned, and every day she got distracted by someone needing a hug or a game that they desperately wanted to play. There barely seemed time enough to give each of the children the attention she wanted to between making, serving and cleaning up meals, much less any thought to the wash. Motherhood is an impossible job, she'd decided, and the war against the mess unwinnable. More often than not, she just gave it up and read someone a book. Benji was working himself into a hysteria that threatened to wake up Julie and Lydia, a.k.a. the Giggle Twins. She didn't think she could muster up the energy for twin four-year-olds and a colicky baby before six A.M. and got herself together to go scoop up her son.

Like a light switch, screams became smiles when Penny entered the room. He was drooling as though he had sprung a leak, and the tiniest white hint of a tooth hit the first light coming through the window.

"Ah-ha!" whispered Penny. "My nemesis shows itself." She picked up Benjamin, who squirmed with delight. "You just send that tooth back, you hear? There are another three solid months of sleep I'm supposed to have before those things grow in and wreck it all. When will I be lulled into thinking you'll sleep through the night forever?"

She nursed him sitting in the rocking chair her grandfather had carved himself during the Depression. The morning crept across the nursery and settled on the golden hairs that framed Benjamin's face. Her husband, Hal, was already at the office, and she wondered for the hundredth time if he studied their children the way she did. He looked at them, she knew, but did he count and recount their toes? Did he drink in each fleck of color in their eyes? Inside her mind she kept her own album of moments, collected at the times her heart felt most connected with her children. Penny told herself, *Remember this second forever!* but she felt like someone carrying water in the cup of her hands. Before long, her three children would be grown. She could swear the twins had just been born, and here they were already four. Next year they would be in school all day. How had that happened so fast? When the bus came to drive them to kindergarten, Penny wasn't sure how she was going to stop crying. Her friends told her she'd get used to it and would start dancing a jig at the beginning of each new school year. But Penny didn't think so.

She stopped rocking. There was a nauseousness growing in the pit of her stomach that was taking on a more serious edge. In the back of her mind she denied even a hint of a shadow of a remote possibility she could be pregnant again. She had had her tubes tied the day she delivered Benji, so sure had she and Hal been that they were a complete family. The baby factory was declared closed. Then she saw an article about a woman who had gotten pregnant on the pill, had her second eighteen months after her husband's vasectomy and had twins right after her tubal ligation. Penny felt that she had that same zany Lucy Ball kind of a life and began to worry. The baby had fallen back to sleep in time for another vicious wave of dizziness.

Food had always been her favorite cure-all and she headed into the kitchen to throw some crackers down her throat. She made it to the sink before dry heaves wracked her body. The sound her overturned stomach sent up reminded her of the twins' favorite dinosaur cartoon as she threw herself back at the sink for another round of throwing up.

"Mommy?" Julie, her soon-to-be four-year-old, stood behind her. It was six thirty. Penny felt cheated out of her usual half an hour of solitude before everyone was up, and felt guilty for feeling that way.

"Good morning, honey. It's not time to get up yet." Penny bit her tongue and tried to hold her stomach down. She turned partway to look at her daughter but remained in sink range, pasting a smile on. Two long sets of morning sickness and she was a vomit expert. She got a brief flash of understanding of why dogs crawl under porches to die.

"Mommy." Her delicate eyes were filling up. "I had a bad dream."

"Its okay, love, let me help you back to bed."

"Noooo!" Julie's bottom lip stuck out in defiance, her arms crossed in front of her chest as she had seen her mother so often do. "Mommy, you went away in my dream. I couldn't find you. You got lost." She began to cry loudly and was swiftly joined from across the house by her younger brother. No one cried alone in Benjamin's company.

Jesus, Mary and all the latter-day saints, Penny thought, *not today.* She desperately could have used one of those everybody-sleeps-so-late-I-have-to-go-in-and-check-to-see-if-they're-breathing kind of mornings.

She scooped up her daughter and held her tightly, thankful for the thousandth time that her kids couldn't read her mind. Her mother-in-law, who had raised four kids of her own, often said the only difference between a good mother and a bad mother is the good one thinks about throwing her children out of a window, but only the bad one actually does it. Penny sank into a kitchen chair and whispered into Julie's ear, assuring her that she was going nowhere, that she loved her and would always be there. She sprinkled kisses on her daughter's wet, salty cheeks and looked at the clock to start the countdown of when her husband would be home.

The flu had passed her up that year in favor of everyone else in the house, and she wondered if it was coming back to collect what it was due. At the time, Hal had said he was jealous that she wasn't so sick and that she should consider herself lucky. After changing twelve diapers, being thrown up on twice and giving three emergency baths before lunchtime, *lucky* wasn't exactly the word she'd been thinking of. She tried to keep her growling down to a minimum, but a little time on the toilet with a good book had sounded almost good. Now she wasn't so sure. Besides, mothers don't get sick days. She tossed around the idea of calling Hal. Even if he gave her a half a day in bed, she would end up spending the next six cleaning up. How is it that men know where to retrieve something but somehow don't connect that information with the idea that it also goes back to the same spot? she wondered.

It was too late to get Julie back to bed, and Benjamin howled like someone was killing him. Penny's head joined her stomach, beating in time with her son's wails. She would get through the day. Her girls were easy, good-natured, and they would help her keep Benji amused. If she could just make it to nap time, she could lie on the couch while the twins watched a movie. Julie went to wake her sister and Penny tried to get her son changed. Halfway done, she threw up into the diaper pail, holding him on the table with one hand and grounding herself to the wall with the other.

Lydia made her first appearance of the day. "Mommy, why you spittin' in Benny's garbage?"

"Mommy's belly is a little sick, honey, but it's okay."

"Is it a 'mergency? Should we go to the pee-trician?"

Penny laughed in spite of it all. "No, sweetie. Mommy's fine. Please go get dressed. You help sister and have sister help you."

"Anything we want?" Lydia's eyes got big and round. She and Julie had an eclectic taste in clothing—of the Clown University fashion department genre, as Hal put it. The twins had the ability to mix two perfectly respectable outfits and come up with something she thought of as "modern waif."

"On second thought," said Penny, "let's have pajama day."

"Pajama day?" Lydia sounded skeptical, not ready to give up the clothing free-for-all.

Penny leaned against the changing table and rested her forehead in her hand. "That's when you keep your pajamas on and watch movies all day."

Julie was standing in the doorway listening, then jumped up and down, hugging Lydia. Penny was a strict television minimalist. After an hour of PBS it was usually off for the day, the three of them reading together or making a craft. A whole-hog TV day would be quite a treat. For the second time that morning the house defied gravity and swayed softly around Penny. "Go make your first pick of the day," she said, and watched as the girls bounded down the hall, squealing with delight. She followed slowly with Benjamin gurgling in her arms and headed for the phone to call Hal for the first of many times that day.

Chapter Two

Jetta Rizone had been in the hospital just under a week and knew this would most likely be her last time there—or anywhere else, for that matter. She broke her hip trying to get the sweets her daughter hid from her in the top kitchen cabinet. A long history of diabetes and hypertension made her a terrible candidate for surgery, but the shattered bones protruding from her skin spoke otherwise. A day after being installed with a set of patented stainless steel hip rods, she showed signs of pneumonia. By day two, her kidneys had given way, crushed under the weight of a failing system. Jetta's heart was blocked almost entirely, and its inability to pump efficiently caused her body to fill with forty-five pounds of excess water.

It occurred to Jetta, as she looked up at the hospital ceiling, that she would rather have five more children than this painful chest, and she wondered if it was just that, looking back, everything gets out of perspective and somewhat softened. Her youngest son had taken her and Johnny sailing on a friend's boat when he graduated college as his thank-you gift to them. Days before the trip, the weatherman claimed in convincing tones that it would be in the nineties the whole weekend on Chesapeake Bay, so they packed tank tops and shorts and considered themselves lucky to be getting such great weather so early in the season. It was ninety all right, for the first day. Everyone got their unexposed winter skin burned and unready for the fifty-degree day that was to follow. It rained so hard the next day, they wore everything in their suitcases in bulky layers that still failed to cover their arms and legs. Raincoats stuck to their raw skin and somehow managed to make them all the more cold. Jetta went down into the galley to escape the icy rain and would be seized by nausea almost instantly. She would fly up the stairs to the deck, where her teeth would chatter as if they had a life of their own. The minute the cold would set in, she was sure that motion sickness was the way to go and headed back downstairs, only to be convinced within seconds that freezing was clearly the better choice. She wondered, if she were thrown into labor this instant, if she wouldn't be screaming for this chest thing back.

The nurses clucked to themselves when they treated her; it didn't take a brain surgeon to know a dying woman when you saw one. Doctors prescribed heart medicine, dialysis, blood pressure stabilizers and diuretics, trying to drain her body, but it resisted, filling and refilling like a self-contained Niagara Falls. Nurses' aides tried to make her as comfortable as possible, but most didn't get especially attached, as they knew it wouldn't be long.

Jetta didn't give them much trouble. She had raised seven children during an era when "Be fruitful and multiply" was a relevant, weighty doctrine. She was, after all, happy to be lying on clean sheets and have someone else cook and tidy up for her. Her late husband Johnny's pension plan from the Electric Workers Local No. 311 included hefty medical coverage for Johnny and family until well after his death, and Jetta was denied nothing.

Mostly Jetta reflected back over the last eighty-seven years. There was an ache in her, wondering what she would say when she got to heaven. There she'd be, she imagined, standing before gates so tall she couldn't see to the top, and when Saint Peter peeked through the bars, asking her if she'd earned her way in, she guessed it was anybody's bet on how it would go. The final act of contrition, which the Catholic Church said would absolve her if she said it in her last moments and was truly sorry, supposedly covered it all. It just seemed too easy, and Jetta couldn't wrap her brain around such simplicity.

The nurses changed her and hooked up her body to the various tubes and wires and fed her, but all Jetta could do was think. She weighed every piece of her life, each act, good and bad. Having seven children, the labor alone ought to get her through the door. Did it count, the nights she walked the floor, holding a head and patting a fanny, the hurts she soothed, both real and imagined? Would it be weighed in her direction the number of meals cooked, stories read, boo-boos kissed, hands held? Was there a celestial accountant tallying up good deeds done and evil brought forth? And what if there was? Did the good nullify the bad? Could the bad be erased only by direct reparation to the injured party? Another humdinger of relevant inquiry she found herself sorry she hadn't looked into before, considering all she could do now was pray for forgiveness. Even if she ventured out to make restitution to anyone she'd hurt, wouldn't it be just for earning points? Twelve years of Catholic school and six thousand masses later, she found herself wondering if there was a God at all.

What if Saint Peter asked if she'd fulfilled her life's purpose? Had she? Was her role of wife and mother her ultimate gift to the world during her lifetime? Not that it would have been a shabby contribution, but Jetta had a terrible nagging suspicion that there was something else she hadn't accomplished yet, and here it was, too late. She felt like a puzzle with one key piece missing. It made the overall picture of her life feel incomplete. Maybe everyone thought they would perform one heroic deed, one spectacular act of importance. Jetta could almost convince herself it was just her own overexaggerated ego, but her heart refused to do this. It said no, there was still something left to do. She couldn't fathom what it might be.

Priests traveled the rooms, saying Mass, giving the last rites. Jetta mostly passed, though she knew she qualified for both. It was the kneeling. A true celebration of God had always involved such a tremendous amount of kneeling. It wouldn't feel right to be just lying there. In thinking this, she realized it was no wonder she had no answers if her main definition of religion was centered around a body position.

The next time Father Connors knocked on the door with his "Communion?"—not much different than the young boys selling the paper with their "*Times?*"—she croaked out a "Yes, Father." In walked the priest, looking the part, clean and holy and eager to administer.

"Father, I don't want the communion."

"Oh, I'm sorry, am I on the wrong side?"

"No, I called you in, but I want to talk about the hereafter."

The priest glanced at her chart, noted her name and the lack of a red psychiatric flag.

Jetta was already talking. "What's going to happen to me, Father?"

"Well, Mrs. Rizone, what have your doctors said to you?"

Her breathing labored, she wheezed, "No, no. I know I'm dying and there's nothing they can do for me. I mean when I die, what's going to happen?"

"Well, if you confess your sins and have your last rites, you'll go to meet the Lord, Mrs. Rizone."

The priest blinked and hid nervous hands beneath his Bible, hands that had started to kick and flutter. He hated the hereafter questions. Who knew for sure? Of course, he wasn't at liberty to reveal that.

"What if I've been a hideous person my whole life?"

"Short of grave mortal sins, you'd be absolved in confession."

"So if I've tortured my children, beat my husband, cheated, lied, stolen and gossiped all of these years away, in a matter of minutes I can wipe the whole slate clean and die in a state of grace?"

Father Connors didn't like the direction this conversation was headed in. He had just defended the pope in 5B and it was getting on to lunch. Why couldn't anyone just take the communion anymore? Everyone needed a big explanation. He had gotten too old for a parish and, standing there that second, he wondered if he shouldn't hang up his collar entirely. He nodded silently and hoped she would fill in the gaps; most people did. It was clear to him why God rarely spoke to anyone, as most people don't really listen. He'd be on his second word to an answer to a lengthy theological question and the person would butt in and offer up his own opinion. No one cared what the Church had to say anymore. Wafts of aroma found his nose from the hospital cafeteria distracting him further from Mrs. Rizone, who was haltingly discussing something about forgiveness in wheezy rasps. Father Connors rooted around in his pocket, checking for the oatmeal raisin cookie his sister Clara had sent him on Tuesday.

He waited patiently for a pause and wondered how anyone so ill could go on so. During a particularly violent coughing spell, Father Connors interjected what he thought might wrap things up. "Mrs. Rizone, God is looking for a pure heart, not a perfect track record. If you are truly sorry for your sins, you will be at his side." He smiled broadly and as convincingly as possible with his stomach growling.

Mrs. Rizone frowned. "Father," she gasped, "I have a theory."

Oh, Lord, no, thought the priest, *anything but a theory. Why couldn't I have gone to the Little Sisters' Meditation Center and spent my retirement in quiet reflection like I wanted to? Why do you torture me so, Lord?*

Jetta Rizone spoke in breathy bursts, fighting the sea that was rising in her chest. "Of course, I can see murderers and thieves going straight to hell, Father, but I think hell can come upon a person slow and sneaky, like. One minute you're holding and loving your children, and the next you're telling them to shut up during your favorite soap opera or screaming at them to leave you alone for God's sake because you can't remember the last time you peed by yourself with the door shut. You walk down the aisle, Father, and fifty years later you're thinking about burning all of your husband's underwear because the millionth time you pick it up from the floor, you have visions of wrapping it around his throat until he turns the color of one of the Fruits of the Loom. I think hell is filled with ordinary people who made ordinary bad decisions and never went out of their way to do anything extraordinary for anyone but themselves. Or maybe with people who had some outstanding goal God wanted from them and they didn't do it. What if they didn't hear God? What if they didn't know what it was He wanted them to do? I'm so afraid I may be one of those people."

With that, Jetta Rizone's heart monitor went flat and Father Connors was whisked to the side of the room as the Code Blue team began to thump on her chest. Indignantly, he gave her last rites, then made his way down to the cafeteria, annoyed that someone who thought she had all of the answers called him into her room at all.

Chapter Three

*P*enny called International Supplies, Hal's job site for the last five years. "Hello? I would like to speak—"

"Can you hold, please?"

"No, I—"

Too late. Penny knew Betty in the office watched the blinking Hold button and filed her nails while she waited the mandatory thirty seconds the company wanted you to be on the other end, thinking how busy they were. The kitchen lights were hurting Penny's eyes and she dimmed them, pulling down some shades. A coldness crept into her and she put on another sweater even as a sheen of sweat glistened on her brow.

"International Supplies, where we can build you a new life. We're so grateful for your business. How can I direct your call?" Betty read from their call greeting card and looked at the calendar countdown of how many days were left until the computer message answered the phones and she was left to her nails in peace. She would only have to respond to "Press 0 for an operator at any time."

"I need to speak to Hal Chaney, please, it's urg—"

"Connecting to voice mail."

She got Hal's voice mail message and felt like screaming. She was going to have to be pushier if she wanted to have him paged. Hal's voice was saying, "I'm in the field right now, but I'll be happy to return your message as soon as possible. Thank you so much for calling." *Beep*.

"Hal, it's Penny. I'm sick. I've got a fever. Please call."

She hung up and tried to get some food on the table, sticking to cereal and juice. It wasn't going to be a Breakfast of Champions, strive-for-five kind of a day. The bowls were laid out and she sat down to pass out the napkins. Sweat was dripping onto the table and she stripped off the layers she had just put on.

The phone rang and Penny jumped at it so quickly, she almost lost her balance. This would be a record for Hal. Relief washed over her and she started rummaging through her phone book for the doctor's number.

"Hal!"

"Penny? It's Joan. You sound weird! I wanted to let you know our in vitro is today and I'm sooo nervous. Jack said this is our last try because it's so damn expensive, and you know the Chaney brothers: still have the first nickel they ever earned, right? So, anyway, maybe you could send us some positive energy or something, okay?"

"Sure, Joan. Listen, is Jack's mom home today, do you know?"

"No, they're up at Mt. Sinai Hospital with Jack's father: He's having his annual heart appointment. Oops, doorbell—gotta go. I'll talk to you soon. Cheer up, honey, you sound like you just lost your best friend. Laughter's the best medicine and all that. Wish me luck."

Click.

Penny started to cry. All of her in-laws were forty minutes away and they were her next hope for baby-sitting so she could get to a doctor. Her own parents had passed away, one after the other, when she was first married. They'd never even had the chance to see her children. Her other relatives were five hours north, and she kicked herself for the millionth time for moving out of her hometown.

Lydia walked in. "Mommy, the video's done and Benji just rolled over to that plant he always wants. Mommy, why are you crying?"

"I was just chopping onions, honey. Everything's okay."

"I don't want onions on my cereal, Mommy."

"Okay, love, no onions for you." She went to get her son out of the ficus plant. He was covered head to toe in dirt and she knew she didn't have the energy to give him a bath. He was brushed off and the dirt stayed in the carpet. And, for the first time in her life, she couldn't give a damn.

Penny took her temperature in the bathroom with Benji crying in her arms, and she found herself wondering who had been feeding him rocks while she wasn't looking, he seemed so heavy. He weighed in at twenty pounds at their last well-baby visit, and she couldn't understand how he could have gained so much weight so quickly. Standing on the mat, she pondered this question, finally realizing she was just too tired to hold him. The thermometer read 103 degrees and she shook it down: It couldn't be right. Penny had never had a fever over 101 her whole life. Her whole family ran only low-grade fevers even when faced with chicken pox, mumps, measles. The second reading said 103.5 and Penny watched three Benjis rolling around the bathroom floor. She needed help.

Penny located the real Benjamin after her hands had gone through two ghosts of him, and she put an arm out in front of her, trying to find which door would actually lead her into the hallway. The mother instinct inside her began a loud alarm, begging her to get the children somewhere safe, especially her son, who could not take care of himself to any degree. She put him in his bouncy seat, propped up a bottle straight from the fridge and called the girls to the table.

Penny tried Hal's office again as her children ate. Hair

hung in her face and stuck to the phone. A picture of herself electrocuted by the phone presented itself in her mind as front-page news. Each ring sounded far off, as if she were calling another country. Eleven, twelve, thirteen rings. Betty must be in the bathroom. *Ring, click* . . . "International Supplies, building America one project at a time. We've never had a call we didn't want to answer. Please leave your name and number and a convenient time to get in touch with you. After all, customer convenience is our first priority. *Beeeeep* . . ."

It was the voice of Tom Carlson, Hal's boss, and, judging by the beeps, they hadn't checked their messages in a week, customer convenience be damned. The truth was, they had so much business, they just couldn't do it all. Putting people first had opened a floodgate of referrals, and Hal had said they were turning into everyone else, greedily starting a great number of projects and having trouble fulfilling their end of the contracts. Hal was most likely overseeing a half dozen work sites spread throughout the county.

"Betty, this is Hal's wife, Penny. Please pick up if you're there. It's an emergency. I'm very sick. I need Hal right away. Please pick up, someone. Please. Hello? This is Penny, Hal's—"

Tom Carlson cut the message off mid-sentence but left the phone in its cradle. Hal was indeed out in the field and the weather bureau was calling for heavy thunderstorms tonight. He was looking to quiet some bristly customers sick of looking at half-finished homes before the rains came. No housewife with a headache was going to slow down what he hoped would be a very productive day.

Penny held on to her kitchen table, trying to steady herself and the sickly swaying scene around her. Julie was watching closely, not eating much. "Mommy, why you drippin' on the table? You need my napkin, Mommy?"

Lydia looked up and mirrored the worry in her sister's face with her own.

"Mommy's going to take an aspirin and I'm sure I'll feel much better," Penny said. She tried desperately to smile and knew these two would see right through her. Benji started to cry. His bottle fell onto the floor and was making a cloudy puddle on the tiles.

Lydia turned to him. "Benny, Mommy's sick, you have to be nice today."

Julie had already hopped down and was holding the bottle in his hungry mouth, her own breakfast half eaten and forgotten. She had her tiny hand on top of his head, rubbing the downy tufts of his hair just as Penny did. Penny watched numbly as her four-year-old put her infant to sleep. All she wanted to do was put her head on the table and sob, half out of the fever turning her insides around and half for the flood of love she had for her gentle children.

"You two are just the perfect sisters." Penny focused on keeping her voice steady, trying to put a lid on the fear that was growing inside of her like a fungus. The girls smiled and came to her, sitting on her lap. "I love you both so much. Why don't you go into the playroom so Benji can finish his catnap?" she whispered, and ushered them out of the room, giving each a kiss.

She watched them sit in front of their play castle, ignoring the running television, taking up the characters and making voices for each. Blackness was spreading into the edges of her field of vision. Tiny black dots danced, coming together and spreading apart, threatening to take her over. *I'm not even going to make it to lunch*, thought Penny. She'd never been this sick and realized she would have to be much more aggressive in getting herself help. Hal and Penny had an agreement that she would only call him on his cell phone for dire emergencies. Up until this moment they had never had one. If there was a desperate need for diapers or milk, Penny just left a message on his voice mail and knew Hal would take care of it. Hal had also been good at giving her a call once a day just to see how things were going, but his job in the last few months had been crazy, and the calls had dwindled down to two or three times a week. She didn't think there was time to wait for him. Clearly this was an emergency. Their address book was filled with bits and pieces of paper and business cards embedded in almost every letter, and Penny desperately looked for Hal's cell phone number, which she had written on the back of a coupon.

"I think it's orange," she mumbled, trying to ignore the grayness the room seemed to be collecting in its corners and the strange sound her voice had taken on. "Come on! *Where are you?* I'm going to die in the middle of my kitchen with no help all because I haven't organized my phone book?" A giggle escaped her, and Penny didn't like how nervous it sounded. It was the giggle that used to betray her as a child when her mother accused her of something.

"Penelope Ann, did you go through my jewelry box?"

"Of course not!" Giggle. It was the sound of someone caught and scared but trying to sound nonchalant. Hal. Why wasn't Hal home yet? *Oh God, I'm not thinking straight. It's only 9:15.* The idea of calling an ambulance danced around in her head just as the coupon for Sal's Bird Land with Hal's cell phone number slipped out of her book and landed in front of her. She thought she might have to bronze it when this was all over. Tremendous hope washed away some of the fuzziness fogging up her thoughts, and she listened to the rings with her head on the table and the phone perched on top of her upward ear, like a bird nesting.

It rang. And rang. And rang.

The phone picked up and Penny started shouting into the receiver, unable to hold herself together at the sound of help. *"Hal, I'm sick! Come home! I need to get to an emerg—"*

Her lips moved and her words continued very much on their own accord, but Penny heard, despite herself, what came out of the phone.

"—caller is not in your service area at this time. Please hang up and try your call again later."

It repeated itself twice and disconnected with a monotonous beep, ending just as Benjamin's crying began again. Penny heard neither as she slid down the side of the table and onto the floor with a thud.

Chapter Four

Southlawn Hospital was bursting at the seams that day. The time clock was a one-way ticket in with no hope of punching out. Residents were murmuring snide Roach Motel comments, and nurses were making nervous jokes about full moons and Fridays. Cots had been set up in every hallway, and patients had begun diagnosing each other. Anyone who wasn't bleeding profusely or unconscious was sent out to other area hospitals until new arrivals started angrily explaining that they had just been sent from that very hospital.

Jetta watched this flurry of activity from way above as her body was wheeled down the corridor. She had a view of herself, though her features were blocked by a doctor who straddled the gurney, administering CPR to her stopped heart as she was brought to the intensive care unit.

Jetta knew she was dead the way she knew in the summer of 1957 she had been stung by a bee. Their screened-in porch had always been her favorite place to drink in a summer storm, and she loved to sit in the early dark of the morning, alone with the rain. That year a particularly nasty group of wood bees tried to claim her spot and gave her notice with a small but noteworthy collection of stings on her foot. It was still dark and she hadn't seen or even heard them, but the moment they struck she had an instantaneous understanding of what had happened to her. Johnny ran down the stairs, bat in one hand and boxer shorts on backward. Half the babies started to cry.

"What's the matter? What happened?"

"I've been stung by some bees!" She had started to cry herself, which always threw Johnny off his game. He had a habit of getting angry when she dared to let herself, the woman he loved, get hurt.

"What'd you go and do that for?"

"I didn't exactly climb up a tree and stick my foot in a hive, John. I was just sitting here."

"At least put a light on, Jetta, it's pitch dark. How do you even know it was a bee?"

That's when one stung Johnny. "He got me!" His screams could be heard down the block. Jetta laughed so hard, it took another bee sting on her fanny to get her to shoo them both back in the house to nurse each other.

"I don't think you got stung," she teased him all the way to the bathroom. "After all, it was so dark, how can you be sure?"

"Very funny, Jetta."

But that was the thing. It was so striking to her at the time that she had never experienced a sting before, yet it was so clear without even seeing the bee what was happening.

It had also been that way with her first child. As she floated along, a scene of her in bed next to John enveloped her and she went with it.

A much younger Jetta nudged her then strong husband. "Johnny, the baby's coming."

"It's three A.M., Jetta." He snored.

"John!" She turned on the light.

"Jetta, you're killing me here. I gotta be up in a few hours."

"John, the baby is coming."

He opened an eye. "Are you in pain?"

"Not really; I just know it's time."

"It's probably just gas, honey. The baby's not even due yet. Call the doctor." He was sleeping before she even picked up the phone, only to get the medical version of her husband's message.

"I'm driving to the hospital and delivering the baby myself, I suppose, whether you or my husband is there!" she had yelled at the doctor before hanging up on him.

John did drive her and the doctor did meet her, because she sounded hysterical enough to be having a baby, if not in enough pain, and she had John Jr. twenty minutes after they arrived. Johnny cried like a baby himself when he met his son, and had to endure years of "It's probably just gas" from Jetta whenever he doubted her.

Death was just as clear. One minute she felt as though she were below a thousand bricks crushing upon her chest, and the next she was above, watching a young man working on her old body, and she didn't need to see the bee to know this was the final sting. The gurney rolled and Jetta felt herself being pulled along with it, like a balloon on the sheerest of threads. Staying with her body, she watched as the outcome of what she thought to be her last moments unfolded, but as she moved forward she also passed through all of the events of her life. She tasted her first wine, looked into the eyes of the first man who said he loved her. Her children rolled within her womb, each in turn, then took their steps, spoke their first words, had their tumbles, held her hand. She wept heartily as the school bus took them one by one off to kindergarten, and her heart broke all over again as they drove off to college. The funeral procession for each of her parents passed through her, and she stood at the graves of everyone she had ever loved and had to say good-bye to. There were a million achievements and perhaps even more failures; each lived in its entirety within the time frame of each fraction of an inch traveled toward the intensive care unit. Being both an onlooker in the real time she had lived in for eighty years and a traveler of the space occupied by each of her life's events seemed almost commonplace, so easily did her spirit allow her to be with each.

She watched herself with an objectivity never before possible, seeing the terrible mistakes she made and the tragedies that had happened and how each had altered her course. Sometimes she learned and sometimes she hadn't. She saw how very, very beautiful she had been, and what a pity it was that she never felt that way, either inside or out. Because now she could see the effect she had on others. She saw into the hearts of her children and the love they had for her. It was astounding. Something as small as an ice cream cone given up when theirs had fallen had been much more important than she could have guessed. The times she choked back a scream and used kind words instead had planted seeds of patience in each of them. She had always assumed that they could somehow read her mind and know when her heart wasn't in it. They just knew she was there. A string of adolescent events flew by her, and instead of the pain she thought was most prevalent for her kids, she saw herself next to them and understood their knowledge that she and Johnny would always be there. It had made things easier. How long had she struggled, thinking she had not made an impact on the world?

There was one last memory she watched. At an unfamiliar place, with people she didn't recognize, it was the only "bubble" of time she didn't know the intimate details of or the ending to. It was a powerful and disturbing vignette, and only as she finally floated away from it did Jetta realize it was time she hadn't yet lived, the true heroic purpose of her life. It was exactly what she had been born to do. She wondered why she hadn't been able to fulfill this destiny, but she let it go as she became detached from her physical body. A piece of her felt relief at not living out what looked like a frightening, bloody scene. She floated easily away from the gurney, lingering again within each of her other moments, savoring before departing.

Jetta watched her body being lifted onto the stark white hospital bed. Nurses shifted back and forth, calling various machines into service. It seemed as though they crudely tethered her body with tubes and wires just as her soul had been attached, though more eloquently. When the last attendant stepped out of her door in that noisy room, Jetta felt a last release. Doctors stormed back to her side and there was tremendous noise, but Jetta almost smiled. She knew it was no use. When the water sac breaks inside a mother's womb, there is a gentle explosion and no turning back. She glided, leaving each of her memories behind. The hospital room was no longer in her sight, only the journey ahead.

In the next moment Jetta hit the wall. There was an electric shock and she felt confusion. All around her there was nothingness. She was expecting the usual white light, a tunnel, angels. Maybe God Himself would be too much to ask—but nothing? Jetta was surprised her Johnny wasn't already with her. Was her assessment of the value of her life too generous? She tried to keep herself from panicking, but there was already an air of chaos all around her: She could feel it like a needle piercing her skin. Seeing nothing, she tried to pick a way to go and felt drawn to a direction. It was a long time before she saw a group of people in the distance. Jetta was relieved, assuming it was her welcoming party, and looked forward to seeing everyone she knew who had passed. There seemed to be thousands. What a joy it would be to have her John again. Reluctantly she admitted to herself that even more than Johnny, she wanted to hold the children she had lost. There were two whom she had still birthed and one, her fragile Emmaline, whom measles had taken. She wanted to squeeze her and kiss her and say how sorry she was that she had somehow failed to be the protective mother a world with advanced medicine and immunization would later have let her be. And that there were rarely two days strung together that she hadn't thought of her, even after fifty-some years. Jetta approached slowly, but the thought of Emmaline sent her running, propelling herself forward in a way she couldn't comprehend. Would she still be a tiny two-year-old with gentle curls and a breathy giggle? Who had taken care of her? She started to scream, "Emmaline, Emma, Mommy is here! I'm here, baby!"

Just as Jetta was close enough to make out the individual faces of the people, her yells died in her throat. They were all strangers. She recognized no one and couldn't get anyone to speak or even look at her. Their faces were turned with a vigorous concentration toward something at the front of the group, which she could not make out. They moved toward it with a constant writhing and squirming motion that made Jetta deeply afraid. Something was terribly wrong.

Chapter Five

Lydia and Julie played with their castle in the playroom, doling out characters and fighting over roles. Enemies were crushed, extravagant balls were held and dragons were befriended. Each had periodically stopped and listened to their brother's fussing, anxious that he should be crying for so long. They had a sense that they should stay out of their mother's way, yet there was also a pull inside of them to help her. Their games led them to just outside the threshold to the kitchen and back to the playroom.

"Lydia, why is Benny still crying?" She held a play dragon and tugged its tail.

"Mommy says he's teefing. His teefs are poking through and hurtin' his whole head."

Julie was sufficiently impressed. "But Mommy's not singing to him. She sings when he cries."

"Maybe she's whisperin' singing."

"I'm goin' to see." Julie marched into the kitchen with Lydia at her heels.

"Lydie," Julie whispered, and reached for her twin's hand. "Mommy's sleepin' on the floor. Why's Mommy sleepin' on the floor?"

Lydia's thumb found its way into her mouth. They went to their mother, kneeling down and touching her with a poke.

"Momma . . ."

Lydia whispered and picked up Penny's hand. "Mommy, wake up Mommy."

"Mommy, it's Julie. Benji needs you, he's crying. Nap time is over."

Lydia shook Penny's shoulder back and forth and her voice rose with her fear. "Mommy, wake up!"

"Lydia, we got to get help. We need help, Lydie."

Tears streamed down their faces and the panic that plagued their mother that morning began to prey on them.

"Lydia, we got to call the 'mergency number. We got to call the nine and the ones."

Lydia heard her sister but had already found her role. She retrieved her brother's bottle and was feeding him. When she got it propped up, she dragged his seat next to their mother on the floor. She crawled under her mother's heavy arm and nuzzled up close to her.

"I'm keepin' Mommy company, Julie. She needs me. I'll be with her. You get help, Julie." Lydia sucked her thumb with a brutal intensity and closed her eyes.

Julie's own terror found its way out in motion. She had to find the phone. That's how you get help. That's what Mommy said. But the phone wasn't in its cradle and the room suddenly felt bigger and somehow foreign. Penny carried the phone everywhere with her, and Julie couldn't remember where she'd seen it last. In her confusion she went through the house, tripping on toys and running in and out of rooms.

Everything was in its place; she could see the cookies her mother baked just yesterday in the glass pumpkin cookie jar they bought last Halloween. There were the marks on the kitchen door that showed how tall they were and how small they'd been. It was all there yet it was all wrong now. A picture of last Christmas's art project in preschool swam in front of her. They had gotten paper candy canes with fire-truck–red stripes to be glued on. Julie used the glue stick from the teacher's desk instead of the sticky white paste given to the children to spread on with their fingers. Julie liked feeling above the other children, not putting her hands into the messy pot. She was a lady. Her mother always glowed over what a grown-up girl she was. But when she got home, the thin glue from the stick couldn't hold the heavy construction paper. The stripes had fallen off, leaving her with a plain white cane.

Julie understood now why Benji cried so terribly when Daddy was left to care for them. He did everything Mommy told him to do, rocking and patting, feeding and changing, but she could see now that Mommy was the glue. And without her, even the pictures nailed to the wall seemed horribly out of place.

The rooms were searched on the eye level of just over forty inches, Julie now racing haphazardly between her own landmarks in the house, the toy box, the potty, the television cabinet, the snack shelf. A sense of disbelief began to encircle her, choke her. The phone was nowhere.

"I get that phone, I get that phone," she murmured, holding herself above her fear the way she kept herself afloat at the beach, holding on to her mother's side.

Throughout the house, Julie glanced out of the windows she passed, wondering if there was anyone on the block who could help them, who would hear her if she screamed. When the Chaneys first moved to this block, they had done so for the closeness a development of houses brings. They had seen bigger homes for less money out in more remote areas of the county. Penny didn't want to live where she couldn't borrow an egg or a cup of sugar from a neighbor. She was very much hoping for friends. Their first weeks there she had spent hours with the babies in their ridiculous triple stroller, a spectacle difficult to miss, trolling the neighborhood for potential playmates. After the first month Penny began thinking of it more as a search for signs of life. Huge wooden swing sets with matching heavy canvas tents adorned the yards, keeping watch above inground swimming pools, animal-shaped sandboxes and more toys with wheels than a person could shake a stick at. Yet, Penny couldn't catch anyone actually using any of these items. She would return home, discouraged, and tell Hal she was sure some biological war had been fought in the neighborhood and that only their family had managed not to succumb. It was the need for a two-income family these days, Hal said. Penny didn't understand why anyone would put their kids in day care so they could go to work to buy them things they couldn't use because they were in day care. Hal insisted it was more complicated than that. Penny tried to be compassionate, but mostly she was just lonely, especially those first few months. She had a secret desire to break into those quiet houses and live in a different one each day, as if the houses themselves, in being used, would somehow bring the neighborhood back to life. Instead, Penny walked past the trimmed hedges and professionally manicured lawns, pushing her children until they could walk through the quietness on their own two feet. And she learned to enjoy the scattered few who were home, mostly retirees who worked in their gardens, giving her their extra tomatoes and advice on the latest weekly grocery sales before heading off to the senior center or their own children's homes.

It was no surprise, then, that Julie expected nothing when she glanced out of the window onto the block and could very well imagine screaming for hours with no hope of anyone coming to her aid. In the back of her mind Julie listened instead to her own house. Benji had fallen back asleep, comforted by his sister and weighted with the exhaustion of a morning spent crying. Lydia sat encircled by the heavy limbs of her mother, waiting for a movement that didn't come. The quieter the house grew, the more frightened Julie became. She was emptying drawers she knew the phone couldn't possibly be in, and she understood the emergency plan her mother had taught her wasn't going to work. There was crying somewhere in the house again, a desperate keening wail that echoed around the tiny rooms and shook the plates in the living room hutch. As each drawer revealed more nothing, the cry became a scream and Julie was shocked to hear it was her own.

"Help! Help!" escaped from her small body in tidal waves as she made her way back into the kitchen.

The stillness of the scene around the table almost broke her. She wanted to be Lydia; she longed to have her mother's arm wrapped around her. She, too, could sit quietly and wait, guarding her mother with her presence. She wanted to sleep. It made her furious to be the one to solve this problem. It was too big. She was just too little. And, like anyone put under enough pressure, she snapped. Julie Chaney threw herself at her mother's rigid body, shaking it back and forth with all of the might of her thirty-five-pound body.

"Mommy, you didn't teach me 'nuff! Where is the phone? You didn't say no phone! How can I call help? *Get up! Get up right now, Mommy!*"

As she shook her mother back and forth she saw under her side the smallest bit of the phone's plastic antenna innocently poking out as if it had been waiting there for her. Julie's tiny face was framed with beautiful brown wet ringlets stuck along her forehead. Relief brought the color back to her round cheeks.

"Lydie, you gots to move. Mommy's sleepin' on the phone!"

Lydia sat staring at Benjamin, her lips slack over a glistening thumb.

"Lydie, I can't move you and Mommy. Please, Lydie, we need that phone!"

No one moved. Julie started to cry again. She placed one foot on her twin sister's bottom and another on her mother's side and held on to the phone antenna. She tried wiggling it free, but it was in too tight. Tugging at it did her no good. One big pull was all she had left, and she thought that if she couldn't get the phone, she would take up watch under her mother's other arm for sure. She wrinkled her face into a tight ball of determination as she gave a count the way her father did just before he lifted her off of the ground and into the air.

"*One . . . two . . . fwee!*" and she jerked her whole body. To her surprise, the phone broke free and sent her flying backward through the kitchen and slamming onto the linoleum floor in what her mother would have called a trip. "Had a nice trip, Julie? Go to France next time!"

Julie picked herself up, holding the back of her head, feeling the throbbing there that was the beginning of an egg. An ordinary fall on the sidewalk seemed like a treat, and she wished her mother were consoling her or running to the freezer for the Boo-Boo bear. Nevertheless, she had gotten the phone and was going to save her mother! She almost had help! Everyone would know. Grandma Ellie would probably let her have Mr. Peepers the cat all to herself the next visit. "Let Julie have that cat. She's the brave one that saved her Mama, you know." Daddy might take them all out for ice cream sundaes in her honor. He would hold his up and say, "Here's to my brave girl, Julie!" and they would clap. She would be a hero. Most of all, Mommy would get better.

Then she spotted the phone at the far end of the floor. It had taken its own trip and lay in the corner as silently as Penny, its frame and innards now two separate entities.

"Nooooooo!" Julie fumbled with the wires and buttons, pushing them into the plastic frame again and again, only to have them pop out. Nothing fit together. The red Power button had broken and lay next to the step stool by the pantry. Julie stopped crying and in violent frustration picked up the phone and threw it at the bay window that held Penny's prizewinning African violets. Five feet of glass showered the front lawn.

Chapter Six

Hal was overseeing the building of a six-bedroom colonial. He watched the early spring rain, which wasn't supposed to arrive for hours, pour into the hole that would become the foundation. Today it was just a giant mud puddle. Hal fought the weather over two counties, scrambling to put up tarps and gather tools at all of his various homes in progress. He had been playing his own frustrating game of phone tag, leaving Tom Carlson message after message, trying to get him out in the field to help. The impossible deadlines and overbooking were taking their toll on all of their employees, and Hal thought it was finally wearing him down. A mountain of paperwork waited for him back at the office, but as Hal's truck came upon the fork in the highway instead of going on to the next job, he took the road that led him home.

A nagging sensation lingered in him throughout the morning, as if he had forgotten something or had done something wrong that needed to be repaired. It was the feeling he swallowed when he forgot an occasion or didn't rave over a new dish of Penny's. The month ticked through his mind as he tried to recollect birthdays and anniversaries. He wondered why men were always in trouble with their wives, and felt certain there would be significantly less divorce if there were no holidays at all. The center of town flew past and with it a last opportunity to bring home flowers, as well as the hope Penny would tip him off to the event without his having to admit he'd forgotten whatever it was. *Better not to have the flowers*, he justified. *Penny always sees right through me anyway and gets twice as mad.* As he pulled into his driveway Hal debated with himself on the pros and cons of showing up empty-handed when he was absolutely positive he had forgotten something terribly important, and was just about to turn around and head back to town. He threw the truck into reverse but spotted the widow Mrs. Greavesly, his seventy-five-year-old next-door neighbor, peering through the bay window at the front of his house.

Hal's first reaction followed closely his feelings about holidays. He was just pissed off. *The nerve of her*, he thought, *looking so boldly through my window—in the rain no less! As if she doesn't spend enough time peering through the bushes.* Penny and he had often joked about putting a chair in front of that very window for her.

He parked the truck halfway across the lawn, ready to throw Mrs. Greavesly over the hedges, the clumsy part of his brain eager to focus on something other than the feeling of dread it had been laboring under. The more insightful, subconscious part of him, however, was warning him loudly, pointing out the triangular shards of glass skirting his little ranch. It noticed the milling of what seemed like dozens of neighbors in his kitchen through the open window and the steady wrenching cries that he could pick out as his Julie's. He sped up to Mrs. Greavesly, finger in the air, ready to make several points about privacy and neighborliness. He called her name and demanded her attention, which couldn't be had as she focused so intently on the innards of his home, and he couldn't bring himself to look until she finally turned to him saying something that he couldn't understand. She reached out for him, her tiny shrunken body guiding his six-foot frame toward his front door.

Neighbors led him over the threshold and buoyed him down the hall toward the kitchen with helpful tugs. The sheer number of people in his home amazed him. He couldn't remember seeing this many out on a sunny weekend, much less in his own home. They spoke with the same pattern as the widow and he realized he was panicking. He nodded and moved along, wondering who was hurt, trying to calm himself down, trying to breathe, but the rain must have been stuck in his throat because he couldn't get control of himself. In college physics Hal had learned about Einstein's theories of time and its flexibility within the microcosm of a moment. He thought the theories didn't make sense to anyone because they were just wrong. How could something virtually no one could understand be correct? He studied with the intent of just passing another course. Yet, here he stood, a decade later, and he was sure he was encased in that very dynamic snapshot in time Einstein spoke of that refused to behave itself, and his epiphany told him it was all relative to his panic. Things moved so slowly and so much action competed to be held in that moment, Hal was sure he could feel his mind bending, unable to comprehend any of it at all.

It was so bright in the kitchen, he almost didn't see her lying there. She was out of place, as though on his daughters' favorite show when you see three boxes that go together and one that doesn't belong. The song turned on in his head and he found it almost welcome. If he could play it over and over, perhaps the three other boxes of his wife in various everyday settings around their house would just reappear, the most likely box overtaking the other three and filling their life screen again. He wished it were a holiday—an anniversary, even.

Their neighbor, Janis Mitchell, was holding Benji in a corner by the refrigerator, swaying back and forth mindlessly as all women do when handed a baby. He recalled Penny commenting on becoming a psychobiologist just to study the instinctual sway factor in maternal and nonmaternal women alike. Another neighbor, Georgia Mullen, tried to extract Lydia from under Penny's arm. Lydia was missing a shoe and Georgia was wearing pajamas. The number of bizarre details seemed endless. Julie had somehow appeared at his leg. Someone was pulling her off of him, and his hand, he saw, was holding her there for the instant before she was scooped away.

His wife. Dana Levin, from the blue bi-level across the street, cradled his beautiful wife's head in her lap. He had never more than waved to her the whole time they'd lived across from one another, and here she was on his floor, holding his wife. Penny was terribly, terribly still. Rain poured in through the window, and he felt he should run out now and cover it with plastic and duct tape, because that's what men do: They fix things and work. They don't come home to find their wives motionless on the floor with their heads in other people's laps. He noticed he was crying.

Hal couldn't move beyond any of these observations and stayed stuck on the first square of linoleum that offered him a glimpse of his wife. He was saying something he couldn't even make out himself, his voice rising rapidly with greater and greater volume until another one of his neighbors, whose name he didn't know, moved over and gently shook him, apologizing as he rattled Hal around. Things began to move at a much more manageable pace again and his thoughts came back into focus.

Hal nodded, mopping his face on his sleeve. "Is she . . . ?" He wouldn't even say it and he was ashamed that he couldn't go to her until he knew. The neighbors stared and Hal stayed on that same safe square of linoleum, watching them shrug their shoulders and pat her limp hand. Mrs. Greavesly quietly joined them in the kitchen, and Hal saw her open the cabinet under their sink and pull out a bottle of ammonia. She went to his wife and passed the bottle under her nose. Penny's eyes flew open with a start that knocked everyone in the room back a foot.

"Penny!"

Everyone was yelling and there were looks of relief, which reverted quickly to fear as they reassessed the situation.

"Has anyone called for an ambulance?" Hal was looking at the sweat pouring off of Penny's pasty-white face. She said nothing, but he thought her eyes were pleading with him for help. He had to do something before his panic seized him again. He was sure he could hold it off as long as she was alive.

Janis Mitchell stepped forward. "We just called as you were pulling in. They should be here by now." But there were no sirens in the distance. Hal finally went to her. He told himself again that as long as he had her, he could keep himself together.

"Penny, did you fall?" He knelt down but didn't want to move her if she had hurt her back. Penny shook her head ever so slightly.

"Do you know what happened to you, Pen?"

A "No" croaked out of her that sounded so unlike his wife it threatened to pull Hal under.

"Can someone open the door?" Hal scooped his wife into his arms and carried her over the threshold into the driving rain. "I'm taking her to the hospital myself. She can't wait. Will someone stay with the children?"

There were many nods, which Hal didn't see. He was already in his truck with his limp wife next to him, tearing down the road toward the emergency room. When Hal looked back later on their ride, he had to admit that he couldn't remember any of the streets he drove on. He tried to recall the windshield wipers, which must have been fighting a losing battle against the storm they tore through, or the flooding on the bridges they went across. Maybe he was on mental autopilot—he would have even believed the truck drove itself—but either way Hal only remembered working to keep his wife alive.

Hal thought that if he could keep her talking, he could keep her conscious. "Penny, did this happen all of the sudden?"

Penny's voice was so low, Hal had to strain to hear her. At one point he tried slowing the wipers, but the road became lost under all of the rain. Hal had to settle for shouting himself to somehow make up for her whispers.

"I was feeling sick."

"Why didn't you call?"

Penny thought her brain might seize up trying to decide between laughing and crying. "Hal, I tried to . . ." She faded and Hal grabbed her arm, giving her small shakes.

"Penny, stay with me! You have to be able to tell the doctors what's going on, honey."

"Hal, did you hear that?"

"What? That's just the storm."

"No, Hal. I just heard a voice. It was a woman."

"Penny, it's the rain. It's coming down in buckets."

"She called my name."

"Penny, it's the fever. Try to focus on my voice. I'll turn on the air; maybe it'll clear your head."

"There it is again, Hal. Clear as day: 'Penny!'" Then she added as an afterthought, "I think she knows me."

The chill that ran down Hal's spine was so icy, he thought for a second the rain had found its way into the cab of the truck.

Penny's Gift

"Penny, please! Should I put on some music? You need to be awake, Pen. I've heard that if you've hit your head you should stay conscious, and since we're not sure what's happening with you, you should do whatever you can to be awake."

Hal heard himself babbling on and on and felt himself slowly becoming unhinged again. The Southlawn Minimarket blinked at him, advertising a two-for-one hot dog special, and Hal knew he was only a few miles away. He cursed at himself for living so far from the hospital; he cursed Penny in his mind for letting herself get sick, and took it back quickly, knowing he was just angry that he wasn't sure he would get them there in time. He was furious he hadn't done anything special for her lately. They hadn't been intimate since Benji was born, and what if she died not knowing how much he loved her? He felt her hand go slack in his.

"Penny!"

"It's okay, Hal. She's with me now. I can see her."

"No! No, Penny, don't look! Don't look at her!"

The truck skidded out along the muddy road and Hal almost lost control.

"She's beautiful. Her light is in my eyes. She wants me to go there, Hal."

"*Nooo!* Penny, I . . . I forbid you!"

He couldn't tell if it was the fever in her cheeks flushing her face red or the glistening of the tears that were streaming from her eyes or his own, but Penny seemed to be glowing, and Hal felt he was losing.

"Penny, think of the children. Julie! Lydia! Benjamin! Penny, I can't raise them alone."

"It's my grandmother, Hal. It's Nana."

Penny's lips quivered and then found their way into a gentle smile. Her eyes rolled back into her head and Hal heard the click of the seat belt catching her slack body.

His arm shot out, straightening her up, trying to hold her, trying to keep her.

"Penny! Penny!" Hal's face contorted with a terrible grimace and he wept as he begged her.

"Please, Penny, I love you, I need you."

The smallest of movements came through her body, a shudder of a breath, and he strained to feel another, which did not come.

From the window of the emergency room booth the security guard watched them drive in and hoped they would be moving on to the main entrance of Southlawn Hospital. It was only two o'clock and he was looking down the barrel of ten more hours of duty. The idea of being soaking wet at the outset made him scowl. Typical of a stormy day, any number of loons would be driving up to his door, expecting him to hold their hands all the way to the check-in desk. Sam had been working this job for thirty years and, having seen it all, couldn't count the number of non-urgent situations he had to escort through the doors, embarrassed to even be standing next to the people. He remembered a man with a sprained pinkie, no insurance as it turned out, who showed up in the middle of a blizzard. Sam wanted to break the guy's arm just so he'd have a real emergency. It reminded him of being a little boy and his mother saying, "I'll give you something to cry about."

The newspaper had been reporting a proposed change in legislation whereby if you sued someone and lost, you'd have to pay for the cost of the other guy's lawyer. Sam thought the emergency room ought to work the same way. Come in with a stupid complaint, leave with a compound fracture instead—that was *his* philosophy.

Sam had a cup of coffee on his way in and cursed as he looked over his shoulder at the men's room. His prostate had him peeing like a pregnant woman, and he couldn't wait to get the damn thing out. It was declared cancerous a year ago, and he'd gone both the medication and the radioactive implant route, but it was proving stubborn. Lately he was up around the clock, passing his three dribbles of piss before flopping back into bed to watch the ceiling. As soon as this truck went by he would duck into the bathroom.

He watched it pull into the ambulance chute and rolled his eyes. Probably someone with a torn fingernail. Sam pictured himself screaming down the hall for the emergency manicurist and laughed at his own joke. His smile fell off sharply, though, when he saw the man get out of his truck. Sam was a man's man and something inside of him innately flinched as he looked at Hal's face. Even through the pouring rain he could see Hal had been crying, and Sam wanted to give him an elbow to the ribs and say, "Buck up, man." He had seen thousands of parents send their calm children into a frenzy by getting hysterical. Honestly, he thought parents shouldn't even be allowed into the hospital. The kids did better without them. But that thought soon dissolved when he saw Hal pull Penny out of the passenger side. The color of her face alone reminded Sam why he just guarded the door and didn't work inside. He knew what death looked like.

He grabbed the intercom and sent his voice howling up and down the emergency ward. "*Code Blue! Code Blue to the emergency bay! No medical personnel on-site! Code Blue to the emergency Bay!*"

He could already hear the thunder of feet and the scrambling of wheels approach him from behind as he turned his attention to Hal.

"Leave your keys in your car, sir!"

Hal looked up, and Sam saw he was not registering anything at all except getting that woman into the E.R.

He went to Hal, patting him down as he ran, looking for his keys to move his car in case another emergency should show up by ambulance. Judging by how fast this one came in and the standing-room-only in the hallways, it was going to be a long day indeed.

"My wife . . ."

"It's okay, pal. I'm just gonna move your car."

"My wife . . ."

"They're coming. Keep running, man." And as an afterthought, as he stood in the rain next to Hal's truck, Sam whispered, "Good luck."

The medical team met them at the door. Penny was laid out on a stretcher, collared, assessed and in resuscitation attempts before Hal could answer even one question. A rolling cart carried his wife and he watched them pound on her chest and force air into her lungs. The storm outside had followed him in, manifesting itself in showers of doctors and nurses.

Chapter Seven

Hal thought they should call Code Blue what it was. It fooled no one trying to cover the potential loss of a patient in hospital jargon. If the screaming sirens and beeping machines didn't give it away, surely the stampede of the entire staff converging on one room would. Visitors and relatives stiffened when the code was blasted through the intercom system. Hal could almost see the hair on the back of their necks stand up and watched as they fell all over each other to scurry back to their loved one, reassuring themselves it wasn't one of their own. Even the janitor, whistling a soulful Billie Holiday tune under the sound of his mop, skipped a beat and turned toward the commotion.

As his wife "coded" twice, Hal found himself washed aside in a sea of stethoscopes and sucked down into the undertow of helplessness and anger. It would have been entirely more honest if he could hear "Penelope Chaney dying in curtain area three." Perhaps he could better accept what was happening and feel that they were there helping the woman he loved and not just a case to be worked on, charted and sent off. He overheard the nurses refer to her as "the virus coma." They transferred her to the intensive care unit, where she was placed between the "broken-hip pneumonia" and the "diabetic enlarged heart."

Hal was terrible at waiting. He rushed in for the ten minutes on the hour that he was allowed to be with his wife, fearful they might be his last. The nurses physically directed him out of the room to confront the time left until he saw her again as if they were fifty individual enemies keeping him and Penny apart. The intensive care unit hummed and buzzed along with Hal's nerves.

A steady stream of doctors paraded through Hal's waiting. Little was known about Penny's condition, and they seemed to spend most of their time telling Hal what she did not have. It wasn't meningitis, diphtheria, streptococcus B or AIDS. Her heart was pronounced sound (except for that pesky habit of stopping, thought Hal sourly) and her breathing strong. Penny apparently had a different doctor for each major bodily function who confidently told Hal in a variety of ways that she was a complete mystery.

At the end of the afternoon, one specialist explained to Hal, "We're fighting her fever and running tests to get a clearer picture of why your wife's system appears to be in such tremendous, um, distress."

Hal studied the man intently, trying to remember what area of Penny's body he was in charge of. "You have absolutely no clue, do you?" Four solid hours of being in the throes of losing his wife had rendered him exhausted and unable to bear another "I don't know," no matter how medically eloquent it was said.

"Well, sir," said the doctor, turning crimson over his yellow hospital pallor and tugging at his collar, "the body is a system, you see, and as such, it is quite often difficult to determine which piece of the puzzle is throwing the whole picture off."

"No less than ten doctors have marched up to me today and told me that the 'system' they are in charge of is working just fine, thank you very much, and have signed off on her. How can eleven men, with decades of medical school between them, tell me there is nothing wrong with my wife when she is lying in the ICU in a coma, for God's sake?"

"I understand you're upset Mr. . . . uh"—the doctor looked to the chart—"Chaney."

"You understand nothing! That's what I'm upset about! How can someone die three times in one day with a raging fever and you say"—Hal squeezed his face into a red bunch and found his most mocking tone—"'All of her primary *systems* seem to be functioning quite well!'" Hal was well beyond shock and settling quite nicely into the anger stage of his grief.

"Please, Mr. Chaney. So far, it looks like your wife has some sort of virus. I assure you we will do everything in our power to save her. She's getting fluids and several types of antibiotics, and we're monitoring her around the clock. I'm sorry I can't be more specific about the cause of all of this, but I'm as much in the dark as you are."

Hal looked at the doctor, who nodded and scurried back down the long hallway. A couple passed the escaping doctor, heading toward the intensive care unit even as he hurried away from it, and Hal recognized them as his parents. He could make out his mother's red lips moving quickly and her arm gesticulating in every direction, a handkerchief erupting from one hand with only a sharp pointer finger free, punctuating her conversations with apparent physical exclamation points. His father, her polar opposite, shuffled beside her, scowling, inches shorter, his back bent and his arthritic legs bowed into virtual submission, taking four painful steps for each of his wife's two in order to keep up.

His mother engulfed him when they approached, patting Hal with the same blows she had used to burp reluctant pockets of air from his infant self. Hal's father stepped up and shook his hand, at the last minute extending his other arm to briefly brush against Hal's shoulder in what could have become part of a hug. His eyes avoided his son's by looking around, checking to be sure no one was witnessing such an overt display of affection. He stationed himself in an orange bucket seat under the glass window of Penny's ward, arranging his mangled legs with a wince and opening that evening's paper.

"Hal," his mother began, "Penny's sisters are at your house, taking care of the kids. They'll be here later when we switch places. Someone named John Linden—"

"Jim," corrected Hal.

Mary Chaney waved her handkerchiefed hand, dismissing the importance of Jim's name.

"Your neighbor," she continued, "replaced the glass window, and a scary little Italian woman dressed in black lent us her cordless phone for the house."

Hal briefly considered asking what had happened to the old cordless phone, but found he didn't have the energy.

"That's our next door neighbor, Mother. You've met her."

"Well, you know what they say about first impressions and all. Do you even remember her, Harvey?" Somewhere behind them, Hal heard his father grunt noncommittally.

"Anyway, as for the rest of the troops, Jack and Joan are resting from the in vitro. It was unsuccessful. Under their insurance they're not candidates for any more procedures. They'll be here tomorrow."

"Please call them and tell them it's not necessary. I'm sure they need to cope with such devastating news—"

"They insisted," she said, cutting him off and closing the subject from further debate. Hal let it go, not up for their usual thrust and parry, which his mother invariably won.

"Your sisters are at your house, making enough dinners for everyone for the next few weeks."

Hal often wondered why his mother had never joined the military. She could have easily commanded entire battalions to victory while simultaneously making sure they all got a good night's rest and ate right.

"We're here to help you wait. Right?" She looked his father's way.

"Harvey!" She yelled at the newspaper.

"Absolutely, Mary," he mumbled from behind it.

"How is she?" she asked, the way a CEO asks how the Dow Jones performed that day, as if Penny's rating as a daughter-in-law hinged on her ability to stay well.

Hal took a minute to steady his voice. "She's in a coma."

"Why? What's wrong with her?"

"They're not sure."

"Not sure? Are they wavering between a few possibilities? How many doctors have seen her?"

"They said maybe a virus."

"A virus? Oh, for God's sake! That's ridiculous! Nobody goes into a coma over a piddling virus! Have they checked her blood sugar?"

"I'm sure they have, Mother."

"We'll ask a nurse to be sure. What do the nurses say? They always know the truth, though they'll never tell you."

Hal wondered where his mother got some of her ideas. He was sure she would tell him.

"Aunt Thelma was a nurse. You knew that, right? Anyway, she said a team of wild horses couldn't have dragged a diagnosis from her even though she said she was on the money every time. Where's the nurse? I'll get her to talk."

"Mother, I really don't think you should do that," Hal said to her back as she walked away from him down the hall.

Hal sat next to his father, head in hand, glancing every

minute or so at his watch, waiting to see Penny again. His father handed him part of the sports section, which Hal pretended to read.

Mary arrived back in the hallway, flanked on both sides by nurses speaking to her in bubbly tones. They stopped halfway and Hal could see his mother hand them both what he assumed was a twenty-dollar bill and smiling as if the pleasure was, truly, all hers. Having made their deal, they each went their separate ways, Hal's mother approaching with an air of satisfaction.

"Mother, why are you paying the nurses? That's what medical insurance is for."

"That's what's wrong with your generation, Hal: You don't know how to show your appreciation to the hardest workers."

"Please let me handle things in my own way."

Mary sent him a hurt look, which he knew better than to take as real.

"Look, I don't want to argue with you, it's on the hour. It's time to see Penny."

"Oh, that restriction has been lifted. They said you can stay with her at all times now." She shot him a look of victory.

Hal lifted his eyebrows but knew when to move along.

"Come on." Mary took him by the elbow, waving to Harvey. "Harvey, come in and say something to Penny. I've heard that's what brings people out of these states. The nurses, surprisingly enough, agreed with the doctors: just a very nasty virus. Maybe something someone brought with them from another country, although Frederica said she's never seen anything like this before."

"Who the hell is Frederica, Ma?"

"She's the Peace Corps nurse who works here now."

"You've been here twenty minutes and you know the staff's résumés?"

Mary had no time for the barb she was going to send Hal's way about how she was only trying to help.

Penny was unrecognizable. Her coloring resembled a pea green and she was virtually lost under wires and tubes. Mary bit her own tongue and surprised herself by needing to hold on to the guardrail to keep herself from falling over at the sight of her daughter-in-law. Harvey looked around as if he were assessing the room for a possible paint job.

Hal took Penny's hand. "I'm here Penny. I'm with you. Please, Penny, come back to us. We need you. It's okay if you need rest, but please come back. Wake up so I know you're all right." He looked up at Mary and Harvey. "My parents are here. They're going to keep me company until you're back on your feet. Everyone is pitching in." Hal's voice was unsteady and began to crack.

Penny responded only with silence, her frame so consumed with stillness that she reminded Hal of a statue. Mary grabbed hold of her hand, trying to encourage her to wake up, but was soon restless at making no headway. She pronounced Penny too cold and was heading out to get her another blanket, putting Harvey in charge of holding the hand she had. Hal's father reached over the guardrail and picked up Penny's hand the way he held the fish he processed for thirty years at the downtown plant. There was a way he had of holding a carp with as little of the fish's skin meeting the surface area of his hand as possible. Yet, Hal always thought there was a hint of an apology in how he cradled the fish before he threw it into the vat for processing and reached for a towel to wipe his hands. Harvey studied the flowers Hal brought up from the hospital gift shop. He and Mary hadn't brought anything of that sort with them, as Mary was more of an organizer and doer than a flowers-and-cards type of person. Besides, with Harvey's legs being in the state they were, more often than not they took the most direct route to wherever they were going.

"Dad, I can get you a chair."

" 'S all right," Harvey grumbled.

"Maybe if you say something, Dad. Penny's always liked your low, rumbly voice."

Harvey looked at Hal as if he were being asked to throw himself out of a window. His big, bushy eyebrows knit together and Hal felt sure his father was going to run out of the room. Not that he thought his father didn't love Penny; Hal imagined he did. It was just his father's way. "He's not a talker," his mother would say to him as a child. This would be the final throwing up of her hands in the air after she had exhausted "He's tired, he works long hours and he's taken on another job to feed you kids." He wanted to know what he had done wrong that his father seemed so incredibly uninterested in him. A scream or even a beating had at times taken on a wonderful appeal to him because it meant input from his father above and beyond a grunt or a half glance from behind the day's headlines.

One morning during his childhood, Hal remembered sitting next to his father at breakfast. It was the day after the Little League opener where almost every father could be heard shouting his boy's name, berating the umpires and pleading with the coach to play his kid. Hal's father was, as always, absent from the stands. Hal gave Harvey ten minutes at breakfast to even ask about the game, after which he was going to pronounce himself a defector from the whole family. He was hoping Matt Brewer's father, who had gotten into a fistfight with the third-base coach, would agree to adopt him. A bowl of cornflakes floated untouched in front of him as he looked back and forth from his Mickey Mouse watch to his father's face, which hung behind the sports section. He sat and stewed, becoming more and more angry with each minute that passed without the desired "How was the game, son?"

As Hal watched, craning his head around the side of Harvey's paper, he noticed something unusual that turned his anger upside down. Hal saw that his father's eyes were not moving. At first he thought perhaps he was studying a picture, a particularly outstanding slide into home plate or a shot of a team in action. But Hal saw the page was filled only with words, which Harvey looked through and not at as he ate his breakfast—using the paper not to read but to shield himself from his family.

Hal shook the memory from his head. "It's all right, Dad."

"No, no, I'll . . ."

Hal looked at him, waiting for him to finish his sentence, knowing his father's arthritic legs couldn't stand for very much longer. The beeps and hums of the monitors were suddenly deafening in their persistence. Harvey clenched Penny's hand painstakingly with both of his own and looked at her face completely for the first time since their arrival. A surprise seemed to force his eyebrows carelessly to the top of his head, revealing Harvey's dark eyes, which grew wide. His face drained of color and just as quickly flushed as red as a fire engine as it screams down a city block.

"Dad! Oh my God! Are you all right?"

"Penny moved!"

"I was standing right here, Dad. You must have moved her hand yourself."

"She moved!" At the edges of Harvey's mouth there appeared the beginnings of a smile.

For Hal, his father's smile was out of place. An unusual occurrence in and of itself, on top of the grave situation, it gave the scene an out-of-kilter resonance that threw Hal off balance. Stepping back, he watched Harvey gaze down at his wife and suddenly realized that the smile was not the only piece out of place, that didn't belong; he had a feeling he was looking at a funny-page puzzle challenging him to find the ten things wrong in a room. Hal couldn't see any but the look on his father's face.

"I can't believe you're smiling, Dad," he said, gritting his teeth.

Harvey just looked at him as if he couldn't understand what the problem was.

"Dad, she didn't move! It won't help giving me false hope!"

At that moment Mary walked in, carrying what looked like the hospital's entire supply of blankets. "What's going on here?" she barked at Hal, turning to see her husband's face. "What's wrong with your father?"

Harvey turned and looked his wife in the eye. "Penny moved, Mary."

"She did not move!" Hal was shouting and nurses were beginning to file into the room.

"Don't yell at your father, Hal! He's got to be careful with his heart." She covered Penny, checking and rechecking her hands to gauge her temperature. "Maybe you just didn't see it, Hal. I would think you would be excited at the possibility. Anyway, we ought to go: It's late. We'll be back tomorrow. Hopefully, Penny will be able to greet us. Let's go, Harvey."

For just a moment Harvey looked down and seemed surprised to find himself still clutching his daughter-in-law's hand. He put it back at her side with exquisite care and reached across the room to replace it with his wife's. Forgetting herself, Mary smiled and accepted it, following him out of the room with a brief backward glance at her son, who sat seething in a confusion he didn't quite understand.

Hal watched them leave, walking down the hall side

by side, still holding hands. It wasn't until the elevator had closed behind them that Hal finally realized what had been so wildly wrong. He hadn't seen it until he watched from behind as his father kept in perfect step with his mother's long strides. His father's legs were no longer bent.

Chapter Eight

Louis Klotz watched the news with his face encompassed in a breathing mask attached by a long tube to a nebulizer. The mask had fish eyes and aqua gills put there to amuse young asthma sufferers into wanting to keep it in place for the duration of their treatment. Louis needed so many treatments a day, he couldn't afford to sit around holding the mouthpiece adults used to inhale the lung opening medicine. His lack of any chin to speak of at all and his thin, rodentlike face made only the child-size mask fit properly. It condemned him to lock his door and pull down his shades for fear someone would catch him looking like an oversize Charlie the Tuna with a smoking habit. His fears were completely unfounded, though, as he had not had even one visitor since moving into his studio apartment three years ago, and being on the ninth floor assured only the birds would get a chance glimpse at his medically necessary but ridiculous getup.

Early in his life Louis had tried his hand at writing fiction. He dreamed of being a world-class writer and creating the next Great American Novel. A very strange mix of luck met Louis on this road. He found himself quite prolific in his ideas and his ability to capture any moment and put it on the page. He was, after all, predominantly a spectator in life, having watched it mostly along the sidelines from behind a mask, an inhaler or an oxygen tent. The pains of his childhood were numerous and slid easily into his writing. The trouble always arose with his characters. They seemed to have a life of their own, saying and doing things Louis had not intended them to. After an intense writing session he would find that his hero had run off with the heroine's daughter, or his heroine had killed herself despite her positive circumstances. It baffled him. He tried outlines, structured story plots clearly designating what would happen to whom and how. Nevertheless, his characters continued to display an unnerving free will on his pages. They were like rebellious teenagers over whom he had no control. The outcomes of his stories were consequently always startling. They sent messages Louis had never intended and frightened him into long bouts of insomnia.

Nonfiction turned out to be much safer. He could solidify his story with facts, cementing the real-life characters into what could be proven they had actually done, verified by multiple sources.

Louis waved away the mist escaping from the sides of the mask, trying to get a better look at the television screen. He watched the nightly news, which, being centered around the city, always held the promising assortment of vicious crimes and freak occurrences that Klotz kept his eyes peeled for. A long writer's pad held a list of possible stories for him to pursue, prioritized according to their gruesome or volatile nature. His latest piece had gotten a great deal of attention, its sensational quality earning him both praise and disgust. Having his disability meant Louis could not chase a breaking story or push ahead of a pack of reporters for the first gem of information. Instead he had to pick up the crumbs of what was left after the initial story had been told and see if a meal could still be made of it. He had developed a sixth sense as to what was still warm and could ignite with the right handling and what was dead in the water.

The news dragged along, offering nothing that piqued his interest until the very last segment. On the surface it read like any other suburban tragedy. House fire causes small boy to jump from second-story window, said the newscaster. Brief film footage was played showing the soot-covered family weeping under a tree. Klotz's ears perked up and he studied the film with the eye of someone searching for holes. The father and mother were reaching out for the boy as his stretcher was loaded onto the wailing ambulance, but they stayed on opposite sides. He thought he caught a glimpse of anger from the mother to the father and noticed he wore no wedding ring. Divorced, but both were together when the fire broke out and the boy was upstairs alone. Someone was doing something wrong, he thought gaily. There was his story. A prefilled knapsack full of medicine and emergency snacks and writing pads waited at the door. Louis drove to Southlawn Hospital like a hungry lion approaching its unwitting prey.

It was easy to slip into the emergency room from the main hospital when things were busy. Louis had developed the ability to look like a part of any group he was next to and could travel to the bowels of any department by hopping from family to family. He trolled the ICU looking for the boy jumper but instead came upon his most reliable emergency-room informant.

"Hey, Beth!" Louis was thrilled to see her and tried to keep up as she ran from station to station.

"Not now, Klotz."

"It's Louis to you, honey. We're friends."

"No, Klotz, you're a necessary evil. I can't talk right now. I'm swamped. Every flu case in the county is here, throwing up all over my equipment."

Louis waved a fifty-dollar bill in front of her.

"Put that away! Are you trying to get me fired? A lot of good I'll do you if I don't work here anymore!"

"I need you, Bethy." He added a twenty to the pile as his eyes drank her in, head to toe. He wasn't sure which he loved more, her chest or her gambling habit.

"Five minutes at the phone on the hallway to oncology. I'll see if I can get her chart."

"Her chart? Her who? I want that boy jumper, Shane Ellston."

"Whatever. Five minutes."

As promised, in five minutes Beth picked up a phone, put in a quarter and started talking to Louis, who was right next to her, responding over the dial tone to the opposite end of the hallway on his own unworking phone.

"So what do you have?"

"Kid's got some third-degree burns, some smoke inhalation, but it's his cracked skull and spine that's gonna do him in. I doubt he'll last the night. What's so special about this kid?"

"I'm interested in the family. What were they like?"

"Very weird. No one talking to each other, mother and father sitting at opposite ends of the waiting chairs, talking to different doctors."

"Did they say anything unusual?"

"I thought I heard the mother say to the father, 'You'll pay,' or something like that, but I don't know what she was referring to. The fire marshal called, trying to track them down, but that doesn't really mean much. A lot of families are all pissed off at each other when a kid gets hurt, especially one this far gone. He has no brain activity at all. It's just a matter of time. Here's a copy of his chart."

So his instincts about them were right, he thought.

"So where are they? I looked all over the ER."

"They're up in ICU."

"Already? Damn! There's so much less access up there. How did he get in so fast? It's a madhouse today."

"That's actually what I thought you came in for. The suits are all pissy about it. Seems that some little grandmother with a broken hip and double pneumonia on a ventilator wrote a note asking to get it taken off. Doctor's orders are respirator, but the intern and nurse comply with the patient's wishes. They extubate her off the machine, no less than four nurses and a respiratory therapist listen to her chest and find no sign of the pneumonia. As a matter of fact, she's talking to them like she's as happy as a clam, according to the nurses. Certainly not like a dying ninety-year-old woman with a fractured hip."

Louis is waving his hand in a circular motion, eager to get at the boy's chart and onto the story. Where was she going with all of this?

"So everybody up there is practically breaking a leg to get to a phone to call the doctor so he could cover his ass over screwing up the diagnosis, and when they get back to her room, she's gone. That's how a bed opened up for the kid."

"Someone bring her in for the wrong test or something? That's been done; I'm not really interested in—"

"She walked away. Aren't you listening to me?"

"An orderly could have wheeled her out to—"

"Bonehead! People with fractured hips can't sit on the john, much less in a wheelchair. Her hip was shattered, with bones protruding from the skin before they operated. Kinda hard to misdiagnose that."

"She still could've been wheeled—"

"Her sweater was gone from the closet. The janitor and the candy striper swear they saw her walk onto the elevator. *Walk*. How grossly incompetent is this hospital? There's your story, Klotz."

He paid her and headed up to the intensive care waiting room. Seeing some incompetent heads roll while taking the boy's family out would be icing on the cake of nabbing an interesting story. The fire marshals should be moseying in anytime now as well if his instincts were on the money.

He set up camp in a row of chairs just outside the ICU waiting room. There wasn't a chair available in there anyway, but he liked being able to eavesdrop on the conversations held when relatives thought they were alone. With any luck he'd get the kid's family on tape. It was also a great vantage point for seeing the main desk, which faced away from the waiting room. He could stare without being noticed, getting a good feel of the rhythm of where everyone was and how long they stayed there.

Klotz listened to what he figured was no less than twenty relatives of some patient tell and retell stories of their childhood or their experiences being her grandchild. He thought he might puke and had half a mind to shout through the doorway, "Save it for the funeral!" The smells of the homemade cooking wafting out to his chair, however, made him hold his tongue, hoping enough of them would leave so he could sneak in and nab a little for himself. He didn't have to wait long. A woman walked back to the large waiting room from the short row of chairs in front of the windows to the ICU rooms and stopped. She took one look at Louis, glanced at the table in the room filled with food and shouted to her sister, "Rosalie, there's another waiter out here. Has anyone offered him anything?" Surprised heads shook a series of nos and shoulders shrugged all around. A gaggle of women came out to where Louis was.

"Hi, I'm Frannie. My mother is in the ICU." She stuck out her hand, which shook Klotz's clammy, limp paw. "You look pale. Come in and have something. Look!

Tina's making you a plate now." Klotz was dragged into the waiting room, his stakeout post abandoned and his pleas of being full completely ignored. Tina handed him a plate.

"You'll have to excuse my sister. Italian women don't seem to be happy if they're not feeding someone. It's eggplant parmigiana. If you find one better than the one in that plate, it's probably not of this earth." Everyone laughed.

He was introduced to a few Franks and a couple of Vinnies and realized every child there was named after another adult in the room. He was confused almost immediately. He thanked them for the food and tried to smile while escaping. Rosalie cornered him. "You haven't told me who you are, Mr. . . ."

"Um . . . Louis. Mr. Louis."

"Who you here for, Mr. Louis?"

"My poor aunt," he said with a saccharine smile. "Family is so important, I thought I'd visit."

"Oh, we couldn't agree more." Yet another sister spooned something else onto his plate. He tried to get it out of anyone else's reach and backed toward the door. "Thanks—really."

"Here, you need a napkin. You've seen your aunt already, I hope. There is an elderly woman missing from the ICU, you know."

Louis tried to make his face look as shocked and frightened as possible. "Oh, dear. When was this?"

"Just last evening. Anthony and little Ralph saw the whole thing. It was getting late and they were sitting in the chairs in front of the windows to the rooms. Mama was resting and they were waiting for her to wake up. They were talking to Hal—that's the poor man whose wife is in some kind of coma next door to Mama—when the door on the other side opens up and a little old lady about Mama's age walked out. She said, 'Good afternoon, gentlemen'—just like that: "Good afternoon, gentlemen"—and went to the elevator. She could have been any visitor at all. Well, the nurses come back with the doctor, go into the room and start screaming. Security was all over the place and Anthony and Little Ralph had to answer the same questions over and over."

"Really?" Louis had a journalist's mental memo pad out. "What could they want to know again and again?"

"Little Ralph?" A young boy just on the brink of adolescence came forward, awkward and pimply and obviously wanting to help.

"They wanted to know if she was limping, if she looked sick at all. And they kept showing us pictures of her, mixed up with pictures of other old ladies to see if we kept picking the same one."

"And did you?"

"Oh, yeah. It was her. Definitely."

"And did they find her?"

Rosalie turned to the group. "Was that lady found?" No one seemed to think so.

"I bet her family was pretty mad, huh? Did they come after she left?" Louis gauged Rosalie's expression to see if his tone was too interrogating.

Rosalie seemed excited that he had finally arrived at that particular question. "They fainted dead away, directly on the floor, all three of them: her daughter, son-in-law and neighbor, flat as pancakes. Knocked Hal right out of his seat out there."

Louis looked up across the nurses' station to the row of chairs and saw what he assumed was the back of Hal's head. Hal's name had come up twice, and Louis noted him as a good source for whichever story he chose to follow.

"Couldn't an orderly have come and wheeled her somewhere by mistake? Don't hospitals do that all the time?" As a matter of fact, Louis had done a story on a switched patient not that long ago. At the time it seemed to be a hot piece but had proven on the dull side, which was why he was reluctant to pursue another one of the same ilk now. He'd heard nothing to convince him that this was anything other than a colossal mix-up and civil law suit. Louis finished his eggplant, and noted it was certainly worth the time he had wasted here. Surely this missing woman would be found in a birthing suite off the pediatric ward any minute. He began backing toward the door until he got stuck there, caught by something Anthony said to Little Ralph: "Well, it shouldn't be too hard to spot her, wearing the hospital gown and all."

"Yeah," Little Ralph responded, "she still had the IV tape all over her arm."

Louis filed that thought in his head, making a note to find out what had eventually become of that woman, and headed across the ward looking as if he knew exactly where he was headed. He smiled, loving the beginning of the hunt.

There were many rooms along the corridor, and Klotz found an old woman with a chart still in its holder outside the door. A rattling breath could be heard from the hall, and her papers said she'd been there for a while. It was quiet, with no family pacing around her room or holding her hand. Louis adopted her as his fictitious aunt and headed toward the chairs to bemoan her fate with everyone's apparent friend, Hal. Before even meeting him, Louis disliked Hal merely for how often he'd been mentioned. Popular people had left a bad taste in Louis's mouth throughout his life. A forced smile was pasted on and he continued forward but found himself looking at his watch. Two and a half hours had slipped by without him noticing, and, like Cinderella, Louis's magic was on a very short leash in terms of time. The familiar whistle of his bronchi found its way into his lungs, the air tubes constricting slowly but surely, cutting off his oxygen. He had been careless in not setting his watch and would have very little time to get back home to get himself on his breathing machine. Hal would have to wait.

Klotz picked up his pace as best he could without further compromising the amount of air he would need to ingest until he reached his car. Three inhalers were on key chains in his various pockets, and they gave him the crutches his withered lungs needed to get a feeble line of air until his car started. As the linings of his lungs pushed together and met, Louis coughed violently, struggling to pull any oxygen into his system. The ride was almost too long. He parked along the pavilion to his building, his Handicapped sticker thrown across his windshield and his keys left under the car where they fell before he hurled himself through the door into his building. Every time he found himself in this dire situation, he promised himself that he would be more careful, that his outings would never be more than two hours. When he slammed open his apartment door and fitted the mask across a face, now a brutal blue color, he sank to the floor, vowing yet again that he would be more careful, more exacting with his time. He chided himself for being sucked into the nonsense about the woman, which had distracted him from the piece with real potential. Tomorrow he would root out what Shane Ellston's parents were hiding and what had really happened in that fire. As his body fed on oxygen, his mind feasted on the prospect of exposing the things he imagined the family had done. It would be a pleasure unraveling both the story and their lives.

Chapter Nine

The bridge stretched ahead of Penny, far enough that she couldn't see where it ended and what it connected to. A whiff of Nana's perfume wafted around her, but she could see no one at all in any direction she looked. She found herself in the middle of the bridge and looked to either side, searching for water or maybe land; perhaps it was some sort of overpass. It reminded her of a bridge she had crossed with her family on a vacation they had taken when she was just a little girl. There were no heavy metal girders or elephant-leg–sized cables, just support beams holding it up from below. Then as now, there was fog obscuring the sides of the bridge, and they had all commented on how it felt as though they were riding over a bridge that spanned the air instead of water.

What she saw above her was a starless sky that was both dark and light, and she wondered if it was morning coming on or night settling in. The deep blueness of that sky hinted at thunderstorms, yet it had an obscure brightness seeping out from beneath the bridge or behind the clouds or up ahead, depending, it seemed, on which angle Penny cast her eyes. She was thoroughly frightened and completely exhilarated and stood mostly in one spot, trying to get ahold of herself. Her mind held on to the knowledge of her body lying in a hospital bed the way a young boy fiddles with a rock that he has found: She fingered it in an inattentive way, becoming familiar enough with it until she could put it in her pocket for safekeeping, where it would join her collection of other inexplicable and quite unabsorbable facts that she decided to coexist with for now.

The bridge was beyond colossal. In either direction away from her it was the size of a football field, and neither beginning nor end could be spotted. She took a tentative step forward and felt the bridge give slightly, and she had a strange picture in her mind of the entire structure flopping violently, should she decide to suddenly jump up and down. She had an overwhelming urge to move across the bridge in the direction she was facing to look for her grandmother and whatever else seemed to be drawing her to it. A stallion in a stampede doesn't get pushed: He moves forward with the pack because the energy around him demands it. Penny was getting pulled as she looked about, unaware of how easy it was to give in to its strong tide. But from behind her a wind blew gently at her back. It carried the whisper of soft voices, and every once in a while she could hear Hal calling her name on a passing draft. Penny wasn't sure how long she stood on that one spot, listening to the conversations that traveled to her. When she could, she gathered her strength and turned around to head toward her husband's pleas.

It was what Hal would have called one long-ass bridge. If they'd been driving across it, Penny was sure he would have made jokes about the first cross continental structure connecting Europe to the Americas. She became leery after a seemingly endless journey, wondering if she should have gone the other direction. There seemed to be no end at all, the way she was heading, and she just about gave up and turned around to go back, when she finally stepped out of a particularly thick pocket of fog and came upon the end of the bridge. A shock went through her. It was a jolt like no other, mental adrenaline that threatened to shut her down. She fought to keep a conscious mind but was overpowered by what she had seen and passed out.

When Penny came to, she was on the bridge, standing again in the spot she had originally started out. She wondered how many times she had done this. A vision of the situation that met her at the other end of the bridge gave her a breathless, panicky feeling that melted together with the sound of her children calling to her. Their voices were clearer than Hal's, louder and somehow closer.

"Mommy, wake up!" She almost laughed at Julie's commanding tone and could picture her fists at her hips, elbows jutting out. Somewhere inside of her she wanted to understand why she didn't have the urgency she felt she should have to get to her children. It didn't overtake her. It didn't send her screaming across the bridge back to her family. Nonetheless, it was enough to fight the pull forward and turn her around again. This time while she walked she tried to come to terms with what would greet her and thought on how she would get beyond it. It took her less time to get there, she supposed, because she dreaded it.

The horror threatened to overtake her again as she looked down instead of out, clinging to her spot on the bridge. She had reached what she thought was the threshold, an entranceway that sloped steeply to meet a small expanse of earth. Beyond that ground was indeed an ocean, but it was alive, made up of hundreds of thousands of people. Every eye looked up at her, beseeching her for some sort of help of which Penny had no clue. They were terribly silent, interwoven among themselves so that Penny couldn't tell where one person began and another ended. There were no colors but black and white on their naked bodies, which were dirty and raw, as if they had been rubbing up against one another in an attempt to climb over the mass of bodies to get onto the bridge. Their movement made Penny think of a giant bowl of restless worms. If she looked out at the sea of people, she felt herself get dizzy and nauseous, her hold on herself beginning to slip, if only for the sheer number in front of her. She looked at each person, trying to make out their individual characteristics. So many had pieces missing from them. And they were faded, transparent in some spots, as if only part of them were there in front of her, only a part of the essence of their whole selves. There was a little girl who, like the others, stared directly into Penny's eyes, as though she had just asked Penny an urgent question and was waiting for an answer. Only one of the little girl's arms and half of her upper torso stuck out from the crowd, and she swayed from side to side, trying to keep a clear view of Penny, to maintain her piercing stare. Penny was drawn to the girl's beautiful round blue eyes but sickened by what looked like gaping holes in her body. She could see the writhing body of the man behind the girl by looking through the missing pieces in her arm and chest.

A thunderstorm threatened to unleash its fury here. Heavy oxygen clung to the air. She wondered if the girl would drown when the rain filled up the holes in her head. As Penny looked out from the elevated height of the bridge, she felt like a motivational speaker who has arrived in front of her audience and forgotten all of her lines. If asked, she would have to admit that she couldn't remember what she was supposed to talk about.

There was a woman in the crowd very close to the foot of the bridge. Penny had seen her farther off when she arrived, but the woman wiggled her way among the bodies to get to the front row. She was tiny, with a bright smile, but Penny could see through the skin of her chest to her lungs, which took up all of its space, squeezing the other organs down to her waist. Her hip was cracked and her body leaned to one side like the number seven. It horrified Penny terribly and she flailed around, looking for something to steady herself. All of the tiny old woman was visible, now that she stood in the front row of the crowd, and as Penny tried to get a grip on her fear, the woman stuck out her hand. It wasn't the gesture of a handshake, someone introducing themselves or welcoming her somewhere: It was the reach of a woman being tossed about among wild ocean waves and from under the water, hoping for a strong hand to pull her out. Her fingers were splayed and her arm was held up above her, an extension of her pleading eyes.

Others behind her continued to push forward, following the woman's lead, pulling an arm out from the thick of the crowd and raising it when they approached the foot of the bridge. Those in the back moaned, but as they made their way toward Penny they put their energies into their arms. They wanted her, but Penny also sensed a demand. A crying baby doesn't ask: He expects and is angered by a slow response, upping the intensity of his screams. A mother can do nothing but run to attend, as if the baby's wails controlled strings in the mother's limbs, almost making her muscles move involuntarily. Penny could no more refuse this hand than she could stand around while her Benjamin wanted her—or burn her own flesh, for that matter.

Penny took a step down off the bridge, both her arms rising to meet those of the woman, whose name she knew instantly was Jetta. Without so much as a touch, knowledge of Jetta flooded into Penny, and like a sponge she was somehow able to absorb it. She thought she stood in the space between sleep and wakefulness, the time just before a dream grabs you out of reality and into its web but where consciousness watches the changeover. Penny had passed through those few seconds her whole life, having moments of clarity, of seeing the connections and why things made sense and losing them always to a maze of dreams that stole them greedily from her waking self. She would say briefly, "Yes! I know now! I must remember this!" and it would never fail to slip away. When she stepped forward and down from the bridge, she stood in the thick of it and felt herself tingling with the confusion of a body whose mind is both asleep and awake. She wanted to hold on to every moment of understanding, every thought that showed her where her dreams were and what they meant. She had been there before.

It took her a long time to reach Jetta. The bridge still had a hold on her and gave her up only with great reluctance. Each movement away from it was a great struggle. She was losing her physical sense of herself, feeling all at once larger than the bridge itself and small enough to blow away like a fragile but hard lead glass center surrounded with billowy robes. She was the dichotomy of body and soul, so different but laboring to stay as one.

Only when she was able to grasp Jetta's hand were both of them whole again. Penny felt the two pieces of herself come closer together and saw Jetta's lungs drain of their fluid until they again took up their rightful space. Her upper body arced sideways and found its way upright, reminding Penny of a graceful dancer regaining her balance after a particularly difficult jump. There were no holes in Jetta, and her coloring came back. She freed her hands from Penny's and took a strong hold of Penny's face, drawing it to her own. Penny could smell wild jasmine and knew it to be the flowers Jetta's mother grew on their farm when she was a child. Sweet breath exuded from Jetta and flowed to Penny with the intimacy of a kiss. Jetta stepped back, glistening with newness as she turned to face the writhing masses behind her. They parted in front of her easily, like a hot knife through butter. She walked down the aisle they made, touching each with a hand as she passed, the way a child draws a stick across a picket fence as she goes by.

Penny watched until she couldn't see any part of Jetta in the distance. The upstretched hands waited and the moans that defined the wanting continued as Penny began pulling each one to her. Every story sang through her head like music, and Penny knew their sadness and pain without asking as easily as she knew the secrets of her own heart. Their bodies healed, each finding its wholeness. The suffering they had endured stayed with them in memory, a piece of who they had come to be. Penny cried with them, and each left their tears with her before they turned and made their way back to the world.

When Penny could only see people approaching from far off in the distance, she turned back to the bridge in a gesture of farewell and was stunned to see someone there watching her. She had not sensed his presence and could feel no pain emitting from his body. With a sense that had just begun to be a part of her, she reached out to him, feeling for what his need was, what she was supposed to make whole.

"Am I supposed to help you too?" Penny asked innocently. She could sense the creature's great amusement and hear his laughter somewhere deep inside of herself, like the sound elephants make when they trumpet to their mates from miles away. Her heart moved with its vibration.

"I'm sorry!" She was humiliated. "I don't know what exactly is happening."

"We've been waiting for you for a long, long time."

"I feel as though I've been here a lifetime already."

"Hardly." He studied her, waiting patiently, watching.

"I'd like to go back to my children."

"That is one of your options. You have many choices to make before you move on."

Penny didn't understand the choices in her head but felt them in the tug of the undertow of the bridge, pulling her back to it and contrasting the voices of her children, her life. With just the turn of her attention toward the being, she found herself again on the threshold pulled easily into the circle of light flooding him and now her. Each step brought her greater peace, and her family took on the feel of a former life, something long ago. She watched the struggle within herself like a fan at a tennis game between her two best friends. She wanted both sides to win, and so the final victory was destined to be a blow to someone dear. At the very last moment, before she was completely engulfed in the accepting warmth of the bridge's keeper, Penny broke the connection, turning and pulling away.

"You are very strong, Penny. There is very little time to help you to understand. You have been chosen. Only the one who sends back the travelers can be the one who saves them."

Penny stood dumbfounded. What could he possibly be talking about? She entertained the idea that she had gone completely crazy. Standing there in the profound silence, she thought, *So this is what it's like to be nuts. How interesting that it doesn't actually feel much different from being sane.* The immensity of what she started thinking of as her delusion was impressing her. Penny never saw herself as particularly creative, and she was wondering if she had just been repressing that side of herself all of these years. She wondered which mental hospital her family had put her in. She would just humor this dream being until it all broke up into a circus scene or something else less bizarre. Maybe if she closed her eyes . . . ?

"You must pay attention! You just healed those souls. They could not cross with you here. Only one other before you has been able to do this."

"This is absurd! I don't know what you could possibly be talking about. I'm sorry if I did anything wrong by touching those people, but I don't want to stay here. Please, let me go."

"The balance of the world's heart is measured by what it does. For all of the tragedy of time, good has always been one step ahead. Evil hasn't ruled with such strength in two thousand years. You know. You've seen it."

And she had. Just this month, Penny's college roommate had called to tell her how her son had been among those shot at on the playground at school. An eight-year-old boy had killed seven before turning the gun on himself.

"You must go back into the world to help it find its way again. It is an ignorant world. It will ask to see and even then it may not believe."

"I don't see how I can change anything for millions of people. I don't think I'm who you're looking for." Penny reflected on herself. She was a housewife and mother, a career she thought highly underrated in its complexity. After all, she was a little bit like an airline running itself with only one full-time employee. She was the skycap collecting everyone's possessions, the ticket agent directing everyone to their gates, the baggage handler loading everything onto the plane, the pilot flying the course and the stewardess making sure it was a pleasant flight. Hal shared these duties with her when he was home, but it was a busy, full life. There was barely time to take a shower every day. And she herself was so imperfect.

"We don't even go to church every Sunday."

There was also that little shoplifting experience she had had in high school. She thought of the people she had cut out of her life when they made her angry and the cross words she used when she was upset. She and Hal had been pursuing the American dream of a big, fancy house, a minivan and a yearly vacation for as long as she could remember. Neither of them had volunteered for anything but an extra nap since their twins burst onto the scene four and a half years ago. Other more monetarily fortunate families were, she admitted to herself now, the object of her jealousy. It couldn't be her. She felt that she fit more of the profile of someone needing help, rather than someone giving it.

"Honestly, I'm sure you have the wrong person. What would I tell people?"

"You'll know. Only one other has been able to turn people away from death."

"And we all know how *that* turned out! No, thank you!"

There was a silence between them for a while, and Penny squirmed under it. "I'm not a perfect person. I'm average. Possibly below. I'm clumsy. I can barely keep from tripping over my own two feet if anyone is watching. I'm not religious. I'm not a public speaker. I'm not particularly strong. I can't watch dance recitals because even other people's children make me weep when they dance. Two days a month, if anyone says hello, I tear up, wondering what they meant by it. I stay awake nights, hoping I didn't permanently damage my children that day. If I played with them, I'm sure I'm overcrowding and they will grow up dependent and coddled. If I let them alone, I'm sure they'll feel abandoned and insecure. So you see, I don't think I'm the best person for whatever job you have in mind."

Penny turned to go, sure she had cleared things up, ready to head back to her life.

"Can you say no to them?" the entity asked her as she

stared into the eyes of the hundreds who had quietly collected behind her, waiting, hands outstretched.

"Do I have a choice?"

"Everything is a choice of one sort or another."

"But everything has a price. I'm not so simple that I can't see it might be a dear one."

"This is no different. You can come across the bridge now and not help even one more soul."

"But then I won't be with my family. Can I go back without this 'gift'?"

"That is not possible. It has already awakened inside of you. It will not go back to sleep."

"What would the sacrifice be if I went back to help? How can I choose if I don't know?"

"If you knew that on Thursday your foot would be torn from your leg, would you enjoy Monday, Tuesday or Wednesday? Man benefits from taking things as they come."

"I have too much at stake to decide without some idea."

"If the fisherman unhooks the fish, he saves its life for another day. If he brings it home to his hungry family, they eat and are nourished, but at the expense of the fish."

"You need to get someone else for this. Someone holy. There are people who've dedicated their entire lives to this sort of thing." Penny's voice broke. "I can't decide. This is beyond me. I can't bear this burden."

"Can you bear to leave your family when you could have had a little more time with them? And can you also bear the burden of not heeding this call when you know you can do so much good . . . despite the sacrifices?"

Even as she asked again, Penny knew what the price would be. It showed itself inside of her like a mad virus, growing already. The last scene, her payment for helping the world, would begin on a slate path with the tinkling of keys, and she pushed it away, knowing the end but unwilling to watch each painful moment collide with the next. It would come in its own time. Of course, she could just walk onto the bridge now and have no part in any of what was to come. She could spare herself so much pain. She closed her eyes and wept, her spirit agonizing and wringing itself with despair. So many people needed this gift. The needs of the many were measured against her own precious few. With her hands still wrapped around her grimacing face, she nodded her consent. Turning around, she made her way through the pulsing throngs of the almost-dead who went with her back toward life. The weight of the choice she made followed her as she received again the weight of her body.

Chapter Ten

Heart monitors kept uneven time throughout the hallway in the ICU. Caryn Woods made her rounds of two A.M. medications and charting data, directing the staff of orderlies and nursing assistants. Caryn had been the missing woman's main nurse before she had gone off to God-knew-where. A disciplinary committee was investigating her personally for extubating Mrs. Jetta Rizone without a doctor's approval, despite the signed consent form in her favor and the fact that Mrs. Rizone had basically yanked it out herself. Hospital politics demanded a head to roll, and Caryn was getting a nasty itching feeling around her own neck. Tonight would be an exercise in dotting *i*'s and crossing *t*'s. As head nurse, she had every available hand sterilizing the ward, doing top-to-bottom infectious-disease-prevention protocol, although it was not called for until the beginning of next month. She knew it was ridiculous, considering the patient hadn't died from lack of sanitary safeguards but had suddenly became healthy. She almost laughed at how upside down that was.

There was a note in Caryn's box at the beginning of the shift from her friend, daytime head nurse Jenny Kol. It said Jetta Rizone had been found in her daughter's home that evening, breathing fine and walking better than ever. The family had apparently retained a lawyer and was considering suing on nine counts of negligence, including, among others, lack of supervision and misdiagnosis. Caryn wanted to scream. In the meantime she would follow every hospital guideline down to the fine print. If a doctor had to be called to dispense an extra bedpan, she would be on the phone, three A.M. be damned, with full documentation to follow. The rules and regulations manual was out and open on the nurses' station.

She walked the floors. She checked the waiting room. The family that had recently taken it over had broken up the party and left it spotless. Caryn loved considerate families. They had posted a schedule of who would sit up all night with their mother and which two would sleep in the waiting room as backup support. Relief always arrived promptly at seven A.M. Extra blankets were supposed to be strictly for patients, but Caryn used some now to cover Rosalie and her son, Little Ralph. They were both snoring loudly, spread out over each of the matching avocado love seats. One of the Franks sat quietly beside his mother in her room, holding her hand. Her chart read the number of times she had coded that afternoon and how difficult it had been to bring her back. Caryn would keep a special eye on her tonight.

Next door, Hal also sat up in the chair beside his wife, but with a head that alternately nodded and came to attention with eye rubbing thrown in between. Caryn came in with James, her best orderly, who helped her switch Hal's chair for the hospital's idea of a lounger—not all that much more comfortable, but he could put his feet up and his head back. Hal insisted he didn't need it at all, even as he, too, began to snore unsteadily. Penny's sisters slept in chairs in the hallway, their heads supporting each other.

The next room was Shane Ellston's, and Caryn slowed

her step as she approached. There was something horribly upsetting about having a young child in the ICU. They were spared the real little ones, who went to the neonatal ICU, but somehow anyone under heart-attack age just seemed out of place. Shane sported what the staff called "the works": ventilator, nasal oxygen, heart monitor, catheter, IV, etc. The machines were sustaining him physically but his own life signs were virtually nonexistent. Caryn had seen his EEG, a printout of his brain activity that was starkly quiet. His heart was strong, though, and would maintain his broken body for what could be years if he managed to make it through the first critical days and if his parents allowed it. A doctor from organ donation had already been there to talk to them about letting Shane go.

She could hear the mother weeping as she stood on the threshold, about to walk in and do her job. Families of older clients were so much easier to be with. When they're older you could assume they've lived a full life and their families have had some time to prepare themselves. Every death was taken hard, of course, but most times it was expected. Even after ten years Caryn sometimes locked herself in the supply closet for a good cry after being in the rooms of dying teenagers. It was the mothers' eyes. They looked like what someone's expression would be as they arrived in hell: a strange mix of incredulousness and shattered dreams with a terrible, desperate hope. They were never resigned to the fate of their children. They clutched at straws of reflex movement and drowned in front of Caryn's very eyes. It was painful to watch; it must have been excruciating to live.

She steeled her will, ready to introduce herself as the head nurse for the night, answer any questions if she could, see if they could be made comfortable. The first full night was always the hardest. It wasn't surprising to see Mrs. Ellston crying profusely with a smile pasted across her face for what Caryn thought was her benefit. Introductions were made, though Mrs. Ellston couldn't seem to speak. When Caryn turned to Mr. Ellston, he was also carrying out that crazy combination of smile crying that Caryn took as a sign that he was dangerously close to the edge and should be handled carefully.

In retrospect, she wondered how long it took before she digested the whole scene. She went from crying parent to crying parent, spilling out her song and dance about being there to help and bringing comfortable bedding and I'm-so-sorry-about-your-son's-accident. Maybe five minutes passed before Mrs. Ellston finally thrust in front of her the note she had been holding out like a small shield and Caryn's mind, ever on the mission to keep things rational and sane, had been avoiding. It held a shaky message written in innocent-enough-looking blue ink and said simply, BREATHING TUBE OUT! Caryn's mind seized up as noisily as a motor with no oil.

When she got herself together, feeling like a cartoon character that has to gather up large, chunky pieces of its body from the floor and reattach them, she turned to Shane, who looked back at her, defying his EEG. He blinked and raised a hand to point at the respirator tubing engulfing his mouth. Caryn sat down in the visitor chair and put her head in her hands. It was hideously unprofessional of her, and she had an overwhelming feeling that she was having a nervous breakdown. This was how last night's craziness had started.

"Oh my God," she said quietly. "Oh my God."

The mother and father just wept happily.

In what she considered unprofessional act number two, Caryn ran into the hallway and started screaming for James. He rounded the corner at full speed, followed by everyone else on staff, most with rubber gloves on and smelling of disinfectant.

"Shane Ellston is fully conscious and requesting to be extubated," she said breathlessly, not believing herself. Everyone just stared. They had read the night's charts. She thought they couldn't have looked at her more strangely if she had just stripped naked in front of them and was proceeding to belly dance.

"James, please guard the door. Staff can go in, but keep the parents there if you can. Shane is absolutely not allowed to leave that room." She thought for a minute that she could almost read James's face to the letter. It said, *You have gone nuts*. She pulled him inside to see Shane's very alive eyes. He saw, his own eyes blowing up like saucers, and he stood in front of the room, his face ashen. The whole staff filed in, one after the other, needing to see it to believe it.

Caryn had trouble dialing the phone. The doctors gave her no grief about a three A.M. call and must have flown in on their own wings, they arrived so quickly. They were met by hospital administrators, board members and their lawyers. Shane Ellston was extubated, examined, re-ex-rayed and –CAT scanned. Everyone interviewed him. Twice. By the time the breakfast trays were rolling in, he was declared completely fit and utterly healed and no one could think of a reason to hold him there. The administrative suits congratulated Caryn for keeping Shane in the hospital, and, together with his parents, she began to wonder when she turned into some bizarre nursing catcher in the rye.

In the meantime, four other patients on Shane's wing improved enough over the course of the night to be moved to regular hospital beds. Hoards of families were sobbing collectively over a continental breakfast in the waiting room. Every note on every patient Caryn had attended to that evening was snuck out, copied by James in triplicate and returned. She was taking no chances this time. She was also not talking about it, per the request of the hospital board, which convened a five A.M. emergency meeting and after two hours came up with "No comment" as the best they could do. What was there to say? There was a boy who jumped out of a two-story window, shattering parts of his spine and skull, leaving him brain dead, but now he's just ducky?

By the time Jenny Kol had come to relieve Caryn of her responsibilities at seven, it was an almost entirely new floor. She, too, sat down when she heard the news.

"That's impossible. That is just not possible, Caryn."

"Someone must have screwed up. I guess he didn't get hurt that badly in the fall."

"I personally saw his X rays. I took his vitals. I saw him stop breathing."

"I don't know what to say. I really don't. Look, there's something else. . . ."

"There's more?"

"Stu Ballard, the chief administrator, has a niece with leukemia." Caryn rolled her eyes.

"Today is not a good day for a bone marrow drive, don't you think?"

"No, it's not a drive. They're putting the little girl, her name's Sophie, in the room Shane Ellston had."

"*What?*"

"They could put her in any room, actually. Everyone's flying out of here like it's an airport instead of an intensive care unit."

"So, no status reports on anyone?"

"Just one holdout—Penny Chaney—and she's status quo: coma, no response, vitals holding. Everyone else came in during the night."

"Is Stu's niece end-stage cancer?"

"They give her two months, tops."

"How can we justify holding a bed for someone not in immediate crisis?"

"Actually, they just want her to sit in the room. They think something in the room is making everyone better."

"It's mean to give her and her parents hope that is based on no sound evidence. She'll be in the way during this shift. What if I need the bed?"

"Jenny, Stu approached the chief of medicine and said he would consider it a personal favor."

"So that's that."

"Pretty much. Here they come now. You better go welcome them. I'm going home and hope the media doesn't get wind of this. Maybe I should update my résumé just in case." She wished Jenny luck and almost ran down the hall.

Louis Klotz passed Jenny as she hurried to her car, trying to shake off the sense that everything around her was tilting wildly out of place. Louis was shaking too. The medicine in his nebulizer was basically a form of adrenaline, designed to open his lungs but affecting his whole body. He tried to focus and appear normal. His watch was set for two hours, giving him plenty of leeway to get home to his machine before he was gasping for air. There was a picture in his mind of a dog attached to a clothesline leash that, when it saw a cat, would run frantically to capture it, only to be snapped back at the last minute when the slack ran out. Louis figured he was that dog. If he hurried, maybe he could snag the story before his time was up.

The first thing he noticed was one of the Franks leaving a dozen roses at the nurses' station. As he passed the waiting room it was empty of that talkative family and their sitting schedule was gone, leaving only the thumb tack that held it above the fake geraniums. The sadness that Louis felt at what he thought was the old woman's death, despite his never meeting her, surprised him. One of the family greeted him fleetingly as they passed: "Hey, our mom recovered! Hope your aunt's better!"

Louis barely had time to lift a hand in response. He rounded the corner and noticed an abundance of what he assumed were hospital administrators talking closely and pointing out things in various rooms. Hal was in his seat as though he had never moved, and Louis thought the guy looked as if he had been whipped through a blender. It was obvious he hadn't slept in way too long. He passed Hal and slowed down, peering into Shane Ellston's room. There was a little bald girl, skinny, barely moving, with a sickly green glow about her, wrapped in a homemade quilt and watching cartoons. Shit! he thought. He was just here! If the kid was already dead it would be such a better story, but it would be hotter and more difficult to score. At least with him in a hospital bed, he could always find the parents. He sat down in chairs next to Hal's skeletal smile.

Turning to Hal, he said, "I'm sorry about the boy. I had hoped he would make it."

"Actually, he went home." Hal searched Louis's face, trying to see if he knew him from somewhere.

Louis stuck out his hand, putting on his best we're-in-this-together expression. "Louis. My aunt's down the hall."

Hal took his hand gingerly. "Hal. That's my wife's room," he said, pointing beyond the glass.

"So the boy went home. I guess they felt more comfortable taking care of him there."

"I guess. He walked out on his own two feet, so I don't know how much caregiving he'll need."

"The boy was standing and walking?" Louis forgot himself completely, his voice loud and full of surprise.

"Did you know him?"

"No, I just . . . I mean, I'm surprised. I had heard his situation was dire."

Louis just sat there stunned. He didn't care how much time this Hal had spent in this damned hallway. He had to be wrong. He had the chart. The kid was brain-dead. Holding his pen, his hands shook from a crazy combination of medicine and suppressed rage at a story clearly slipping out from under him. Abruptly he got up and went back to what he considered Shane's room. He almost laughed at himself. What was he going to do, look for him under the bed?

A woman with a bald child looked up at him as he paused in the doorway, an expectant, hopeful look on her face. "I'm Sophie's mother. Can I help you?" The little girl's eyes moved toward her mother's gaze but her head seemed uncooperative, staying still, refusing to move. Amelia lifted her daughter's head gently for her and replaced it on the pillow so she could view the television from a better position. Both mother and daughter seemed like branches of the same tree, limp and tired from weathering one too many storms.

"Um, actually, I was looking for the boy who was here." He took a tentative step into the room, searching his mind for the right face, the right words, to extract from this woman what she knew about what had happened to his story.

"Oh, yes! He went home. Isn't it exciting news that he's better?"

"I thought he was terribly injured."

"Apparently everyone did." A smile crept across her face. "We hope Sophie will get—"

A shadow fell across the door behind Louis. "Amelia! What are you doing? Who is this?"

Louis whirled around. "I'm sorry. It's my fault. I was talking to the boy's mom and dad and was just wondering if he was better since I didn't see him." He smiled, trying to look silly. *Just a friendly guy, that's me.* "I'm visiting my aunt. I'm sorry to have taken your time. Good luck with your little girl."

"I'm sorry." The man said quickly. "We're all just nervous over Sophie. I didn't mean to snap. Hope your aunt has a speedy recovery." He stood tall with a look that, Louis realized, had experience in excusing people out of rooms, and he recognized him as one of the administrators skulking about the ward. With just a step out the door over to the left and an untying of a shoe, he was in position to hear the fallout from what he thought was a wife who had obviously, with one sentence, said too much.

Stu Ballard hissed at his sister. "Amelia!" Louis could barely hear him. He was whisper screaming and he sounded very frightened. "I've put my job and reputation on the line for this. I'm sure the entire hospital thinks I'm out of my mind. He could be the press! Please, she has to stay in the bed. ICU patients don't sit around in chairs."

"You know she can hardly move! And who's going to care? It's only families of patients here. This was your idea, and stop yelling in front of Sophie!"

Louis could hear Stu pacing and hoped he wasn't coming to the door, where he would be spotted. He strained to hear.

"Amelia, when word gets around about how many patients are just walking out of this hospital after being on their deathbeds, the press is going to go crazy. Two gunshot victims were here this morning. They were operated on and after two hours they were asking to leave. Two hours. One had lost a lung." There was a pause, and Klotz could picture Stu mopping his beefy brow. "It's going to be impossible to keep people from talking, but I have to be believable when I end up in front of a camera and say there's nothing unusual happening here. I don't need some smart-aleck reporter asking why my sister's kid is sitting in an ICU room on a hunch if everything is normal here at the hospital."

"What if people *do* know? So what? What if something wonderful is just beginning and you are a part of it?"

"But we don't know why it's happening. We don't know what we're doing right—or wrong, for that matter. What's even more important is, if people from just this state find out, do you know what kind of a stampede we would be facing? This is a small hospital; we're not equipped with the kind of manpower it would take just to turn the people away, much less treat them."

Someone sat on the bed and Louis thought he got everything from Stu that Stu himself knew. He sat again where Hal had been and drew a diagram of the ward. When there was a lull in the hallway he walked along it, taking down names, attending physicians and making best guesses at what people were there for. He would sit and watch them come and go. There had to be a pattern surrounding who was taking care of them or what they were taking. Had a doctor found some new drug and was using the ICU as his testing ground? Was there an orderly dispensing a new age herb? Maybe there was something placed in one of the rooms that was giving off a medicinal effect that was being ventilated into surrounding rooms by the heating ducts. A full page of his pad was devoted to theories, which he would try to eliminate.

Louis had almost the grace of a ballet dancer, moving around nonchalantly, blending in, and being the type of person who never gets a second glance. It had been the source of incalculable pain for him while growing up, yet it was the key to his reporting success. It worked like a charm today, and before long he had the name of every nurse, nursing assistant, orderly, doctor, janitor, respiratory therapist, administrator and intern with a name tag who placed a toe in the intensive care unit. He mapped their paths through the rooms. During a quiet moment he stepped out to the lobby and used his cell phone to call his contact at the airport, where he would get a summary of every person's travel itinerary from the last six months. In the middle of running down the lists and spellings of names, Louis Klotz's watch alarm went off. Reflexively he shut it off, making a mental note to run home and get his portable nebulizer. The list was endless, and when it was done, Klotz was promised he could call for results in exactly an hour.

Louis knew this was a tremendous story. He called his editor to lay claim on it as his territory and to give an outline of the piece for this evening, which would be mostly questions, speculations and buildup for the discovery. It was nearly written already. Finally he went off to the cafeteria to grab a quick cup of coffee before returning to his stakeout. When he returned to the ward, he noted the changes that had taken place in the short time he was away. Some patients had already been moved to a regular bed in a different floor, their condition upgraded despite being there so briefly that morning. Two teenagers, car accident victims, were being discharged completely. Klotz pored over his map, looking at the variables, trying to locate a pattern. He started taking a time record as patients came in, just to see how long they stayed.

The ward was getting crowded as the morning progressed. More and more doctors were finding their way there as whispers and rumors circulated around the hospital. Administrators wandered around and Louis scorned their unorganized approach to the situation. He wished they would clear the halls, as the extra people were getting in the way of his map. He was having a difficult time keeping up with the changes and those attending to them. At one point he finally threw up his hands in disgust, almost ready to abandon it all. His stomach was growling and he headed for lunch in the cafeteria, where he would scrutinize what he had and try to find some connection.

Louis slid a tray filled with pizza, a hamburger, a hot dog and two packages of cookies along the conveyor belt that snaked through the packed dining area. It was way too much for him, and he wondered where he had gotten such a big appetite. He stood in front of and behind doctors rooting around in their pockets for money when his watch alarm went off for the second time that morning. His panic was too large to hold. He had done it again, and this time he had no extra minutes to spare at all. Louis dropped his tray and his things scattered, most of it ending up under the salad bar, moving with a disarray that seemed to begin inside his mind. He stood ready to sprint to his car, knowing he would never make it, confused that the usual signs of distress hadn't warned him. He banged his pockets and looked for inhalers and all at once saw his headline go yet again to someone else.

"Are you all right, sir?" One of the kitchen staff came over with a chair.

"No, thank you," Klotz said, declining the proffered seat. "I have to get my medicine...."

A doctor approached him, guiding him to the chair. "Can we help you?"

"I'm sorry." Louis stood up. "I have acute asthma! I need to get my treatment." Now he was shouting. "Get out of my way! Can't you see this is an emergency? I could die!"

Louis probably would have sprinted out of the door if he hadn't seen the smirks on the faces floating above the white coats surrounding him. His anger kept him staring at them, not wanting to retreat. He would give them a full account of his lung disease, a count of the absurd number of times he had been pulled just inches away from death. He was a very sick man and they were laughing at him. How cruel! They had taken an oath! What kind of people were they?

"But, sir, you're not even wheezing."

The kitchen staffer said most eloquently, "You screamin' loud enough. Sounds like you got plenty of air!"

And Louis knew she was right. Everyone was moving on with the business of getting their lunches, streaming around him, and he stood there forgotten, a false alarm. His breathing was just fine. He sucked it in and blew it out, and it was the first day of his life, some thirty-five years, that he had gone from breakfast to lunch without being hooked up to a machine. Louis felt crazily free. It was as if gravity, as a law, had suddenly been lifted for being too restrictive. He was untethered and wondered if it would last. He was still the dog, the collar to the electric fence lost, but flinching as he approached the perimeter of the jail that had always confined him. The only home he knew.

Air poured into his lungs with a wholeness Louis could almost taste. A motor that had revved unchecked for over thirty years had finally been shut off, and in enjoying the quiet, he was able at last to see how loud it had been. Tears streamed down his face, and someone asked him if he was in line. Louis turned to the man and said, "Yes, I am most definitely in line."

It was the worst food and the best lunch Louis could recall ever having. He was barely able to focus on the maps he had created, he was so busy just breathing. But as he sat there he desperately tried to make sense of the pieces of information he had compiled. There was no consistency with the doctors treating patients; no one— doctors or nursing staff—had been anywhere exotic in the past year; and even as the shifts changed, the patients consistently continued to respond the same. Two distinct things popped out at him from among the clutter of facts. Everyone but Penelope Chaney was getting better, and the healing spread out in circles around her. The closer the patients were to Penny, the quicker they healed.

Louis almost ran back to the intensive care unit, knowing now where his focus should be. When he returned, the first thing he saw was little Sophie's bald head bobbing up and down the long corridor. She was skipping.

Chapter Eleven

Penny emerged from her sleep like a woman who had cliff dived beyond her capacity and was breaking the surface with a terrible urgency for air. Her gasping breath lifted her head at the same moment Louis Klotz's first article about her was lowered onto newsstands everywhere in their county. The wave it set off joined the whispers of the doctors and administrators who had already abandoned their posts in droves, seeking out their sick relatives. These whispers would quickly roll themselves into bold shouting and build to a roar before too long.

This news story, the stone thrown into the once quiet pond of Penny's life, sent ripples through the community like any newsworthy topic of the day. It was debated, mostly tongue in cheek, over the airwaves at the local radio stations. Callers dismissed its truth with gusto. In more intimate settings at work and schools, however, there were those willing to put forth the hope that perhaps this Penelope Chaney could heal. The most desperate went directly to the hospital.

While quiet country route 83 to that very hospital became overcrowded, there was another, smaller street across town that filled up with its own share of cars and hurried drivers heading to Isaac and Daisy Rourke's house like bees to a hive. Daisy Rourke opened and closed her screen door.

Above the handle was displayed a decal of the man whose outstretched arms threatened to jump out and hug someone unsavvy enough to be standing still for too long. The figure had a large head made into a globe and fingers that snaked toward opposite galaxies. Members of Isaac Rourke's movement found spots along his living room walls, bare but for two naked seventy-watt bulbs and their dull reflections on dusty uncarpeted wood planks. Most sat on the floor, packed tight and murmuring with excitement as they waited for the others. This was where the movement met. It was the kind of place where every movement in every city that Isaac Rourke ever began would meet. He and Daisy rented a modest house with a large living room on a country property with viable parking space. It was not bought and was never decorated. That would be materialism. They were to own nothing but the clothes on their backs, the bowl they ate from, a blanket for sleep.

Isaac much preferred the word *movement* over *church*. Movement suggested a vibrant membership guiding the volition of the group with a singleness of thought and ideals. It lent itself to being whatever it needed to be without conforming to any preconceived notions of what people expect from church. Isaac Rourke thought of himself as a sculptor of sorts and wanted his materials raw and unsuspecting.

Isaac and Daisy had been stationed in Southlawn for only eight months and had tremendous success in building a group of followers. Southlawn was their twentieth city in as many years and was slated to be their last. At each they brought to light the message of the heaviness of all that we possess, particularly money. Isaac was able to show the weightiness of things owned as a spiritual albatross wrapped around each person's neck and was more than happy to help unburden their souls.

Upon arrival into a new town, Daisy joined the local

senior citizen center. She would cook, deliver meals, volunteer to run the sewing club. Her secret was eye contact. Daisy looked deeply into the eyes of people who woke up one morning to find themselves approaching eighty. If asked, they would say they were genuinely shocked by the news. Most clung to their middle-age mindsets like someone holding on to a weak limb over the side of a cliff. Most would not look down and denied their stage of life even as that thin branch broke with a deafening snap and they plummeted to earth at breakneck speed. The snap was often the death of their spouse, the arrival of senior citizen status for their youngest child, a broken hip or the sale of the home they had lived in for the last fifty years. When they hit the ground, their mortality left them wounded.

Daisy could see on their faces the grandchildren who never called or the dream they hadn't lived. With a complete attentiveness and a gentle brush of a hand, she connected with them. Daisy had been raised by her elderly grandmother who beat her when the welfare check didn't arrive on time, and ran over her to get out the door when the spry widower across the street stepped out to collect his mail. She plucked the coarse white hairs from under Granny's chin in the evenings and watched that same neck quiver when Pastor Ellsworth complimented the dress she wore four Sundays in a row. Daisy knew their needs and how they wanted to be seen.

"Mrs. O'Leary, is that a new dress? It's absolutely stunning with those earrings!"

"This old thing?" they invariably said. But Daisy saw the color rush to their cheeks and their hands, like traitors, sneak down to smooth it out.

"Mrs. John, you look a little peaked. Come sit down. I'll get you some water. I insist," she told the ones always bemoaning their poor health.

"I have been a touch under the weather lately."

"I'll come by with a soup this evening. Split pea is your favorite, isn't it?"

Within a few short weeks she knew their tastes, if they liked to be complimented or coddled, their pains and their stories. She got into them the way a pleasant chill will ride your back when it is rubbed. It was easy for them to fall into the comfort of her services, and when she looked away, they fought among themselves for her attention. Daisy gave to each of them until they forgot how they had gotten along without her.

It was easy for her to let them do the talking. Her own granny had kept a roll of three-quarter-inch masking tape on the television stand for occasions when the child her daughter left her to raise became too talkative. Granny thought the axiom "Children should be seen and not heard" was one of the commandments. When it came time to drop the first lines about the movement, Daisy's seniors were always caught listening, so rare was it that Daisy wasn't asking them about themselves, bringing them somewhere or fixing something for them. She brought it up like an afterthought, a quiet secret among confidants. They were flattered to have a tidbit of information the others didn't. And, of course, they always let it slip.

"Daisy told me she and her husband don't own any furniture. Helping others is their most proud possession."

"Well, she told me her husband visits the sick ward at the children's hospital every day. They must be a good match, those two."

"I heard her tell Ida they hold prayer meetings every night, just them and a few friends." A jealous tone would creep into the teller's voice.

"But Daisy told me she's not any religion. How can you have a prayer meeting with no religion?"

Daisy would begin arriving late to the senior citizen center and smile to herself, reveling in the hushed quiet when she stepped through the doors. *They're talking,* she would think. Soon they'd be showing up unannounced at her home with pies and breads they had to take a handful of aspirin to knead out. They would be expected.

The seniors brought their daughters, women who tagged along to guard their inheritance, women who became the object of Isaac's keen, penetrating stare. It reminded them of how long it had been since their husbands looked at them that way. Soon they would bring their own children.

Most were already there that morning and Isaac came in to address the group. "I know you've read this morning's paper, and, like you, I am both excited and concerned. It has always been this group's sole purpose to find the next messiah and give Him all of our support, to help guide this world into a more holy existence in line with God's wishes. We've sold our monetary goods as individuals and come to be a part of the family of God. Is this person, this Penelope Chaney, the One? It has always been expressed that the One who would save would be of male figuration. That is the first point that gives me pause. We have also expected an immutably holy individual. By all accounts and some checking I've done, she is of average birth, leading a rather average existence. I caution us all to not become excited and remember that evil often does good to trick the pure of heart into its web of deceit."

A shaky voice came from the floor. "My neighbor said she healed her niece—said her niece had only weeks to live."

Isaac stood taller and lowered his voice. "It's possible she is healing people—I can't deny this—but we don't know what her intentions and connections are."

"So how will we know?"

"The One to represent us will be much quieter. This woman is in the news. She has no commitment to God that anyone knows of. We want to test her to be sure she is ours before we give her the backing of all of the resources we've gathered, before we let her in."

There was a reflective pause among the group, an expectant air. They looked to Isaac, in whom they had stored all of their trust and, more importantly, their cash. "How much have we gathered for the One?" someone called out, voicing a question everyone wanted to ask. Isaac squirmed and was temporarily relieved to hear the distraction of a footstep that arrived with a loud knock and an echo on the cold wood floor. Every eye looked up at Jetta Rizone.

Jetta spread her hands out to both sides of her, unaware that she was imitating the icon that stuck innocently onto the sliding screen door. A smile sat on her face, gathering all of the light in the room. She needed only to whisper the three words that blew apart the operation of Isaac and Daisy Rourke.

"She's the One."

Control of the room collapsed around Isaac. There were sobs and quiet screams that wound themselves into prayers and gasps. Some stood, ready to go that second. Daisy looked around, wondering how things could have unraveled so quickly, so completely. Isaac tried to get everyone's attention, seat them and assure them that Penny would be looked into thoroughly, convince them no action should be taken until they were sure. Yet, he couldn't be heard above Jetta's quiet nods and raised eyebrows, which accentuated her one brief sentence. She was irrefutable with her mere standing presence. The blow of her testimony was then made complete. "I was dead and she brought me back to life."

Mrs. O'Connell, the dentist's wife, fainted. Daisy locked the front door and stood blocking it, hoping she wouldn't be crushed in the onslaught of people rising and heading toward her. Somewhere in the kitchen she heard her one glass fall to the floor and break into what she would later discover to be two large jagged pieces. She marveled at how every substance has its own sound in its breaking: Glass, wood, human bones all admitted their defeat distinctively.

"Please!" Isaac was shouting. "Please! Everyone, settle down. Please, sit. We are a group. Let's work this out together."

The floor filled up again and there was a quietness Isaac saw as probably his last opportunity. Looking at them all in their anxiousness, he felt as though he were addressing a crowd of race cars, parked but idling. He could hear the hum of their impending motion. Truth be told, he, and in turn they, had little idea of what to do. The movement had always been about waiting and watching. It centered on getting ready and how to live. It was in the collecting of funds. Isaac was careful not to give Jetta the floor again and searched feverishly the annexes of his mind for something, anything, that would give them pause.

"My friends, I fear in the depths of my soul an imposter sent to mislead this righteous group away from its mission of waiting for the true One. I fear this woman's motives. She is not the pure heart we have sought out. We want to think it will be in our lifetime but we have to put our egos aside and know we work for the generations to come, to create an antimaterialistic society devoted only to holiness. Only when these ways are all of our ways will the true One appear. We will not be fooled by evil imposters looking to lead us astray to divert out attentions."

"But what if she *is* the One? Look at Jetta!"

Isaac knew Jetta was an undeniable argument and would have little means to refute what had transpired. Daisy looked at him with eyes that brought him to attention, focused him on everything they had worked for over the last twenty years, what they had planned to retire on after this last dismal town. A light sheen of sweat encapsulated her face.

"We will set up a schedule to watch her around the clock, to track her movements in order to determine her motives." Hands flew up around the room to volunteer.

"Daisy and I will meet with her and see if we can't feel out her intentions. We want to be careful, folks." Isaac ignored Jetta's hand, which was raised and swinging wildly about. When she got up to speak to the group anyway, Isaac hurried to throw out his last idea, shouting to bring the focus back to himself. "She may have beat her own death, if reports are accurate, and she may even have the power to heal, as we can readily see with our sister, Jetta. But we want to know for sure what her true nature is. Others are flocking to her like sheep. We will be more cautious. If we are to give her all of our allegiance, all of our resources, we must take care. We will monitor her and see who she is. If she seems to be the One, we will have to test her. Only the true One will be unstoppable, able to survive the hands of someone seeking pure holiness, an apostle of righteousness."

With the weight of Isaac's desperate words, one last moment of quiet was thrown into the room. An essential question was eked out before the frenzy of activity began.

"Are you saying we'll have to kill her to be sure?"

Chapter Twelve

Helicopters circled Southlawn Hospital with an impatient chopping, darting toward traffic as if they could shepherd it into submission or frighten it away. At only nine A.M., when most offices and schools took up their tools at the start of the day, the hospital was deeply embroiled in what already felt like a lengthy battle. Every parking spot for two miles was taken, and lines snaked around the modest blocks that watched the sick wait patiently for a turn with the Mother Healer, as Penny was being called. Newscasts over the last day had been recounting her life and, as it had not been particularly exciting or overly juicy for a feature piece, mentioned primarily her role as a loving mother to her three small children. They had started out calling her the mother who heals, and with time being of the essence and sound bites of information coming together, Penny was transformed on the long line toward the hospital into the Mother or the Healer. It would run itself past enough lips and through enough conversations to meld into Mother Healer, a title they would call her until her given name was nearly forgotten in the cascade of exchanged facts about her, real and imagined.

Penny could feel the hoards of people as she took her first conscious gulping breaths and before her eyes were even opened. Their need reached her the way the sound of a bell finds your ear the moment it is struck. In that vein, this new sense she had was as unyielding as hearing or smell in its veracity to work despite a desire to dampen or shut it down. She tried to find the lids to close, the means to stave off the stimulus, even as she looked at Hal for the first time since their ride to the emergency room. Hal looked terrible, and she felt the exhaustion in his chest. But his eyes lit up, watering with relief as they met Penny's.

"Penny! Thank God! Nurse! She's awake! Oh my God, Penny!" He threw himself at her, alternately pulling himself away to check to see if she really was with him and surrounding her with arms that were suddenly alive and strong.

"I had the strangest dream, Hal," Penny whispered, not knowing how else to put things, needing him to know right away.

"Shhh, Pen. Just get your strength together for now."

Nurses came in followed by an entourage of doctors, hospital staff and security guards, all of whom had already read Louis Klotz's article. They looked at her the way her twins looked at the visiting exhibit at the zoo each summer. It wasn't quite the fear the lions evoked or the laughter of seeing the orangutan, but more like the mix of amazement and awe of being too near the elephant should it suddenly stand on its hind legs and trumpet. A team of nurses unhooked her, one taking her vitals with an almost complete lack of skin contact and an inability to look her in the eye, another changing her sheets as though she were giving her a massage. The first fled from the room and the last touched Penny's hand, asking her to bless her.

"Nurse Joan!" Stu Ballard, the administrator, scowled at the nurse, who backed out of the room, bowing respectfully, keeping both eyes on Penny until the door was closed on her.

"I'm so sorry!" Stu smiled, as a sheen of sweat made its first of many appearances of the day at his temples. "We're glad you're awake. We have quite a bit to discuss here."

"My wife needs a minute to reorient herself, don't you think?" said Hal. No one responded. "Please everyone." Again no one moved, either to examine her or to leave. They were statues.

"All right! Get out! I said my wife needs a minute! Is this how you treat all of your coma patients? Examine her or get the hell out!" Hal had already gotten a terrible glimpse of the shape things were taking. He had to hold his hands up and shoo them out like a gaggle of mute geese. Hal scowled as he physically guided them all to the door. One nurse stayed, giving Penny a drink of water and helping her to sit up in bed. Penny watched the antics carefully, her head tilted as if she were listening for something while she offhandedly tried to disconnect each of the wires attached to her.

"Hal..." she croaked in a weak voice. The group, halfway out, froze so abruptly, their eyes fixed on her like little marble soldiers called to attention, that Penny laughed. She was living one of those old E. F. Hutton commercials and she knew she was not going to enjoy it in the long run, but for now, for the very first time, the humor of it blindsided her. She hoped they wouldn't think she was insane.

"The security guard..." Penny's eyes searched the group, looking for him as he stepped toward her. The length of her arm seemed incredibly short now. What had been spread out like a giant blanket, enveloping much of the hospital and healing all in its path, was now rolled up inside of Penny, but it had lengthy feelers, monitoring almost constantly those around her, both near and far-off. Penny saw at once that she could no more reel them in than she could shut off her sense of hearing. She held out her hand, and Sam, the security guard, scooped it up like the winning fly out at the World Series. They looked at one another and Sam began to cry immediately, heartily, over what had passed between them. Bawling and keening, his bones lost their rigid stance, sending him down on his knees, collapsing into their handshake, his forehead resting along her cool arm. He could feel the cancer lose its hold on his prostate and see the microscopic piece that had metastasized on his lung float serenely out of his system.

Hal and the others watched with awe. No one moved anything but their eyebrows, which shot up in unison, and their mouths, which they didn't technically move, but which rather dropped open of their own accord. Every hair on every square inch of every body in the room stood on end, and all at once there was the cleansing smell of heavy oxygen that complements the end of a rainstorm or begins a crisp autumn morning. When it was over, Hal went over to Sam and helped him to his feet, escorting him and the others out of the room, closing the door even as they stood there, still looking in.

"Please," he whispered, "I just want one more minute with my wife."

Hal and Penny stared at one another from across the room, already swept up and rushing down some strange river. It seemed almost impossible to stop it all long enough to go back and discuss where it all began. Hal came over, sitting down in his chair-bed and feeling whatever was coming from Penny touch him like the heat from a campfire.

"How are the children?" Penny asked, making a stab at normalcy, trying to step away from the situation to pretend for a minute it wasn't there. But as she listened to Hal describe who was caring for the children, what they had said and the cards they had made for her, she could also feel the nurse who passed the room hesitating in the hall, then moving on again and again, hoping her breast cancer would be healed before the mastectomy procedure she had scheduled for the next week took place. Penny nodded and smiled at Hal and tried to give the nurse what she needed but somehow couldn't.

". . . and Benjamin won't nap for anyone. Thank God you're all right. I think he's become delirious in the last twenty-four hours. You know how he gets when he doesn't sleep."

"I think I need to actually touch the people to heal them now."

Hal hesitated, screwing up his mouth and sitting down. "People have been walking out of the ICU since you got here, Pen."

"Yes, I know. I met them."

Hal stopped. "I think I'd like to hear about that dream now."

Penny described it all in as much detail as she could remember—the bridge, the figure, the people—trying to relive it for Hal so he could somehow be there with her through its reenactment.

"Penny, what you're saying is impossible."

Penny gaped. "How can you say that? You're the one who's witnessed everyone being healed. Why is what I'm saying so much crazier than that?"

"Because . . . I don't know, just because it's too much. Why you?"

"Thanks, Hal."

"I don't mean you're not a great person, Pen. I love you. But let's face it, you and I are pretty ordinary."

"I tried saying that; it didn't seem to make a difference."

"Well, did the being you met say why they picked you?"

"No, not really. He didn't make it sound like I was picked; more like I had this quality when I showed up."

"Well, didn't you ask why?"

"I did, but I didn't really get an answer."

"There has to be a reason."

"I'm sorry, Hal. Would you like to bop me on the head and send me back there so I can get all the little details ironed out?"

"Sorry."

"No, *I'm* sorry. Not exactly the patience of some great healer."

Penny and Hal waited quietly while a nurse came in to remove Penny's IV. The beeping of machines and squeaking of white shoes filled out their background, making everything sound so normal and ordinary. Only the bustling outside the window of the sick lining up and pushing in on the police lines around the hospital gave Penny and Hal the sense that the world hadn't changed in their minds alone. Hal stood, pulled back a heavy drape and peeked out at the swarms below Penny's window. A brief glimpse of his face through the crack of the curtain was enough to send murmurs through the crowd that led to screams. Hands reached up toward Hal as he whipped the curtain closed again, trying to make it block out the picture in his mind as well as the one in front of his eyes. He knew the children would not be able to visit Penny today. There would be no getting through. He wondered how they would ever get Penny out. A vision danced through his imagination of the room being dismantled piece by piece and sold on the Internet: "Penny Chaney's IV bag, bidding to start at ten thousand dollars."

"I can feel them out there, Hal," Penny said as the door closed behind the nurse. "I know what a scene this already is."

"They're out there praying. What are we going to do?"

Penny's face fell into a grimace. "I don't know, Hal. What will I tell them?"

"I have no idea. They're already making you into some kind of a religious figure. You're all over the news. I think the Catholic Church is sending in their miracle authenticity group. They're probably flying out of Rome as we speak. Kind of like the Messiah SWAT team." Hal chuckled in a high pitch Penny had never heard before.

"This is not funny, Hal. How can you make a joke at a time like this?" But Penny did laugh, too, before she started to cry.

Hal held her and searched his mind for answers he didn't feel he had the resources to acquire. "Pen, you're going to have to tell people something. Otherwise, they're just naturally going to make what's happened a religious thing." He added, "Maybe you shouldn't do it anymore."

"This gift has no card attached to it—no sudden understanding of what it all means or why. It should be accompanied by some kind of instructions, some insight into the bigger picture. What's wrong with me? Maybe somewhere inside of me is the answer, but I just don't know how to read it. I don't want to be on a pedestal. I don't want to be some kind of messiah. I don't fit the bill. It's almost sacrilegious."

"Almost?"

"It is sacrilegious. I think I should use this ability to heal but why can't I just heal them and send them on their way? It would be the most honest way to handle things."

Hal rolled his eyes. "That's too simple. I just don't think people will let it work like that."

"I wouldn't be believable if I started talking about religion. I don't know anything about it even in a theoretical, book-knowledge kind of a way. Honestly, I'm not sure I can fake it. And I don't think I'd want to pretend to be something I'm not. Isn't just getting their health back enough of a statement? I don't want to say things I don't believe."

"But you said you're supposed to change people's view of the world."

They both fell silent, listening to the chants of the prayer circles that had formed under the window. Penny felt cheated. She really had no choice after all, and she couldn't imagine making an impact on people who had already decided who she was without her even being conscious.

"What if I tell them to go out and be a better person?"

Hal thought. "What if to them that means going to the gym more often. Everyone has a different opinion of how to work on being a better person."

Penny chewed on a fingernail, a habit she'd quit when she was in college. She suddenly regretted not being a chain-smoker or having a drinking problem.

"What if I say, 'Get right with God'?"

Hal screwed up his face. "That's very corny, Pen. It sounds like something out of a movie. What if they ask you how to do that?"

Penny threw up her hands. "This is a ridiculous situation. I don't want to say something superficial, but I also don't want to tell people to go do something I don't know how to do myself."

Hal thought he had something. "How about 'Love thy neighbor'?"

"Kind of general. What if their neighbor is a beer-swilling, drug-selling thief?"

"Then I guess they'll have a harder job to do." Hal sat with a sigh. "We have to get home, Penny. I can just imagine what's going on outside of our house. What I can't imagine is how we're ever going to get you out of here."

"How does 'Embrace your religion' sound?"

Hal rocked his head from side to side, mulling it over. "It does cover everything, doesn't it? You wouldn't be starting a new religion, just asking everyone to go out and make a commitment to their own."

"It's still so trite. I'll go down as the Greeting Card Savior."

"I've been meaning to bring that up."

"What?"

"You've already been labeled."

Hal described how the title Mother Healer had come into play and went into some depth on the coverage she'd gotten in the last twenty-four hours.

"It sounds like I'm a little old nun."

"If you haven't noticed, you're getting no calls. I had to have the phone shut off. Everyone in any media capacity in the area wants an interview with you. There's a guard posted outside of your door."

Penny was stricken. Hal hadn't seen her so white since he carried her to the ER. "Penny! Are you all right?" At that moment Hal thought he might never recover from this event, possibly living the rest of his married life feeling as though his wife were attached to him by a single fragile spider-web–like thread that could simply float away at any time.

"Every new piece of knowledge about what's happening paints a clearer picture of how we are never going to have our lives back. Ever. The morning I collapsed was my last morning as a normal person." Penny sobbed, choking out her words with a mourning Hal was beginning to feel himself. "Our children will never know a normal life. I'm not going to be able to walk around the block with a baby carriage. I won't be able to go food shopping."

Hal could think of no argument. Of course, she was right. The lives they knew were now over.

"Penny . . ." he said hesitantly, trying to boost her back up, "Maybe we're looking at this all wrong. Maybe this is really a great honor, to be able to do good for so many people. But my gut tells me you shouldn't do this at all. I think you should just walk away."

Penny shot him a look, a little embarrassed. "I tried to get out of it."

Hal smiled briefly. "Only you would say 'No, thanks' to possibly saving humanity. What did you say, 'I'm too busy with the kids'?"

"Well, I am," she said sheepishly, hearing how ridiculous she sounded, how ungrateful.

"We can just disappear and step out of the spotlight. You can choose not to do this. You can also pretend it's all been a mistake or say you don't have the power anymore. Although, judging by whatever you just did for that security guard, I don't think you're going to be credible."

Penny wanted to share with Hal the options she'd been given on choosing to participate or not but held off, afraid. Only half of the memory of what had been said seemed clear, and her mind fought off the other half, wanting to bury it away behind the clutter of thousands of days where it would be less potent, less frightening.

"How about a disguise?" Hal suggested.

"My picture's been all over the news."

"What if everyone thinks you've been dramatically changed by what happened to you and you now look different? Maybe old, wizened."

"I'll still have the same features I always have. I didn't just fall off the turnip cart, but I certainly don't look eighty, either."

"We can spread a rumor that the experience has made you unearthly-looking."

"*Unearthly?*" Penny frowned.

"Okay, maybe just different." Penny frowned again

but Hal persisted: "Just hear me out! What if we say by seeing the face of God—"

"I'm not sure I saw the face of God."

"It's a rumor, Pen. We'll say you'll only go out in public in a head wrap and veil. If you heal some of the people surrounding the hospital in that getup, it will get plenty of coverage. That's what people will start seeing in the news. When people picture you, it will be in that outfit. That way, when you're out with the kids, you can just dress normally, be yourself and blend right in. Everyone will be looking for a woman in a head wrap and veil."

"That's so bizarre, I think it might work."

"Let's do it now, before you're exposed to even one more person."

Hal headed for the hospital linen closet and Penny flipped on the overhead television, where she found herself on most of the morning news shows. She was thanking herself for spending the extra time getting ready for her high school senior picture as that was the shot everyone was running. The array of facts that were made up about her was fascinating, and Penny wondered if she wouldn't have to say anything at all when she healed people. Perhaps the media would come up with something for that as well, she thought cynically. An E-mail address flashed across the screen where the Mother Healer was supposed to be holding an on-line chat at noon. Penny was dying to log on to see what she would be saying. For brief moments it was almost possible to believe they were talking about someone she had never met, and in some ways that was true. She made a vow to never read another gossip magazine again, and even the thought of glancing at "Hollywood Grape Vine," one of her favorite sections in the local paper, made her queasy.

A pile of pillowcases and sheets hurried in with Hal's legs scurrying underneath. Hal helped Penny into her jeans, sweatshirt and sneakers and they set about creating a covering for her that tried to hold her anonymity inside it, allowing only her frightened eyes and clammy hands access to the world.

Hal felt as though he had recaptured some control over the world. "Penny, I made some calls while I was out hunting for these."

"Are the children all right? Did you find out about the children?"

"They're upset. Our house is surrounded by people looking for you."

"What about the police? Can't they move them back, tell them I'm not there?"

"They're doing their best. But I have a plan to get us all out of this town completely until things settle down."

Penny was torn between a desire to fly to a remote corner of the world and her commitment to the hordes of people that waited for her.

"Hal, let's try to help these people first." He began to wrap her up.

"It takes such a short time to heal them—seconds, really." She spoke from behind a mask of bleached linen, feeling somehow protected. "If I give them what they need, they'll go."

Hal couldn't even put into words how wrong Penny was. It was as if she had said, "It's okay, Hal. If we both have a pail and start right away, we can empty out this sea in no time at all." He thought about arguing with her, telling her she might be able to gather up the foam, but the waves of the ocean are infinite and relentless in their onslaught. Instead he just led her to the window and drew open the curtains with a snap.

The crowd came alive. Those who could rose to their feet, setting off a push toward Penny that began three stories under her and continued three miles off in the distance, its end lost to view. It was noon and they already surrounded the buildings in all directions, swallowing up each feature that made up the city. There were no cars or sidewalks, mailboxes or curbs; instead there were people, as never ending as grains of sand. The city seemed to be losing its identity in sympathy with Penny and her very thoughts, which didn't have a fighting chance over the shouts of the crowd, now calling, crying, keening, wanting.

And Penny saw that Hal was right. If she could just hold up a hand and give them what they needed, it would be easy. But by the time she got to each of them individually, it would take days, maybe even weeks. By that time others would have arrived to take their place. This was not the bridge with its timelessness. Each second was solid and real, taking with it another moment from her, another opportunity to be with her children. . . .

"Some of them are so very desperate." She stepped away from the window.

Hal threw his hands up and raised his voice. "Penny, you could get crushed, then you won't be able to do anything for anyone. This isn't a controlled setting. Let's find a place where you can do this safely."

Penny's voice was steady. "Some of them won't make it. They've already come a long way and have been waiting."

Hal tried to stare her down, but the only part of Penny that was still showing was her strong eyes, and he lost before he even realized they were arguing.

"I think I'll need a megaphone or a PA system or something," Penny said tentatively.

They gathered up their things and had their meetings with the administrators, assuring them that she would try to disperse the crowd peacefully and asking them to call off the policemen until she could see what she could do. Penny signed out of the hospital against her doctor's orders. She stopped along the way to help those who had come to work that day for her: the nurse with breast cancer, the elderly volunteer whose cataracts had settled into his eyes with a firm grip but who was desperately afraid of surgery, the janitor whose heart housed a small leak.

She made her way back to her third-story room, an entourage of suits in tow, and threw open the windows, Hal holding on to her from behind as she leaned out and shouted through the hospital sheets into the emergency megaphone that Sam, the security guard, had found for them.

"Please!" The antiquated sound device squeaked, and hundreds covered their ears. *Great,* thought Penny. *That's exactly the opposite of what I want them to do.*

"Please," she tried again and watched as those who could raised their eyes to her and settled down. It took a few moments for those in front to pass the message down each of the overcrowded blocks. All Penny could think of was the telephone game and wondered what a simple word like *please* would turn into over three miles.

"The hospital cannot function with so many people blocking it from every side." There was a roar of defiance, a massive wave of disappointment on the faces of everyone Penny could see, which traveled outward as her words got passed along. She could hear crying both in her ears and in that new receptacle that absorbed their pain. *Okay,* she thought, *that was bad. Start with the good news first. Make a mental note to start with the directions from now on.* "If you can, please move carefully to both sides of the road to the ambulance bay."

Penny waited, watching for movement. A few people fell.

"Please move slowly so no one gets hurt!" It was like reading a quiet poem at a football game. She was thoroughly convinced that not one soul had heard her. Both Hal and Penny gasped when a path snaked out from the hospital as if a pair of giant, invisible scissors had cut through the fabric of people. It was a ribbon, then a narrow walkway, and grew slowly into a road, stopping when there were policemen and yellow sawhorses butting against the sidewalks. Classical music wafted toward them from somewhere off in the distance, fighting off the unnatural quiet.

Their team took the elevator down to the hospital's main entrance. Penny and Hal were surrounded by the administrators, security guards and state troopers, one of whom was explaining why Penny had to take the newly opened path and drive away.

"You-all don't have a license for a parade or formal public gathering. It's unlawful for you to address this crowd at this time without a city permit. You're also in an essential emergency area of the city at which no permits for such gatherings are ever given."

Penny and Hal stared at the officer. At only one o'clock, it was already the longest day either of them could remember.

"Are you saying that if Penny interacts with the crowd in any way, she'll be arrested?" asked Hal.

"They've come a long way to be helped," Penny added.

"We need to listen to the officer, Pen."

"I'm sure you'll be able to find accommodations for them at some other lawful gathering," the policeman said, stressing the word *lawful*.

"Fine," said Penny after a moment of thought. "Allow us to walk up the road and tell them where the location will be so they'll leave peacefully. I'll use the megaphone."

The story of what happened along that road away from the hospital got terribly twisted, as all amazing events do. The ten administrators who surrounded her as she exited the emergency room doors turned into fifty, the three circling news helicopters became thirteen, the fifty local police officers keeping the peace were five hundred in later accounts. Instead of walking along, briefly holding hands with those who came to see her, some said she shook their entire bodies until their maladies fell out of them like coins from a bank. Her eyes were reported as ice blue, sea green, lavender and black. They swore they could see the face of God in them—even those who had been standing two miles away. One news reporter interviewed fifty people who said they had personally touched her and fifty who claimed to be in close proximity and came up with one hundred different messages they said Penny had passed on to them. "Embrace your religion" didn't appear anywhere in the bunch. For all of the facts that everyone seemed so sure of, no one could quite possibly pinpoint when the crowd had rushed her or how the police had been able to extract Penny's limp form from under the swarm that engulfed her. The only thing everyone agreed on was that it all got ugly fast.

Chapter Thirteen

The question hung in the air: Was Isaac seriously suggesting Penny would have to be killed in order to test her validity as the next messiah? "Of course," replied Ronald Miller, the retired librarian. "How else will we know for sure?" Jetta was astounded. For someone who had seen eighty years of life frame by frame and thought she had put her finger on some of the world's greater truths, she now saw only her own naïveté.

On the ride over, Jetta had reflected that in retrospect getting old was one of the worst things that had ever happened to her. There was tremendous rhetoric about growing old gracefully and the wisdom of the years and all that. In truth, there was a lot more indigestion, gas, hemorrhoids, and arthritis than wisdom. It had been about losing things, your hair, your figure, your sex life and, most painfully, the people you'd grown up with. Jetta found her circle of those she loved like an October tree. Every time she turned around, there were fewer leaves. She herself had dried up, hanging precariously to the last brittle twig when Penny Chaney brought her back.

And brought back she was. Fully. She could feel juices flowing in places she had forgotten all about. Her aches and pains had scampered off to areas unknown, leaving her dizzy with an energy she didn't quite know what to do with. Days had formerly been filled with getting to the bathroom on time. Fixing a cup of coffee entailed three cuts across the kitchen and maneuvering past an open refrigerator she named Cape Food, the door had seemed so big and far around. She often counted her steps to fill the space of seconds between each, trying to keep them steady and firmly planted. Her children helped move her, elbow extended, arms pulling her along. Days were scheduled with a nothingness that seemed to take up all of her time. Now, somehow, that had all been lifted—suspended, Jetta thought, somewhere above her—so that if she looked up, she was afraid she might be able to see it ready to crash down around her, bringing back the former weight of her limbs.

All of the questions that plagued Jetta on her deathbed seemed to fly out of her in the car on the way to the group, and she had let the sun buoy them up where they could slip out of her driver's-side window unnoticed. The crank had turned easily to let the glass slide out of her way and she had thrown her arm into the rush of air she sped through. Life, like speed, was terribly intoxicating, and Jetta gulped it down heartily. When she arrived, she walked in free of the many aches of old age and small pangs of everyday life, excited to share with her friends the elation of discovering the very thing they had all been searching for. The friends who cried at her bedside only days ago, she thought, would again be crying, this time with relief. She was counting on marking this day on her calendar and in her heart. The greeting she imagined she would get in just minutes bounced around in her head, and she savored it like the penny candy she favored as a child. Isaac and Daisy Rourke's was the group she felt most a part of since leaving the Catholic Church. Jetta never imagined she would be anything but Catholic, and technically she still was. Enough rosaries passed her lips to send a legion of souls from purgatory when there still was a purgatory to pray people out of. She still went to confession every Saturday to ask forgiveness for not going to church the Sunday before as well as her premeditated intention to be absent the following day. There were nights she woke up with the Our Father trailing from her lips as if her subconscious self were trying to make up for her daily transgressions. A Catholic who considered herself on temporary hiatus, she wondered how you could live a whole lifetime and not at some point resist the rote movement of hundreds of thousands of prayers so ingrained in your memory that you could pray for an hour and also plan out your shopping list at the same time. Jetta had just wanted to stretch.

She knew everyone in the group and they all knew her condition. It was prideful, but on the way there she had thought how thrilling it was to be the concrete evidence of the miracle they had all joined the group looking for! They would be astounded. How satisfying to describe the peace she felt at Penny's touch, the wholeness, not just physically but spiritually. It was as if she had spent her whole life at attention and finally had been given permission to be "at ease." There was a doubt in her whether she could convey this with the depth of meaning she felt, but she wanted to try. Never much of a public speaker, she let that thought pass through her. *We'll cross that bridge when we get there,* Jetta decided. She knew now she would have to be electric to win the group's trust. She wanted to see Penny again, to bring all of them to help her. All of Isaac's people across the country could be merged into a network of support for Penny's work. She had touched Jetta for only a moment, yet Jetta felt as though they had been joined somehow. In her mind she called to her: "Don't worry, Penny! We're coming! You don't have to do this alone!"

Instead, Isaac's doubt and skepticism spread through

Jetta's friends like a virus. The world felt as though it had spun completely the wrong way on its axis. What was up, to Jetta, was now down, and there suddenly seemed to be nothing to hold on to. Conversely, Isaac and Daisy couldn't believe their luck in turning the group against her, fanning the fire of their confusion and trying to ignite opposition in those who remained reasonable and reserved.

"We've been waiting for this moment to weed out deceivers. Others have died waiting for it. Will we turn away from it with cold feet or tepid sentiments?"

Isaac got a mild response. The opposing murmurs had settled down and he knew he had to act fast to keep the momentum going. "Will you let evil take over in the name of goodness?

Some mild replies of "No" and some of "Of course not."

"I said," Isaac shouted, "will *you* be the one to let evil take over in the name of goodness?" He pointed at the strongest man among them, a retired engineer. Everyone looked the man's way. Isaac's arm was a steel rod. Stronger "No!" responses, and he knew he was gaining them back.

"Will we let the world be fooled by this imposter?" He was inches from their faces.

"No! No! No! *No!*" A chant arose, sounding around the country lane and pushing farther and farther out with each question.

"Will you be bought off by the evil one's magic?" They were being accused and stiffened against whatever Isaac condemned.

"*No!*" The room shook.

Isaac knew instinctively amid the shouting that there could be no more discussion of whether Penny was the One. There could be no waiting and seeing. That was how the group would be lost. Of course, he and Daisy could just take the twenty years' worth of other people's earnings and head for their offshore account. Their middle-of-the-night discussion turned heated argument revolved around just that. Daisy thought they should call it a career ender. Isaac thought this could be their most profitable time, their most noble coup. After all, surely this Penny woman was no one, as worthless as her name indicated. Whatever had happened around her would be debunked and she would go back to her obscure life. His group would see her for what she was and invest with even greater gusto in finding the "true" One. There would be great pride in keeping this path clear for the One. They could retire victors in every sense of the word. They just had to hold on.

Jetta seemed to be the fly in the ointment. "You're all wrong!" she tried shouting above the voices of people she thought she could trust.

Daisy took her aside. "Jetta, you've been through a terrible ordeal."

Jetta was having none of it. She turned back to the group, "You all saw me! You saw the condition I was in! Betsy," she said, eyeing one of her oldest friends, "you visited me!"

Isaac thought briefly that he should have been a lawyer. It was when things got most heated, most chaotic, that his mind worked best, as if oiled by controversy. He could think twice as fast on his feet. "You have been tainted by her!" he screamed, sending both Jetta and even Daisy back a step, caught off guard, surprised by the power of his voice.

"I can describe what happened!" she appealed to her peers, people she had grown up with. "Judge for yourselves! I can tell you about being healed by her!"

They looked at her, and in the microcosm of the instant that Isaac hesitated, Jetta thought she saw the flicker of doubt in their eyes, the idea tangibly crossing their minds that perhaps they should listen to her. But when Isaac stepped back up to the plate with "She has been affected by this woman! Every word of her testimony is tainted! Will you go under her spell too?" Jetta saw only sorrow and fear in their eyes. For her. Their eyes said, *The lines have been drawn, Jetta. We're here and you're there and we don't know exactly how things fell out the way they did, but we're not on the same side anymore. You'd better go, Jetta. Hurry.*

Around her his voice reverberated: "Will you listen to this evil testimony?"

"Nooooooo!"

Jetta backed away, reaching behind her for the door and turning the latch back and forth, only to find it locked.

Isaac asked his group, "Will you let this evil testimony be spread?"

"Noooo!"

"Will you let this evil force influence us?"

"Noooo!"

At some point the ocean doesn't need the wind to sustain its storm. Crashing waves perpetuate themselves. The group no longer shouted but screamed, as if each and every one was beyond any rational decibel level. As their cries became louder and more pronounced, they sprang to their feet, their bodies following their voices in the call for action. When they reached a climax that threatened to burst Jetta's eardrums, Isaac called for silence with both of his long arms and tightly clenched fists thrown up to the ceiling.

Only the crickets could be heard. There seemed to be no breathing at all. The old house stood stock-still and held its creaks in check. Isaac bathed in the ionized energy of full, almost volatile attention, holding it with those fists and his wide-open, wild eyes.

If one of Jetta's friends, any one of the many who had known her for over fifty years, or a neighbor who had greeted her across the counters of the Shop Quick for more decades than they cared to count, had asked a question or even made a sound of disapproval, the momentum of the group might have faltered. Jetta might have had the extra seconds she needed.

Isaac's wiry hair, usually slicked back into submission, was now scattered around his head in separate tufts long enough to brush against his arms as he thrust them toward Jetta. They were no longer arms, really, but floodgates opening to allow the mad crowd out. Jetta ran. One last pull told her the front door had been dead bolted and she wasted no more time tugging at it. The living room was tiny, made smaller by the number of people packed into it. They would be on her in seconds. Daisy Rourke blocked a wooden archway to her left leading into the living room. Jetta could already see a clever throng coming up behind her from its back entrance through the living room. All she could think of in those terrible moments was how fast they were, like a lion let out of its cage, its sleepy naps and lethargic pacing pure trickery to hide the truth of its deadly speed. She jerked herself to the right and was almost thrown off balance, she was so unused to her body's regained agility. There was the side door, opened to the screen at the rear of the long kitchen, and Jetta saw her car in her mind's eye, parked at the end of the row that extended from the house. She would throw herself against the door and jump off the three-step porch. They wouldn't really hurt her, she said to herself again and again in those quick seconds that she ran into the kitchen. Leda Maynard had been in her wedding party. Tony Elliot had fixed her first refrigerator and sat on her steps drinking lemonade she had squeezed fresh for him and her children one hot August. Disbelief slowed her down as she felt the first scrapes of fingers against the nape of her neck, the hands snagging her sweater. Some had found access to that side of the house via the dining room leading into the kitchen, and she saw their shadows cross the threshold, threatening to head her off only feet from her escape. She let her sweater go as their hands grabbed at it, thrusting her arms backward and pulling them out to ward the group off. In that free second she gained enough ground to make it to the last cabinet in the kitchen and forward to a set of tarnished coat hooks on the threshold to the exit. From the corner of her eye, flashes of color came at her, all arms reaching.

It was unfortunate that the screen door opened inward. Jetta threw herself against it and the breath was knocked out of her as its hinges held and the first dozen or so piled against her. Someone pulled her gold chain off of her neck. The cross that it supported was thrown aside. Someone else had their hands in Jetta's hair and was using them to bang her head against the wooden bar separating the long screen door into two symmetrical squares. As Jetta pulled her head down to avoid the wood, her body ripped through the bottom half of the screen, leaving behind large surface areas of her hair and scalp. Blood dripped carelessly onto the three concrete steps. Jetta left a footprint in each as she scrambled down them, trying as she did to get the world to steady itself.

She almost had a fighting chance while Daisy was inside, screaming for everyone to back away from the door, screaming that they were crushing each other. Senior citizens who could barely bend were trying to climb out of the three-foot hole in the bottom of the screen door. The few who got through dogged her, chasing her down the aisles of cars with clumsy steps and harboring some inexplicable dread should she be allowed to get away. Jetta spotted her car; she had veered away from it in her fright and now began weaving among the rows, trying to close the distance to it before she could be caught, bending down to try to stay out of sight. Only ten feet more. She felt a vague, almost painful morsel of hope that she would make it. A bloody streak, her handprint along the windows of the cars she crouched alongside, gave her away to the mob. But Isaac, who had already used his key to open the dead bolt of the front door and been standing on the porch, observed her movements. Jetta slipped on the dark gravel, reached up to open her car door and felt her ankles ensnared by Isaac's strong hands. Her head hit the ground, and as the darkness rolled mercifully over her, she remembered she had left her car keys in her purse, which was still in the house.

Chapter Fourteen

Penny's first true conscious miracle came to her on the crest of a passing thought. This was not unusual for Penny. She had long subscribed to the notion that her mind—or anyone's, for that matter—worked as a sort of a tremendous filing cabinet with a variety of drawers containing thousands of pieces of information. The idea that what you received on your tenth birthday could somehow be thrown out of your memory seemed absurd to her, as it was just another, if minute, block in the whole construction of how your persona came together. Retrieving that particular piece of information was another story altogether. Perhaps, Penny had theorized while changing a diaper or folding a towel, there were drawers for levels of knowledge in some sort of order of importance. More immediate knowledge would be in a top drawer, easily accessible with arrows and highlights; your favorite actress's maiden name was in there, too, just buried deeper, somewhere consciously inaccessible.

Like everyone else, Penny sometimes found herself with something "on the tip of her tongue." She would let her filing-cabinet theory of memory work for her by envisioning her subconscious as a sort of managing-secretary part of her brain. She asked it to get whatever it was she couldn't remember and gave it time to peruse through the available files. Hal would ask her what the puppet's name was in the movie *Magic* and Fats would pop out of her mouth an hour later. The key was to let it do its job without nagging. Pressing her conscious mind to find it seemed to get in the way of the process. Her subconscious would send it up in a bubble of thought if she was patient enough. She wondered what Freud would say.

Penny felt this was why she had passed out when the throngs of people rushed her. Her inner voice, her subconscious self, knew there was a better way to fix the situation. It had an answer but no time to make Penny stop panicking or tearing her hair out in an attempt to determine how to help all of those people.

Even as Hal patted her hand and face, rousing her, Penny's mind was focusing on telling her she already knew what to do. It was sending her thoughts of a time when she and Hal had bought their first house. A real fixer upper, it had been auctioned off by the state at a rock-bottom price. When it was finished, Penny never wanted to see another paintbrush for as long as she lived. In the basement, in what Hal said was more of a cellar, there was a tiny pantry that also housed the electrical box with its switches and fuses. One winter night in the middle of dinner they lost all of their power. Assuming it to be a blackout, they were amazed to look out and see all of their neighbors' houses still warmly lit. Hal felt around for their flashlight and headed down the stairs with Penny in tow. Penny could still smell the mold and hear the drip of the sump pump echoing as they squeezed into the cramped space in front of the fuse box. She tried to keep the spiders that lived down there out of her mind. The flashlight shone and Penny held on to Hal's elbow, feeling safety in his proximity. He reached out to flip the main breaker and relight the house when Penny saw a spark fly. Hal's hand came to life, thrown backward by the surge of energy, and Penny watched his body contort even as she listened to herself scream. She felt her body slam into dozens of cans of peas and bottles of laundry detergent, she and Hal rag dolls among the fallen shelves. The electricity had found her through Hal, and of course that was the answer.

Hal and the policemen were now arguing. How could they have let that happen? Pandemonium had obviously taken over. The thud of heavy objects could be heard hitting the side of the building, making the emergency-room doors slide wildly open and closed. One of the policemen was bleeding from a generous gash across the forehead, another limping and wincing. The crowd outside would not be put down. Someone in the blur of background said *riot gear* and Penny thought she heard talk of rubber bullets thrown around in the heated conversation. Hal was wearing handcuffs and another pair was making its way toward Penny, shiny and solid.

"I know we can do this peacefully," Penny said, her voice quivering. She barely believed herself, the way it sounded. She tried to appeal to the police officer who snapped the cuffs tightly behind her: "If you march us out in handcuffs, there will be terrible riots."

"It's hard to riot under tear gas, lady."

"They're sick people. Many of them can't even walk on their own."

"They seem to be able to throw things pretty well."

Hal reacted badly at the sight of Penny shackled and prostrate on the floor. He knew he was no match for the police in a normal situation but struggled nonetheless. "Uncuff me! I haven't done anything wrong."

The bleeding policeman told him, "Look, pal, don't make me club you."

Hal looked up at him from the cold tiles of the emergency room floor, his eyes looking wildly around. "Penny, what are you doing? This is crazy! Let them take us away from the crowd. This is dangerous." A red light flashed warning circles off the sliding doors as a police car backed up toward them.

"Here's your limousine, lady. We're ready to go now," the policeman said as he approached her, dripping blood onto the floor through his handkerchief.

She would have no other chances and she considered that it would be better for her to let things go, to go along with Hal, to get into that police car and let the crowd disperse, feeling cheated. It would help her get back her life if they thought it was a hoax.

"If I can heal your head, would you let me heal the crowd?"

"You can turn yourself into a leprechaun and sing 'Danny Boy' and I still wouldn't let you anywhere near that crowd." There were some muffled laughs, but the room quieted down and there was some whispered arguing between the ranks.

"I won't have to go out there to heal them if my theory is right."

Hal looked at Penny. He remembered her comment on needing to touch people to heal them. His face questioned her and he looked as if he were saying, "Let's just go." She turned away from him.

"Officer, if I can heal your cut, will you at least listen to my theory?"

He was about to say "No, thank you" when the captain, a gentle man whose wife was suffering from MS, stepped forward. The police officer from the patrol car came through the sliding doors, waving what Penny assumed was a warrant for her arrest. The captain held up a hand to him, holding him off, keeping his eyes on Penny.

"We can't uncuff you, ma'am."

Hal was saying, "Penny, please, this is enough!"

"Just have him hold on to my arm, Sir."

Captain James Elian took a step back and looked around at his fellow officers, who were stone silent and watching him with an intensity they usually reserved for stakeouts. The number of policemen had reached twenty-five with the newly arrived team from the precinct. Elian's reputation as a captain was at stake: Should he agree to let what they probably thought was another whacko do anything and it didn't actually work, he would be the precinct laughingstock for the rest of his career. It was difficult for police officers to take orders from superiors they didn't respect. On the other hand, there was his wife. Only a person on the sidelines watching their loved one die a slow, painful death fully understands hope in its every manifestation.

Captain Elian knew the distance between "I hope the Yankees win the Series" and "I hope my wife lives." He didn't think it should even be the same word. Worse yet, he did hope his wife would live, though he knew in the space of that same thought that she simply would not, not with the disease that plagued her. Penny was a wild, crazy, absurd kind of hope he knew he had no business being in the same room with. It would hurt too much when it didn't pan out and he would lose face with his men all at the same time. He was ready to utter his official "No, thank you" when one of his other men raised his voice. Marc was his old partner before his promotion, a man whose life he had watched over like his own during the span of their duty together—a man who knew about his wife and was smart enough to see his dilemma. He was the only one who wouldn't compromise the captain's position by speaking out.

"The road won't be cleared for a few minutes, Cap. Let her do her hocus-pocus; it'll be good for a laugh later," he said, without a trace of humor in his eyes.

Someone else chimed in, one of the captain's poker

buddies: "Prove them wrong now, they'll be more compliant when we bring them down to the station."

"Someone check on the road! You got exactly one minute, lady. Start talking."

"I know I can heal your officer if he touches my hand or even my elbow...."

The captain nodded impatiently, rolling his hand in a get-to-the-point-and-fast motion. Hal's face became beet red and he mashed his lips together as he watched Penny try to convince them.

"What I think might work is if your other man, the one with the cut, touches only your limping officer, who touches me and also gets healed. If I could move it through a line..."

The captain turned her plan over in his head briefly, again wondering if he was going to be called the station idiot in the morning. Penny caught his eye and looked hard at him as she asked her next question: "I'm also wondering if it would have an affect on people related to the person I'm healing."

Captain Elian froze. She could feel his wife all over him the way you can see the clothes people wear. The hurt inside him reached her at an inner-ear–splitting decibel, and she ached for his misery. He could feel her look shoot through him.

"Roger," he croaked, trying to control himself, "go over and touch her elbow. Clemens, make sure you watch her back. Has she been patted down?"

There was a bustle of organized motion. In the middle of a day that would never find itself in any crisis manual, the relief of some bit of standard procedure was comforting. Roger dripped over to Penny, his handkerchief not stopping the flow of blood, just slowing it down. He reached out, but just before they made contact Penny yelled, "I want the man with the limp too!"

Captain Elian rolled his eyes and nodded him over. Officer John Reitz limped over, wincing, and was also about to touch her elbow when she let out another cry: "No! No! Please!"

Two policemen in the group showed their frustration, complaining, "Come on, lady!" "Let's get moving" and "What are you doing?"

Penny ignored them. She looked up at the injured officers. "Please hold hands, and only one of you touch me."

The two looked at each other. Penny instructed, "You with the limp, please hold that officer's free hand, the one not putting pressure on his wound." They looked at the captain as if to say they had clearly not signed up for such nonsense. What could he be thinking?

"Just do it so we can move along to arresting them before the other half of the state gets here," he said.

It was quick. John reached out in a fast, embarrassed motion, held his partner's bloody free hand, then used his other hand to touch Penny. That was the last second of doubt. Those standing around felt the rush of warmth, the smell of newness. One thought of the moment the doctor handed him his newborn son. Another remembered the day he pitched a perfect game as a teenager in Little League. Their hair stood on end and their hearts swelled with their own private moments when life had been situationally orgasmic. It was warm and womblike and somehow left the footprints of peace within them.

The bloody cloth fell to the ground and Roger touched his head gingerly, searching for the wound he already knew was gone. Millions of cells had healed, sewing his scalp skin together, reuniting itself in a natural motion the way water fills a receptacle. The officer had felt every last connection take place. He turned toward the group, who gaped as if on cue as he held his hair up and away from his forehead. He was still holding the hand of his partner John, the officer who connected him to Penny.

John hopped around, walked and did some jumping jacks. Everyone else was still busy gaping. A few men sat down, overcome.

Penny was afraid to lose her moment. "If we can make a human chain out the door and the crowd is told to hold hands, making sure everyone is connected to someone else, I think we can get them helped and dispersed in no time at all," she suggested.

Captain Elian tried to collect himself. He cleared his throat. He tilted his head to the side, like a dog listening to some far-off sound. Finally he said, "I think we can uncuff them."

"This is Brad Lofton for WKAZ television, reporting from our roving chopper. We have been circling the site of the hospital where the woman now being called the Mother Healer is. Since early yesterday evening, some ten thousand people have surrounded Southlawn Hospital in this formerly sleepy little town. That number rises hourly as buses and trains pull in its small transit station. Jackie Wen has the traffic report. Over to you, Jackie. . . ."

"Thanks, Brad. It's pretty much a parking lot as far as the eye can see. There's zero movement along all of the major byways. These are narrow country roads not designed for this amount of cars. We've been watching people just leave their vehicles on the highway where they stopped. Most are carrying their loved ones on makeshift stretchers or pushing them in wheelchairs, wagons or carts. It looks like a parade, folks. There are no signs; people are just merging and following the crowd. The advice from here is, don't bother trying to get to this end of Southlawn by car. It is impossible. Everything is at a complete standstill. Back to you, Brad."

"Thanks, Jackie. Earlier we saw the Mother Healer

emerge from the emergency-room exit at the eastern corner of the hospital. Let's go to the video playback. It's been assumed she is the cloaked figure in the center of the group of policemen. Based on her outfit, there has been much speculation about her ties to Muslim extremists. You can see the Mother Healer pushing out of the ring of security around her, trying to make contact with the crowd, reaching out to several people at a time. It's difficult to determine from our aerial camera angles, but it appears she is either kissing those in the crowd she encounters or trying to make some sort of communication with them. Ground crews are still trying to penetrate the thick throngs of people packed tightly around that area. At this point in the footage, if you look into the crowd, beyond the front line to where the Mother Healer has already passed, there are people falling, trying to push forward to reach her. Several small groups are rushing her from both sides in an attempt to make contact, and the Mother Healer is being pulled under them.

"For those of you just tuning in, the Mother Healer has been trampled by those waiting to be seen by her. She was pulled out, apparently unconscious and rushed back to the safety of the hospital by the policemen guarding her. We have received no update on her status. I repeat, we are unsure if the Mother Healer has survived being rushed by those waiting outside of Southlawn Hospital. It has been forty minutes, and those in the crowd who can are responding violently. Of course, there are many in the crowd who cannot even move on their own." The camera zoomed in on a woman who was just a torso, no arms, no legs, perched on a wheelchair. She swung her head back and forth, giving WKAZ a physical example surrounded by dozens of others.

"Going to our live air cam now, you can see the restlessness and the debris being thrown around. This is a desperate crowd. It seems that all eyes are focused on the doors the Mother Healer was carried to when she was last seen. Over to the left there is a police car with its lights flashing, trying to get through the makeshift road. People are pounding on its hood as it passes. Here's a shot of the ambulance bay where the policemen are three and four deep, in riot gear, holding back the crowd. We would like to repeat, for those just tuning in, we are unsure if the Mother Healer is still alive...."

"Wait! We may be getting word. There appears to be a group of policemen coming out of the doors. They are addressing the crowd. We are going to live audio...."

" *'Please hold hands! ... Please hold hands! ... Pass it on! ... Please hold hands! ... Pass the word down! ...'* "

"This is Brad Lofton of WKAZ television reporting at Southlawn Hospital. You heard it here: The police department is asking the crowd to join hands. This situation gets more unusual every minute. Are they going to have a prayer service? No report has been made on the Mother Healer's status. The crowd is responding. Hands already clasped are being held up, perhaps to show they've complied. It is a spectacular sight. It is a surge of hands moving toward the back of the crowd in a wave. If you look on the left side of your screen, you can see a line of police officers coming out of the hospital doors and squeezing through the barrier. The odd thing is, they are holding hands too. Look carefully, folks: The policemen are holding hands! The line of officers is running from the hospital to the crowd. We're doing a close-up. The first officer in line is reaching out to someone in the crowd. What are they doing? They're—"

WKAZ television, the number-one most popular station in most of the state and broadcast generously in three surrounding ones, had its first full minute of dead airtime in fifty years. The aerial camera was running a panoramic view, which started at the chain of policemen linked to the hospital and ended three hundred yards out into the crowd. Anyone watching needed no commentary. The faces captured on tape spoke reams for themselves. Among them was the woman whose legs and arms erupted from her truncated torso into a very whole body. A silence sang out until the very last person at the very end of the crowd was reached, and the hold everyone had on each other was only broken with tremendous reluctance.

Brad Lofton, of WKAZ television, ended the on-air silence with weeping, apologizing to his audience repeatedly that he was unable to even attempt to describe what had just transpired, professionally or personally. The clip of him sinking into his seat in the helicopter, crying into his hands, would be played over and over both nationally and around the world.

Chapter Fifteen

Freedom caught Louis off guard. He had longed for it for as long as he could remember, but it was a fancy, an unattainable thought. Even in his imagination it was difficult to get beyond the idea of having no schedule of medication or blocks of time spent in his chair, the one with the imprint of his body as permanent as if it had been built that way. His day doubled and his spirits soared, but he was like a rocket ship loaded with thousands of gallons of high-octane fuel but no distinct flight plan. Sitting and expanding his lungs artificially through drugs was time-consuming, but it was his time to think, to plot out the facets of a story he would highlight and trim the fat of legwork to include only the most crucially relevant. That had all fallen by the wayside, seemingly unnecessary.

Other things had changed for him also. Since being healed, Louis had a series of disturbing dreams that threw him up from sleep with a silent scream trying to rip its way out of his throat. The sheets would be soaked with icy buckets of nervous perspiration that clung to him as the remnants of the dream did, leaving him cold. It was an innocent enough dream, really.

Louis would be watching a narrow cobblestone road from the shelter of an evergreen bush. The road would be covered up top by a thick canopy of trees, making the day unusually dark and casting heavy shadows in every direction, even though Louis knew in the dream it was almost exactly noon. Just when the sun should have been directly overhead, he would hear a sound off in the distance down the road. A few times it was reminiscent of nails being brought agonizingly slowly across a chalkboard. Other times he thought it might be bones moving without the aid of lubrication—a joint with no cartilage to cushion the scraping and gouging of bone ends working against each other. This sound chilled Louis so completely that the first few times he woke up having wet the bed before the road could reveal to him what traveled along it. When he was able to watch and wait, he felt, even in sleep, the hair on his body stand at complete attention. If his voiding into his bed—something he hadn't done since he was five—wasn't enough to awaken him out of the imminent danger he felt, he would be forced to stand in his hiding spot, his dream eyes fixed in the direction the sound came from. The closer it came, the louder its noise, and Louis rediscovered again and again that the sound was much like his own former raspy breathing, wet with mucus and fighting to suck in oxygen through the narrowest tubes.

Fear, Louis would later think, is a fascinating subject, with every individual responding differently to different things. There is such a wide range of items and creatures that send people into all kinds of full-blown anxiety attacks and nervous tics. What dragged itself down the sleep road that lived only in Louis's imagination stumped him completely every time in its ability to scare him so entirely that when he awoke, bathed in his own sweat and urine, he often threw up right into his own lap. He was absolutely sure it was only a matter of days before he died in his sleep, aspirating on his own vomit like some drunken rock star. Only for him it would be over a turtle.

What scraped across the stone path, emerging from behind a bend, was a simple turtle, wheezing and dragging its shell as if it couldn't possibly go another inch yet somehow did. And it sported Louis's face. He recognized the Gorman nose, from his mother's side, the Klotz hairline, his own unique frayed eyebrows. It was clear he couldn't allow the turtle to get to him. It knew Louis was there. It looked straight at him, through the bushes, its eye contact saying Louis couldn't hide. Louis would try to make a break for it, intending to go the opposite way down the path, out of that dark forest. He would try to move, sending mental messages down to his legs that if ever they were going to work, now was the time. But of course Louis knew dream rules as well as anybody else. There was no running. The greater the desire to escape, the slower the body would go, if at all. The turtle was only painstakingly creeping along itself, but Louis was stuck like set cement both in his legs and his eyes, which were forced to watch it approach him step by step.

Even in the midst of the dream, with an aeon seemingly spent watching it draw near, Louis couldn't put his finger on what exactly horrified him so. It was your standard run-of-the-mill turtle. It had no sharp claws, no big teeth, and it wasn't overly large, he thought during the daytime when he tried to reason with his dream self. There was no clarity even for him on what would happen if the turtle actually reached him, but it drove him wild with terror both in and out of sleep just the same. On top of that, it got a cobblestone closer with each dream. When the dream first started, he would awaken with calculations in his head as he scurried to count the steps left between himself and the turtle that had somehow stolen his face.

As the dream ran its course six or seven times that first night, the tape of his subconscious apparently stuck, unable to play another feature, there would eventually be a second disturbing presence moving up behind the turtle. This one crashed along as if it were leaving craters on that narrow path, and Louis fully expected to see a pair of huge feet descend from somewhere above the trees any second. Repeatedly he hoped it would crush the turtle and go right over him as if he weren't there. Again and again he was bowled over in wild astonishment at the rabbit that sprang out from the same bend as the turtle. Unlike the turtle, though, the rabbit was huge and made of heavy concrete, so that each step it took sent pieces of the path flying in all directions with rabbit-size holes marking its landing spots. As it hopped along like a tacky oversize lawn ornament gone crazy, Louis would invariably notice that the rabbit, unlike the turtle, had a cat's face imposed on the rabbit's body and had managed to fit Louis's favorite sneakers on its feet. It hopped over the turtle, always missing it by centimeters and proceeding down the road with seemingly not a care in the world.

Louis knew the rabbit was in terrible trouble. With a colossal effort he was able to turn his head and yell at the cat-rabbit to stop. It never listened, but went on to meet whatever horrible fate Louis was sure awaited it. Always, at this point, Louis would turn around to find the turtle in the bush with him. He would wake up screaming.

With all of this, Louis's sleeping hours were turning out to be more challenging than his waking ones. Yet, he still had enough energy for what he thought would be about ten men. Something inside warned him to slow down, to watch that he didn't burn out. Louis imagined this was what people on drugs or with a coffee habit must experience. The drug for him was oxygen.

He ran out the door early in the morning, bagel in hand, taking the steps down two at a time instead of the elevator, just because he could. A hardy spring sun hit him with hints of the force and brightness it would have in just a few short weeks. In the car he had the yellow pages open to the religious organizations in Southlawn County and had plans to visit each one regarding their take on Penny Chaney. The radio blasted out news of the crowd gathered around the hospital, multiple teams onsite reporting on every detail of the wait for the Mother Healer to emerge. Louis crossed off each church in his book as they were interviewed over the airwaves, ignoring the traffic as if he weren't driving. No reporter wants their story to be old news or, worse yet, redundant. At a light, not sure of where he was headed, he thumbed through ads until a small box with ISAAC AND DAISY ROURKE, MESSIANIC VISION caught his eye. Without a second thought, Louis turned his car away from the stalled traffic toward the other end of town. The reporter's instinct inside that had never failed him sang wildly like a divining rod over water.

There was another instinct buzzing alongside the one that sniffed out a good story. This one, though, was unfamiliar to Louis. Instead of studying it, he left it, in his hurry, by the wayside. On a normal day, Louis would have a succinct list of pertinent questions, a distinct angle of attack and a story tone he would be seeking out. He would have already researched the group on the Internet and through the community and paired his findings with a background check performed by one of his many investigative contacts. His editor would have all of this information and they would confer on what he expected to find, what snags might come up. Today he just went. He thought what he felt was pure exhilaration, the raw hunt for the story, played wildly.

Fate led Louis down every country road on the west side of Southlawn and through every cow farm he never wanted to see. Louis had never been on this side of town and hadn't printed out a route to follow. His map seemed unusually uncooperative. The new, impulsive energy surging through him wanted to tear the map to shreds and throw it out of the car window. He tried to find some of his former patience. Isaac and Daisy's road was a private one and Louis finally had to break down and ask for directions.

The gas station he chose looked deserted as he pulled in. His car door sounded like a cannon as he slammed it closed in the quiet lot. Among dusty oil bottles and cigarette ads was a sign that stood out perpendicular to the window, saying OPEN if you walked to it from behind the garage, CLOSED if you saw it approaching the office. This wasn't terribly surprising to Louis. Most of the county was busy standing around the hospital. Louis mentally patted himself on the back for his continued unique genius as a writer. Let everyone else on earth get the same story: He still liked the odd angles. He squinted through the dirty glass of the office, looked around him quickly, then inched over to try the door. An empty can was blown across the pitted concrete of the gas island and Louis turned toward it to find himself inches away from the proprietor.

"Help ya?" Mo Beard said, blowing twenty-eight chain-smoked cigarettes toward Louis with his breath.

Caught off guard, Louis squeaked and grabbed for the inhaler that no longer lived in his pocket. A fright like that in the past would have sent his lungs into a shut down.

"Jumpy little fella, aren't ya?"

Louis heard snickers off to his left where Mo's cronies sat in the shade just inside the garage. They'd been watching him the whole time. Louis made a note of his lapse in observation and turned red at his own amateurish behavior. He ignored that instinctual voice for the second time of the morning, the one trying to tell him he wasn't as thorough as he usually was, that he was lacking caution. A funny snatch of the concrete cat-rabbit hopped through his brain.

Mo stared hard at Louis. "Look like a man caught with his hand in the cookie jar. Thought we'd be gone to the hospital with every other fool in the county, did ya?"

"Actually," Louis sputtered, "I'm lost!"

"You know how many times we heard that one? Bud over there has the garage's trusty sawed-off shotgun for boneheads like you who gets lost."

Louis threw up his hands. "I'm a reporter. Honest!"

Mo stared at him some more, moving his silver aviator glasses up with a wrinkle of his nose, keeping his hands free, sizing up something in Louis although Louis couldn't quite figure out what in the world that something could be.

"The hospital is that way." Mo pointed.

"I'm not going to the hospital," Louis said.

"Just where do you think you're going around here?" a shaky voice from the shadow of the garage asked.

A third man chimed in. "There's nothing here. Buy some gas or go home."

Louis couldn't help but think of the episode when Bugs Bunny throws some cartoon gangster into an oven and, throwing himself across it, professes, "He's not in this here oven!" The gears in his mind skipped a click and his eyes worked to focus on the men in the shadows. He stepped around Mo toward them, noticing how they looked unshaven, mussed, half dressed, hurried, as if they had called each other five minutes ago and hauled ass over here without so much as a morning pee. They stood as he got closer. A crate fell over. All of their coffees were steaming, full.

Louis pulled out of neutral, back into drive. "I'm looking for the Rourke place. Messianic Vision?" He said, "I know I've got to be close," and watched their eyes grow round and one of them spill his coffee down his shirt. The sawed-off shotgun made its appearance.

Oh, shit! came and went through his mind like so many bats tangling his rational thoughts up into knots. After years of assuming an asthma attack would get him in the end, he soaked up the irony of possibly being shot to death instead.

"Never heard of 'em!"

"They're on the other side of town!"

"They moved away."

"We don't know who you're talking about."

They spoke simultaneously and two of them hit the garage door switch together, making it close, then jerk open halfway, only to close again with a bang.

Louis turned around, jangly, unsure, only to come face-to-face with Mo yet again. Louis's heart flopped for a second time. He thought the man should be made to wear a bell.

"You heard 'em." Mo said more quietly, making Louis back toward his car. "We don't want to have anything to do with what's going on over there."

"So you do know where it is." Louis felt infinitely more courageous with the garage door between himself and the shotgun and the idea that, as usual, his instincts were correct as to where the stories were.

Mo's eyes turned on and off, flickering, and Louis knew he was battling with himself about letting Louis walk into whatever situation was going on at the Rourkes'. That alone should have been enough to give him the heads up he needed, should he even find this group out here in the East Nowheresville of the county.

"Two lefts and a right a mile down. Watch yourself," the proprietor whispered, his back to the garage, Louis needing to read his lips more than hear the words. And for the sake of his cronies the old man snarled, "Buy gas or get the hell out! Does this look like the damn Triple A or something?" He hit the back of Louis's car as it fishtailed off the lot.

Mo's eyes followed Louis's car down the road and his heart yanked at him in the way it did when he sold an underage kid a pack of smokes. He always figured a man had to make his own decisions for right or for wrong, and the reporter was nothing to him—maybe less than nothing, as he had no respect for people whose job was to tell about other people's business. What kind of work was that anyway? On the other hand, in his opinion, that group was a bunch of crazies. He knew enough to suspect there would be more trouble than one reporter could handle. Although if all it took to scare off that guy was one little unloaded shotgun, maybe he'd be all right. His buddies, John and Michael, had come here when they woke up to empty beds, wondering what they should do, their wives already there with that crazy bastard Isaac Rourke. Rourke had never done anything personally to Mo, but Mo knew crazy when he saw it. His own sister, Molly, had been sent off to what his mother called the resting place and the rest of town referred to as the loony bin. She had gone after them with his father's Thanksgiving carving knife one night. Molly had never had the look of the rest of the world in her eyes. When Mo saw the war and the young men who came back from it with that same look, not ever recapturing their lives, he knew it was just the look of crazy. Isaac Rourke wore that look like it was going out of style, and it made the pit of Mo's stomach queasy. He couldn't understand how the women in the area could be so devoted to him. Mo could barely stand to pump the man's gas.

Sal's wife, Ellen, had called just before the reporter pulled in; their property was adjacent to the one Isaac and Daisy were renting. She said she heard screams and banging out there. Should she call the police?

Most of the people at this end of town were either in Isaac and Daisy's little group or knew it to be the cult that it was. It wasn't discussed much, mostly out of embarrassment by those whose loved ones were devoting entire days there. Families were fighting in whispers so neighbors couldn't hear. Some were coming home to empty bank accounts and missing spouses. Mo's own group of friends was spending more and more time standing around looking at their shoes.

Mo scratched a two-day-old beard and sighed. The hand in his pocket folded and unfolded the only bill he'd earned this morning, usually his busiest time of day. If he were a betting man he would put money on all of the law enforcement available being at the hospital. Not much chance of getting even a speeding ticket today. He watched Louis's exhaust leave a trail off around the bend then he fiddled with the gas pump hoses, dumped the week-old windshield wiper bucket no one ever looked at. No, never mind, he thought, pushing his conscience down and away. Every carton of cigarettes has a warning on it and he shouldn't have to tell a man if you go looking for trouble, most times it'll do you the favor of finding you first, usually by biting you right in the ass.

Louis's experience with trouble was, of course, previously only of a self-contained, biological nature. He turned onto the narrow country lane and knew he was in the right place. All kinds of cars were lined up on either side of him, slanted in toward the gullied dirt road. He glanced up in the distance toward Isaac and Daisy's house as he foraged for the press badge under his seat. Everything was quiet and he wondered if everyone from the group had gone to the hospital. The stillness was so profound that, for the second time that morning, Louis's car door sounded like a shot going off as he closed it. If they were still there, would they let him into their meeting? Would they allow themselves to be interviewed? He would make it a point to get back to that garage and get them to talk to him somehow. Questions paraded around his mind like flow charts, various angles unfolding with the responses he imagined he might extract from what he thought of as simple backwater people. He wondered how anyone gets sucked into a cult, how foolish one would have to be. Louis rolled his eyes in advance and caught a piece of the canopy of leaves along the edge of his vision. Stopping and looking, he wondered where all the birds were that it was so quiet out here.

When Louis was a little boy his illness would take such terrible turns, his mother would park him in various places around the house. She learned quickly not to put him at their front picture window where he could see the neighborhood boys play stickball and roller hockey and where they could see him sitting in his late grandmother's wheelchair with her afghan wrapped around his shoulders. The boys would laugh and Louis would cry until breathing was almost impossible and they would end up whisking him back to the hospital for another round in the oxygen tent. When he made it home again he was restricted to the back window with a view of the pieces of all of the cars his father never put back together before he left them. Louis had hours to wonder why his mother never threw any of it away. Mentally he tried to piece it all into some sort of working vehicle and in between he watched the neighborhood tomcat.

Louis supposed if he had been a cat, his yard would have been his favorite also. The lids never seemed to make it onto the garbage cans, and when they did, it wasn't long before something tipped them over again.

More importantly, though, Louis's mother had put up a bird feeder, which hung from a planter's bracket off of the garage. It was perched more than six feet over the driveway and she had to carry out their kitchen stepstool to refill it with seeds. What a production she always made, invariably falling off the stool or spilling the seeds, shooing away imaginary swarms of hungry bees. It had embarrassed him as a child that she made everything so difficult, but he realized now she had probably done it all to amuse him. What she didn't know was that Louis's favorite part always came when his mother was long gone into the house and on to other tasks.

There would be a cacophony of birds announcing the feeding site, squawking their claim to its contents and ensuring swooping fights for the right to stand at the tiny perch in front of the seed hole. Tinier birds would gather at the bottom, picking through the spoils, having their own skirmishes over specks of food. The truly amazing moment, though, came when the old yellow tom put just one paw through the rotted hole in their fence and, with a piercing scream of warning from the fierce blue jays, there would be an absolute silence.

It was as if the tom knew the language of the birds, knew they were feasting, knew that the hunger they had would somehow be worsened with the tease of the taste of even one seed and it would make them do foolish things. He sauntered into Louis's yard with a smugness that was always justified. It was all just a matter of waiting. The cat had taught Louis the lesson of patience. Below the feeder he would sit up at attention in the shadow of the corner of the garage, moving nothing. That was it, the tom's whole plan. And it worked every time. The birds were always their own undoing.

The silence held for a long five minutes, birds moving their heads back and forth in jerking motions, spotting the cat again and again. In the periphery Louis would begin to see some movement, nervous hopping first where they were, then from branch to branch. The cat would just sit. Louis would imagine what the birds said as their peeping began. "What about the seeds?" "Watch out for the cat!" "Where is the cat?" "We're hungry!" "He can't jump that high!" "The seeds are just sitting there!" The older, larger birds never fell for it, though they were the most vocal. "I don't see him. He must've left. He's probably sleeping sitting up!"

Invariably a young fledgling would think itself bold and fly down to eat a few luscious seeds while every tree was stock-still again, watching as the cat's meditation was broken and he threw himself up to consume his prey. The tom took his victim and the birds resumed their feast, the sacrifice made.

Anyone else but Louis might have dismissed the quiet at the Rourkes', not felt a panicky discomfort that there were no songs here at this Messianic Vision meeting place, outside in the trees or coming from inside the house. Louis heard his footsteps echo off the dry gravel and with each one he had the growing memory flashback of the ridiculous surprise on the faces of those fledglings he had seen caught in their own foolishness.

When Louis looked down the path he saw a large, dark haired man, yards away, near the house next to an old Ford, its trunk open. He held what looked like a large black plastic bag over his shoulder with a dark liquid leaking out of the bottom. Isaac's people watched Louis from behind the trees, some close enough to hear his breathing speed up. As Louis turned back to his car, he knew deep down the cat had already sprung. It was really no surprise to him when he felt the rock strike the back of his head or saw the ground rush up at him into blackness.

Chapter Sixteen

Penny was disguised as herself. Her big-sheet costume was thrown into an abandoned linen hamper and they made haste in getting into the parking lot to try to look like other members of the crowd going home. They took up the tail end, reveling in the conversations floating around them. To their left was a teenager who had been plagued with spina bifida, a birth defect of her spinal cord. Today was the first day she had ever walked. Her parents held her arms like a toddler's and they smiled at her first steps, some sixteen years late. Behind them was an old man who had lost his sight in a factory accident fifty years earlier. He was looking into his wife's eyes, which were a hundred times more beautiful than he remembered. A woman stood on a corner and just moved her arms in circles, watching them swing about, shouting to people as they passed, "They work! I forgot what it feels like to have no pain!"

Policemen flanked Penny on all sides and Hal kept shooing them away, saying they were blowing their cover. But in truth most people were so engaged in their newfound health that Penny doubted if they would have noticed an elephant stampeding by.

A red flashing light greeted them on their way into the patrol car where Penny would not be arrested, but skirted off to repay the debt she knew she had incurred with the captain. She reflected on how easily she had gone from one side of the law to the other, the line between outlaw and hero a fragile one. Before stepping in, Penny turned to look back at the hospital, trying to somehow solidify what had happened, if only in her mind to make it make sense. A handful of stragglers remained but the rest of the scene spoke of what had occurred more than even the event itself. The grounds surrounding the hospital looked strangely like an ocean drained of its water. Littered as far as the eye could see were surgical pieces catching the sun like cold metal bones. Wheelchairs were overturned, their wheels still spinning, some facing the hospital, packs still strapped to their backs with buttons and embroidered names, empty bodies waiting for new patrons to assume their identities. Casts lay about in the shapes of various limbs, cracked open and keeping quiet company with the leg braces, empty IVs and forgotten crutches, which were stuck in the rain-softened grass like life-size exclamation marks. Penny wished she knew what particular point they were emphasizing.

It all should have been a perfect good. Everyone was better. She felt their illnesses drain out of them, each and every one, followed by a filling up of elation at their mending. Yet, looking out at the abandoned pieces of their lives, Penny was plagued with doubt. The car pulled away and snaked through the walking throngs. Hal pulled Penny toward him in the backseat.

"Hal," she whispered. "Hal, you're looking at me funny."

Hal smiled and held her gaze. "Penny, you've just changed thousands of lives. How should I look at you?"

"Like I'm still the woman you married. The one you bought oven mitts and a fire extinguisher for on our first anniversary." Penny began to cry quietly in Hal's arms, a mix of relief at heading toward home and confusion over where she was going with this healing. It reminded her of the day she sat in the backseat of their old Toyota, flanked on both sides by twin screaming babies who they were finally taking home. Penny thought the hospital was crazy to let her have them. She was in a panic over how she would possibly care for them. "They don't come with instructions?" she had said in a scared voice before checking out. "You'll just know," the weary nurse had replied, probably for the thousandth time.

In the rearview mirror Captain Elian's face was covered with a continual flood of his own tears, and Penny looked forward to helping his wife even if it delayed their journey home. He had come through for her. She hoped to do the same for him.

"Hal, where does the captain live?" she whispered.

"You can call me James, ma'am," the captain answered for himself from the front. "We're over on Deer Acre, not far from your house. I took the liberty of looking you up on the scanner, ma'am."

"Call me Penny," she said, though Captain James Elian wore a look similar to the one Hal sported, and she knew he would probably call her nothing but ma'am even though she was half his age.

"I'm sorry I doubted you, ma'am. I've had such little faith that my wife would ever get well." He looked at the road, his face red and scrunched with a regret that made Penny feel as if she had personally done something wrong. She searched for something to say. Anything. The silence held her until they arrived at the captain's house.

His was a small cottage stuccoed a country blue and trimmed with flower boxes and gingerbread. From the front Penny wondered how the captain fit through the doorway, much less lived there with any modicum of comfort. She imagined him walking sideways down a hall and hunching in his shower, always holding his well-over-six-foot frame at bay. On each of the flower boxes were hearts, and Penny knew that the captain's wife was everything there, the decorator, the hub of the home, his princess.

They stepped out of the squad car and Penny could feel her pain as it seeped across empty flower beds and into Penny's head. She looked around for her, knowing she was close by, and found herself staring into her eyes through the front window, a little bay adorned with purple African violets like Penny's own. At first Penny thought the captain's wife must be very tiny, as her eyes barely lit over the top of the sill, then connected the picture in her mind: She was in a wheelchair, of course, and her head listed somewhat to the right, her mouth hanging open just slightly, all enough to make the casual passerby register in their mind that something was not quite right, but not be able to pinpoint what that something might be. Penny walked to the door, the captain leading with stunning urgency. For some reason the last minute is always the longest wait. His wife's eyes continued to stare into the space Penny had occupied and she knew that the woman could not see.

Introductions were easy. His wife was Midge, named after her late mother's favorite cat. "Herrow," she got out over tongue and mouth muscles, which were no longer cooperative. She knew Penny. She had been hanging on the broadcasts of her miracle all morning. Captain James called ahead and Midge had been painstakingly setting her modest table with an heirloom tea set no one in her family had had a grand enough occasion to use in two generations. It was aged an antique yellow and as fragile as their hopes that rested on Penny. Setting out four cups, some spoons and a ruffled pile of napkins had taken her forever. She looked exhausted.

Captain Elian never stopped crying. It had become like

breathing and he hardly noticed it at all now. Penny's extended hand brought him to his knees and he sobbed loudly in a prayerful position as Penny and Midge connected. Hal braced himself like someone in midair the moment before they plunge into a warm bath. Each time was uniquely satisfying, and Hal got a glimpse of what drug addiction felt like. He shivered with the heat of it.

Midge looked into Penny's eyes, this time registering her features. She stood, shaky and in some shock but with each of her nerve endings firing with sentience and in unison the way they were meant to. Despite that, Midge and James collapsed to their modest parquet floor, a heap of joy, and Penny turned to Hal, ready to head back to her own three little miracles whom she ached for. Hal led her to the front steps, where they waited, giving the reunited couple their privacy.

"Hal . . ." Penny looked down at the hairline cracks on the Elians' front steps, watching the ants carry their loads. "I just want to go home. Enough of all of this for now. The world can wait one more day for more miracles."

Hal shifted uncomfortably. He listened to the continuing sobs of happiness that resonated throughout the little house behind him. "Pen, we're not going right home."

Before Penny could shout her protests, Hal held up a hand. "You know we won't be able to go there for at least a while. I diverted media attention away from our house, but I'm sure that won't keep them away forever."

And with that, her house was gone from underneath her. She ran her mental tongue along the place where it had been rooted, the space gaping and empty now, somehow permanently lost. The sounds of joy were very far away from her, as if she were listening to them from down a long hall. Hal was smirking, and the incongruity of it was almost too much.

"What did you do, Hal?"

"I'm actually very proud of this plan. I called and set it up at the hospital. Your sisters agreed to it wholeheartedly."

"My sisters?"

"Yes, both of them dressed in the same garb as you were in today, sheets hiding everything but their eyes. Then they put Janice Mitchell in the same getup. All three left the house at the same time in three different cars with a different set of kids, none of whom was ours. While the cameramen chased in three different directions, my parents slipped out with the kids."

" 'Slipped'?" Penny looked doubtful.

"My Dad is a new man. He's the one I relayed the plan to. He was very excited. It doesn't even sound like him, Pen." Hal looked like a kid at Christmas.

"So where did they take them, my sister's ski house?"

"Too obvious."

"Your parents' favorite hotel?"

"Nope."

"Where?"

"Aunt Myrtle's."

"*My* aunt Myrtle? We haven't seen Aunt Myrtle since our wedding. I thought she was in Florida."

"She is. My mother, God bless her controlling soul, is airing out her house upstate, taking care of every minute detail, I'm sure. Aunt Myrtle never had the heart to sell it. She said we could use it indefinitely if we promise to fly down to Florida sometime soon and relieve her arthritis.

"Well, wherever we're going, let's get there. I won't feel right until I'm back with the kids. Then maybe we can put some kind of plan together."

"I thought the plan would be to fade out of the spotlight for a while. You just healed thousands. That's got to be enough."

At that moment the captain and Midge came through the door, somehow managing to bow and bend down four concrete steps. They threw themselves on the sidewalk in front of Penny and Hal, who could only gape, noticing that neighbors were beginning to come to their doors to look at the sound of their weeping.

"Please," Penny whispered, looking at the neighbors' windows. "Get up."

Each reached out to put a hand on Penny's feet, simultaneously thanking God and thanking Penny and calling her the Mother Healer. She thought one of them was chanting. Penny put her head in her hand and just shook it. This was ridiculous. She'd done housework imagining it to be an Olympic event with thousands of captivated onlookers cheering her on to a gold medal in dusting. She was the original Walter Mitty in that regard, but this was just too much.

"Get up, please," she said more emphatically.

With eyes cast downward, James Elian begged, "Let us come with you."

"Thanks," said Hal. "We need to get back to our car."

"We'll take you to the car, but I mean we want to join you wherever you're going."

Hal and Penny looked at James and Midge smiling at them, and neither could think of anything to say—except that they were looking forward to being alone for the first time in a week or perhaps to tell them that they were private, quiet people who generally enjoyed their own company. Instead they just gaped at the lack of doubt in his voice.

The captain was firm: "You're going to need people."

Actually, Penny thought, the whole problem was their need for *fewer* people. She was so overrun with people, she needed more people for those people. But she got his point, and who better to assist them with security and crowd control? She hoped that Myrtle had bedrooms to spare.

"If you *do* come with us," Penny said, "please don't worship me. Could you treat me like a friend instead? Please, get up." She helped them to her feet. They looked at her as if they could never comply with such a request.

"Yes, Mother Healer, we'll do whatever you say." From beside Penny, Hal grimaced.

No, no, no! thought Penny. *That's not it at all!* Instead she said, "I need friends. Please just be our friends. Call me Penny." And when they looked at her with doubt, she said more strongly, "I insist."

Aunt Myrtle's was quite a drive from the low, flat land of Southlawn into the heights of the surrounding mountains. Aunt Myrtle and her late husband, a quiet accountant, had fleeting dreams of living off the land in a secluded woody spot. God bless Aunt Myrtle, thought Penny, but did it have to be so far? It would take them three hours just to get to the winding path that led up the side of the mountain to the cliff-side home. Penny supposed she should be thankful that Aunt Myrtle's idea of roughing it did not include outhouses or bailing water from streams.

The small city flickered by in groups of buildings and clusters of homes. Penny had grown up only a few blocks from a railroad crossing much like one they passed. When her walk to school crossed the eight-thirty freight, she would come as close as she dared to the red-and-white-striped arms of the safety gates. The flashing lights would surround her and Penny would allow herself to be enveloped in the rushing motion. If she focused on one spot, the train would suddenly stand still and turn its speed over to Penny, who felt herself whip by, the one now moving, leaving the train and her town behind. The mental rush of that ride was always sweetened by the bellowing blast of the horn jolting her back. This ride was real and everything was indeed moving behind her. She wondered if there was a psychological form of Dramamine for emotional motion sickness.

It was no easier to watch the inside of the car. Hal was looking at her with that mixture of fear and awe. Midge was flexing her fingers into an open high five, then into a fist over and over again until apparently her toes were feeling left out and she tugged at her shoes and pulled off her socks, leaving them in careless balls. Up and down her toes moved, and Penny could reach out with her inside and find only peace coming from Midge, tossed in with a small hunger that reminded Penny that none of them had eaten since she'd been dressed up in sheets about a million years ago that day. Midge's tea had been left behind in a flurry of departure, their suitcases flung into the squad car and later bouncing in the bed of Hal's truck.

At every other light Midge would stop flexing and turn around to face Penny, her whole being emitting a gratitude Penny would not have thought humanly possible, and she wondered if it was just that feeling another person's emotions blew them all out of proportion. Penny did her own flexing, trying to reel in that feeler again, and was again unsuccessful. It felt a lot like peeking into someone's bedroom window, and Penny felt ashamed despite an inability to control it.

"Let's stop for something to eat before we leave town," she suggested.

Hal turned from the wheel. "I know you want to get to the kids as soon as possible. We'll make it quick. Anyone have any preferences?"

James suggested pizza or Chinese food, looking to Penny for a sign of approval. Midge, speaking in a beautiful, steady voice, said, "How about the diner across from the lake? It's on the way to the mountain road." She, too, looked to Penny for confirmation.

As everyone was mulling it over, Midge added, "I would love to order for myself somewhere without just pointing to the menu." So it was settled.

The day had sneaked past them and they arrived at the height of the dinner rush. They waited in line for a table, and Penny tried to fend off all of the colossal need packed into such a tiny place. James, Hal and Midge made awkward small talk and Penny nodded, trying to smile as if she were a part of the conversation. There was a man in one of the old plastic booths staring out of the dirty window, his fork poking unambitiously through the meat loaf special. His wife sat across from him, worrying her hands across a paper napkin and ignoring a spaghetti-and-meatballs order long since gone cold. Gingham curtains, a cheery lemon yellow, boxed them in like a cartoon strip gone wrong. Their teenage daughter had run away three days before. The mother knew the girl was schizophrenic, as her own mother had been.

It took everything inside of Penny not to scoop them both up by the hand and find the daughter. It was as if she needed to heal them the way she needed to eat. Sitting back to back with them, in the adjacent table marked with a bold, crooked number three, sat a truck driver angry from waiting too long for his meal (which was cold on arrival) and consumed by the pain in his big toe. He had the gout and he reflected crankily about it with every bite. Virtually every table had its own misery, and Penny was nauseous with the overload. She breathed a sigh of relief when they were seated. The sooner they ate, the sooner she could leave and stop the influx of other people's hurts.

They ordered and James turned to Penny, "I know we barely know each other. Thank you for letting us join you."

Penny gave a half of a laugh. "I didn't think we had a choice."

"You could have said no."

Hal added, "I suppose. But you're right, we're going to need some level heads to help us work this situation out. I'm worried about keeping things reasonable."

"Have you always had this ability, Penny?" Midge added quietly, afraid to offend Penny or be too forward, and Penny sensed that in some way Midge was somewhat afraid of her.

Penny's mouth dropped. "No! This is all new to me."

Midge and James said at almost the same time, "How did it happen?"

"I had some kind of odd virus and I went into a coma. While I was out, apparently everyone around me in the hospital was healed. When I came out of it I could still heal; I just had to have direct contact with the person to do it."

Penny thought the condensed version would serve just fine. She forgot James was a policeman—and, being a captain, obviously not a shoddy one at that. His wonder emanated from him in nothing less than buckets.

Penny tried to distract him, not wanting to go back onto the bridge, the place where all of this craziness started, even if just mentally. "So is it okay with the Southlawn police that you're leaving for a while?" she asked.

"I'm overdue for retirement. Now seems like the perfect time. I have vacation coming to me until the paperwork goes through. We can be with you as long as you need us." He looked down as if worried she might send him away on the spot.

That was all Penny could think to say, and she knew James's questions were cropping up. Where was dinner?

"Did the virus change your body somehow?"

Hal looked at Penny, wondering if she wanted to get into it.

Penny shook her head. "I don't know. I don't think so."

Midge pressed on: "Did something happen while you were in the coma? I know I've been wondering what would happen to me when my body finally gave out. Did you see anything?"

Their food came, giving Penny a moment to think, to decide how much she felt comfortable sharing. So much of it was fading, she wondered if there would be a time that she didn't remember it at all. Midge took small bites and stared expectantly at Penny, waiting.

"I knew I was dying...."

"She 'coded' three times in the first half hour we were at the hospital," Hal added, not noticing how quickly the hospital jargon had become a part of his vocabulary.

Midge asked. "Was there a bright light? Everyone in my MS support group said they felt so assured when they thought that would be the first part of their death experience."

Penny squirmed. She didn't want to blow someone else's vision of death, especially if it was comforting. "Um, well ... not exactly."

Midge stared at her, a glimmer of something flickering out of her for an instant too short for Penny to put her finger on what it was.

"Maybe I just don't remember that part," Penny said apologetically.

"What *do* you remember?" James asked.

"There was a bridge." *Aha,* thought Penny. *That's usually something people see in near-death experiences.*

"Could you see across to the other side?"

Penny frowned. "No. It was very, very long. I never got to the other side."

"Hmmm." Midge ruminated over her food and Penny's responses. "Did you see any angels?"

"I did see a person who told me I would have to go

back and use this gift I had for the world." Penny felt justified, as though her near-death experience was somehow more normal with that information revealed.

"That person wasn't an angel?"

"Well, he wasn't dressed all in white or wearing wings, if that's what you mean."

Midge turned white. "I didn't mean to upset you, Penny." She was stricken that she had somehow insulted Penny, and Penny felt the wave of doubt that began inside of Midge. Midge expected her to be perfect, to never get angry, to have the right answers for her on how things would look at the brink of death.

"It's okay, Midge. I just feel as if I'm disappointing you. I know my experience was not the cookie-cutter version of the entrance to heaven everyone is familiar with."

Midge's curiosity at hearing the word *heaven* overcame her desire to keep Penny calm. "Could the person you spoke with have been God?"

"I don't think so. It didn't feel that way."

"Was God at the other end of the bridge?"

"I really don't know."

"How about relatives that have passed on?"

Penny perked up. "I heard my nana's voice at the beginning, but I never got to see her. When I arrived on the bridge, she wasn't there."

Penny's story left the detective in James unsatisfied and wondering if she was leaving something important out. Oftentimes, when questioning a suspect, he would find they produced odd answers that were so off the expected track, he would literally have to go back to the beginning of things and start all over again with a whole different line of questioning. Instinctively he went there with Penny.

"Penny," he said, "you didn't enter a bright light, see any particular place, pass relatives or angels as people have described in the past. . . ."

He paused here, unsure of how to ask her what he was thinking, not wanting to show a scintilla of doubt in her and also wondering if she had asked herself the same thing. "How can you be sure you were on the bridge to heaven?"

Penny had no answer.

Chapter Seventeen

Somewhere, someone was taking a rather large watermelon, bringing it up to an obscene height and dropping it over and over again onto a cement floor. Or so it seemed to Louis, who could hear the sickening thud at a regular nauseating interval. His strange dreams of the forest seemed to have left him, and he came out of sleep in small bits of awareness instead of his usual hair-raising jolt. His mind felt out the territory of consciousness haltingly and with a great deal of confusion. Who was throwing down the melon? Why was his bed shaking? Louis kept his eyes closed until all of his senses came to him, even if somewhat muted and with great reluctance.

Sadly, the melon was his head. With each heartbeat it drummed its own thump of pain, and Louis figured it was probably the size of a watermelon as well, based on the difficulty he was having lifting it. When he did finally raise his body enough so that his head had no choice but to follow, he struck it on something above him, sending little white stars across Louis's eyes, which were now wide open. Aside from the stars, all he could see was black. Had he gone blind? Where was that part of the brain anyway? Louis's Uncle Albert flitted through his mind, both for the jokes he told every Thanksgiving and because he was blinded in the Vietnam war by a well-placed piece of shrapnel in his brain. He tried to remember where the scar was that Uncle Albert showed him, annually leaning his head across the cranberry sauce and always dipping dangerously close to the candle centerpiece Louis's Mom had lit. That blind Uncle Albert never went up in a ball of flames was somewhat of a yearly holiday miracle.

The scar was on the right side of his head, if Louis remembered correctly, and he gingerly lifted a hand to his own to make some kind of investigation of the pain. His arm was not tied but blocked from a full range of motion, and he heard a sound he knew was familiar. There was something all around him in the darkness, a covering of some sort, and Louis's mind knew it knew what it was but didn't care to share it with him. Pictures of his kitchen came to him. He was cooking a TV dinner and eating it, then he threw it away. The garbage was full. He could see himself replacing the bag, shaking it with a snap for the air to explode through. He was in a garbage bag or a plastic bag of some kind. Whoever put him here didn't bother to tie him up. Louis guessed they had taken him for dead.

And that gruesome byte of information led to several others, also unpleasant. The movement meant he was in a car, and judging by the head clearance, he had the privilege of being in the trunk. Someone had been lifting a large bag into a car when he first arrived on the scene of Messianic Vision. How long ago was that? Unfortunately, based on the cramped legroom, he was probably next to that other body, most likely a corpse.

Louis froze like a deer in a car's headlights and later understood why that fear reaction has some survival benefits. If he had started thrashing about and screaming, there was a chance he'd be found out and he'd end up as dead as they thought he was. Ice cream danced around in his head, his lucky sweater, the Pulitzer prize. *"These are a few of my favorite things. . . ."*

Louis wanted to pull himself together, but it had been a hell of a week. Rational thought seemed to have turned its back on him in every shape and form. His eyes darted around in the dark, not knowing what they were looking for. He wondered where his assailant had gotten such a big plastic bag, much less two of them. He snaked his hand up to reexamine the back of his head, which was mushy and oozing. Mostly he was wasting his time spending his energy pushing down his panic.

The bag he was in felt as though it had no hole. When Louis collected enough of his wits to try to get it off, he got hopelessly stuck on the idea that he was literally the personification of someone unable to find their way out of a paper (plastic) bag. He got caught up in a fit of hysterical laughter that was one hundred percent terror and zero mirth. After that terrible cackling ceased, Louis's second snag was the notion that they had somehow sealed the bag. His mind lit on the top of the idea and bounced around there for a while. This was not at all unusual for Louis. Watching movies, he often found himself greatly distracted by the minor details left unaccounted for. If the main character put up a pot of tea and never got back to it, it would just plague him until the very end of the show. Or if the mother was putting together dinner when an adventure began, he was completely unable to go with the flow of the action. Did the meal burn? Had anyone picked up her children from school? If they had, what would the children do when they arrived home to find their mother gone? This was his literary stumbling block as well. Everything had to be accounted for. Surely it was another factor in cutting short his ambitions of writing fiction. His mind was equally mobile now, at a time Louis most needed to focus on saving his own life. He might have died wondering how many people it took to get him in the bag if the next three seconds didn't jar him so forcefully.

In the midst of his reverie, he had been feeling around, rather offhandedly, for the opening in the bag when he inadvertently touched the body next to him. His hackles rose and his breakfast threatened to revisit him. He was desperately trying to ignore his proximity to a corpse when he heard the rustle of what he assumed was a garbage bag very much out of sync with his own movements.

The plastic moving around the corpse roared like a fire engine in Louis's frozen ear. He tried to will it quiet, cowering into a corner and pushing up against radio speakers that compressed his painful head. A hand wrapped itself around his ankle. With this fright, Louis came unstuck, screaming and tearing at the plastic, which flew in and out of his mouth along with his gulping, panicked breaths. While his hands flailed and tried to tear the bag, slick with the moisture of his own condensed sweat, his feet kicked and fended off the body now reaching for his upper arms.

"*The dead body has me, the dead body has me . . .*" he scream-whispered in a high-pitched voice his vocal chords hadn't produced since he was twelve.

The car continued to roll along, now over a slightly rougher terrain, pitching the two giant bags close enough together so that Louis could feel the other body's nose find its way into his ear. When it spoke, Louis was sure his heart stopped completely.

"*If I was dead, I wouldn't be talking to you,*" a female voice whisper-screamed back at him, more than a little annoyed. "I did the dying thing. Trust me, this isn't it."

Louis squeaked incomprehensibly.

"*Shut up before you get us both killed.*"

Jetta had regained consciousness not long after Louis, aware of what Isaac had done to her and examining her own hurting skull. Jetta had always been, first and foremost, practical. Raising five children, it was practical or dead. Whenever there were stitches, broken bones or other craziness (such as when baby Joey got his head stuck but good in the iron bars of the back porch), Jetta acted calmly and fell apart later when Johnny got home. That, and the fact that she had been practically raised from the dead not two days earlier, made this situation seem almost comical, bordering on annoying. *Well, God, do you want me dead or not?* she wondered. *Or maybe you figured you'll keep me around to torture me a little bit more?* She would work on getting out of the trunk and getting to Penny as best she could. She had heard so many stories of young children hiding in trunks and getting stuck, unable to open them from the inside, that she had her doubts.

Of course, if she couldn't even get out of the bag, the obstacle of the trunk was irrelevant. It struck her as horribly ironic that in fifty years Johnny could hardly get down their driveway without the garbage bag bursting into shreds of paper products and remnants of the meals of the day. Finding no opening, she tried holding it taut while ripping it with her nails, two of which were jagged from the scramble down Isaac and Daisy's concrete steps. Soon she was out and moving on to extract Louis's head from his bag like an obstetrician delivering a reluctant baby. The dark was still between them and Jetta wished she could see into his eyes, know how much coaxing he would need to be helpful in escaping from the confines of the trunk.

"I'm Jetta," she whispered, not expecting a handshake but hoping for any sign of life. "Run your hands along the ceiling of the trunk. See if you can find a latch to open it." He still said nothing, but she could feel his arm bump into her own as it swept along above her. She was just happy she hadn't scared him to death. Her eyes rolled pointlessly in the dark. "I think this is the back. I can hear the driver using his blinker if I put my ear up against this wall. Let's try the opposite end."

It was a struggle in such a small space for both of them to turn around, and as they maneuvered themselves, Jetta listened to Louis's reedy breaths and understood for the first time how wild animals smelled fear. Even his jerky movements spoke to her of his panic. Not that Jetta wasn't afraid, but her fear was not getting to Penny in time to warn her how much danger she was in. Her only desire was to get to Penny and be a part of her team, to facilitate her work. There was tremendous strength in not worrying about her own self.

They ran their hands across the top edge of the trunk for a few long minutes, finding only wires and holes that led to more wires. Jetta could feel the heat of Louis's sweat next to her. In the center of the ceiling they both tactically explored a round piece of metal soldered into place with another link hooked around it. Louis examined it with his hands and spoke with a voice he was trying to keep under control.

"I think this is it." He went back to it, tugging from both ends, then pulling on it while trying to push open the trunk.

"If we get it open, we have to be careful the door doesn't pop up where the driver can see it," Jetta cautioned.

The hope of escape was steadying Louis. "At least we'd be free to defend ourselves. I'm Louis, by the way."

"Jetta," she said again.

Their introductions were cut short by a distinct change in the car's progress, now climbing a steep hill. They were further smashed against the front of the trunk. Rocks and gravel hit the undercarriage and Jetta and Louis pulled and pushed on the latch from every possible angle. Visions of being pushed over the side of whatever mountain they were climbing while still encased in the trunk seemed decidedly realistic.

"It's not working!" Louis said desperately. "You can't get it open from here!"

Jetta tried to think of another option.

Louis just started to scream, "Get us out of here!"

Jetta reached out blindly in the dark and clamped a hand over his mouth. She could feel his sparse mustache and sharp nose. "Don't lose your mind, Louis."

He shook free of her. "If we shout, the driver will have to open the trunk to investigate."

She whispered, "Or he'll shoot us through the top. Or he'll hurry up and push the whole damn car over a cliff. Either way, we'll still be stuck in here. Let's take a minute and think."

"We don't have too many more minutes! We have to do something right now!"

Jetta was suddenly very angry that women were always depicted as the weak, helpless sex. If there was a fight, they were supposed to be the ones standing in a corner with their hands over their mouths, screaming or running on the tops of tables at the first sight of a spider. The truth was, she always saw men's and women's strengths as of a very different nature. Her daddy had been a firefighter. Running headfirst into a four-alarm blaze was nothing to those men, and they were highly admired and decorated with citations from the little town she lived in, and rightly so. But Jetta often thought that brute force and a rush to action was their advantage, and that if they had to stop and stand outside, watching the fire for even a few minutes, a lot more firemen would have been librarians.

Jetta knew that a woman's strength was her endurance. In Jetta's day it was not unheard-of for a woman to withstand forty hours of labor and produce a twelve-pound baby without even the hint of pain-controlling drugs. And those same women went on to have more children. Her mother's generation stayed up half the night with sick babies and got up three hours later to work fields that would feed their families through the winter while their husbands went to jobs that paid next to nothing. Most of the men took to drinking while the women taught each other how to knit and crochet so they could sell things in town once a month for pennies. Church was filled with these women, and Jetta as a child had always wondered where all the men were. It was clear now that their endurance was fueled by hope. Women don't pull the rope that hard, they just keep pulling and don't stop.

Jetta's mind returned to the trunk. *Can't get the trunk to open. Is there another way out?* Jetta had a flash of her cousin Betty, who took her out once a month to the movies. Betty had a trick knee and would store her walker in the trunk with one of the backseats down!

"Louis!" She felt him come to attention. "The backseat! Maybe it folds down. We can grab the driver from behind."

The button that folded the seat stuck up like a flag and seemed to ask why they hadn't thought of it before. As Louis released it and Jetta pushed the seat forward a hair to look out and get her bearings, the car came to a stop. There was just the driver, and he dialed a cell phone while looking out over a precipice. The sun was going down, and at any other time it would have seemed a beautiful view. Jetta put her finger to her lips while looking into Louis's eyes for the first time. They listened.

"I'm at the place to dump them." It was Ronald Miller, the retired librarian, and his voice shook with an uncertainty he hadn't felt when he was next to Isaac. When he was with Isaac, everything made sense, even things he couldn't understand. Out here, alone with what he thought were two dead bodies, doubt had crept in.

"Are you sure we shouldn't leave them where they can be found? What about their families?"

Louis and Jetta listened to the mumbled response coming from the earpiece and noticed Ronald was wearing latex gloves. For people who were only supposed to own bowls and blankets, the Rourkes had turned out to be more resourceful than Jetta could have ever imagined.

"But I—" Ronald was saying before another long pause. Then, "Maybe we should just—"

The mumbling from the phone became shouting, though it was still indistinguishable. It ended, and the old librarian looked for the button that would end the call.

Louis took advantage of that moment of hesitation to spring forward. Just as the cell phone was shut off, Louis knocked it out of his hand toward Jetta and surrounded the confused librarian with his arms in a headlock that was dangerously close to cutting off Ronald's air. Jetta was as surprised as the librarian, and judging by Louis's expression, he was a little shocked himself at being part of the action instead of just reporting it. He looked to Jetta as though asking, *Okay, now what?*

Jetta crawled out of the trunk and reached over the seat to grab the car keys. "Where are we, Ronald?"

Ronald looked as if he were going to be strong and hold out, but Louis tightened his grip.

"Okay, okay . . . let up," he whistled through clenched teeth. "We're at Mt. Pleasant."

The irony of the name didn't escape any of them.

"We should kill you, Ronald," Jetta said. Louis looked at her as though she were crazy. He shook his head and raised his chin toward her as if to say, I'm *not killing him*, you *kill him*.

Happy her new sidekick wasn't a killer, Jetta said, "Get out of the car right now, Ronald, and run away."

He looked up, appealing to her with his eyes. In saner

times he had helped Jetta find books about learning disabilities when her son Freddy had been diagnosed as a difficult student. He had almost single-handedly done all of her research regarding her diabetes. *This is probably why there aren't more murders in small towns,* she thought. *People just have too much history together.*

"Open the door, Ronald. On the count of three, this gentleman will release you. Start running."

He was walking slowly on the main road as they drove past him back down the mountain. Jetta knew they were lucky it hadn't been Isaac getting rid of them or they would already be at the bottom of the cliff.

The sun had sunk down at last, leaving the sky dark and starless. It took only five minutes of conversation for Jetta and Louis to agree to find Penny. Jetta wanted to be by Penny's side, but Louis wasn't sure what he wanted. He wasn't sure if he was objective enough to write about her. At any rate, he told himself, he owed Penny his life and, at the very least, was obliged to warn her what was coming her way.

Penny and Hal were not used to being fugitives. Hal had thought himself clever. But with just one call from the librarian's cell phone, Louis found Penny's and Hal's mothers' maiden names on their various marriage licenses through his source at the town hall. It was the information age, after all. With a computer and a sense of where to look, anything could be found. This same source searched real estate holdings under both names, noting those with two addresses. The home most remote but still in driving distance would likely be their destination. With this one well-placed call it was frighteningly easy for Louis to use his contacts and instincts as a reporter to pinpoint Myrtle's as where she would probably be. Louis shuddered, knowing that if he could locate her so readily, anyone could.

Chapter Eighteen

The car moved with the fog that developed along the edges of Mt. Pleasant's steep turns. Penny looked out at the evergreens, so solid in the mist and so plentiful, it seemed they were the very force that held up the mountain. There were patches of green revealing themselves under the giant boughs of the pines, and she had the urge to go out and sleep under them alone. Her children waited for her, though, and she could envision them padding along in feety pajamas, chairs drawn up to a roadside window, waiting. Hal spoke to his mother from a pay phone at the diner and he assured her everything was fine, but Penny had overheard Benjamin crying.

Houses were scattered around them, and as they moved cautiously up the single-lane road she studied them for signs of life; waning piles of wood or smoke billowing out from end-of-the-season fires were intended more to scare away the dampness than to warm. Shades were drawn and driveways sat barren, boats and snowmobiles somehow absent. She wondered if they were between seasons, or if these homes had been abandoned for more popular getaways. The town had always been teeming with life when she was a little girl visiting Aunt Myrtle with her grandparents. The neighbors reminded her of the old woman who lived in the shoe and had so many children she didn't know what to do. Aunt Myrtle's house was on a double lot and had been built to accommodate her as one of six children, but most of the homes around them were cottages with pull-out couches serving as bedrooms.

The area was skeletal with the hum of life missing from it, and Penny didn't need that extra sense to feel its absence. Instead she thought of the lake and its rowboats, which her grandfather had paddled around with her, the sea queen, at its helm and him the captain. His stories of things he remembered from his own childhood were stored in her mind like jewels in a treasure box, and his passing was almost unbearable here, where her memories of him lived most vividly. He had always told her she would do something remarkable, he was so sure of her greatness. She wondered if this whole episode counted. She had not earned it the old-fashioned way, through education or practice. This had been thrust upon her. Something obtained with such ease seemed terribly unreliable now, she felt, thinking of her grandfather in his steadiness.

They turned a familiar corner where a small road led down to a cluster of larger homes built directly over the lake, and Penny recalled the name of the family that had owned each. Most of the houses had fallen into disrepair, and she felt a terrible sadness slip over her at the thought of everything so changed. She would like to go up onto their porches, push aside the ivy and moss growing unchecked and run her hands along the gray stucco for some knowledge of where her comrades in play had ended up.

There were no children here now, and Penny searched her mind for some alternate plan for her kids. Julie, Lydia and Benny needed playmates, and she and Hal couldn't afford to hide out for long. They just barely paid their bills as it was, with her at home with the kids in a two-income world. This was a great vacation spot, a good getaway, but she didn't think they could stay here more than briefly. And how soon would it be before the world found them? A one-lane mountain road wasn't much of an escape route.

Aunt Myrtle's house stood out among the pines ahead in the distance. Facing due east, it wore the sunset at its back like a veil trailing behind it. The children were surrounded by the light in the picture window that faced the road, so that Penny could only see their silhouettes, their features obscured and undistinguished, blotted out by the dying sun.

She was out of the car before it stopped. The house greeted her as she grabbed hold of the long banister leading up the wooden steps to a porch that surrounded it in its entirety. She imagined she could feel its creaks and broken floorboards, the manifestations of its age. Could she also heal a house? She laughed at the thought.

The children's voices easily came through the four-inch thick antique door: "Mama! Mama!" They raced to her before it had even swung open. Hal was pushed aside and the strangers ignored for the rock that was their feeling of security, that home-safe feeling that had been desperately missing for days on end without her until unfamiliarity began to be the most familiar feeling and the safe one odd and distant.

"Mama, you're back!" They held her, one at each leg, Benny vying for a spot so that they were all stuck at the doorway, unable to move, Penny unable to walk and trying to pick everyone up at the same time. Instead she just bent down and kissed each one of them over and over again until she thought they couldn't stand even one more.

"Are you better?" Julie asked her while her sister insisted, "You're staying with us now, right, Mommy?"

Benny just cried and Penny, breaking the logjam of people and getting them through the door, took a good look at him even as the twins rattled off the millions of things they had done since they had arrived. She nodded and listened and held her son as he settled down and put his heavy head on her shoulder, going into a doze in mid-scream.

Hal introduced Midge and James and Penny thanked her mother-in-law for being with the children. They were a whirlwind as they made their way out of the foyer and into the great room Aunt Myrtle had filled with overstuffed couches and chairs and an old player piano that was never dusted but had often been played. Windows were set all around it and Penny felt as though she were in the clearing under the pine that she longed for earlier. She sat, shifting the sleeping Benny in her arms and feeling at home with the girls on either side of her. She watched Hal and his father and wondered why they seemed so unusual together. They were making eye contact, sustained for longer than she could ever remember; that in itself was unusual, but she supposed it was more the content of their conversation that was odd. Harvey was telling Hal all about showing the girls the lake and the pine cone collection they had turned into bird feeders with peanut butter and bird seed. Before she could wrap her mind around any of that, she noticed that Lydia had slipped away from her and was on her grandfather's lap. She couldn't recall Harvey ever even addressing any of the children directly: That was just the way he had been. And now it wasn't.

Penny got up and held Benny throughout the tour her mother-in-law gave her of what she had done with the house to get it ready for them, the bathrooms she had cleaned, the mattresses she had turned, the linens she had freshened up.

"Mom," Penny asked her, "what are all these wreaths on the doors?"

Her mother-in-law blushed. "Those are from your

father-in-law." She paused. "He's been collecting them with the children and making them as"—she scrunched up her face, trying to look as if she highly disapproved or thought him ridiculous, but also looking extraordinarily pleased— "love gifts, as he calls them." She changed the subject quickly as they came full circle from their tour back into the living room. "I don't know if it's just because you've been gone, but Benny hasn't been right."

Hal looked up from his conversation with his father and the Elians. "Hasn't been right, how?"

Penny shifted Benny's sleeping body, checking his forehead and cheeks, slipping two fingers under his collar to feel the temperature of his upper body. "He feels warm. Did he eat today?"

Mary Chaney looked uncomfortable. "He hasn't eaten well since you've been gone. He's been running a low-grade fever for a day. I've been afraid to bring him to your pediatrician because I didn't want us found again by all those reporters. Also, I thought you would just . . ."

Penny looked at her. Of course! Why hadn't she thought of that? They all looked at her as if to say, *Well, aren't you going to do something about this?* "Has he been sleeping well?"

"No, not really. He hasn't been napping at all. I thought it was just all of the confusion, all of the fuss and change."

Again the group looked at her expectantly, wondering what was keeping her from doing her thing, helping him with whatever he needed. At the very least, finding out what was wrong. A fear stole over Penny, and it fit her the way the old house did, filled with memories that were in most instances vague feelings rather than concrete recollections. Benny stirred, his mouth hanging slightly open, because his nose was too stuffed to breath through. Penny reached out to him and they all watched her intensely, waiting for that glorious feeling of her gift rushing through the room.

"He's got an ear infection," she reported, not looking at Hal, not knowing what to say to him. "We should get in touch with the pediatrician. Maybe he can recommend someone up here and keep our hiding place secure. You know, doctor-patient confidentiality and all that."

Hal's mouth dropped. What was Penny doing? She could make him better right then and there in the next second. "Penny just heal him. Do what you did to Midge."

Penny tried to stall him, put him off. "He's just a baby, Hal."

"There were tons of babies in the crowd outside of the hospital, Pen. You saw them yourselves. You made them better."

"This is different, Hal. He's my son."

"I don't think you could hurt him. Is that what you're afraid of?"

Harvey, a world away from the man he was a week ago but still not up to any major confrontation, tried to steal out of the living room to put the girls to bed. "No!" screamed Lydia. "I want Mommy! I want Mommy to put us to bed!"

Penny took her opportunity to escape, whisking Benny up the broad staircase and into the nursery her mother-in-law had put together for him. He seemed deep in sleep, and she covered him gently. She remembered her cousin Lily sleeping in that very crib when she was just a girl and wondering at how tiny a baby could be. The girls followed her into what was now their room, and she read the books that were scattered there and said every prayer she could think of with them to put off her confrontation with Hal. He would want answers, answers she was very unclear about and not ready to give him yet.

Their bedtime routine was unchanged, even a hundred miles from their front door. It was the same back patting and reassuring. Penny sprinkled imaginary "good dream juice" on each of them, head to toe, twice for good measure. Directions to the Dreamer's Ball (Hal's invention) were reviewed, and they described what they would be wearing so they could find each other in their respective gowns. Lydia said she would be arriving by unicorn coach, Julie by flying dragon. Often Penny actually dreamed they had met and danced in some far-off castle, but the jubilation of the experience was muted by the knowledge that it was just a dream even as she twirled her two daughters, one on each side. She tucked the covers under their chins and wondered if other people had dreams in which they knew they were dreaming.

Musty smells wafted around her. The girls were in twin beds covered by sheets that still smelled of a fifty-five-degree setting in a seldom-used cottage. Pictures of seashells accented the walls, and Penny smiled at Aunt Myrtle's vision of a summer house being associated with the shore instead of the woods. Even as a child she thought that trees and squirrels should fill the frames instead of whales and sand art.

She was so happy to be with them, to be back in her role of mother only to her rightful children and not be responsible for everyone in the world, if just until morning. Being with the children made her feel somewhat grounded again, as looking at one object does when you're spinning to keep your bearings. It came to Penny that all of the great religious leaders didn't have any children, and that suddenly seemed so clear and sensible. Who could run around bringing people back to life or meeting with thousands when children needed schedules and routines and a sense of normalcy? She was sure Christ never would have lived so radically and been crucified if he had had a wife and family to answer to. Surely Mother Teresa wouldn't have risked bringing everything from leprosy to diphtheria home to her own offspring. Who would have watched his children when Gandhi was jailed for his peaceful protests? There was a freedom needed to heal that she neither had nor wanted.

The girls slept soundly for the first time in many nights, and Penny stopped and stood outside their door, listening to them breathe, snoring peacefully with their arms wrapped around their animal lovies, their world somewhat restored. In the next room Benny started to wail and Penny bumped into Hal, both of them racing from different directions to get to him. Penny scooped him up.

Hal whispered from the doorway, "James and Midge are all settled in. They're going to work on security tomorrow, come up with a plan."

Penny carried Benny back downstairs, looking for where Mary put the bottles. Benny whined uncomfortably.

"Penny," Hal said with some anger, "I don't understand why you don't just heal him."

"I don't understand why you're pressuring me!" But Penny knew Hal was standing on different terrain than she was, one in which logic prevailed and ruled the law of action. Penny didn't feel like a resident of that place anymore.

"He's your son. I'm surprised you can sit and watch him suffer when you know better than anyone how he's feeling."

"It's just an ear infection, Hal," she retorted, and she could hear the whine in her own voice that mirrored Benny's in its helplessness.

"An ear infection would've sent you running to the doctor a week ago."

"Well, things aren't what they were a week ago, are they?" Penny snapped.

Hal was taken aback. "I just don't understand at all."

"I made some promises on the bridge, Hal."

"Promises? What kind of promises?"

"Promises about the decision to use this healing power."

"What are you talking about?"

"I don't remember it all clearly, Hal."

"Well, what do you remember?"

"It's all so cloudy now." She walked to the sink, handed Benny to Hal and washed out a bottle, as she had a million times before. If she could just keep doing normal things, she could keep moving, keep breathing, not freeze up.

Hal stood, mouth open, looking at Penny with confusion and an anger he couldn't pinpoint. "It's not so cloudy that you don't remember making the promises. What the hell were they? I want to know now, Penny. I am affected by all of this, and obviously our children are too."

Penny stood her ground, wanting none of this conversation, not knowing where to go with it.

"You're holding out on me and I resent it." He tried to hand her Benjamin and she backed off, not putting her arms out for him.

"Let's call the doctor now, Hal."

"Not until you tell me what the hell is going on here. You heal him, Penny. You heal him right now."

"I can't do that, Hal," Penny whispered.

"You can't, or you won't?" Hal shouted, and the vein that always stuck out on his neck when they discussed the monthly bills showed up, throbbing. "You're his mother: He should be more important to you than anyone around that hospital today."

She reached out for the baby, taking him in her arms gently and looking into his curious eyes. Penny pushed out that healing force, trying to wrap it around her tiny son. Hal felt it billow through the room like a warm spring breeze but also felt it dampen quickly and die out.

"What's the matter? Why didn't you finish, Pen? It was working."

Penny, unsurprised, looked at the floor. "No, Hal. It wasn't. I tried. I can't heal him."

Chapter Nineteen

As soon as her eyes were open, Daisy knew Isaac was gone. Even at midnight Isaac's very presence was missing from the house and there was a palpable void where his towering self used to be. Isaac couldn't boil an egg without a certain amount of bravado and drama. He made you think his method of boiling was so far superior to any other in the history of man, you ate it like manna from heaven and begged for another. It was all in the advertising, he always said: "It's easy to sell people what they want. They want to eat good food. They want to be loved, to solve the mysteries of the world, to save the planet. I just convince them they are."

The spark of that electricity was never quiet, and Daisy didn't ever awaken to birds singing or quiet rain against whatever windows on whatever house they called home at the time. A pet project of the day in all of its excitement would always be in full swing even as Daisy dreamed her last dream of the morning. Once she had come down at five A.M., the world still dark and Isaac already selling bonds in India to soy farmers. His words melted into theirs, and five minutes after he scored three hundred thousand dollars, a perfect English-Hindi accent still lilted around his voice like a prize. "People trust who they know," he said again and again. "You have to be them to get them."

His pillow had no indentation—the proof in the pudding, her grandmother always said. Not that Isaac ever really slept, the way most people do. Isaac took power naps, even his rest needing to be large and purposeful. He lay down on his back for twenty minutes at a time a few times a day, and even then it looked more like intense concentration than sleeping. Daisy rarely saw him with a hair out of place, and it was hard to feel at all on top of his every game when he had an entire extra third of the day without her at his disposal. She tried to keep up with him when they first joined forces and ended up with a coffee habit and a killer case of mono. Thinking seemed just short of impossible, words becoming soupy and even basic ideas elusive without a minimum of five consecutive hours, and she just didn't know how Isaac pulled it off.

Dropping just one hour a night in an attempt to surprise him and find out which pots of trouble he was stirring up made her exhausted and ill. Isaac, on the other hand, seemed impervious to all physical sickness. Lying there without him, she tried to remember if she ever saw him holding a tissue or taking an aspirin.

They were together for twenty years, and she wondered when Isaac had begun to seem normal, when she stopped being in awe of his gift for pulling the sting on whoever was unlucky enough to have aroused his interest. She accepted things as par for the course eventually, and knew to glance away when a voice inside of her set off a bell of alarm. Isaac had become the king of scam and she the perfect partner, which included not looking back. When they blew out of a town, there would be hundreds of thousands of dollars resting comfortably in some offshore account. When asked about it, Isaac invariably said, "Don't worry, I'll handle everything." She should have asked for numbers, demanded passwords. The doubt ran through her like an underground stream.

At first, whenever they left a town, it was under the

guise of starting a new branch, referred to affectionately by Isaac as "another arm of brotherhood." He smiled at this and every other phrase of deceit, which made him laugh when they were alone, his steely blue eyes the only party not to get the joke. Daisy would stay in touch with whoever they had left in charge, trying to keep the followers' own doubts at bay, giving them only cell phone numbers for contact. Invariably, though, someone would grow suspicious and the questions that seemed positively absurd when Isaac was near bubbled to the surface and grew contagious when his rousing speeches and piercing stare were gone.

There was a sleepy little town called Hamptonburg where they spent ten months a few years ago: lots of old money sitting around, getting fat—so much so that they had probably run out of things to spend it on, Isaac would say. They left on the expansion excuse, and Daisy made her follow-up calls to keep the scam from going sour and to the authorities. It was way back, early in their formation of the Messiah-seeking pretense they eventually got great at. Daisy got in touch with a Mike Doogan, an old man no younger than ninety who had been left in charge, picked because he was a strong personality and a big believer. She had never heard the age in his voice until their last static-filled conversation that winked out intermittently with the passing solar flare.

"Daisy! Thank God!" Mike had started out saying, and she already knew the jig was up. "Jim Myers said he was going to the state attorney the day after you left. He said our group was a scam cult. He wanted all of his money back."

She wondered how Isaac's spell had been broken so easily. Daisy went into the song and dance she and Isaac had rehearsed and polished in the car for just such an occasion, but Mike interrupted her.

"Yes, yes. That's what Isaac said when I talked to him a few days ago."

Daisy stood stock-still outside the new senior center she was working at halfway across the country. A car was pulling into the lot, its passengers short in its seat, the driver with her chin held way up to see over the steering wheel. Each head was an identical steel-wool gray.

"That can't be, Mike. Are you sure it was Isaac?" Isaac had made it clear he wanted her to do all follow-up so he could concentrate on their new location. That small alarm bell went off again like a not-so-gentle poke in the back.

"It was Isaac, but he never got back to me." Here the old man's voice broke and she thought she heard the thump of an awkward body sitting down. "You see, Jim Myers is missing."

"Missing?" Daisy said noncommittally, the way someone would say *Pass the salt* or *Yes, I think it might rain*.

"He left a note saying he went fishing with his brother in Florida and wouldn't be back for a while...."

"There you go," Daisy said, feeling almost better.

"No, you don't understand. That's not Jim. First of all, Jim is a scheduled type of guy. If you'll forgive me, but he doesn't even fart, if it's not on his daily calendar. His wife, may she rest in peace, dragged him all over the place to travel and then just gave up and started going with her sisters. Jim told me he'd have to be pulled out of that house kicking and screaming before he went further than the corner drugstore. I believe he meant that. Also, we've been friends for fifty years. We have coffee every morning." His voice broke again. "I know how many sweaters he has. Five. Do you think he would get on a plane and go somewhere to do something he doesn't even like to do without telling me? He doesn't even eat fish sticks. Why in the hell would he go fishing?"

Mike Doogan went on like that for a while, and Daisy tried hard to wonder sarcastically why the man never argued before the Supreme Court, he seemed to have so many damned reasons for everything. Yet, a growing dread was filling her stomach in the pit where her fear lived.

When asked about it, Isaac had replied evenly, "Many older people adopt new hobbies at a later age." His eyes had glared directly into hers, unafraid and daring her to challenge him. Some arms of brotherhood stayed attached. Others were severed off if they became gangrenous and threatened the viability of the entire body.

With everything they'd accumulated, Daisy couldn't understand why Isaac couldn't just retire. Of course, that was assuming Isaac was just like her, done with it all. She had been done three towns ago. Isaac wheedled her, "We're almost at eighteen million, Daisy. Let's make it an even twenty then hit the Bahamas." He took her to Vegas for a weekend, and the taste of opulence kept her going. Coming from food stamps and Salvation Army clothes, it was all about money for her. To Isaac, it was only about power. He was the king of scam in the way of the king in a game of checkers, double-stacked to see higher than everyone around him and having no morals to stop him from going any direction he chose. The difference was that he was almost invisible in his movements, having been born with an overabundance of the two other qualities besides intelligence that cinch a scam: old-fashioned charm and an extraordinary amount of luck. Daisy wondered if luck was indeed a personal quality or something measured out at birth. Could you use it all up?

She looked at the pillow next to her on the blanket they slept on to keep up the appearances the scam called for. She had lived onstage for twenty years, the very utensil she ate with a part of the plot. Not that they never indulged, but Isaac always itched to get back to the game.

A dawning light came on in a corner of her brain that had covered itself with the desire to stay with Isaac, and underneath it found the ultimate humiliation that she was just another mark, a victim of Isaac Rourke. But instead of just money, he had stolen her time, a chunk of her life that people called the prime. She had nothing: no family, no babies, no home or community. *Well*, she thought bitterly, *not exactly nothing. I have a blanket, a pillow, a pot, a toothbrush, a comb and a fucking spork. What else could I possibly need?*

The clock said twelve-thirty. She went down the creaky old stairs, not expecting to find anything of Isaac's at all and wanting to throw something hard and heavy. With no knickknacks to speak of, she settled on the small aluminum pot and headed into the kitchen to wrap her hands around it, hoping to feel some release from the stupidity of being scammed herself. If it were the Olympics, Isaac would be walking off with the gold, because scamming a fellow con artist was the pinnacle of accomplishment among thieves. On the counter was a hundred-dollar bill—a slap in the face to Daisy, who, after twenty years, instead of half of the earnings was getting a whore's one-night pay. This was unacceptable.

Looking down into the cabinet below the stove for the pot, something caught her eye. Her rage was muffled momentarily, overcome by her curiosity. The garbage sat in the adjacent space, looking unassuming. She reached inside of it, closing her thumb and first finger around a small piece of cellophane. The paper bag serving as their garbage can tipped over and Daisy was left holding a wrapper, which glistened in the dull light of the kitchen's sixty-watt bulb. It came from the variety store in the next town, and a smiling neon butterfly sticker announced it was a buy-one, get-one-half-off item. Its mate lay at Daisy's feet, also torn open, its shell sliced horizontally under the brand name and content description. It had contained 100-percent cotton percale sheets, white, 240-thread count, and at first Daisy thought he was going someplace luxurious where he would be sleeping on the sheets she never got to have. Visions of a home with a spoon rest and curtains cluttered up her mind so that she couldn't think clearly, or at least think the way Isaac would think.

Furiously, she started pulling things out of the garbage, looking for further evidence of the extravagant lifestyle she had been denied, always waiting for the payoff. It was a cornucopia of oddities, at least for them. In addition to the sheet wrappers was a slim box with two staring eyes shrouded by dark brown round coverings. Underneath it said 20/20 VISION, 24-HOUR WEAR. The last item was a shoebox, empty, showing a computer generated picture of a leather sandal on its side, men's size ten and a half. Besides a brown banana peel and a burrito wrapper, there was no other trace of the man she knew as her husband for two decades.

Group members began knocking at the door a short fifteen minutes later, demanding answers, asking to see Isaac.

Chapter Twenty

Anyone who has stayed awake all night walking the floors with a baby with an ear infection has a clear picture of where bad parents go when they die. Benjamin screamed all night and Penny heard it both in her ears, which throbbed to the rhythm of his wails, and in that place that felt his pain. It was as infuriating as an itch that one couldn't reach to scratch or the mirage of an oasis in a desert that is perpetually in the distance. When the time came up on four in the morning he was all cried out, exhausted, and as any good pediatrician will tell you, most ear infections stomp around a good bit but make their way off all on their own. He had turned a corner and was asleep, his white blood cells now winning the war. Maybe Hal would go out for antibiotics later when the true morning arrived, if only for something to do.

Penny herself slept in the enormously uncomfortable rocking chair in the nursery, a hand on Benjamin's crib constantly feeling out for him and her head bobbing up with a jerk whenever it got too close to her chest. At five, with only an hour under her belt, she gave up, leaving Benny's side after propping him up carefully and assuring herself he was doing better. She was completely awake and felt strangely rested, as though she could put on a pair of sneakers and go jogging. She didn't think this was possible and was afraid she would crash later. It would be her first full day with the children and she wanted to be fresh, so she slid in next to Hal and tried to get some more sleep before the troops bugled reveille. Sleep, of course, is at its most evasive when it's most needed, and Penny finally threw up the white flag at six and whispered to Hal she was going out for a walk.

The morning was lovely in its quietness. Penny enjoyed the time of day when the sun was stealing in to take over the night. It was just below the tree line, and stars still twinkled stubbornly in a sky that was a deep twilight blue. There seemed to be hundreds of birds, and she could feel their chill and hunger as they looked for breakfast as they rose up out of their nests. She made her way along the dirt path down to the lake, pausing once at the foot of an old hollow tree, the home of a family of squirrels. The mother squirrel had been pecked on the head by a blue jay and its wound had become infected. Penny felt the sickness rising off of the squirrel and settle into the base of her stomach. Its babies squeaked, hungry and frightened. She knelt in the shallow mud and peeked into their hole. The mother's eyes were swollen shut, but she smelled Penny and made a halfhearted effort to snarl her away. The healing was quick and it quieted the morning sounds of the forest down, the birds gliding in circles over her in their curiosity.

The cobbler's children have no shoes, she said to herself, and thought of her own father in his grave now; almost a mythical figure in her mind, she had so little to hold on to in terms of her connection to him. Penny would go to her aunt's house after school some days and her aunt would say, "Your father told me you got A's on your report card. He's so proud of you," and Penny would look at her and wonder if he really was. Or wonder, if it was true, why her father hadn't told her himself. He would look at her report card and nod and Penny was always at a loss as to what that meant. Perhaps all it indicated was *I see you've been attending school* or *Yes, that's definitely a report card*. The word *proud* never really came to her mind as a possible interpretation of what that stoic look on his face meant. He was a mystery to her, almost twice as much so when she saw him with other people. His father, her grandfather, had passed a machine shop down to him, and with customers her father's face came alive as he shouted above the din. He would lead them into the back office, where Penny heard laughter and was left to wonder what those people did right that they could elicit such a response that she, his own daughter, had been unable to. That he would even comment on her doings to her aunt seemed unfathomable and quite absurd. The words her aunt repeated, *He's proud of you*, hung in the air above them both somehow, unable to be processed. She fought hard always to find her children in the midst of their everyday lives, to look into their eyes and talk to them. She wanted to tell them her own feelings. Now, like her own father, she couldn't give them what she could easily give to strangers and even animals.

Penny wanted out of this deal. The path was muddy and as she walked, the cloudy water speckled the legs of her pants and ran across her sneakers. A giant stone jutted out of the brush, large and boulderlike, a familiar piece of landscape she remembered climbing many times as a child. The old footholds were there but had shrunk proportionally to her own growth, and she struggled to mount the rock. It was flat on top, smooth and cool, and from it Penny could see over most of the lake.

She wondered what she was looking for. Lake Pleasant was full of the growing sun rising with precision over the water. Everything moved along on its regular schedule, an ordinary sameness Penny didn't think possible. Even the smells surrounding her on the rock evoked memories some twenty years old as if it hadn't changed in any way and would stand here two hundred thousand years in the future, a damp freshness of ferns and woody cattails still wafting about. Everything was different and Penny was astounded that the world didn't reflect it. She didn't know what she was expecting but was annoyed all the same that it wasn't out here where she thought she might find some answers. A bird lit on a nearby branch, folding its wings and settling in to look at Penny.

"What do you want?" she asked it. She felt its hunger and suspected there was probably some other person who frequented this rock, perhaps with bits of bread. The bird turned its head to rest one steady black eye on her.

Midge and James's questions about heaven and the origins of her healing plagued Penny. She was embarrassed at how little she knew, academically speaking, of theology. She winced at the childish ideas she had of God, visions of Him, a gigantic human being with clouds for a beard, sitting on a throne somewhere above the earth. On the rock, she put her face up to the sky and imagined that to be her only way of seeing Him. At the same time she felt extraordinarily foolish. Her own background was, for all intents and purposes, mainly secular. Christmas was about Santa Claus and reindeer; with Easter the focus was mostly on bunnies and eggs. Her mother collected Longaberger baskets, and they would spend many an evening pouring over the spring catalog in search of that year's Easter limited edition. They dressed up and ate ham on both holidays, her mother scouring the house weeks before whatever aunts, uncles and cousins were expected actually arrived. It was about bonnets and the perfect navy or plaid outfit, each occasion calling for a dress and a hat. Penny had inherited her father's sister's head, a bit big for her body, and her mother took her from store to store to find a hat that didn't teeter precariously or leave a ring around her forehead, threatening to cut off all circulation entirely. On those two days she and her siblings were sent off to church, where they would stand in the back with the other two-holiday-a-year participants to whom the homily often appealed to.

Penny could only remember praying on her own twice, with opposite yet strangely similar results: once, when her cat had gotten run over by the mailman's truck, some errant metal part from its undercarriage ripping him into pieces of fur and blood too gruesome to avoid looking at. She asked God to put Misty back together, and at the time she felt sure He could do it if He wanted to, if she pleaded enough. Misty stayed undeniably dead, and when her mother had cleaned him up somewhat, she had for the first time a true understanding of what life feels like. Misty was cold and his limbs frozen forever, but more importantly, that spark of somethingness, that movement within us, even when we are perfectly still, that marks our being alive, was irretrievably gone. Feeling its absence, Penny knew God would not be bringing Misty back no matter how hard she begged.

When asked, her mother told her to try to accept what had happened. Penny mentioned that she had prayed to God to bring Misty back, and her mother said God had His own plans, which people cannot always understand. Penny asked then what the point was of praying at all if God had His mind made up about things, and her mother sighed with that look she got when Penny asked too many questions. She told her to go wash her hands for dinner.

On the other hand, the second prayer Penny participated in outside of the rote recitations of her biannual church visits was by outcome quite successful. Her older brother's close friend, Victor Lanugo, a friendly and popular boy, had been stricken with leukemia. She went with her family to visit him at the hospital, peering into his semiprivate room as her brother gave Victor his prize Mickey Mantle baseball card to prop up on his night table or hold during any painful procedures he might encounter. Victor smiled, his teeth looking frightfully huge set against his round, bald head, yet somehow maintaining the look of an adorable kid. His roommate, some other boy similarly afflicted, looked on despairingly from the next bed, and Penny noticed the overabundance of cards and toys surrounding Victor, a virtual mountain compared to the bareness of the other boy's side.

The schoolchildren met each morning around the flagpole and prayed diligently for Victor's recovery, Penny taking part just once when her brother was staring at her, shaming her into it. There were collection boxes and bake sales to offset the Lanugos' doctor bills, and the newspaper ran his picture in support.

Victor recovered marvelously, and the whole town seemed to take credit in the pride of the prayer movement that they claimed saved him. Penny ran across the other boy, whose own picture was also in the paper—not on the front page like Victor's, but set against the short paragraph of his obituary, which was filled with the additional despair of divorced parents and a string of former addresses. His name was Max Treadwell, and Penny was angry for him. He hadn't had an entire community praying for him. Was that how it worked? Popularity? Her voice asking for Victor Lanugo's returned health felt like a vote against Max Treadwell, and Penny no longer wanted any part of it.

It was no wonder she didn't know how to start a prayer, or even a conversation, all of these years later. Each of the stars winked out with Penny just waiting, expecting some sort of angel or voice from above. She took a few long, deep breaths trying to be patient. A fish thrashed his tail off toward the middle of the pond, and Penny could see others nipping at the surface in search of their breakfast. She zipped her sweatshirt up around her neck and watched the sun pull the last of its orb out of the lake.

"I've changed my mind," she said out loud, looking around for a response. The small brown bird continued to wait expectantly across from her.

"I didn't realize what I was saying yes to," she said a bit louder. "I was on that bridge and I wasn't myself, but I'm more convinced than ever that I'm not the right person for this at all."

Two loons called to each other in the distance. Actually, thought Penny, make that three loons.

She raised her voice. "I don't know how to manage it all. I need a plan. I need to know exactly what to say. I think those people that were healed are probably as confused as ever." She looked around, truly expecting to hear a voice in response.

"If I can have some sort of phrase..." The silence grew bigger somehow, quieter.

"Okay," Penny said, her heart pounding. "What I really want to say is, I don't want to do this. I'm giving too much up. The price is too high." She stood up, her finger pointed at the sky, and she used it to emphasize her words, yelling now at a God that seemed to ignore her, unmoved. "I thought I could make this sacrifice, but I can't. It's too big."

Small ripples hit the shore of the lake, thrown off of a distant boat riding out to mine its fish. Penny didn't care. *Let everyone in the world hear me,* she thought.

"I mean it." Her voice shook, and she frightened herself with what she said. "I was tricked. I was on that bridge and I thought I was going to die if I didn't agree. But all of the choices were lousy. *Lousy!*"

A small flock of birds took flight from a nearby tree, and Penny noticed the small brown one was gone from his perch next to her. A toad croaked. She threw up her hands. "You have to talk to me! I cannot bear this burden. Hell, I can barely figure it out. There's been some big mistake. I'm sure of it. This must have been meant for someone else, someone who doesn't have as much to lose."

A car door slammed up the hill above her. The morning chill was burning off, revealing a hint of the spring that was almost upon them. Penny stood, hands on hips, scouring the landscape for some kind of sign that she had been heard. Somewhere in the woods a baby bird fell out of its nest and to its death. Penny felt it take its last breath, knowing it was too far off for her to get to in time. She hopped down off of the rock, turning, looking down the rows of trees. Reaching out again, she lost all sign of it.

The morning was getting on. The children would be waking up and she wanted to get back into some sort of routine with them. It was a more challenging route back up to the house, climbing the steep incline. Sweat ran down her back and a chill reached inside of her jacket. Dried twigs lined the path up the hill, and Penny stomped on them, enjoying the crisp break when she landed on them just right. Perhaps she would just stomp her way right back to her own home, she thought. With no word or sign, maybe that would be enough to break the deal. They could just camp out indoors for however long it would take for the media to get bored. How long could they stake her out? Surely she could become yesterday's news if she did all of her shopping on-line and didn't run around saving anyone.

It all started to sound right. Just fade away. Hal had said something like that at the hospital, hadn't he? She knew he didn't want any part of this situation. And if she didn't use this crazy thing, maybe it would just go out of her. If she didn't have to see them, she wouldn't be tempted to do any healing. Like a use-it-or-lose-it type of a thing. Or a glass of water set out in the sun to dry up. Yes. God hadn't heard her and was at present completely incommunicado, as they used to say on her favorite detective show as a child. If there had been a sign, she'd missed it, and signs so subtle were obviously used for unimportant events. Her mind rambled, justifying her decision to pack it in and head back. She felt she had given it that good old college try and had honestly come up empty, and without some sort of guidance she was positive she would mess everything up. What if she did more damage than good? Someone had to be thinking of the negative effects she could have.

Her thoughts went on and on and the whole situation was beginning to take on a new lightness. They could leave this morning. How had she let anyone talk her into coming all the way up to Aunt Myrtle's? She had a calendar full of responsibilities and felt like someone who went out only to remember that she had left the iron on. If she hurried back, she could savor her thoughts over a cup of coffee before the children got up.

In the midst of her joy at coming to a decision on ending the madness that everything had turned into, Penny had stopped paying attention to the path. She was embroiled in her mind and already living out her plans and, in doing so, barely noticed that she had finished climbing the hill. Her feet followed a map stored in her memory as if of their own volition, and she turned the last corner on autopilot. A faraway look played in her eyes, and although the house loomed large ahead of her in the dawn's first light, she didn't notice anything amiss until she was already up the front stairs.

The bareness of the porch acted like a camouflage

against the whiteness of the sheets wrapped around him. He had been in the shadows, waiting, and only the old boards gave him away as he rose off the wicker swing and came toward her. She jerked her head to see his large frame advance like some surprise ending to a book she hadn't read yet. He reached Penny before she could turn the cold doorknob and return to the safety of the house.

Chapter Twenty-one

Milo Davis watched the people pour into the Beaver Hill bus station and was reminded of an Animal Channel special he had watched about lemmings. There was an old gray sign in the lobby saying MORE THAN 83 PERSONS IS DANGEROUS AND UNLAWFUL, with the big 83 hammered on, slightly off center, and Milo seemed the only one concerned. Just when he thought they couldn't fit one more person into the waiting area, ten more showed up and Milo could only get to number forty or so before everyone shifted and he couldn't remember who'd been counted and who hadn't. Every time he lost count he wondered how they had come up with eighty-three exactly. He knew he was no great shakes in the math department, but why that particular number? Who decided eighty-three was still safe but eighty-four clearly made the situation unlawfully dangerous?

Milo was hired to manage the night shift of incoming Greyhounds and Martzes and the meager flow of patrons that trickled in and out in a fairly regular fashion. He made a circle on the record sheets next to the incomings and put a check inside of it as they departed. He loaded bags and swept up the terminal. Hell, he probably could have sold the tickets, too, and actually had done just that the weekend Betty, the woman at the counter, was out with her gallbladder attack. Betty was also in charge of the pay toilets that everyone just climbed into from underneath. Her cleansing ritual included sweeping up and spraying a particularly lethal-smelling antibacterial agent on every available surface. It leaked down from the stained sinks, across the Pepto-Bismol–pink tile and into a drain that led to God knows where. Milo thought if that drain ever backed up, they were all in a heap of trouble.

He stood back and watched the bustle. Milo had taken on this job because it was at night, during the wee hours, when anyone with any sense at all was still in bed. It made for a colorful clientele, but at least there weren't many of them. Most people sat in the orange plastic bucket seats and tried to get the pay TVs to work. They haunted the bathrooms for as long as they could stand the smell and crept around the corner to smoke a cigarette with their heads down, their eyes nervously sweeping the landscape for their bus out of there. It all suited Milo just fine.

Today, though, he stood like an island in a stream of distinctively different people than his usual pale night travelers and picked at his long fingernails with a *thwack, thwack*. He rubbed the yellow wattle that hung down from his chin and started his count for the fourth time. A rental bus suddenly filled the glass window, its American-flag logo streaming by in the stop's power lights. Milo ran to direct it into an adjacent lot, where it would be joined by nine of its sisters and a moving van for what he assumed was the extra luggage those buses couldn't hold.

Milo guessed he hadn't talked to so many people in the sum of all of his forty-six years as he had tonight, and it was only a few hours into his shift. If the numbers those people were throwing at him were right, all ten buses would be filled to capacity by sunup. He walked back, his neon vest hanging halfway across his narrow back and down off one shoulder. A woman approached him. She waited for his eyes to reach hers and she smiled widely as she asked, "Mt. Pleasant?" Milo just pointed with a straight arm to the lot, now holding four double-decker cruiser buses, others filing in quickly.

"Are you coming?" she asked him, as if Milo could pick up that moment and leave. Milo just looked and backed away from her, tripping over a nearby family.

"She's for everyone," the woman reported as she turned and walked away, swinging her suitcases as if they held nothing at all.

Milo could hear something tinkling inside of her bags and decided he really did not want to know what it was. He scanned the area for ones not associated with this group, the men checking their watches and looking over their shoulders. They each had a story, he knew, most likely very interesting and somewhat unique, but Milo never gave them a second thought. Police cars and even sirens in the distance were guaranteed to send some of his customers scurrying away like roaches from the light, but he didn't spend his shifts making up stories he imagined them living. It wasn't his concern, and those people were, he thought, less frightening than the group that had piled in the station tonight.

They stood in circles, laughing and hugging each other. Betty worked the phones and the counter with one finger in her ear and her eyes scrunched up as if that would help her to hear better over the crowd. There were a dozen or so people going from cluster to cluster, imparting information the others listened to as if their lives depended on it. Booklets were passed out and the pay TVs stood ignored as the orange chairs were filled with people poring over the slim pamphlets. Checks were exchanged and Milo lost his never-ending counts and recounts, distracted by watching the stiff rectangular pieces jump around from hand to hand. They all eventually ended up with one dark-haired woman who stood one step outside of each circle she passed. She spoke on a small cell phone and tucked the promised money inside a waist pouch. Milo thought she looked more like one of his regular customers than any of the others she was with.

At five A.M., just as Milo gave up all hope of everyone standing still long enough to be counted and decided it was time to clear the place out, eighty-three or not, the groups merged and began heading toward the distant pack of waiting buses. Drivers descended, opening up the luggage portals, manning them on the sides, waiting for them to be filled. Milo temporarily put aside the rule about being the only employee allowed to load the bags. He made a half-hearted attempt by walking out there, if only to organize things somewhat. When he came up to the rear of the dozens of queues, he stopped and watched. Each person on line knelt on the asphalt, and as Milo started to turn back toward the station, not wanting any part of some group prayer, he saw they were all just opening their luggage.

"What the—" Milo uttered under his breath as Betty joined him to get a closer look.

"What are they doing?" she asked him.

Milo had no answer and found himself even more speechless, if that was possible, when media trucks from three local television stations swung into their terminal. Boom microphones emerged from behind the buses like futuristic giraffes feeding in a metal jungle.

The travelers were unconcerned. They continued pulling things out of their trunks and knapsacks and carry-ons. It took Milo a few seconds longer than Betty to figure out they were holding sheets, flowing and white. The group members wrapped one another up, pinning and repinning, helping one another cover every inch of themselves until all that could be seen of any of them were their eyes.

It struck Milo that, even at a dozen paces and with only lids and lashes and irises to go by, he could tell they were smiling. He wondered if it seemed that way just because that was what they were doing inside the station. He smiled, experimentally trying to feel the effect around his eyes just as a camera flashed a picture of him. Milo thought of his wife and four unsupported children half a continent away who would be extremely happy to get their hands on that picture. The reporter was swallowed up inside the white churning mass before he could open his mouth in protest.

Many of the larger suitcases lay stacked in groups of ten along the concrete median dividing the rented buses. Drivers shrugged when Milo shouted to ask if those were to be loaded. Milo stopped a person on the periphery. She turned to him and he could see there was no place to look but into her eyes, the total whiteness of her outfit reflecting everything so that his own eyes spilled up into hers. It was stark, and Milo felt trapped there.

"I—" he started. "You can't just—" Milo took a breath. "What about the luggage?" he finally spit out.

A fold of cloth crinkled above where her nose would be, and Milo inferred another infuriating smile. "We don't need those any more. We're traveling light, not weighing down our souls."

Milo tried to crinkle his own nose, but with a frown. "What am I supposed to do with all of them?"

The side of her sheet came up over her straight arm, and Milo looked to see a sign hanging four cases up on a hunter-green Pierre Cardin bag trimmed in calf leather with an embossed handle. He didn't see many of those. It said, simply, in upper-case block letters, FREE. When Milo turned back she was gone, indistinguishable from her companions in any way.

A final regrouping was made—by what means, Milo

could not tell—and ten lines were formed. Before the buses were boarded, each line wrapped around, grasped hands and held their arms and faces up to the sky, chanting something as a group that Milo couldn't quite make out.

"What will they reveal?" Milo asked Betty.

"Not reveal. Kneel. They said, 'We will kneel.'"

"Actually," claimed a passing reporter, "I think they said, 'We will heal.'"

No further clarification was made as they climbed up the big steps and into the cavernous seats, giving Milo back his station. The buses roared off like giant hurried caterpillars. A bright sun was just rising and they drove right into it, the metal of their casings seeming to liquefy into the road as they disappeared over the first hill.

On each bus a group leader took a last roll call, then sat with individual members to hand out maps that described where they would be located and what their particular job responsibilities were. The top of each map said JANET FINCH, REALTOR, with a glowing computer-generated likeness of her hovering in the corner. Janet Finch, realtor, had been up since just after one A.M. Emma, her secretary (actually her neighbor, who sometimes made copies for her), had been up since one-thirty. Four hundred initial real estate offers were drawn up, substituting only addresses and amounts on form sheets. Contracts were already written, waiting for signatures. Janet woke up Brad at the town office-supply store and bought up every fax machine he could get his hands on.

Prices ranged greatly in keeping with the mountain that Mt. Pleasant is. The highest plateau, on which Myrtle Halloway's house—the only house not for sale—sat, was the pinnacle location with the surrounding houses in view of it calling for the highest prices. Each was getting four times its worth, and even the smallest shack at the bottom of the hill, the opposite side included, was selling at over twice its market value. After fifteen years of sporadically renting moldy cottages and selling nothing worth more than a few meager thousands' worth in commission, Janet thought she'd died and gone to real estate heaven. She just prayed this Peggy or Piggy or Healer-whatzit stayed put. At exactly one forty A.M. she'd made it crystal clear to Emma that if no one called Myrtle in Florida, giving her any kind of heads up, she'd give Emma a ten-thousand-dollar bonus. As they made each of the middle-of-the-night calls, they read from a script on how the buyer was sick and her last request was to die in the foresty mountains and how her quaint (dumpy) cottage had caught their eye and blah, blah, blah. The most important thing was to make it sound as if it were just their house alone. Janet hoped it all went over. She'd be happy never to see another lease or For Sale sign for the rest of her natural life. At six P.M. she was hoping to be sleeping on a plane to Maui. It was a one-way ticket. If this Healer person saw everyone move in and then left, well, that was just not her problem.

Janet met all ten buses at the bottom of the mountain, where she had constructed a roadblock, a sort of last-minute insurance policy. She'd have everything signed and then let them loose to scrape, bow, genuflect or whatever else they felt they needed to do. Janet was more of a practical person than all that. She had a breakfast bagged and waiting for the busloads to ensure that no one would revolt and get up the hill before their business was settled. Her good friend Lenny, a pickled real estate lawyer, represented all of the buyers, and his partner, John, some new kid with a mail-order degree, represented the sellers. It went like clockwork. Garbage, remnants of breakfast, were discarded as contracts were handed in. Faxes were sent and deals were closed. Cash is a beautiful thing where expediency is concerned, thought Janet. Let the banks ask everyone else for eleven more documents. They'd just go and buy the houses the way you buy a Coke at the corner deli.

When Janet finally gave the go-ahead for the roadblocks to be dismantled, the groups disembarked, waving away the buses, which left in every direction, a motorized army disbanded. She asked one of the leaders if they didn't want to be driven up as she went around troubleshooting, making sure everyone had gotten the right keys and made it into the homes all right.

"Oh, no," the leader said to Janet. "You can't do that."

"It's not a problem. It's the least I can—"

"No," he said more firmly. "You don't understand. No vehicles are permitted up the road except for the holy family's."

Somewhere deep inside of Janet, in the place in our brain where we all stay little, where there are always monsters under the bed and bogeymen in the closet, something stirred. She couldn't put her finger on it and it showed itself in a crawly feeling around her skin. A question passed through her mind as to whether she had been a party to something dangerous, and she quickly tried to shrug it off. She raised a hand in a farewell to her departing customers, shook hands with Emma, Lenny, and John and wished herself Godspeed to the airport.

She got into her car and watched through her rearview mirror as two persons in sheets set up guard at the edge of the upward road. Janet shivered and, without noticing, crossed herself reflexively.

Chapter Twenty-two

The blur of the mountainside ripping past that night was all wrong. It was dark and the trees huddled together in small angry groups, and Jetta was pitched toward the windshield with the forward angle of the car going back down. She found it ironic that she should have any fear at this point, considering that they were driving the path instead of being flung over the side, the original plan for their descent.

"We're lucky we're getting to leave here in one piece," Louis pointed out. "We'll never find Penny's cottage in the dark. It's tar black up here," he added to the list of reasons they should get home and try again tomorrow.

Even in the dim glow of the car's light, he could see the lines on Jetta's face, worried and pleading with him. Louis's mind was on his editor: He had gone far enough without him, and with every hour was losing a grip on what was out there in the news, what had already been covered. How long had he been unconscious? He needed to get to a phone and a fax.

Jetta was saying, "I don't think you understand what kind of danger she's in."

"I'll come back first thing in the morning, before breakfast, and give her a heads up," Louis said. "I'm sure she'll be fine until then." He was wondering if that was where his focus should be when he interviewed Penny.

That would probably draw a higher price per word, and he thought he could get more out of her by telling her about his own healed asthma. He wanted to lock it in with the paper and get a special deal. Maybe he'd walk the finished copy in past the guys that looked down their noses at him and called him Leonard and Larry at the staff meetings. There was nothing holding him back now and he knew he could get more coveted stories. If he could get this covered, it would cement his standings, he just knew it would.

"Louis!" Jetta was shouting at him. "You're not listening to me," and Louis also knew he couldn't bring this little old lady with him, scaring Penny Chaney so that she wouldn't feel relaxed enough to sit through his questions. The focus would be on how much danger she was in and how she had to leave right away, and he could see his story going off with her in her suitcase.

"Give me directions to your home. I'll bring you to Southlawn and turn around and come back to warn her," he said. "Maybe she shouldn't be bombarded with too many people at once."

He could see Jetta look at him in his peripheral vision, her whole body turned to face him head-on. "Stop the car. I'll get out here and walk the mountain until I find her."

"What are you talking about? You'll fall off the mountain in this dark, or at best you'll run into our friend the librarian."

"It's hard to believe you're not falling all over yourself to warn that poor woman! She has no idea what she's in for. You just got a headful of it yourself and you don't see the urgency."

"What I see are two people with dried blood caked all over their clothes. Have you looked at yourself lately?" He turned the rearview mirror to her.

"Maybe it will convince her that what I'm saying is true."

"Or scare her away so she'll be afraid to talk to you."

"It would be for her own good."

"Look, there's no one here for miles. Let her get some rest, for God's sake. I'll come back at dawn and not a minute later," Louis promised.

She looked almost ready to take him up on his offer, ready to be driven home and relieved of the burden of being a messenger with bad tidings. She felt like someone falling in a dream, her body forgetting to jar her awake. Louis stopped the car at the bottom of the road and turned to look at her, and when she saw his eyes she said, "Drop me off at the nearest hotel."

They stayed at the Crestview Cottages, five shacks in a row that each smelled like a big wet dog had just run through. Louis had cottage number one and Jetta had number five. After receiving their keys, they went their separate ways without so much as a good-bye.

Louis made his phone deals sitting with one cheek on the corner of a bed made up with a spread of Dutch girls among faded tulips and wooden shoes. His editor, Jack, promised him the world, the most precious perk that it would all be his exclusively. "If you know where she is, she's all yours, kid," Jack said.

Louis was sure after this story he would not be called *kid* ever again.

"Remember, if someone else finds her first, all bets are off. And I have to tell you I have three other guys on this, Lou." Jack laughed through the earpiece. "It's dog-eat-dog, Lou. You know that. You get it and it's all yours. But if someone else gets there first, all you get is a big goose egg. Welcome to action reporting, kid," he said as he hung up.

Louis thought Jack needed a cliché-ectomy. But he was

right: There was no time to sleep or to go back to Southlawn to get his car or drop off his unwanted sidekick. He would shower, get an earful of CNN and whatever local news he could, then skip out. Granny Jetta would just have to call one of her kids; he couldn't risk her distracting his subject. He flipped on the motel television set, old enough to still have wire rabbit's ears for reception and a knob to change the channels. Even at four A.M., still the heart of the night, the story was hopping all around the dial. And when Louis switched on the cable box, for which he'd had to pay almost half of what the room itself went for, the box strained to leap ahead a quarter of a century with its inadequate machinery. Louis waited for a glass tube to blow. One of the major networks' sister cable stations bleated out its all news format, four A.M. be damned.

Louis left the TV blaring and the door to the bathroom open. He stripped and stepped into the shower, which was decorated in another lifetime in avocado green that was somewhere just this side of puke. The dark color was helpful in letting him imagine the stall to be clean and that underneath the mustardlike tile trim there wasn't a few decades of filth. Mostly he was worried about it because of the gash in his head. It protested under the water, grinding the gravel from Isaac's former home further into his skull and inviting a whole new session of bleeding. Red ribbons fell at Louis's feet, and he held himself up by the Hot and Cold knobs. Bits and pieces of news from around the world filtered in to him through the steam. It was all Mother Healer this and Mother Healer that. There were exclusive interviews with the staff at Southlawn Hospital, the state troopers under Captain Elian and patients from the mass healing, which had been universally labeled the first modern miracle.

There were enough religious theologians for commentary to last through the thirty-two pebbles Louis picked from his wound and the time it took to hold back the flap of his scalp and wash it clean. He tried to scream during introductions and commercial breaks. Hydrogen peroxide found its way onto his list of things to do, though somewhere at the bottom.

Louis only needed until he was dry and dressed to have a good sense of where the press was with its coverage and where the public was with its appetite for the story. No one had the Mother Healer's own voice, but every station had its own experts interpreting the fragments of what anyone claiming to have been a witness said she preached. Everyone was very clear that she was a religious figure, though every major religion seemed, to Louis, majorly pissed off. She didn't fall under anyone's umbrella, and those who couldn't lay claim to her—which was pretty much everybody but the oddest fringe fanatics—tried to disparage her. The stations all had someone with an air of authority opening up a book (or scroll) big enough to choke a mule, pointing at it and using the word *not* repeatedly in conjunction with various text references. Muslims from around the world not only said she was not one of them, they issued a statement saying that she had laid on them the highest magnitude of insult with her covering up as if she were one of them. Anyone interviewed from the Nation of Islam started and ended each sentence with the words, "She is not one of us." The Catholics were also hopping mad but only because she wasn't a man, and Head Rabbi Someone or other was saying something about hell freezing over as Louis started flipping through the channels, looking for something different, an angle the others hadn't caught.

He pressed the remote quickly, sitcoms and infomercials flying by in droves. Mary Tyler Moore smiled. He paused at a spaghetti Western, then sped ahead, summarizing shows in seconds and moving on.

Under the pressure he felt to hurry, Louis almost passed by the little news station based an hour south of Mt. Pleasant. A training ground for interns and fledgling reporter wanna-bes, it featured an abundance of stuttering and mispronunciation, knocking knees and old, washed-up newscasters. Louis had the channel blocked from his own remote at home so that it was skipped right over on the way up and down, along with the Spanish station and cooking network.

Under the fuzzy black-and-white snow across the screen, there was a glimpse of a person covered in white. Louis's thumb kept pressing but his mind threw up a flag. Was that her? He did a U-turn and headed back down the dial. Ricky was telling Lucy he was home. Did someone get a glimpse of the Mother Healer? Was she heading this way only now? Was it a live telecast or a tape rerunning and rehashing it? If it was her, everyone else would know where she was, and that couldn't be it because the networks would be screaming her location. Monster trucks rolled over a row of Volkswagen Beetles, a dog show blared thunderous applause for a yellow poodle named Sunshine. Where the hell was it? Shit! Shit, he screamed inside his head.

There! A bus depot! There were piles of luggage, and Louis tried to put it all together and it was like a bizarre three-dimensional puzzle that refused to yield into any understandable shape. Everyone was dressed up in sheets and getting onto buses. Was she with them? The reporter was talking about the Mother Healer's following and their new community on Mt. Pleasant. He was reading a pamphlet over the air and summarizing their religious outlook. He interviewed a woman named Daisy and then the buses pulled away. Louis waited for the reporter to name himself and give his site. Maybe Louis was wrong about the location. Maybe they were farther away than an hour. And would he say, "Live from . . ."? That was most important. If it was happening this very instant, he could beat them up the mountain. He stole a glance at the clock bolted to the table. Six-thirty, and a faint light was showing through the window. How had he wasted so much time? There it was, the end of the spot.

"This is Jim Ryan, reporting from Beaver Hill."

They flashed back to the newsroom, where someone named Cindy was dressed in pink and saying, "That was the overnight report feed as it happened at three o'clock this morning. We'll be going on scene shortly to give you the live update on the Mother Healer's group." They went on to sports, high school basketball and a new seniors tournament.

Louis ran his hands through his hair and winced at the pull of the new scabs forming there. His belongings were scattered and he used both of his arms to grab in all directions, gathering his few things and throwing them together. No bigger than a closet, the cottage worked against him and he fell over the corner of the cot they called a bed. Louis saw stars but ran through them on his way out the door, pausing only to get the car keys.

Jetta's cottage was dark against the lightening sky and he allowed himself the smallest sigh of relief. At least he would only have himself to worry about. All of his equipment was in his own car back at the Rourkes', and he floundered about in his mind both with the problem of not getting to Penny before everyone else and what to write or tape her with when he did. He wondered if they had passed any twenty-four-hour mini-marts on the way. He kicked himself for the first of hundreds of times for coming down the mountain. He should have listened to the old lady. Would he even have time to stop? Maybe he could just remember and paraphrase her. The car was unlocked and he threw himself in, pulling open the glove compartment even as he closed the door behind him. It was full to the brim, surely there had to be a pen and something to write on. There was no time left to stop and he thought he'd gotten his second break of the morning when his hand bumped into an old envelope that could be ripped and opened up for writing. There were two pencil stubs that would just have to do, and he was infinitely grateful for them. Louis straightened up, feeling as though maybe his luck was changing.

The key went into the chamber. "I thought you might try to leave without me," a voice from the backseat said.

Louis jumped so high his head hit the roof of the car, and this time there were no stars but a grayness that threatened to send his face into the steering wheel.

"Damn it!" He looked back at her, ready to scream and kick her out of the car.

"I'm coming with you," she said, as if they had known each other their whole lives and he was going out for a gallon of milk.

"The hell you are."

"You don't look very good, Louis." He tried not to give in to the urge to look but he found he couldn't. In the side mirror he saw bloodshot eyes and hair that stuck up in every direction. Jetta's clothes were still spotted with dark patches of dried blood but she looked bathed and as rested as if she'd slept for nothing less than eight hours.

"I was just warming it up anyway," he said, not looking back at her. "I was going to tell you I was going to warn her."

After her fourth child Jetta found she could spot a lie before the very breath was projected and syllables formed across the fabricator's lips. She told each of them that when you lie, a dark spot appears on your forehead that only a mother or father can see. The guilty party would always be caught climbing up to sneak a peek in the bathroom mirror, but it was just an affirmation. She always knew before that.

"We'd better hurry," she said, hands folded across her lap, eyes straight ahead.

The car flew out of the motel's dirt parking lot. Louis knew every second counted and he couldn't waste any time arguing with this woman. They would get there together, that's all. Surely he could outrun an eighty-year-old, and he sniggered to himself at the thought, wondering in his exhaustion if he had done it out loud or only in his own mind. He hoped Penny would offer him breakfast when he got there. He tried to calculate how many hours it had been since he had eaten or slept. His head felt cloudy and he couldn't seem to count it out.

They approached the road up to Mt. Pleasant so quickly and without incident, Louis thought he had beaten the buses. Their car was alone on the two-lane highway, and at first glance, as they approached the road that led up the mountainside, everything looked deserted. There was no camera crew or lines of sick people. Media tents had not been staked outside the area. Louis turned the first corner up the mountain in fifth gear, smiling at his own craftiness and speed. He had landed on Park Place and was just about to stack it full of hotels.

The dream died the moment they hit the roadblock, sawhorses two layers deep manned by ten followers in white sheets. Louis leaned on the horn, rolling his window down and cursing. "Media," he screamed, his head poking out of the window briefly and his car moving forward as if he would just mow down the blockade if it weren't moved that instant. The ten stood behind it, not budging. Two spoke into cell phones.

Louis flew out of the car and into a rage, his hands flying around his body.

"I have an appointment up the hill. Now move!"

One of the followers stepped around the edge of the last sawhorse and came up to Louis. "I'm sorry, no one but the holy family is permitted up the hill."

Confusion burst a hole in Louis's anger. "The holy family?"

"The holy family," the follower said, his voice muffled through the linen wrapped over his nose and behind his head.

Louis couldn't believe this was happening. The mice had stolen the cheese out from under him as he lay sleeping right outside their hole. It was unfair and he stood, completely flummoxed at how close he had come, only to have it slip through his fingers. Someone else would get this interview! Someone else would receive the fame that was rightfully his! If only he had listened to the old woman! Damn her for being right! He spun around, looking for her as a place to lay guilt. This was somehow her fault. If only she had been stronger, had insisted more, he would already have his piece going to print. Her curly gray hair could not be seen in the backseat. She was gone and he tried to remember if he had seen her get out of the car behind him.

"Sir," someone was saying, "you're going to have to leave this area."

Louis could have flowed into his natural investigative mode right then and interviewed them. He could have asked about people coming to be healed and where they would be sent. Hell, he could have made up a story about how he himself, while being a reporter, was already a seeker in need of the Mother Healer's help. He could have left, gotten some white sheets and taken his chances at a hike up the backside of the hill. Any of those options would have yielded him a story nobody else, as of yet, had gotten. But, finally, having the whole loaf in his hands made eating the crumbs an unsatisfying meal. He was panting and he just couldn't seem to think straight. Where was that Jetta? Had he imagined her? Where was his regular car? The people in white were taking on a funny look, as though he was seeing them through a circus mirror. Some were big on the bottom and long at the top, and why were they talking so out of tune?

"Are you all right, sir?" The voice stretched and bent.

He saw the people in white turn back and forth to one another, whispering and asking questions. It all came together to make sense when they faded into the background and Louis could listen to only himself trying to piece it all together. He had been hit in the head. Someone had tried to kill him. Was that yesterday? He hadn't really slept in too long a time. His award-winning story had probably been snatched from under him. He was driving in what a police officer would consider a stolen car. And the most surprising of the crystal-clear realizations that came to him in those seconds was that in less than a week he had forgotten all of the warning signs. What was formerly almost the entire focus of his life were now only the remnants of some bad dream, easily brushed aside in the daylight. He dropped in steps, first to his knees, then forward onto his elbows and finally, reluctantly, onto his side. He was wheezing terribly; he couldn't breathe. People in white scurried about him.

Chapter Twenty-three

Penny gripped the door handle and jerked it back and forth. She hadn't locked it, yet it clicked obstinately at her. This man, this large man—he had to be a man, his frame was too big and broad-shouldered to be a woman's—he came toward her. A barrage of thoughts came over her with each of his footsteps. First and foremost, how had he surprised her? Even now, consciously reaching out, she couldn't find him. No signs came from him the way they poured off others. Every tiny creature throughout the woods seemed to have a place in her senses. She could feel the owls settling down after their hunt, and the fading pulses of life of the mice that became their early breakfast. It was overwhelming the way walking along a busy city block bombards a person with neon signs, billowing flags, the smells of hot dogs, pizza and fried onions from open windows, babies crying, horns honking. Hers now also involved the emotional pains, joys and life situations of creatures for miles around. In the same ways as the other five senses, it was all too much and yet manageable. In less than a day Penny's brain was beginning to learn to sift through it and pick out the relevant data the way a person offhandedly listens for oncoming traffic and walks across the street without as much as a glance, confident of his or her safety. Just now she felt Hal stirring from sleep and the captain and his wife making joyous love they thought no one else could hear. And they couldn't. She heard it with that other ear, the one that should have let her know this man was waiting for her here.

He was dressed, as she had been, in sheets wrapped haphazardly around him. Was he the sign she'd been asking for? Was that why she couldn't feel him? It was terrifying, the lack of any signals from him. Last week it would have made no difference to her. But now that she had those extra "hands" to feel with, she felt physically paralyzed in her inability to use them on him. So what if she won her argument down by the lake and her gift was taken? This was how everyone would feel again, but now, instead of that being normal, it would be flat and two-dimensional. And no one would understand. It would be like crying on a deaf person's shoulder that you yourself couldn't hear anymore. Never having had this ability, perhaps they wouldn't understand her grief at its loss.

He came close enough that he had to look down to see her, and she was still pulling on the door and trying to get a handle on what he was.

"I didn't mean to frighten you," he said. His voice had an Indian accent, a smooth, British-Hindi English.

"Hal!" she yelled, and felt him roll over, only one more level away from a deep, tired sleep. Captain Elian heard only his own explosion inside his wife.

"I've come to help you. I thought you might need help." His voice was low and quiet, lilting in the cadence of another culture.

When the captain mentioned security, Penny thought he was being ridiculous, almost comically absurd. Yet, here she was, confronting the fact of how easy it was to find her, and in that moment the world shrunk. Clearly there would be no hiding. And if anyone could trot up the stairs and sit on the porch at any hour of the day, she did indeed need security.

She looked at the stranger, who had backed up, giving her space and waiting for her to say something.

"Why are you wearing those sheets?" she asked.

"Why were you?" he asked right back, and Penny couldn't help but laugh despite herself.

"I was trying to hide my features so I could go out and have a pizza without being bombarded."

"You mean, by people like me?"

"Yes, exactly," and she tried the door again, this time knocking.

"I thought it had some religious significance, and I didn't want to offend you. Also, now across the country it symbolizes what you do. People are saying it is about not paying attention to our outsides but on the humanity of the heart."

Penny heard, in her way, Harvey put his feet onto the cold wood floor and head to the bathroom to relieve a night's full bladder. She knocked louder, hoping he would hear.

"Is there anything I can do for you . . . ? I'm sorry, I didn't get your name."

"Ishaw."

"Well, Ishaw, I really need to get inside to feed my children, who'll be waking up any minute. I'm sorry I can't really talk now. I'm sort of taking a day off."

"I didn't come to ask for anything. I came with a plan for you," he said over Penny's knocks, which had turned into furious hand slaps against the adjacent window and stopped abruptly at the end of his sentence.

"A plan?" She had asked for some kind of a plan at the lake. She couldn't read him, the only person she couldn't read so far, and now he was offering the very thing she'd said she needed. His voice was soothing somehow. It was what she imagined Buddhist monks sounded like in their infinite Zen-like wisdom. She stopped knocking for a moment.

"What kind of plan?"

"A plan on how best to serve the people you're going to heal and your family at the same time."

That was too good to be true. "How would you know how to do that?"

"I had a dream. Someone came to me in a dream." He seemed to fumble, tossing his head to the side as if he were trying to remember it all. "They told me to come and help you and give you a message."

Now Penny wished desperately that she could feel him and read his emotions and intentions. He looked her straight in the eye, and, unlike Jetta, her children were still small and her experience in the art of deception not as extensive. She found herself handicapped in relying on the regular ways of feeling someone out. Her intuition no longer felt reliable. She peered through the glass, knocking, hoping to catch Harvey on his way back to bed.

"In the dream I was told you are a great spirit."

Penny stopped and turned around. "Now I know you are a fake. I have this gift, but I'm just an ordinary person."

"I guess I was sent to tell you you're wrong." He stood watching her.

Penny blinked.

"You are going to shape people."

"You seem to think you know a lot about what I'm going to do."

"I told you: I had a dream that led me to you."

"Well, you may be too late. I'm thinking of going home and putting this entire situation behind me."

The man who called himself Ishaw backed up and sat again on the porch swing.

"How can you think that in good conscience?"

"How is my husband supposed to work in the middle of all of this? Who will take care of my children?"

"With the right plan you can provide for your family and have plenty of time for your children. It just has to be run by the right person. Which is, I suppose, why I had the dream. I am purely a businessman and I can help you with all of the details."

"You're suggesting I use this healing like a business? That doesn't sound right at all."

"But throwing it away sounds right?"

Penny came and sat in the wicker chair to his right. She threw her head back and closed her eyes.

"Look," he said. "Outside of the hospital, people just came and created a dangerous situation. Wherever you go, they will gather and crush each other to get to you. You have to control that. You have to find the right spot to give people this gift, a spot where people will be safe. Where people with debilitating illnesses don't have to stand outside for hours or risk getting run over by others. I believe I can help you do that if you let me."

Penny tilted her head, listening to Hal come awake.

"Watching the news, I know people want more from me than just healing. They want me to be some sort of messiah that I just am not."

"You are what you do."

His remark jarred her. "Setting up a formal business in a permanent location somehow confirms their claims that I am a religion. I don't want to be a church or a religious figure."

"Do you really think you can run away from this?"

Penny looked out at the trees.

"No," he said. "I mean that question. Do you think you can go anywhere and hide?"

There was silence on the porch as Hal's feet swung over the side of the bed.

"I suppose you can go to Canada and find a major city and get lost in it. But how long until a sick child crosses your path who you just can't pass up healing? It would be a homing beacon. How long before this mountain is packed shoulder to shoulder with needy people and you can't walk down it? How long are you willing to run? How good would that be for your children?"

Penny studied the early buds that were beginning to emerge from the bushes beyond the porch stairs.

"It would be an around-the-clock business no matter how you set it up or what you call it. I think I may have some alternatives for you."

Of course, what he said made sense to her. It was all logical.

"I think I can help you get some control over this situation. Will you let me?"

Control was exactly what Penny wanted. It had been gone since that morning she woke up feeling woozy. She'd been fighting the tide, trying to swim upstream. She could let go and let it carry her along, but she wondered if that would be freeing or just suicidal. This whole experience was a bigger wave than she could imagine anyone riding on without wiping out. If she could somehow go along with it but control it, maybe they'd all be fine.

"What do you have in mind?" asked Hal from the doorway, and Penny was surprised for the second time of the morning. James was behind him, tousled but smiling. She hadn't felt either of them, she'd been so wrapped up in this Ishaw's ideas. When her attention was turned to them they came in to her again, clear and vibrant. It was so loud, it made the time with Ishaw seem twice as quiet.

Penny sprang to her feet, and Ishaw sprang to his own in response. "Ishaw," he said extending a hand from under his crisp sheets. "I was—"

"Yes," Hal interrupted. "I heard. I suppose we'll need some suggestions if we're discovered here. How did you know where to find us?"

"I had a dream—" he began, but was interrupted by Penny.

"There's already a group at the foot of the mountain. There are hundreds of them." She sat back down.

"How can that be?" Hal asked Penny, as if she were personally responsible for their arrival through formal invitations. "How did they find us?"

"How do I know, Hal?" Penny snapped. Just when there seemed to be some sort of plan forming, things threatened to get hectic again. "They all just arrived together."

The captain and Ishaw stayed quiet, watching the couple and not getting involved. The man who called himself Ishaw knew when silence was strategically stronger than any possible input.

Hal just looked at his wife. He'd been awake for less than ten minutes, with the sun just over the horizon, and they were already cornered.

"It's not like I alerted the media, Hal. Honestly, I don't know how they did it. I know this is a frustrating situation."

"Are you sure they're here for you? Maybe you're getting your wires crossed with some kind of parade or something."

"Hal, they're looking for me. I just know. I guess you'll believe me when you see them."

Hal shook his head. "Let's get to the plan before we're overrun and don't have time to talk."

Ishaw stepped up to the plate. "I think my dream showed me some kind of stadium where people would buy a ticket for a seat and get healed en masse as it happened outside of the hospital."

"Buy a ticket?" Penny made a face. "I don't know if that's ethical."

"At the cost of a doctor's visit they would have their lives back, or the lives of their children."

Hal and Penny looked at each other as Ishaw went on. "You would need some money to hire security. Based on what you said, you need that already."

James broke in. "I could be in charge of that. I have plenty of buddies on the job who could use an extra buck or two."

"And," said Ishaw, "you'll need someone to sell the tickets. Someone who could weed out who is most needy, who needs you the soonest."

Penny felt Hal being drawn to this Ishaw and calm down upon hearing his plan. "I'm sure that wouldn't be hard to arrange," he offered.

"Also," Ishaw paused, "I don't think, Mr. Hal, you'll be able to return to your place of work anytime soon."

"Just Hal is fine. And no, I'm sure I won't be able to."

"Sensibly speaking, you'll need to feed your children, of course."

"It just doesn't feel moral," Penny said.

"Before this opportunity came to me, I was an accountant of sorts," Ishaw said, and they could see his smile pull the sheet taut across his face. "Money and numbers have been my whole life. I think I can arrange things so that you'll make only enough to pay your overhead and maintain your family."

"I suppose we could be comfortable with that," said Hal, before Penny had a chance to protest. "If you would manage that, we would be very grateful."

Hal put his hand out to close the deal and suggest that they all go inside for some breakfast. He heard Benjamin crying and the twins tramping down the old oak stairs and knew everyone would be hungry. Before his hand reached the newest member of their team, there was a scream down the narrow dirt road. They all turned to see a very old woman running their way. She was a vision of pure juxtaposition, an eighty-year-old (and possibly then some) not just walking quickly or trotting but in the all-out run of a twelve-year-old chasing a blue ribbon at a track meet. She positively glowed in the sweat of it, looking healthy and refreshed even though her clothes were stained with what looked like enough blood to fill two small old ladies with some to spare. She was crumpled and her hair stood out wildly. Behind her trailed two figures clothed like Ishaw in folds of white sheets across every part of them but their eyes. They chased her, closing the distance between them as the road leveled in front of Aunt Myrtle's cabin. Penny wasn't sure whom to root for.

Everyone leaned out and over the railing as the old lady got closer and the sheeted ones tried to reach her. Penny wondered if the people in sheets were with Ishaw and he hadn't gotten around to telling her they were his group. How many more were out there? But that of course she knew. There were hundreds. She had felt them before. They were coming up the mountain.

The old woman was moving as though her pants were on fire, and the two behind her reminded her of ducks for some odd reason. No, thought Penny, not ducks: two of the Stooges trying to put the third one's burning pants out. She could picture them throwing her into a water barrel. It struck her as so ridiculous, she had to stifle a laugh. Of course, it wasn't funny at all. But if people were going to pop out of bushes, chasing each other at all hours of the day, she couldn't be expected to keep a straight face. Maybe it was that Ishaw had offered them some sort of sane plan and she felt hopeful that things would take on a shape and a routine. If healing large crowds of people could ever become routine. At least she had a tickle of the feeling that they could stop running. So a smile did find its way to her lips for a moment, a short moment that got in the way of her assessing the next second—which was fast, shooting by before she could hold on to it and turn it around in her mind.

The old lady came straight toward the front porch. Penny thought she recognized the woman but couldn't pinpoint where she knew her from. It came and went as quickly as the old lady's racing feet, and Penny tried to scour her mind for a name to pair her face with. Even as she ran, the old woman's eyes searched until they found Penny's. She looked relieved when she identified her, as if she could see that the fire was almost out, and she sped up, gaining an extra step ahead of the two in pursuit. But then she did a double take, looking back at the person next to Penny, and their eyes locked and the old woman slowed down a hair, her face filled with a confusion mixed with a terrible brand of horror. Penny turned to see Ishaw and the woman staring at each other, Ishaw's eyes wide and round. Both turned to Penny and began yelling at the same time.

"This woman was in my dream. She wants to kill you!" Ishaw grabbed Penny and pulled her toward the house. Hal joined in with the captain shielding Penny from behind. Penny found herself resisting. She craned her neck around to get another glimpse of the woman. She knew that she knew her. But from where? The woman was yelling, "Don't trust him!" Penny could tell by the sound of the last word that the two white sheets had grabbed her. "That's Isaac Rourke! Penny, please listen to me!"

Ishaw kept pulling at her, but Hal and the captain were stunned. They stopped for a moment at the old woman's knowledge of her name. "Penny! Help!" she screamed from a farther distance as she was also dragged away from down the path. Penny thought she heard her say, "He's going to rob and kill you!" But she was too far away to be sure.

"She knows you from the news," Ishaw said. "Get inside before she breaks free. Hurry!" That broke the spell for the other two men, who escorted her into the house and out of earshot of the old woman.

Chapter Twenty-four

Louis had to die to get up the mountain to see Penny. Not that he wouldn't have volunteered for it if he thought it would get him his interview. He would have, in a heartbeat. The very pride of a reporter is often not in the awards on his mantelpiece but in the time around the water cooler boasting of the lengths he or she would go to nab a story. A scar was worth double points. Louis heard fellow writer Kevin White tell (repeatedly) about the time he sneaked into the mayor's private dinner party by scaling a ten-story building, going from fire escape to fire escape with a projection microphone. He got the mayor on tape telling the city's newest developer he would have no interference from the building inspectors. In this same five minutes the mayor thanked the developers for their outstanding campaign contributions. It was a hot story all right, even after one of the mayor's personal guards caught Kevin on the fire escape and shot him in the leg. The guard would later report he thought his microphone was an Uzi, but not until after he tried ripping the evidence out of White's hands. Shot clean through his lower leg, he still managed to climb back down, his equipment and story intact. That was more than anyone could say for the mayor's job. Everyone at the newspaper had seen Kevin White's bullet wound. Twice. It was a pretty tough story to beat. Any one of them would have offered to shoot themselves—or each other, for that matter—if it got them a story this hot.

Like Jetta, at the moment of death Louis was able to review his life passing from one event to the next in bubbles. His own existence hadn't been all that long, and each memory involved some sort of pain, both his own and that which he had inflicted upon others. He watched the people in white carry him up the mountain. They threw his body into the back of a truck and conferred for a while as to what should be done with him. Louis knew as clearly as Jetta had that he was dead. After a review of all of his decisions throughout his life and a look at how he handled his obstacles, he was plunged into darkness. He couldn't see his body and he was wet somehow, as if he'd fallen into a river on a cold winter's day. A feeling overcame him that he was being watched. Small animals scurried around in the darkness, and he heard something with an uneven walk coming toward him and somehow he knew it was dragging half of its body. Louis imagined it bloody and mangled. Occasionally it screamed. He waited for it to reach out and grab him. He fully expected to be eaten, and as the cold reached an unbearable level, he wished for it.

Penny felt Louis's life wink out at the bottom of the mountain but had been occupied with Ishaw. Louis was in her periphery, weeded out in the midst of the flurry of events that had just overtaken them. By the time the excitement had died down and everyone was situated around the breakfast table, all ten of them now with the addition of Ishaw, Louis was gone.

Hal and James reached for the biscuits Mary had baked, taking huge bites, which sat like lumps in their mouths as Ishaw went ahead and said grace. "Thank you, God, for this food. Help it nourish us as we set forth to do good for your people." He looked around. "Would anyone like to add anything?"

Hal and James shook their heads and closed their lips to keep the biscuits in.

"Amen," Ishaw said.

The twins stared at him. Benjamin, finishing a bottle, burped.

"Why are we fourth, Mommy?" Julie asked.

"No, we're not fourth, like in line; we're setting forth. We're going to do something."

"I want to be first!" Lydia said, and her sister nodded in complete agreement.

"We're going to go where Mommy can make people better if they're sick."

"Are you a doctor now, Mommy?" Julie asked seriously, as if Penny could just wake up one day and be in practice.

"Not exactly." Penny turned to Hal for some help with the explanation but instead found herself staring at Ishaw, who had freed his head of the wrappings she found him in. His jaw was square and firm, his eyelashes thick all around, framing dark eyes. His skin was a deep tan. He sported a thick mustache peppered with a hint of gray. He caught her looking and lowered his eyes quickly, as if ashamed at attracting her attention. Penny blushed.

"I think the wrappings are a good idea," Ishaw said. Penny's blush rose to crimson.

Mary looked out over the table and heartily agreed, also staring at Ishaw now and nodding. Ishaw threw Mary a warm smile, and it was her turn to blush.

"For who?" Hal wanted to know.

"For all of us when we're traveling. I have no desire to be famous. It would be a great impediment if you could go nowhere without being overcome by followers."

"It was Hal's idea for the same reason," said Penny, trying to refocus herself on her husband.

"Are all the people around the hill your followers?" asked the captain.

"I imagine they're Penny's," Ishaw said, then thought of correcting himself: "Do you prefer to be called Mother Healer?"

"No!" said Penny and everyone at the table looked at her. "It's just that the term implies some sort of religious figure. Penny is just fine."

"Penny it is, then."

"So you don't know who those other people are?" Hal asked.

Ishaw had an idea but kept it to himself. "I don't."

"Looks like I have some help with security, whoever they are," James said. "It's been quiet up here since they led that woman away."

Harvey tickled Benjamin in between feeding him baby apricots.

"Are you sure you like other people deciding who you are and aren't going to see?" Mary asked Penny.

"It's the first breath we've had," Hal commented. "It's a good chance to decide what we're all going to do to help us set up permanently somewhere."

"I'll work on getting a stadium or convention hall, something that will accommodate a large number. If we think this out right, all you'll have to do is show up once a day for half an hour, if that." Ishaw thought that at a few hundred a person, things would work out beautifully.

Penny wondered at how much confidence Ishaw had in her. As far as she knew, he had never seen her heal anyone. Would she be able to read him once he did? "Were you at the hospital for the healing there?"

"No. I saw it on a newscast. Quite extraordinary."

James was thinking of his own role. "I think I'll go talk to the people in white, see where they stand and what they're doing to keep the mountain so quiet. I'm sure we can all agree we don't want anyone hurt down there."

Hal would oversee things. "Mom," he said, "I assume you'll be in charge of the house."

"For as long as we're here. We're going to need groceries. James, when you're down there, maybe you could get Midge out to do some grocery shopping. With ten of us, things are going to go fast. Harvey and I will do food and the kids. My daughter-in-law needs her rest. I think we're forgetting she just got out of the hospital yesterday."

Everyone looked Penny's way. "I'm feeling fine, honestly."

"Penny," Hal protested, "I'll set up a couch." He shot her a look.

"Look at me all you want. I'm not going to be away from them another minute. I love Ishaw's plan, if it means ninety-five percent of my day will be with the children." Penny wasn't just putting on a brave face: Indeed, she felt fine—better than fine actually. She had more energy than she had had a week ago, before all of this madness started. She remembered when she was a child being completely awake before her eyes were even open and jumping out of bed every morning. Kids usually hop, skip and all-out run from one place to the next. It hadn't been apparent that she'd lost that energy until it was back in her, boundless and building up. She had the idea that she was experiencing what people on speed feel like. She wanted to do something and couldn't quite place what that something was. A jog around the lake? A run around the lake! No, it was another itch from an unexpended energy. A picture of healing someone danced in her head, and she knew it would satisfy her and bleed out the excess motion swirling inside. It was becoming a need.

"Penny, are you all right?" Harvey was at her elbow, and she was shocked, still, when he addressed her with anything other than a simple yes-or-no answer to a question.

"I'm sorry; I was daydreaming. The original Walter Mitty. You know me."

"I think that proves how tired you are. Why don't you go back to bed?" Mary was standing over her. Breakfast was finished and the dishes were heading to the giant country sink.

Penny smiled, "No, thank you." They couldn't feel inside of her and know how wrong they were. They couldn't read her energy or know how strong she was. For a moment they seemed almost blind to her with their limited senses.

Hal chimed in: "She's right, Pen. Please, we don't need you back in the hospital."

Mary was not used to her wishes being refused. She probably would have won in the end. Penny was outnumbered and before she knew it, several people were herding her toward the stairs. Penny's protests stopped abruptly when there was a knock at the door.

James opened it and, finding no one there, stepped out with everyone emerging behind him onto the porch. The children peeked through their legs. Only Benjamin could be heard in the kitchen, gurgling from his high chair, engrossed in a handful of Cheerios.

At first Penny thought large white monument stones were surrounding the cabin, and the flicker of the idea bounced around in her thoughts, including how they could have been transported up the mountain so quickly. Of course, she knew that was wrong. The life signs of the sheeted people fought for her attention, and she felt their bodies curled up against their knees, foreheads looking down toward the dirt, flank to flank with the others. They were still to the naked eye, but Penny could hear their breathing inside of her. There were so many of them that a person could step off of the porch onto someone's back and walk out of sight down the road without ever touching the ground. Only a small path was made, a ribbon of green leading away from the steps of the house. Penny wondered if this was in answer to her request at the hospital. It was one of the only things she had said there.

Her family, true and adopted, turned to her on the porch. Eyebrows were raised and shoulders shrugged. What were they supposed to do with these people?

"Is there someone in charge of your group that we could talk to?" Penny shouted above the huddled white backs. In response she received an overwhelming wave of confusion. Question marks seemed to litter the air around her. In their eyes she was completely in charge. They chanted the name they gave her, "Mother Healer, Mother Healer," beginning in a whisper and rising louder and faster until the cabin shook with it. At the hospital, people had prayed in their own religions, a rosary circle, rows of davening, songs from every corner and tradition. Here, with their heads still pressed to the damp ground, they threw their arms up and linked their hands until each of them was connected in a human chain. Their chants broke into murmurs alternating "Peace" and "Mother Healer," and everyone on the porch just watched.

Finally, over the quiet whispers, Lydia tugged at Penny's shirt and asked, "What are they doing, Mommy?"

Penny was almost the point of throwing her arms up in exasperation when Ishaw stepped in and crouched down. "They're worshipping your mommy. She's a great healer."

There wasn't enough time to explain how wrong that was to Lydia and Julie, whose hand she was clutching, unconsciously imitating the crowd in front of them. She saw Hal's mouth, a tight line drawn down in sharp angles, and wondered if he would know what to say. Midge and James looked back and forth from the crowd to

Penny as if debating whether to bow down themselves.

"Please," she shouted out over the followers. "Please stand." And, like a sail billowing out with the snap of a strong wind, they were up on their feet as one body, their heads still bent, their interlocked arms still raised in some sort of salute to her. Only one had her face tilted ever so slightly higher than the rest, her eyes peeking out from under the crisp linen wrap. She was in the second row and found Ishaw's gaze immediately before bringing her chin back to her chest. Ishaw stepped back into the shadow of the porch, eyes wide for the second time that morning.

Penny was ready with a speech she'd been composing since her time down at the lake that morning. It was about how she put on her pants one leg at a time and she was really just like them. It stressed how confused she was and how she didn't have any guidance for them at all. She wanted them to go out and do good things. Love the people in their lives and go back to their own religions, where their own leaders could guide them on bettering themselves. How she was just the catalyst for refocusing them on the good they already had all around them. She wasn't a god. She wasn't able to do anything but heal their physical wounds, but after that the healing of their spirits was up to them. It was clear-cut, short and to the point and she was ready to deliver it when she saw the dirt rising up in a cloud beyond the trees. The unpaved road announced the arrival of visitors before any engine was ever heard, and it stopped her before she could begin.

The crowd waited with her until they could hear the complaint of the engine reluctantly shifting gears up the steep drive. It was a pale blue flatbed truck, and it fit neatly between the groups up the path they had made. Frantic followers in white jumped out of the cab and threw themselves on the ground in front of the cabin. Penny started down the steps but Hal and James grabbed each of her arms.

"What are you doing, Pen? We don't know anything about these people." Hal was almost as white as the sheets around them.

"It's okay," she said. "They're not going to hurt me." And she went down to them, bending down and whispering, "Please stand." She waited until they had lifted their bodies, determined to try to get them away out of a prostrate position. "What is it?"

Though they stood, they kept their faces down in a permanent bow and led her to the back of the truck where Louis lay, a strange combination of winter white and blue battling to color his face. His mouth was open as if it were still trying to bring in air even after his body had given up and shut down. Penny gasped, and the group on the porch rushed down to see. Louis's life signs were long gone. Those who brought him looked up. Penny felt every eye on her. What could she do? This man was already gone. Feeling around for him seemed pointless, but that energy was still banging around in her, looking for a place to go.

She tried to get steady and started to reach out to him when she caught herself, knowing she probably could not do anything for him. Part of her understood that this could be all the better in going her own way, apart from these people. It would be a benefit for them to lose faith in her. More frightening, though, was the scintilla of a possibility that she could. It snagged her and stopped her with the idea of bringing his body back to life, only to find him a mental vegetable. Her father-in-law, Harvey, had been healed physically, but psychologically he was different, too, stronger, unafraid of whatever demons had always scared the life out of his every conversation. Harvey was opening like a new flower, but he already had something of a bud, a healthy stem. This man had nothing.

Julie was at her side. "Can you help him, Mommy? He's very sick, isn't he?"

"I don't know if I can, honey. I'm not sure."

Inside the house Benjamin, out of Cheerios, began to cry. Penny looked up to the door and back down at what was essentially a cadaver, cold and lifeless. She should go in and comfort Benji.

Instead Penny moved toward Louis, touching him and throwing her mental feelers out, looking for him. The followers in white felt their skin warm and their hair pull up and away from them, lightened somehow by that energy. They looked at the bed of the truck, watching and waiting, forgetting their reverential bows. It was as if Penny's arm were reaching through a long, narrow, hollow log on a damp forest floor. The things she bumped into felt soft and rotten and made her want to recoil. Despair engulfed her. The blackness around Louis held no hope, and she saw images of hundreds of thirsty animals around a dried-up river. Still she looked, closing her eyes and reaching further and further until she was sure this extra arm inside of her would snap off, having gotten too long and thin. When she reached what was surely her limit, miles and miles down that long dark tube of nothingness, Penny felt herself falter, and she became certain she would be sucked down like a rubber band stretched beyond its capacity and slipping from its original hold. Going only one more breath further seemed impossible, and she was ready to concede failure when she felt a tiny warmth ahead like a warm spring bubbling into a frozen river. She stretched what equaled a half of a pinkie toward it and saw it losing its heat. It was dangerously close to being snuffed out and still falling away from her. Her body shook with the effort of staying in that mean, cold place.

Every ounce of her wanted to retreat. She couldn't breath there.

With what was her last iota of strength she held herself out as long as she could, and although he was still out of her range, he was pulled toward her, her energy attracting the last bit of his life. When she had him in her grasp she engulfed him and dragged him back, sweat pouring off her brow as though she were moving a mountain. Hal stood behind her now, trying to pull her away from Louis, but it was over. Penny's legs gave way. Dropping to her knees, she felt Louis's eyes open. He rose to a sitting position, blinking, and looked out over the hundreds of followers in white, each turned now to Penny, on their own knees with heads down again, arms outstretched, crying and chanting.

When Penny managed her way back into the cottage, it occurred to her how many times she had opened a door to let out a fly stuck in her home, only to have another wander in before the first one could be freed. She was always reluctant with the flyswatter. Louis cried in a corner of the room occupied by an overstuffed tan wingback chair. Harvey sat next to him, keeping him from Penny, whom he tried at regular intervals to hug. James and Midge were on the porch. When Louis sat up in the truck, Midge threw herself on the ground in the manner of the people in sheets. Although James pulled at her to stand, he did so only out of respect for Penny's direct request not to be bowed to.

Hal left Penny and looked around the cabin for any liquor that might have been stored there, prepared to drink just about whatever was available. He knew he should go to his wife and say something, but his search for something to medicate himself with was too urgent. He went up to his mother's luggage, hoping she still carried around a few Valium for emergencies. Mary had already headed him off at the pass and consumed three, the total number of pills she had packed, which seemed at the time a generous amount most likely not needed. She made a pact with herself to carry the entire bottle on her person at all times from then on. In minutes she couldn't feel her feet walking the worn wide-planked wooden floors, and the impression that she was floating along helped her to look at her daughter-in-law. If Mary stood next to her for too long, she got the feeling that she was lying at the base of a skyscraper, unable to see the top. The anxiety of the idea that the building was about to topple and pour every one of its thousands of bricks on top of her was only slightly quelled by sedatives. Cooking was less threatening, and she decided on an elaborate lunch that would take most of the morning to create.

Julie and Lydia began to play as soon as Penny entered the house again. There was a laundry basket full of their toys from home, and they pulled them out one by one, turning them around and over as if they were foreign objects whose purpose would only be determined by intense scientific scrutiny. At regular intervals, in response to some bell only they could detect, they shot up and over to the windows, their heads tilted backward in an attempt to see outside. They watched the waves of sheets, and Lydia was reminded of a Spanish woman she had seen on a children's show whose skirt had tiers and tiers of white surrounding her in flowing ripples when she twirled a dance. It did feel a little bit as though the house were spinning. Plastic princesses and miniature evil knights promised to be much more reliable.

Penny noticed that the girls didn't look over their shoulders at her to explain the name of each of the characters. There was no whining to make her play a part or decide who got to have the prettiest doll with the sequined dress first and for how long. They built a building-block castle that stood firm, without fighting about clumsy feet knocking it down. She realized someone had already put Benjamin down for his morning nap.

It didn't surprise her that no one had anything to say. Penny looked through the giant bay windows and out at the thousands of tiny maple leaves opening. She reflected on the English language and its usage to describe everyday occurrences. What opportunity was there to develop vocabulary around the experience of raising someone up from the dead? We talk about what we live, she thought. Penny also had no words for the place she had pulled Louis out of, or the fear that now lived inside of her and was beyond her every comprehension.

Chapter Twenty-five

Kristy Elton was a designer by trade, recently graduated from the Fashion Institute of Technology with a dual degree in both modern textile and computer applications. The computers were an idea forced on her by an overly practical mother who felt there was no future in design for someone with no name: "We can't all be Paul McCartney's daughter, you know," Kristy's mother had said, forking over the tens of thousands of dollars in tuition only upon approval of a coursework registration peppered with a clear backup plan in case Kristy's "unrealistic dreams" didn't pan out. A's in these classes were expected, and anything lower than a B would find Kristy out in the cold on her "trendy little ass." Her mother was not a woman of mere words. Kristy endured the albatross of a second major like a nineteenth-century child swallowing cod liver oil, all the more determined to make something of herself in a nearly impossible industry. She vowed to throw herself off the highest building before creating Web sites for other designers.

After graduation Kristy got a moderate loan from a woman-friendly bank and opened a small boutique in an up-and-coming New York City neighborhood. The stock was all of her own design, visions she had wanted to breathe life into for the last four years. She manned the store, drawing plans in between a scanty customer flow and sewing at night when she closed down. When her overhead became too high, she moved her personal belongings into the shop, sleeping between the sewing machine and the stained toilet that stood starkly in the middle of the back room. It was nothing but inspiring, and when her mother visited, jokingly looking under the rounders of clothes for hidden customers, Kristy's resolve tripled.

Kristy wasn't the only one on the small commercial strip hurting for business. Each member of their block association struggled from month to month, waiting for their neighborhood to establish itself as a solid commercial area. They made up rules of etiquette on the display of their signs, awnings and fliers. They wanted to be the next Chelsea. Outdoor racks were a giant no-no, as were sidewalk sales.

Kristy was tired. She had a small window to go with her minuscule shop, and, being an original designer, the no-outdoor policy prevented her customers from seeing—and being "sparked" by—her merchandise. If things kept up this way, she wouldn't be able to pay her rent for much longer. To drum up some business, she was developing her own Web site. She worked on the graphics of her product while listening to the early news on a ten-inch television she had recycled from the garbage in a crustier neighborhood. After sewing halfway into the previous night, she wished she could attach a coffee IV drip into her arm.

The turning point in Kristy's business was like a razor in the sun, bright and sharp. One minute she was deciding on the perfect angle for the picture of her new tasseled pushmina wrap, and the next she was staring at the television. It was the quintessential "Eureka!" of the apple falling on Isaac Newton's head.

At seven A.M. the world had found the Mother Healer,

the loser in a televised game of global hide-and-seek. Kristy knew everyone was tuning in. Yesterday the conversations in the bars ranged from discussions about whether it had all been some sort of high-level hoax to bets over whether anyone would be able to find her. There were sightings of the Mother Healer in all corners of the earth, sending news teams scrambling. Having found her, they were delighted.

The news converged like a SWAT team rooting her out for crimes as yet uncommitted. The first shot Kristy saw was one of a mob that had formed around the base of Mt. Pleasant. Like everyone else, she was becoming familiar with the religious groups already proclaiming to follow her and the sheets they wore. A close-up revealed the department-store tags on the linens sticking out at odd angles. A roadside stand sold safety pins. People appeared disheveled and walked in the fashion of the mummies they looked like. They wrapped and rewrapped in small circles when they weren't lying on the ground with their hands clasped together behind their backs and upward in what was surely a painful position. Kristy saw one woman whose sheets were choking her, stretched across her neck and pulled backward by her arms. After several rounds of whatever prayer they were participating in, their "robes" were wrinkled and filthy.

Some people watched these shots and argued religious philosophy and the Second Coming. Others scoured their brains, wondering who in their lives needed this magical healer and how they would get them to her. Kristy saw the opportunity of a lifetime from an angle she hoped only she recognized. Not for the first time that day, she thanked her lucky stars that she had such a bitch of a mother who had armed her with exactly what she needed to succeed in the field her mother hated. Oh, it was going to be luscious.

Kristy picked up a recycled piece of paper with Luciano's Pizza advertising on the front. A number-two pencil flitted across the blank back of the page, alternately scratching in and erasing lines in fits and starts. In twenty minutes she had everything she needed. Her design was simple: an A-line midcalf-length caftan with a square neck and attached oversize headdress. To avoid having it resemble a graduation gown, she tapered the sleeves and scalloped the bottom edge slightly. This crowd seemed to be after simplicity. She did away with the face cover, knowing Americans wouldn't hide their faces for long. The caftan would be white, of course, made of high-grade nylon. Cotton would never do if they were going to lie around in the dirt all day, she thought. It would zip up the front, as buttons would pop off with all that pulling on the ground. A double line of stitching would flow in connected ovals around every edge, and the zipper would have a small white emblem as its pull, two plastic hands touching each other in an off-center patty-cake, copied from the interlocked hand gestures of the followers.

Designing was never really a problem for any of the people Kristy knew who shared her dreams. Finding your customer was the real problem. Kristy's customers were in the millions, according to CNN's latest estimates. They wanted this ridiculously simple outfit and she knew just how to get it to them. She spent the next hour spitting out a prototype and applying on-line for a copyright on the design. Once she was recorded as being in the process, no one would be able to touch her rights to it without grounds for a lawsuit. She sent her model off by E-mail to a garment district sweatshop whose owner was smart enough to know genius when he saw it. After a heated twenty-minute negotiation, he agreed to start mass production with all ten of his worldwide plants, his A, B and C shifts to work in assembly lines around the clock. He wasn't going to waste any time, considering that this Mother Healer fad could blow over the next day.

Kristy went on-line and secured every Mother Healer Web site not already captured. By lunchtime she had MotherHealerrobes.com, MotherHealerwear.com, MotherHealersheets.com, MotherHealerfollowers.com and ten others she thought might snare customers. Temporary Techs, a company twenty blocks away, hungry from all of the collapsed e-businesses and still set up for handling on-line purchases, started processing the orders coming through as the Web sites rolled into action. By two o'clock the orders were so out of control, they numbered in the hundreds of thousands. She did what any savvy businesswoman would do and doubled the price. By three she decided maybe she had missed the ball and contacted a variety of shoe companies specializing in earth-sandal styles and offered them a space on the Web site to pair their shoes with her Mother Healer robes for a cut of their profits. Kristy Elton was a multimillionaire by four-thirty. An evening deal with three of the major national department store chains for gowns with subtle beading and silver thread instead of white (for the more refined followers) capped off her evening by putting her in the ball park for the latest *Fortune* 500 list.

At the same time Kristy began seeing her clothing on the crowds covered by the news, another designer was seeing his own handiwork. Marco Cedicci, a jewelry artist, took the same inspiration from the clasped hands and turned them into his own, his being a slightly more splayed image of the hands touching at almost right angles and curved a hair at the fingertips. His copyright was also applied for within minutes of Kristy Elton's, and they would have a difficult time suing each other.

Instead of the gold and platinum he worked with on a daily basis in his studio, Marco used a cheaper more readily accessible metal that could be cast, packed and ready for delivery in hours. Marco was already an economically comfortable man unfamiliar with computers. He buried his nest egg in television commercials, which offered an 800 number and fended off competitors with the words PATENT PENDING in bold letters. Mr. Cedicci got his investment back fivefold. He wasn't sure which excited him more, the money or seeing his product on literally thousands of chests on television in scores of countries around the world by that evening. *M. Cedicci* was engraved on the back of each pendant. Marco felt larger than life.

The only thing truly larger than life was the movement itself. Claims of thousands of healings piqued people's interest, as any good story will. The reports of someone being raised from the dead snuck into people's morning coffee and refused to get out of the house.

Natural-food stores were shipping out packets of earth that supposedly came from the land around the hospital where the mass healing had taken place and from Mt. Pleasant. Rocks from Penny's home garden were sold at astronomical prices, and all of her personal items from inside her home had been stolen and auctioned off by noon. What was once the Chaney home was an empty shell that lacked even a thin layer of dust to mute the echoes of the footsteps of people long gone carrying out pans, pots of dead flowers, bent forks, their moldy shower curtain. All of these things proved highly worthwhile finds in terms of their resale value.

Crowds began their pilgrimages to Penny's former home and took the complete absence of materials as a spiritual message of self-deprivation and stark simplicity. They walked through her family room, rubbing their hands and arms along the cracked stucco or rolling themselves in the space where her bed once was. Her childhood home was overrun. The poor folks who had the misfortune of living there gave up the idea of privacy and took to selling robes, hand-symbol chains and painted signs that read, WHAT IS IT THAT YOU WANT?—Mother Healer's last words before bringing the dead man back to life. Groups repeated the phrase like a Zen chant in front of the Chaneys' door. Walks through their backyard were fifty dollars a pop. Tour guides had to rotate people away from the narrow slate walkway to keep the customers flowing.

A big story around the nation was the onslaught of people petitioning courts to have their children's bodies exhumed. There were flatbed trucks in lines around the community cemeteries where people in white who couldn't wait for the legal system had shovels and were digging as fast as humanly possible. Parents whose sons and daughters had been dead for twenty years, whose bones were nothing more than dust and cobwebs, cried with true hope. Squabbles broke out. If one kid had been dead for fifteen years, surely one just in the grave had a better chance.

"Please, move your truck!"

"I have a heart condition. My daughter's coffin is almost here. My sons are still digging."

"I can't wait! My daughter was only two. Please! I have to hurry!"

"Where do you want me to go? There are ten people in front of me anyway!"

"Move your damned truck!"

The Centers for Disease Control issued a warning against digging up postmortem coffins, especially with regards to infectious diseases. People heeded these warnings the way they do the ones on packs of cigarettes.

Mt. Pleasant was unapproachable by car. Tents were set up along the sides of the road, and vendors moved in quickly with wares of food, bottled water, camping gear and Mother Healer memorabilia. Kristy's gowns were there, as were Marco's chains. Within ten miles of the mountain, everyone who had something to sell sold it. Cots and blankets would become more expensive as the evening approached.

By late afternoon it looked as though the highway, which was modest to begin with, had never existed at all. More than one spectator commented on the similarities between this odd crowd and rock-and-roll concerts from the sixties or tailgate parties at football games. Most people were waiting for further instructions and debating which direction the movement would go in. Acquiring the same artifacts gave them a great sense of unity. Songs were written and sung.

Others extrapolated from Penny's few statements and her dress and published what they thought were her clear intentions. These writings, combined with the fliers from the first ten buses, constituted an extensive manual for followers. The main idea embraced by the Mother Healer movement was a rejection of the outer self, the covering up of vain physical attributes and the relinquishing of claim to material possessions. It was called the first book of the Mother. Others simply called it *The White Book*. Each fresh edition, copied in the neighboring town of Corvington, was priced higher than the last in 200-percent increments. Eight loads were sent to the base of Mt. Pleasant over the course of the day. Jonathan Ceil, owner of Covington's Discount Books and Pamphlets, thanked his lucky stars he'd computerized his shop a year earlier for speedier product output. It took only minutes to print scores of these books. The price of each subsequent batch, like Kristy's gowns, skyrocketed exponentially. After the fourth load, Jonathan Ceil pulled out a catalog of yachts he'd been filing away for nine years. The seas of the Caribbean were beautiful in the spring.

A 900 number cropped up like a weed, hooked up nationwide ("Must be 18 or older to call, please"). Their quick business license titled them as Healer's Helpers, and after a brief meeting with lawyers changed their slogan from "The Mother's Advice" to "The Helper's Opinions." No one wanted to be legally responsible for overly zealous zealots. Calls were three dollars a minute. The telephone operators were required to skim *The White Book* on coffee breaks, and most tried to fit the opinions given with the philosophies espoused. The majority of the conversations rightly denied knowledge of how to get time to see the Mother Healer herself or where to bring recently deceased relatives for help. Even these calls generated ten dollars apiece. The term *raising* became a familiar part of the world's vernacular.

Holding the crowds around Mt. Pleasant at bay proved to be a challenging task. Roadblocks were yards deep, and most people were deterred by the idea that "the Mother Healer is seeing no one at this time." But the mountain was large in circumference, of a rather moderate altitude and woody. Hundreds tried to blend in by using the white outfit. The current owners of Mt. Pleasant's cabins made lists of the first arrivals—the true followers, as they called themselves—and spent the day ridding the area of intruders. It was an endless battle. It seemed that even people halfway around the globe had one foot on the mountain.

Chapter Twenty-six

Isaac couldn't be distinguished from the other sheets outside. He was tall, but the white wrappings bled away his height and brought their sameness to him. He was sure he had seen Daisy out there, but there was a great deal of movement and an influx of new followers who filled in the kneeling spaces others left behind. He walked halfway down the path and called her name, hoping to catch her instinctively turning her head. He had never given Daisy enough credit, apparently. He still couldn't believe she was swift enough to construct such a counterattack to his leaving.

There was no finding her, and Isaac wasted no more time getting back to the cottage and on the phone. There was a stadium a few hours west of their location, a popular venue for sporting events and Moonie weddings. With fifty thousand in attendance, the place looked empty. There would be plenty of room for his marks. Chiding himself for not coming up with this angle of the modern-day messiah scheme, he had to hand it to this Penny: She was good. It had been almost believable for a moment that she actually brought that guy back from the dead. Only a master could have orchestrated such a perfectly staged swindle.

Clearly, Penny was the ultimate con artist. She portrayed herself as genuine and stayed in character every moment, an entire group of living scenery around her with their own plausible lives flowing. The healing event at the hospital he'd attributed to mass hysteria. People wanted to believe; it was their undoing in every scam. Getting the details of each situation to look real was her forte, apparently. The guy's face looked as dead as any corpse he'd seen. A tape loop ran through his mind, playing and replaying when the man had gotten his coloring back. Had he been holding his breath? Maybe he'd taken a drug timed exactly to bring his body back to normal functioning at the time Penny got to him. Then it occurred to Isaac: It was probably an antidote somehow given to the guy when she touched him. That had to be it. He wondered again if Penny's and Daisy's paths were intertwined, if they'd conspired together before he even left Daisy. Isaac, the man who called himself Ishaw for this particular sting, thought that was the most plausible construct of the scenario. He would proceed with caution and beat them both at this game. In his mind Penny and her group were targets when he first arrived. Now he would consider them full adversaries.

Crown Stadium hung up on him twice before taking his call as anything but a hoax. Everyone wanted a piece of this Mother Healer. It seemed absurd that anyone but a promoter would represent her. Isaac got past the secretary and the booking manager's personal assistant only after hanging up to give them a chance to verify that he was calling from a Mt. Pleasant number. Everyone knew where she was. The cabin phone would be worthless at the end of this conversation, he noted, after the stadium sold Aunt Myrtle's number to the press.

Isaac finagled his way up to the top but couldn't book quickly without either the Mother Healer in the flesh or a load of cash. Penny and her husband had played the moral angle when he'd brought up the idea of charging people to see her. What were they after? Power? Were they creating a new religion, contemporary Martin Luthers with a series of attention-drawing events to bring in the flock? There were any number of things people got off on, and Isaac decided it was all rather irrelevant. He would bend and shape things to his own will. No matter what dance they were doing, they would find themselves moving to his music before they even knew the record had changed.

Isaac's offshore accounts waited like obedient children, eager to do his bidding. He paid for every seat in the stadium at a flat rate up front. If he could get her there, he stood to triple his nest egg. If he didn't, the deal fell under the tough-shit clause. Isaac would lose virtually every cent. Timing was going to be everything. He stood in the doorway to the great room while Penny watched neverending footage of the world's reaction to her. The news of the "raising" was out and the pope was being interviewed. Tape of the scene at the bottom of the mountain was extensive. He would have to get her past all that. It was so sweetly challenging. Penny was the queen on his chessboard.

A few more calls later, he had a mansion not far off from the stadium. An old actress who had gone senile in her last years had had it equipped with surround sound alarms, wrought iron gates topped with three levels of intersecting barbed wire and 100-percent video surveillance coverage. At six thousand square feet, it was a not-so-small fortress. A wire transfer from his remaining Antigua accounts and it was all his.

Another twenty minutes on the phone and a flushing out of his Swiss account bought him two jeeps originally designed for use along Israel's borders and able to withstand the shock of a grenade attack. Iron plates were being drilled under every exposed area, and defensive driving experts were being deployed from somewhere in the Midwest. One had driven for the Shah of Iran. The other had fended off crowds of over-the-top teenyboppers who'd wanted to jump inside David Cassidy's pants. Isaac was assured that God himself couldn't stop these guys from getting through a mob, be it angry or adoring.

It was easy to buy things. Isaac hoped he'd be able to sell the idea of leaving here. Penny looked convinced earlier, but this morning seemed to have happened days ago. They'd be worried about getting the little rug rats out safely. There was literally nothing money couldn't buy. Two days at the stadium and Isaac could purchase his own damn island if he really wanted to. He opened his purse a little wider and made a contact through the jeep dealer, one John Hayes, a former Green Beret who'd had the misfortune of missing every large-scale ground war. He felt cheated and coped by forming his own little army for hire. For the right amount, Isaac could have overthrown a small country. All he needed was to get the eleven of them down the mountain and to the jeeps that would be waiting for them at three o'clock that morning. Hopefully night would bring them some sort of cover and maybe the world would be sleepy enough to have her stolen out from under its nose.

Isaac hung up and walked back into the great room. Penny was on the couch, James and Midge on either side like bookends watching a spot on MSNBC about people who'd been healed at the hospital and had their afflictions return. A young, snappy reporter was summarizing the data and attempting to draw conclusions. According to his research, 52 percent of those claiming to have been healed, with witnesses to verify it, had become ill again with their particular malady within forty-eight hours. At first they had looked along the lines of similarities in diseases for some idea of a correlation. There was none.

Some individuals with tumors bounced up and never looked back, others didn't. Two women with severe cerebral palsy of an identical type were healed. One was marching in a Mother Healer parade later that day. The other had already relapsed, collapsing at a supermarket in the seasonal aisle.

Penny recognized that she'd been turned into a Rubik's Cube. People were wearing Mother Healer T-shirts and baseball hats, but Penny thought more about the ones who wouldn't love her, the ones who'd get their afflictions back or who wouldn't get to see her at all. The world adored John Lennon; it only took one Mark Chapman to bring him down. And what had he ever done but write beautiful songs? The desperation of these people would be powerful and their end a black hole. Penny was still cold from the place she'd pulled Louis out of. She knew his name, his work, his ambitions. She also knew the second they connected that she'd healed him once already. He was one of the ones who'd relapsed. Things were coming into focus. Being in the depths of that dark place gave her her first insight into what she was supposed to do.

There was a knock on the door, the second one of the day, and all Penny could think was "What now?" Her hands grew cold.

James answered the door. "I think you'd better come here," he called.

They walked over and discovered the doorway to be impassable. Up to the threshold and spread along the porch were bags and bags of groceries. Lettuces perched on top and potato eyes winked out at them. Penny thought she saw a fresh coconut resting beneath a bag of marshmallows. A loaf of bread had fallen into the foyer where they stood.

"I told them we wanted to go down the hill for some

food, that you needed some groceries," he said to Penny.

"How hungry did you say I was?" Penny asked.

Hal came into the room, his face a warm pink, his nose a Santa Claus red. Aunt Myrtle's Wild Turkey was just what he needed to come back to the group. He walked with his arms tucked in close to his sides, as if they could hold him up. He looked out the window behind the couch to the side porch. His voice was smooth and relaxed: "Look back here."

The bags wrapped around the house and rode the stairs down like big brown dominoes.

"Let's bring them in and sort through them," Penny said, looking to Midge for help. "We'll take what we need and give back the rest. She turned to James. "This isn't your fault. We just have to be very, very specific when we talk to anyone out there." She made eye contact with each one. "Let's be careful about what we say. We're going to have to assume everything we mention out there will be put over the top and construed in ways we might not mean."

Isaac saw his chance. "I get the feeling they don't want you to leave this house at all."

Hal jerked his head toward Isaac. "You think they're keeping us captive?"

"It does look like they're doing what they can to make us stay. I'm not so sure how they'd react if we wanted to go."

Mary rushed in from the kitchen, the morning's fireworks suppressed in her mind as well as possible. "We can't have these people tell us what to do. Are we prisoners here?"

"I think we're free to go if we like," Harvey said from the corner of the room, his hand still on a weeping Louis's shoulder.

"How can you say that?" Hal asked. "We can't even go grocery shopping. God only knows what's happened to my job and home. All we have are the clothes on our backs. I feel like a prisoner."

Isaac stepped in and looked steadily at Penny. "Do you remember what we discussed this morning about setting up a safe place to heal people, maybe just once a day?"

Hal felt calmer at the suggestion of a move, less claustrophobic already. "That sounds great. Doesn't that sound great, Penny?"

"Actually, I feel safe here."

"Safe?"

"Those people out there are guarding us. They won't let anything happen to us or the children."

"They also won't let us have our freedom. We can't go anywhere."

"Where do we need to go?"

"What about the kids?"

"What about them?"

"Do you think this is a healthy environment for them? Or doesn't that matter?"

She walked over to him and Hal flinched when she got within arm's length, backing up a half a step. He had the surreal feeling that she was not his wife.

Quietly he said, "Maybe you like being worshipped."

At any other time in their marriage, she would have been sucked into the fight. When Hal was upset or confused about a job he was on, they argued about who was ultimately responsible for emptying out the pockets before a wash, the wearer or the washer. If he was feeling insecure about his latest investment, Hal complained about the color of the living room being sage, which turned out to look more like baby puke than an herb. And she couldn't blame him. She'd had her own share of displaced pissiness put into a fight about the front gate never getting fixed.

But this was worse. Hal's underlying theme was fear,

and he was nearly blind with it. Penny didn't want to push him into making any rash decisions. She could feel the alcohol course through him.

"I think there are a lot more people angry with me than just you, Hal."

"All the more reason to go somewhere we know is safe."

"These people are at least on my side. They believe in me and want to keep us safe."

James and Midge edged out of the room and started in on the groceries. Isaac hopped at his chance to fortify Hal's position. "What's between us and all of those people out there? Steps? I've secured a house for us that has a security guard set up with surveillance cameras in every corner of the grounds. I was assured not half an inch is uncovered."

"One security guard as opposed to the hundreds of people out there who would die for me? The children are in danger, Hal."

"This new house is completely gated in with layers of barbed wire to assure privacy," Isaac added.

"And who's to say one of them isn't one of these nutty cultists? They aren't trained to guard you." Hal's voice rose so that heads shot up outside. "They're a bunch of left-wing flakes with their faces in the dirt. This is who you're trusting the children to?"

"Hal, please calm down. We'll talk about this later, when you're sober."

Hal's eyes got wide and round. "So now *I'm* the one off balance? *Me?*"

Penny went up to him, and Hal still had enough dexterity to sidestep out of her reach.

"Please, Hal. Enough has happened today, and there's still a lot I need to do."

"Christ, Penny, you've raised the dead this morning.

What could possibly be left for the afternoon schedule?" Hal's words were slow and sarcastic, and Penny's blood would have been boiling if she couldn't feel his fear radiating like an overheated wood stove with one log too many on the fire.

"I'm sorry this is all so much, Hal. You know I didn't ask for any of it."

"You could have said no!" Hal screamed, scaring even himself with his volume. "You can still say no!"

"Watch the television for three seconds, Hal, and you'll see I can do no such thing. I have to talk to them. I have to talk to the media and settle people's fears. I think I can get people to go back to their lives—at least, some of them."

"All of a sudden you know what you're doing?"

"Please, Hal, lower your voice. You're scaring the girls." Benjamin was awake from his nap and had just begun to cry at a full roar.

"I'm scaring the girls? I'm scaring them? Nothing you've done in the last week has been anything short of terrifying. Now you want to invite the media in here? You have gone completely out of your mind." Benjamin's wails became more insistent.

"If I can be of any help..." said Isaac, stepping in, trying to seize Penny back to the idea of leaving. "This home I found is perfect, and I have a team that can get us there safely. If you'll just let me describe it..."

Penny faced him with steady strong eyes. "I need to speak to the media. I need to help the people I've already healed; they don't know what to do." She turned to go get her son, but Hal grabbed her arm, holding her back.

"Don't bother, I'll get Benjamin," Hal said. "Don't worry about any of the children: You're too busy saving the world to be concerned for their welfare. I'll just get them out of your way." He turned to Isaac. "We'll be coming with you whenever you're ready to go."

Isaac began mentally to count his money and was curious what wonderful thing he had done in a former life to have courted such great favor with the gods of fortune.

"You will not take my children anywhere!" Penny was screaming, and Isaac was thinking he was in a much better spot. If Hal took the kids, surely she would follow. He was waiting for her to calm down, to see reason, but she continued to scream. "They are in danger! You cannot take the children!"

Before Hal could reply, the front door opened and there was a stream of followers in white, all Isaac's height and above. Under the sheets their bulk was unmistakable. Captain or not, James didn't stand a chance of holding them back. One looked at Penny and asked, "Ma'am?"

"I don't want my three children to leave this mountain until I say otherwise."

"You can't do that!" Hal shouted. "They're my children too!"

The largest one glanced in Hal's direction. "Is there anything else we can do, Mother?"

"Yes," she said, looking from him to Hal and back again, her body shaking. "I want a copy of *The White Book* and then I need to talk to the press."

They filed out quickly and quietly, and for a moment Hal thought he must have hallucinated the whole scene. He wondered if Wild Turkey goes bad while he tried to shake the image away. "This is too much for all of us. I'm leaving with the children tonight, Penny, with or without you."

Chapter Twenty-seven

Louis was positively shattered. One of his mental feet still felt as if it were stuck in that place the Mother Healer had pulled him out of. This Harvey person was sitting with him, a hand on his shoulder, and Louis tried not to close his eyes because the moment he did he could smell the odor of the hole he'd fallen into. He could hear the screams of the people scattered around him down there as well as his own howls of fright.

The souls had whispered to him as she dragged him up and back to the light, "You're one of us, Louis. You'll be back." A rotting face of teeth said, "You earned your way here. It's all yours." And he knew they were right with the cemented certainty that told him if he had two apples and ate them both, there'd be no apples left. The sky is blue. Grass is green. Axioms of unwavering truth.

Louis clung to Harvey like a drowning man out at sea. Harvey tried to reassure him with his bright blue eyes that reminded Louis of his cousin Edgar's. Edgar was two years older than he was but destined always to be a child. When Edgar was born he was a perfectly healthy baby full of the screams of life. His aunt Brett reminded them constantly of how Edgar smiled from the minute he emerged. He grinned through all of his early feedings, despite throwing up the milk he took in and shitting with the intensity of a tiny volcano. It was months before the doctors back then could tell Aunt Brett that little Edgar had phenylketonuria and couldn't process the proteins found in most foods. By that time baby Edgar's brain had reduced itself almost to Swiss cheese.

Three months later a law was passed requiring hospitals to give newborns the test for PKU at birth. Thousands of babies would be saved Edgar's fate. A crummy three months, just ninety-some-odd days, Louis would think, and Edgar would have been completely normal. It was like missing the antivenin for a snakebite by ten minutes. You drop dead and the doctor walks through the door.

It always fascinated Louis that, to look at Edgar for the first time, you'd be hard-pressed to find the problem. He didn't drool. His posture was perfect. He had the face of an angel. It wasn't until he walked that you could see the stage of development he was arrested at. His arms didn't swing when he walked, and you could almost immediately infer that things didn't swing too well upstairs, either.

Every so often though, Louis saw a certain expression come into Edgar's eyes, and Louis would swear in that moment Edgar was looking at things with a complete understanding. It was like a lightbulb flickering on for nanoseconds, only to immediately extinguish itself again. Louis found it exhausting to be around Edgar, always half expecting him just to turn those eyes on all the way one day, sitting around rooting for it and knowing it would never happen. And here was Penny, whom Louis knew had already turned on some eyes so they were bright and strong. He suspected Harvey's were one pair. They wavered like Edgar's, but the shutter was clicking in reverse, occasionally bringing him away from the room into his own private reverie for the briefest of moments. Louis reflected that he himself had turned out to be the most like Edgar in the long run. His asthma always seemed to be his biggest problem, and it took a walk in the hereafter to see that he was indeed broken but in many more complicated ways than he suspected.

This new self-awareness had a dampening effect on being exactly where he had wished so desperately to be just a few hours ago, an arm's length from the woman the whole world wanted to know about. He could think of four story installments without even a stretch. His editor's phone number was committed to memory and flashing in big neon lights across his mind. A pen taunted him on top of a monster RCA television console. It stuck out of an old ceramic fruit basket whose bananas looked as if on the verge of turning brown. The curved blank screen watched him.

He said to Harvey, "She pulled me out of hell."

"Yes," he responded. "She did the same for me."

"But her healing doesn't hold. People relapse back to their illnesses like I did."

Harvey took a minute to think. Louis waited the way only a lifelong observer could. Harvey tilted his head and he came back into focus as if some marble had fallen into just the right spot. "I think the people she heals need to do something to hold on to the change."

"Like what? What would they need to do? There's nothing any normal person could do that could come close to what she does to them."

Harvey smiled, privy to some funny inside joke Louis didn't get the punch line to. "I've been thinking about it. It may be a question of balance. If the person's mind or body is made whole and their spirit stays soft and weak, the structure falls in on itself."

"How can they do something as illusive as strengthening their spirit? Some people spend their whole lives trying to do that."

"Penny has the easier job in that regard."

Louis leaned back and looked up at the cracked ceiling. "So if it's basically impossible, what's the point?"

Harvey waited until Louis made eye contact with him again. "I don't think you have to immediately be at your destination. I do think you have to get off the road you're on and turn in a different direction."

Louis slumped down in his chair. The only direction he could go in was back to his apartment sometime soon to get his hands on his meds or this conversation would be pointless.

Harvey stood up. "If you'll excuse me, I have to go talk to my son. He needs me." His eyes were confident and for the moment completely unwavering. By the time Louis could think of something else to ask him he was gone, but his voice sifted down from the top of the house, calm and steady.

Louis sat back, thinking of the argument between the Healer and her husband. Something poked at him, wanting him to know what the fight reminded him of. Rather than a person or a picture, it was the smell of the hole he had fallen into when he died, a smell he couldn't quite put his finger on. Maybe it was the smell of fish shot in a barrel or whales beached on a shore, dying. Whatever it was, it had an oldness to it. Louis had gotten a whiff of the odor floating in ribbons through his mind. It spiked sharply when he thought of Ishaw entering the room, and Louis remembered seeing a smile dance across the man's lips as the voices rose. He thought of a large black bag slung over a tall man's shoulder with a dark liquid leaking out, and the connection was complete.

Harvey was wrong. He wasn't on a path he could turn around on. He was at the hub of a wagon wheel, and each road was urgent. He should go home and get his medication to assure his own life would be saved. He should risk it all, call his editor and make his mark on the world of journalism. Any writer in his right mind would kill to be him here in this house on this day. Another road down which he could walk begged him to warn Penny of the danger he felt she was in. It occurred to him that if that hole was waiting for him when he died, what would be the point of getting his medicine just to put it off? It would be a living hell just waiting for it to happen.

Louis stood and tried to gather himself together. He smoothed his hair, raking a shaking hand across his head. The old floor creaked as he advanced on the stairway, and he wondered if it was encouragement or deep disapproval. Louis's feet found the worn grooves in the faded cranberry runner leading up to the bedrooms. His head could be seen rising as he ascended, then resting on the upper landing. He looked in on Penny's bedroom from floor level.

She was on the queen-size bed, sobbing with her face in her hands. Around her shoulders Isaac had draped his lengthy arm, his other hand gently patting her knee. Louis felt his bowels loosen and his mouth fill with the biting taste of metal. For a second he thought he had made a terrible mistake, climbing back down into the seat of hell instead of up the stairs to Penny. Isaac watched him over the top of her bent form. The recognition was mutual. Before Louis could get to the top stair, Isaac retracted his arm, stood and quietly closed the door in with a click.

Louis was going to need help. He turned back around and galloped down the stairs knowing he was flying by the seat of his pants, not sure which path he'd chosen exactly, wondering when he opened the front door how he would ever get beyond the wall of white and back down the mountain. For that matter, even if he got down, how on earth would he get back up? He had the impression

God Himself couldn't get up here without a note from His mother. He took a deep breath. The size of the front line of followers reinforced this idea tenfold. He stepped forward, expecting to be knocked back, but found they made a path for him. And as he walked forward they reached out for him, wanting to feel Penny's Lazarus. They touched him with their palms, then rubbed their hands around their chests in circles over their hearts. They were gentle with him and he stopped, reaching out with his arms so that some from beyond the path could make their way over to him.

"I'm looking for an elderly lady named Jetta." Hands paused in midair. Eyes turned his way. "Can someone help me? Is she still on the mountain?"

Murmurs ran through the crowd and a woman stepped forward, taking Louis by the hand and leading him down to the main road. Fingers brushed up against his body along the way, a densely packed forest of people with soft leaves. The urgency he felt was tempered with a desire for the contact never to end. Approximately a third of the way down the mountain, the kneeling followers gave way to camps of tents and tables with people scurrying from one location to the next. Some held stacks of white books Louis could see had no writing on their covers. Other people opened plastic bags with white robes inside, which they held out against themselves and stepped into quickly. A food tent, with an odor like school lunch emanating from it, had a cafeteria sign affixed above its triangular door flaps, written in an indiscriminate array of capital and lowercase letters. Similar plaques rode the tops of other makeshift buildings.

Most shocking to Louis, aside from the quickness with which people can create communities, was the way this one was being guarded. Instead of metal or wood fencing around the encampment, which would have proved difficult in the areas of thick bushes and trees, there was a human fence that Louis assumed circled the mountain completely. Followers stood, arms locked tightly, in what looked like an overly serious game of schoolyard Red Rover. It was four rows deep, with the bodies of the front rows standing directly in front of the locked arms behind them, who were in turn blocking those behind them, and so on. Clearly no one was calling anyone over.

In front of the interlocked followers the masses that had been at the base of the mountain oozed upward. Louis saw lines of boxes, brown and black, and he stepped away from his guide and tried to discern what they could be. He expected the walkers and the wheelchairs, the stretchers and the crutches. The boxes were coffins, on pulleys and carts, carried by whole families or just dragged by the desperate. The saddest was a tiny one—most likely, Louis guessed, a newborn, her box small enough to fit in an upright shopping wagon. He thought he could almost hear the bodies thump against the lids as the families pulled them forward, jockeying for closer positions. The front row of the human fence had their heads turned sideways so that they could only see each other.

Louis tore himself away from the view and followed the woman to a large unmarked tent that stood apart from the others. The woman bowed and left him at its entry, two nylon flaps zipped closed. He wasn't sure how to knock or what he would say. For the thousands of people milling about and waiting, the area was unnaturally quiet. Louis was afraid to interrupt it and be thrown over the human fence. Two women's voices could be heard arguing inside.

"We need to get her out of there, Daisy. You know better than anyone what Isaac is capable of." Louis recognized Jetta's smooth tones.

"That woman is no concern of mine. Isaac has nowhere to run with her."

"He'll kill her if she doesn't go along with whatever he's scheming up."

"Maybe she'll be a good influence if she's so wonderful," Daisy replied. Louis could see the shadow of her stand, signaling that she was ending the conversation.

Jetta lowered her voice and Louis strained to hear. "She really is the One, Daisy."

Daisy laughed. "You're a stupid old woman. That was all a scam. None of it was ever true. Isaac has a bank account you could choke a horse on to prove it. He called it his sucker store. You were one of his suckers. Besides, how do you know he didn't plan this all out himself? I wouldn't be surprised if she's his flunky, just carrying out his plan."

"So if you want to get him back, let me convince her he's up to no good. She'll kick him out. You'll have won."

Louis thought he could hear Daisy's sneer and picture the look of contempt she wore. "He'll walk down the mountain and into the arms of all of the millions he stole from me. That's what you consider winning?"

"He won't have pulled one over on Penny."

"If you think he'll just walk away, you don't know him at all. Didn't you learn anything from what he tried to do to you? Isaac doesn't lose. He wins or I imagine he'll die trying. Which is just fine with me."

"And you don't care what happens to her?"

"She's not my concern."

With that, Daisy pulled the zipper down the tent's opening like a surgeon cuts open an exposed belly, rapidly and with no apologies. Jetta was seen to the door, where the two women came face-to-face with Louis.

"Can I help you?" Daisy asked.

"I'm here to see Jetta."

"If you're here for work detail, please go to the sectional tent."

Louis's eyes met Jetta's when she responded, "I'm going that way, let me show you." She tried to walk around Daisy, who stood in her way.

"I'm sorry. You're a risk to our worship," Daisy said to Jetta. "You'll have to leave." She turned to call for help from the security station.

Louis moved to block her way. "The Mother Healer has requested her."

She said to him in a hissed whisper, "I don't care if the pope himself has asked for a private sitting with this woman. She's a security risk."

A group of large followers approached from a few tents away. Louis started to wonder if all of the recruits were football players. He didn't know what more he could possibly do. Without Jetta he had no plan. He was sure she would have an idea about convincing Penny to get rid of Ishaw or Isaac or whatever his name was. Having been down here, perhaps she could also convince Hal that they should stay put. The more desperate people he saw, the more Louis was convinced that Penny was safest up that hill. Penny was a fragile butterfly, maybe the last the world would know with this beautiful gift, but she was in the midst of a meteor shower and Louis felt she was going to get more than her wings singed. Of course, he could do nothing to help her if they threw him out now. He wondered if he'd made the wrong choice. Maybe he should have written a story after all, maybe that would have done more good.

Swirls of robes hurried over, and Daisy's face bent with her determination. "Remove these people, please! At once!"

The large ones looked at Daisy, then stepped toward Louis, their large hands extended forward to grab. Louis considered running but knew it was fruitless. Just when he expected to be scooped up by the collar and thrown like a birdie over a human badminton net, one of them said, "It's the risen one!" Everyone stopped and for a second Louis looked around, trying to see who they were talking about. The giant guards bowed down at Louis's feet. The irony of it, considering where he'd been just a few short hours ago, made Louis step back. His throat constricted and his eyes swam.

"We can't throw this man out any more than we could throw out the Mother Healer herself."

Louis was shocked but seized the moment. "This woman and I need to return to the cabin. Please let us through."

They were whisked away by dozens of people, murmuring and stealing brushes against Louis's skin as he walked. Jetta turned briefly to see Daisy's face turn an angry red and felt safer looking away. A parade of excited worshippers followed them up the path, leaving the sick craning their necks over the fence if they could, trying to get a glimpse of the commotion. Daisy was interested in none of it. She whirled back into the tent, rifled through her bags and brought out a gun. Beyond the human barricade, the dead were jostled in their resting places, shaken by their loved ones, hoping the excitement meant that maybe the Mother Healer had come down the mountain to help them at last.

Chapter Twenty-eight

Isaac had excused himself to attempt renegotiation of the stadium, perhaps delay their arrival for a day. He was confident it wouldn't take much longer than that. He had talked people out of millions of dollars. Getting some housewife from one location to another seemed almost ridiculously easy, especially since he had her husband's complete support. He would have his way and enjoy the game while he was at it. Everyone was where he wanted them to be, he told himself. Women don't like to keep their spouses angry. What difference should one day make? Stepping into the tiny office off of the great room, Isaac closed the door behind him, blocking out the sound of the children's quiet playing, happy that Penny was upstairs, resting, contained.

He got right through to the booking agent. "Bill, this is Isaac Rourke."

"Yes, Isaac. We're waiting anxiously for your arrival. My team has covered the promotional aspects for you as per our agreement. You may have already seen the commercial spots on local WKAX."

"Right. Actually I'm going to need a little leeway here."

"Leeway? We're all set on this end."

"Yes, I understand. But the Mother Healer needs an extra day. It's pretty jammed up over here. We're having difficulty getting her out."

"Then you'll only be using one of the two days you have reserved?"

"No. I'd like to push my two days back. We'll definitely need the full two days to service the number of people we want to."

"I'm so sorry, Mr. Rourke. We have a soccer tournament in three days, booked months ago. You understand."

"Then I'm sorry as well. If you can't accommodate us, we'll move to a different venue." He added, "You understand."

"That's fine, sir. Of course we'll be keeping your deposit. As I explained, it's nonrefundable."

"You'll do no such thing. I'll stop payment from my banks."

"Yes, I'm sure, but the wires have already been processed, Mr. Rourke, and the monies received."

Isaac had fully intended to speak to the men in his pocket in Antigua about delaying the payments until he gave them the signal. He'd been too excited. It had slipped his mind. A bead of sweat appeared on his brow.

The booking agent was saying, "We just book. Whether you fill the stadium or not is irrelevant to us. We're just in the business of making it available to you."

His voice sounded far away to Isaac, as if he'd receded down a long hall. Isaac had never lost control of a scam. He'd never been arrested or caught even by one of his victims. It hadn't been difficult figuring out how to cut loose anything jamming him up. He'd certainly never ensnared himself. A part of him that he would not acknowledge whispered that he'd finally put his foot in it, tricked himself not only out of the sting but out of the profits of his life's work. Isaac was not used to losing.

"I'll get her there, don't you worry."

"Oh, I'm not worried, sir. The stadium will be empty. That's my only obligation to you."

Isaac's face turned crimson and his first bead of sweat was joined by half a dozen friends, who began a race down the side of his head through the cut features of his face. "The stadium will be packed!" he said through clenched teeth before hanging up.

Isaac paced back and forth in the small downstairs office. He ran his hands through his hair and tugged at it to help himself think. During difficult times Daisy used to calm him down and give him another angle. He pushed this idea away and focused singularly on getting Penny off the mountain.

He would do what people at war do, which is to form alliances. Hal was in his pocket already and he racked his brain for whoever else he had pull with who in turn had pull with Penny. He emerged from the room still thinking of the possibilities. Toys littered the living room and Isaac stepped over a pink Jeep with a naked Barbie at the wheel. Midge was dressing a male doll while the twins spoke in high play voices. One of them, nearly small enough to be a doll herself, looked up at Isaac, "Want to play?" Isaac hesitated.

"You could be Ken."

"No, thank you. I'm trying to get us ready to go."

"Go?" Midge jerked her head up. "The Mother Healer doesn't want to go."

"Because she's good and kind. She wants to help everyone here on the mountain. I want to move her where she can help them in a safer environment."

"Look outside. Even if we wanted to go, I don't think they'll let us."

"You also think the Mother Healer's own followers are keeping her prisoner?"

Midge stopped dressing the doll and looked up again. "Of course not. She's not a prisoner."

"By definition, someone who is forced to remain somewhere against their will is a prisoner."

Midge thought this over.

"Besides," Isaac pressed, "what about other countries? Won't she want to travel around and bring her gift to the whole world?"

"I suppose. But what about her followers? Where will they stay?"

"Shouldn't they go out and tell other people about her? She doesn't seem to like it when they bow to her."

Midge nodded. "Yes, that's true. Will she be able to heal people where we're going?"

"Of course. Much easier than here."

"Where exactly are we going?"

"Oh, just a few miles away. What did she do for you?"

"I had MS. She got me out of a wheelchair." Her eyes misted over. "I didn't have much longer."

"Then I guess you want only the best for her."

"Yes." She nodded vigorously. "Yes, I do."

Isaac stood, smiled and wandered into the kitchen, where he found Mary still cooking. They could eat for a month, Isaac figured, based on what was on the table alone. Her mouth was set on her face in a tight line, all of the red of her lips drawn in and mashed against her teeth. Pot lids clattered. James sat at the butcher block that Mary scurried around. A laptop was open in front of him and keyed into a Healer Web site.

"What's the world saying?" Isaac wanted to know.

James looked up. "They're all across the board: She's loved by millions, if what it says here is accurate. Unfortunately, she's also hated, I'm afraid, by just as many."

Isaac chuckled as if in disbelief. "Does that make any sense to you? What has she done but help people?"

"She's frightened the pants off of the world. They scream for help, but they want it to look a certain way. For example, she's not a male. Christians want her to be talking about Jesus but are absolutely infuriated when any comparisons are even subtly suggested. Muslims have totally disassociated themselves from her. Like that. Most of the modern world wants us to raise the dead but have it somehow connected to a form of technology. If Penny were a new drug or immunization, less of the population would be pissed off. At any rate, across the board, she's simply too much to swallow. She's being called by some the biggest hoax in history."

"I wonder if she shouldn't just bow out of the scene for a while," Isaac asked, trying to feel out James's position.

James thought it over, scraping a groove in the old wood block with a fingernail. "I think she should do what she can, no matter what the controversy. It's just that it may be dangerous."

"That's why I'm advocating the move." Isaac nodded, imitating one of the first men he'd ever gotten to give him his savings. The man could nod like gangbusters. *With ya one hundred fifty percent*, the nod said, *five hundred percent, if that's what it takes*. His name was Sam, an insurance salesman used to assuring his clients that everything (nod, nod) was exactly what it should be. It said everything was right as rain, praise God. It went down like gravity and was more convincing. Isaac had practiced it in the mirror until it was his own. He'd used it on Sam himself, as a matter of fact, and had the inkling it would work beautifully on James.

James, though, was a bit of a slippery fish. Speeders liked to nod their heads off and they still ended up holding tickets with James's signature across the bottom. *Nod yourself dizzy*, his face said. "What did you have in mind?"

"I have a secure house, video cameras, twenty-foot fences, sentry posts. There are three access roads, two major, one minor."

James just waited, years of giving people all the rope they needed.

"The only room for kneeling would be smack in the middle of a thick apple grove. Most of this congregation—" he jerked his head toward the window—"would be a mile down the road, and even then it would be packed in tight."

James thought this over, a pocketknife dislodging Aunt Myrtle's old butcher-block grease from under the nail of his meaty thumb. When this was accomplished, he found another groove along the butcher block's soft wood corner and cleaned it out with the same thumb. Isaac wondered how the man had ever apprehended anyone if he moved as slowly as he thought. He was in charge of security and the place was just choking with religious fanatics anyway, and Isaac thought that said a great deal. Maybe he was worrying too much about this particular man's opinion. At the moment he had the impression James couldn't support a tit with an underwire bra in one hand and a horny teenager in the other.

"How would you get her down the mountain?" James asked without looking up.

This was a question Isaac wanted to hear: James was now considering the possibility of getting her to a new location. It was a good sign, his father would have said, although Isaac's father's signs had sometimes proven to be confusing and untrustworthy. A Bible Belt preacher who Isaac was sure was the original source of the phrase *tough as nails*, he had had no identifiable soft spots and tolerated none in the family he thought of as his own little army for Jesus: *Private* was what his father had called him every day of his life, and if he knew his son's name was Isaac, he never gave any indication to that effect. When in his childhood his mother used the term *private area* to mean his genitals, Isaac wondered almost obsessively if he was the only one with these parts that his mother cleaned with her head turned away and her cheeks flushed. "It's from the heat," she'd say, splashing water on herself when he looked at her quizzically.

His older brother Luke had somehow climbed up the ranks to sergeant, although Isaac could never fathom how he'd accomplished such a feat. Most of Luke's days were spent bent over with his hands around his ankles, gritting his teeth against the strikes of his father's iron rod for whatever infraction Luke had committed against this father's penal code. The last piece of bread taken off the plate at supper. The absence of the word *sir!* or *ma'am!* at the end of a sentence. Looking an elder in the eye. Failing to say *Amen!* at hearing the name Christ. The list was mind-bogglingly endless. Memories of himself as a child came through across time in jerky freeze frames of Isaac stopping and restarting, searching every thought, every action, for infractions, proven or potential. Despite the fact that his brother outranked him, Isaac couldn't remember ever seeing him sit down on his perpetually swollen behind. If Isaac slipped between the bars that held those raw memories in check far, far in the back of his mind, he could still hear Luke's teeth clunk shut with the jolt of his body as the pipe struck it again and again. In a corner behind the many frightened doors of his mind was the last beating Luke had ever received and his questions about where Luke had gone off to being met with silence. Later, when the school came looking for him, his parents said that Luke had gone to live with an aunt for a spell.

"Spare the rod and spoil the child" was Billingsworth Rourke's favorite saying. It was the first time Isaac took issue with words themselves and the effect they had when various emphases were put on them. If only he'd interpreted that unfortunate section with emphasis on the word *spare,* as in "Yes, do spare the rod!" Isaac felt it could just as easily have been written with connectors and meant something opposite and wholly different. Do spare the rod and spoil the child. Words were indeed powerful. Words were weapons. Even his father's name, Billingsworth, was loaded with infractions. It was never Bill or Billy. Of course, to the boys it was *Sir!* or the steel. But even with his mother, Billingsworth expected every last one of his long three syllables, and God help all four foot eleven of her if she should skip the last one even in an attempt at familiarity and warmth. The pastor had a rod for her as well.

Isaac spit the memory out like an ice cube too cold for his mouth. If James wanted to know how he would get down the mountain, it meant he would at least entertain the idea. His father had at least given him an understanding of words and their meanings. James also hadn't yet asked if she wanted to go. "I have a group that does just this kind of gig: gets celebrities out of people jams. Kind of like the FBI's Elian Gonzalez removal team," Isaac added.

James's head jerked up. "No guns, right?"

"Oh, definitely not." He puffed his lips out with a breath as if in disbelief that such a thought would cross anyone's mind for even a fraction of a second.

"Kind of a moot point, though, considering she doesn't want to go."

There it was. "Maybe she's so caught up in this thing, she can't see the danger she's in. She's virtually trapped here."

James continued his digging. "Also moot. She doesn't care and seems to want to stay. She thinks it's safe here."

"What if she doesn't know what's best for her?"

Isaac watched James entertain that thought briefly. He ran with it. "If you could go back in time and force James Earl Ray's gun sight a hair or two off Martin Luther King Jr., wouldn't you do it? If you knew a perfect good was going to be snuffed out, wouldn't you fight to keep it alive?"

The digging was done. James looked straight at Isaac. "You could throw James Earl Ray's aim off or tackle him at the last moment, sure, but I wouldn't be naïve enough to think I could go back in time and keep the man out of the public eye. Martin Luther King Jr. was gonna do what he was gonna do, 'Forewarned is forearmed' be damned. I'm sure those in the know were telling him he was a hot item and people wanted him dead. He stepped out on that balcony all the same."

"Does that mean we don't try and convince her she can do her thing just from a safer spot?"

Mary came around to their side of the kitchen, a dripping spoon suspended over her cupped hand. Isaac wondered where she was heading with it when she stopped and turned to him. Mary should have been wearing an apron. A splotch or two from each dish she'd wrangled had found its way onto her front, and she gave the impression she just climbed out of a blender.

"Penny wasn't always like this."

The men looked at her, waiting for her to connect her point to the present dilemma.

"She was just some girl when she met Hal. I didn't think she was good enough for my boy. She worked, I don't even remember where. If she offered to bring blueberry pie for dinner and I said, 'Oh, that gives Dad gas,' she'd bring apple or peach instead. She changed my curtains every spring and fall."

"Don't you think we should move her to a safer place?" Isaac asked, trying to focus them again, especially Mary, who swayed slightly from side to side, dripping gravy onto the worn floor.

"I don't know," she admitted, flinching, as if she couldn't recall having used that phrase before. "I don't know," she repeated, trying it on for size like a bizarre hat she never thought she'd wear. "Anything can happen." Something boiled over on the stove and she went to tend to it, still speaking. "It already has." Turning suddenly, she tried briefly to reclaim her solid, no-nonsense persona. "It doesn't matter where she it, does it? What is happening will happen wherever she's . . ."

Mary stirred her gravy and retreated back behind the thick curtain of Valium that allowed her to function at all. She muttered, "She's too . . . It's all . . ." She stared up at the wood-beam ceiling, looking for words to finish her sentences. James and Isaac waited for the conclusion to her opinion, and when none was forthcoming, they also retreated, into the living room.

"Mary has a point," James said. "There's nowhere to run with her, it seems."

Of course, Isaac didn't especially care on any level but the one that involved Penny at the stadium. "I agree there's no running, but let's get everyone to a safer, more manageable location."

James straightened at the word *manageable*. "All we can do is talk to her. She's running this show. We're just here to help. If she wants to go, then so be it."

"Will you at least come with me to try to talk to her?"

"I can try."

From the corner, surrounded by children and miniature doll clothes, was Midge. "No you can't."

"You think everyone should stay at the cottage?" James asked his wife.

"I think we should be wherever the Mother Healer wants us to be, but that's not what I meant." Midge loved being able to use her voice again. It was thrilling not having to put her every thought into two-word sentences limited to perfunctory meanings because of time constraints. "You can't talk to her because she's not here."

Isaac felt his gonads tighten into the kind of hard black rubber made for racquetballs. He wondered again if they weren't all in some sort of odd scheme designed by Daisy, whom he now considered his ex-wife. "Where is she?"

"I don't know. She was all dressed in those white sheets. She kissed the girls and headed out the door."

"Headed out the door?" Isaac parroted, stunned. "Aren't you going to look after her, James?" he asked, his balls withdrawing deeper inside of him. A seed of doubt had landed on the frightened soil of his mind and was germinating through his senses. He held the door open for James to join him, which he did. The two of them waded through the bent waves of white into a churning ocean of followers farther down the road that Isaac worried he might very well drown in. Isaac's hand felt for his life preserver, a steely piece tucked into his waistband under his sheets.

Chapter Twenty-nine

Penny felt the end drawing near very much the way a farmer knows when the weather will soon turn against him. There was a calm in the center of things, perhaps, but in the periphery she could see the top branches of the trees bending to oncoming winds. And, like any storm worth even half its salt, this one was going to be a crop eater.

Weather like that was to be weathered, she'd always thought. If it was going to rain, all a person could do was roll up the windows and wait it out. But what if it was pouring inside your house? Penny's grandmother loved the word *doozy*. Everything had the potential to be a doozy. That shot with the ball into the apple basket was some doozy of a throw. That penny sale at the five-and-dime was some doozy. This thing is going to be a doozy all right, Nana, a real doozy.

Penny racked her brains for a way to fix it all, to turn around and go back to square one. Hop, hop, hop. We're back at the start. "Do-over!" they'd screamed as children when the ball struck Mrs. McKeegan's old hound lying in the middle of their field. "Do-over! Dumb dog in the way!" They'd yell four ways from Sunday, trying to get the Maltese, Pillbox, to move. Someone would drag the little dog out of the baseline and the play would be redone with at least three more shots available before he'd lumber back smack in the middle of the action. "He really is a pill!" they'd cry. Penny wasn't sure if she could relate more to the batter, interfered with in the middle of a game, or the dog, stupid and somehow sleeping in between the action. She just knew she needed a "do-over" something awful.

If she could just go back and rework the deal—not agree to anything, or choose something different—she was sure things would turn out better. The exact agreement she made on the bridge remained sketchy in her mind, fleeting around her conscious thought like a naughty child in the woods, occasionally stopping to stick a tongue out at her or taunt her with half of one image or a sliver of another.

She'd agreed to use this gift to heal people and to get out some sort of positive message to the world. In exchange, something would be taken from her. No, her mind corrected, she'd agreed to give something up, something precious. That's as far as her memories allowed her. At that point in the flow chart of her consciousness there was a gate up. She just couldn't make out the details, although that, too, was a lie her mind told her. At that point she would turn away. She couldn't look. Whatever it was had to change. The fee would have to be paid in some other way. Surely things could be renegotiated.

It was good that the porch wrapped around the old house. She'd left through the front door but scurried to the back and down into the crowd, somewhat less dense there. On her knees quickly, she'd blended in, unable to be distinguished from the rest. Heads popped up and down trying to spot the person who'd come from the house. It was easy to kneel there for a spell. Her plans had been to duck down and reclaim a temporary anonymity so she could work her way down the mountain. Instead she took advantage of a moment off, listening to the people around her. Mostly they were quiet, but some chanted under their breath and others read the small white book she'd seen on the news, their bottoms up in the air and their arms encircling it under their downturned foreheads. Despite a peacefulness at being surrounded by so many focused, loyal bodies, Penny was struck by the terrible irony of seemingly praying to herself. A low chuckle threatened to break out and it took all of her energy to hold it in. Of course, it was like being in a library and knowing that noise was absolutely forbidden. Penny never found anything funnier. Hal often went to golf matches himself. Just the sight of the rectangular signs saying QUIET! in old-fashioned lettering sent her into peals of laughter. She wondered what the hell was wrong with her even as her body shook with repressed giggles. *Obviously,* she concluded, *I've gone over the edge. Not just peering over the cliff but completely off and careening to the rocks below.*

But there wasn't even a question in her mind about turning around and slinking away. Her plan was clear and it seemed the only reasonable one, despite an unquestionable understanding that the neurons supporting her sanity were becoming a bit stretched out. Giggle. Someone off to her left turned and looked her way, annoyed at her insolence. She took her sacrilegious self down a few rows, and when she was sure she was unpegged as a member of the house, she took to the road, making her way to the camp. The buzz of the people around her was ubiquitous now, much in the way the hum of a row of fluorescent lights goes unnoticed by the owner of the room they illuminate. If she stopped she could hear them all and pick each one apart to study individually. Instead she let it run through her, paying no mind.

It was the coffins she was looking for, and at first she almost missed them. The camp with its myriad tents was so engaging, she let herself be sidetracked to wander from station to station. The people in sheets had created a whole city, and Penny was astounded at its detail, its completeness in servicing the followers' needs. Lunch was being served in the mess hall, a vegetarian split pea soup with a side serving of pita triangles. Penny got in line. Their tiredness and excitement wafted to her much in the same way as the aroma of the soup. They were on the heartbeat of something, something modern. They were working toward a cause, and the togetherness they felt was so strong, Penny thought it was almost in the realm of terrifying.

A woman behind her spoke to a mate: "Where are you stationed?"

A rustle of paper before his reply: "I'm up at the Healer's cottage."

"Guarding or praying?" she asked.

"Praying," he replied. "But I'll work my way up to the third line. I'm big enough to help out if there's a problem."

"What will you pray for?" she asked, and again there was a rustling of paper. Penny turned to see.

The man consulted the back of his assignment sheet. "The health of the Mother Healer."

"Oh, yes," the woman said, gravely serious. "That's a good one." They nodded in agreement, walking past Penny to retrieve their plastic utensils.

Penny picked up a spork, then absently set it down, suddenly losing her appetite. A man behind her was impatient. "If you're not going to eat, get out to the gate: They need reinforcements," he said to her.

"Reinforcements for what?" Penny asked.

"To keep out the crowd." He looked at her as though she'd spoken Chinese.

"Why doesn't the Mother Healer just come and heal the crowd so they can go back to their lives?" she asked.

"The Mother Healer heals as she sees fit. There's no

questioning the Mother Healer. Who are you? Where's your assignment sheet?" Obviously this woman hadn't read *The White Book*.

Penny put her tray down and headed for the exit.

"Guards!" the man shouted behind her. "Reporter!" his screaming insisted.

Penny pulled her sheet over her nose and mouth, pinning it as she went. If she ran she would stand out. A flurry of movement worked its way past her as she ducked into the medical tent. Cots lined either side of one long, high room. There were more sheets on the people walking around than on the beds, Penny thought, and immediately had to suppress another round of not-altogether-healthy laughter. It wasn't difficult when she saw who they were tending to. About a half dozen people had been crushed earlier in the day by a surge of excited followers. They'd run ahead suddenly at the rumor that the Mother Healer had come down. Not long after, another handful had been stampeded outside the gate when the sick had rushed it. They'd been plucked over to the camp side, the last to be accommodated in this way. Orders were that anyone not already inside the perimeter of the fence stayed out. As it was, if any of these people got better, as doubtful as that was, they'd be thrown right back over, never mind what happened to them when they landed.

Attendants scurried about, holding hands and giving drinks of water to their patients. Dressings were replaced and iodine dispensed, but Penny noted the patients didn't seem to be receiving any real medical treatment. The absence of IV bottles especially bothered her, particularly in conjunction with the injuries they'd sustained. One man's leg was positively crushed. It had a cartoonish flatness about it that made Penny feel woozy with empathy. The amount of pain he was in filled up the entire room and shot out of the tent in silent screams. He moaned and thrashed, and Penny could feel the infection building up inside of him.

She went up to one of the medical team, a woman follower with a red cross tied to her right arm. "Is there a doctor coming for these people?"

The woman stopped in her tracks and, much like the man in the mess hall, looked at her as though she'd grown another head. "What are you talking about?" the woman asked.

"These people need medical attention. Aren't any of the followers doctors as well?" Penny didn't wait for a reply. "Where are they? Are they coming?"

The woman turned and ran down the center aisle of cots, and at first Penny assumed she was getting the guards. *I can break my own record on how fast I get thrown out of here,* she thought. Before she could turn to run out the way she'd come in, the woman returned with *The White Book* and was flipping through its pages furiously. It appeared considerably larger than the version she'd seen hawked on television not two hours earlier. The woman stopped at a section titled, "The Great Healing," an account of what had happened at the hospital. She smiled, then flipped forward to a page headed "Requirements," under which the woman ran her finger down page after page, turning when she got to the end of each list. Finally she had what she'd been looking for and thrust the book at Penny, her finger cemented in place. "Number one hundred and forty-two," it read. "Have faith in the Great Mother to heal your ailments and iniquities. Wait patiently for Her grace; seek not the solutions of this world, but Her light only."

Oh, brother was all Penny could come up with. Capital *H*s even. Talk about a doozy. This was actually way beyond a real doozy, and she wished desperately for her Nana to be alive, if only to come up with a big enough word to cover this situation—though frankly Penny doubted there'd ever be a phrase for this. What had happened was a sort of religious kudzu that had wrapped itself around her. And the horns of the dilemma were that she could very well heal these poor crushed people, but if she did, she'd be perpetuating the myths that had already been spun and put into print. She might also lose her opportunity to seek the thing she'd really come for, and that was bigger than this dangerous little white book.

She nodded to the woman—Isaac's nod, she'd be disturbed to know. *Yes, I understand,* it said. "Of course," Penny verbalized, as if it made more sense than turkeys on Thanksgiving. The woman was terribly satisfied and went about her duties, slim and superficial as they were. Behind Penny, an elderly woman who'd had half of her face smashed in whistled her pain through the holes where her teeth had once been. At that very moment her two molars and a bicuspid were still being stepped on by the approaching masses a quarter of a mile away.

Both of the choices she had stung Penny. The woman's pain was so strong, so complete, it was all the elderly woman could manage to attend to with a brain pierced by shards of its own skull. *Fuck Zen chants,* thought Penny. *Nothing like physical torture to really focus a person.* She couldn't leave them like this. Yet, the thinking in *The White Book* was at odds with what she would try to do, what she thought this whole thing was about. "Shit, shit, shit," she murmured. Had Mother Teresa ever said *shit*? Probably not.

In the end Penny decided to flow as best as she could among the red crosses and play a quick form of duck, duck, goose with everyone she came into contact with, getting to be the coveted "goose." She was in the middle of the room before the lady with the restored cranial features began to shout, "She's here! She healed me! Mother Healer!"

The man whose leg was better than it had been before his accident joined her, yelling, "Yes! Yes! Yes!" as if he were having particularly good sex. Another patient, catching up to the others, added "She lives!" as her contribution to the frenzy.

Penny tried not to look back. There were only about eight more beds, four on either side of her, and most of the attendants were rushing toward the victorious screamers. She finished and got clear of the tent without being identified, but the jig was up, as they say, and her presence was noted in voices that were something on the order of town criers'.

"The Mother Healer is among us! She has healed our sick! The One is here!"

People were rushing around. Penny headed beyond the camp and its flustered inhabitants down toward the bottom of the mountain and found herself as floored by the fence, its pickets of the human variety, as Louis had been. *And to think Hal and I were choosing between wood and vinyl,* she mused. *How limited.* The word had already been passed that the Mother Healer was out and about. "She's at large," she heard one man say. Was she some sort of escaped zoo animal? There wasn't a doubt in her mind that requirement two hundred and something stated that the Mother Healer was to be protected (contained) at all times. The fence was told, and Penny thought she could see them squeezing even closer together, now not just to keep out the riffraff but to hold her in. Perhaps she'd go down as the slippery messiah.

Abandoned white copy paper floated around her feet: Sheets have no pockets, and one of the fence's assignment papers had blown away. *Human fence, row two, southside*, it said. *Good enough*, she thought, and adopted it.

"No one's to join the fence at this time," a man said as she approached.

"I got my assignment right here!" Penny said, trying to force annoyance into her voice. "No one in or out. No one's getting past me!" she almost screamed, holding the paper up to his face.

"All right. Get in quick!" Room was made for her, but instead of the second row, Penny edged over and up to the first. One step and she'd be beyond the protective shield of the followers. Her arms were linked and wrapped up tight with the people on either side of her. The determination they projected was fierce. They were ready to die for the cause. Hordes of people faced them, most sitting in the mossy dampness of the mountainside, waiting for her. When they heard the clamor of followers shouting that the Mother Healer had been sighted, the crowd rose to their feet, excited and desperate. They stood on tiptoe, trying to get a good glance beyond the fence. Some, ironically, looked her right in the eye before stretching up to see over.

The fury behind at the camp was more fuel for the fire that was already burning in front of her. The crowd pressed forward for the second time that day, having learned nothing from its earlier injuries. On this occasion, though, one of them inadvertently made contact with Penny, and the power surged through the crowd like electricity, healing everyone in its path. Too late, some onlookers grasped the line when Penny was already disconnected. The crowd pressed in again on the human fence, jarring and knocking it about. Much of the front line was forced apart like the tail end of a train off its track. Penny took the opportunity to let go of her neighbors and step out into the confusion of the crowd.

Chapter Thirty

Jetta recognized the last bubble of her life even as she now lived it. It was the final event that she'd seen before finding herself all alone in the place around the bridge. At the time she experienced that last bubble, she was confused and hadn't known what it was. The country path and the newly formed buds of the trees had come into focus in her dying mind's eye. In that near-death experience this was the final act, walking alongside Louis amid miles of white. It had made no sense to her at the time because, of course, she hadn't yet lived it. And now each step she took unfolded the memory in a chain of events that made perfect sense.

Louis came to seek her help. That was the spark that set off the fireworks, dull at first but picking up momentum with each movement. Louis's face framed under the triangle of the entrance to the tent was like a picture hung in the hallways of her mind, forgotten for a bit but now brought back to her. The snapshot of his long face was like a black-and-white photograph Jetta had already seen once and was destined to revisit. Perhaps, thought Jetta, more like a play in which the actor repeats his lines again, succinctly and with no deviation, show after show. She could not remember how the final scene ended but each line brought with it an "Oh yes, that's how it goes." It was eerie and unrelenting.

Daisy's expression made Jetta think there was something she'd forgotten, some piece of the equation she should have noticed. It was an itch that, when scratched, only became more demanding. Her mind searched for Daisy in the scheme of things. Why was the hair on the back of her neck standing up? Her emotions responded on call, but her mind refused to give up what it already knew. What was the ending? She probed and probed but could not make anything clear until it was near enough to touch and she was actually living the moment. *And what the hell good is that,* she thought bitterly. *I will twist my ankle now,* her memory told her, like tiny crumbs given out by a stingy heart. Looking down quickly, she sidestepped into Louis, trying to avoid the jagged rock she knew would upset her balance. In moving her foot over instead of missing it, she stepped directly on it and her leg rolled in just the right way to twist it awkwardly around in what was obviously the prescribed plan.

I will wind up on Louis, she knew, even as she watched him cartwheel over with the impact of Jetta's body. The ankle was completely out of commission; she didn't need to feel the bolts of pain running up and down her leg to know. Her foresight, or unfolding memory, was running three to four seconds ahead of things that happened to her—not nearly enough time to avoid any catastrophic event. And, according to the ankle experiment, changing the way things were going would be tricky if not impossible. Jetta was certain that things were going to have to be changed or avoided—thwarted, even. Yes, said her heart, filled with regret for something that hadn't even happened yet, something that had to be stopped. She was going to have only a few seconds to recognize the event and throw it off track. *And,* she thought, *on top of that, I can't even move around on my own now.*

Louis put one hand around her waist and she hopped alongside him.

"Maybe we should just rest for a second?" Louis suggested, pointing to a rock up the path where Jetta already knew they would stop. It was a few yards away, and Jetta remembered it would be surrounded by poison ivy.

"It's got poison ivy all around it," Jetta said. "Maybe we can sit somewhere else."

Louis stopped. "You can see that from here?" Louis was a city boy and, worse yet, an indoor city boy. It all looked the same to him. "We both have long pants on, and I don't see anywhere else for you in hopping distance."

If she could change the course of their events, perhaps she could shake it all loose again, like a puzzle broken up into unconnected individual pieces. Maybe they could reconstruct the order of things.

Jetta would die rather than sit on the rock and play out the vision of what was supposed to happen. She let go of Louis and plunked down on the road. There. For a second she couldn't see into the future, as myopic as her vision into it was. There was just the present, and she thought she'd won a victory. *Ha!* she cursed the gods of fate. *Take that!*

Behind them they heard a vehicle that sounded at first like a car and turned out to be a truck: It's grille took up the entire country pathway. Still moving, the truck beeped for Louis and Jetta to clear the way. It was in a terrible hurry. Louis scooped up Jetta and half dragged her out of the way and into the woods. They narrowly avoided getting hit.

"Well, we're probably in the poison ivy now anyway," he said, still pulling her up the hill. They were up on the rock before Jetta could turn around to see it. She was still looking at MACK branded across the back of the departing truck. Her bottom touched the rock, and she couldn't get off of it before Louis also sat next to her, as her memory told her he would.

"Damn!" Jetta screamed. "I told you I did not want to sit on this rock!"

Louis's eyes flew open wide. "I just saved your life! Don't bother with 'Thank you'!"

The memory of how this scene would play out began to flow again. She watched in her mind, Louis stomping off to the road and her hopping along from tree to tree, following him seconds before they did each of these things. Was there nothing she could do to set things on a different course?

"Louis, please!" she yelled when it was clear she could never catch up to him. She would have to apologize before he'd come back to her. No sense avoiding that. "I'm sorry, Louis!"

Stopping, he turned around and joined her again, his face flushed.

"You don't understand . . ." she began, but he stopped her.

"No, it's you who doesn't understand. Penny is in trouble. I think the man who tried to kill us is with her. I think he's going to ruin any chance she has of doing what she's meant to do. I don't think we have time to argue about which rock to sit on."

"Louis, please listen to me." Jetta sat down in the damp dirt. "I'm seeing into the future, a few seconds ahead of time." She gave him a minute to digest that. "It's all a memory from when I was dead and Penny brought me back." Louis stood, unresponsive. "I don't know how things will turn out, but I have a terrible feeling about it."

"So you only know what's going to happen a few seconds before it actually happens?"

Jetta waited for an expression of his disbelief, which never came. Penny had brought him back from the dead, and Jetta thought she could have told Louis little green men were running Washington and he'd have been open-minded about it. Then again, she would be, too, at this point. Nothing seemed beyond probability anymore.

"I'd like to try to change the way things go; maybe they'll turn out for the better."

"That's why you didn't want to sit on the rock? What does a rock have to do with Penny?"

God, he's a literal little man, she thought. "We're on a path with a bad ending. I'm trying to get us off of it and change what will happen."

Louis looked off in the distance as if trying to calculate some tremendous sum in his head. Time was running out and she wished he could absorb the unabsorbable a little more quickly. Although Louis's sponge appeared rather full at this time, he surprised her. "All right," he said simply.

" 'All right'? That's it?"

"Yes: all right. What more do you want? What should we do?"

"I don't know!"

Louis tapped his foot. Jetta's own throbbed in response.

"Let's head up to the cottage." *Think, think, think,* she said to herself. "When I see what's going to happen, we'll try to do something completely different to see if it changes the order of things."

"Well," said Louis, "how will you know until the end?"

"Maybe I'll stop feeling so scared. Maybe the hair all over my body will stop standing up. I won't have the taste of fear in my mouth."

That was good enough for Louis. Jetta wished she could have some time with Louis away from everything. A difference had settled over him since the last time they were together, and she wanted to know about it. Had he seen the bridge, too, when he died? Who stood around the bridge? Did everyone see it the same? She longed for a cup of coffee and a conversation with the man, the kind she enjoyed with each of her grandchildren. Every week those children were shining in wholly different ways, houses with additions being built around the base models. Talking with them over coffee, she waited to be invited in, how she wanted a tour of each wing of their lives. And they took her, telling her about the boy in study hall with the blue eyes staring at her over his geometry books. They debated their colleges with her and confided that their parents, whom they never saw as her children (she was on her grandchildren's side), were too strict and completely out of touch. Listening was her specialty, and when they were finished talking she told them each in turn how special they were, that they could do anything they wanted to if they worked hard. Each felt that clearly he or she was her favorite. She handed them money when their parents' backs were turned and told them to treat themselves to something good. She also told them to make her proud. They had.

Louis looked like someone who'd never had a proper grandparent. His eyes shifted back and forth the way her grandchildren's did when they had too much inside of them and needed someone to spill the beans to. Her children always said the kids came home from her house calmer and more content. "It's all the soda and candy I feed them," she'd joked. Not that she didn't in fact feed them junk: She'd given them hordes. More importantly, it was the information that leaked out between bites. They let the air out of their tires talking with her. Louis looked ready to pop.

But time was against them, and Jetta was sure the delay of her ankle would put them directly in the thick of the action by the time they reached the cottage with little or no time to spare. She had a vision of an old-fashioned dry-goods store like the one her neighbor Mr. Costwick had owned when she was a little girl. He held out a big glass jar in one hand and its giant cork stopper with the other. A label across the jar's front said TIME. "Sorry!"

Mr. Costwick said in his loud voice. "All out!" A canine had been missing from his upper right teeth, and eighty years later Jetta could still see his tongue bobbing and weaving behind his smile, as if it were trying to escape.

"A man is coming," Jetta said, shaking Mr. Costwick out of her mind and letting the bubble memory settle in his place. "We're going to talk to him."

Louis looked stricken. "How do we talk to him about something different from what we're supposed to talk to him about?"

Jetta rolled her eyes. "Let's try to get back into the woods so we can just avoid talking to him altogether."

Louis nodded. As they hobbled sideways, trying to find cover, Jetta added, "Let's try to keep things simple. This whole situation is confusing enough."

Before Louis could reply, a man appeared over the ridge they'd been heading for on the path, and as Louis peeked at him from behind a bushy evergreen, he was struck with the déjà vu of his dream of the turtle and the rabbit. He almost screamed, and his fears mixed with Jetta's as if by osmosis.

The man was moving along at a good clip. Other people in the white uniform of Penny's uncommissioned army passed here and there as well. Jetta's memories, like that of the rock, stopped offering themselves to her; and again she felt some hope that things could still be shaped differently, bent toward a better outcome.

Then the man stopped. He turned and looked around. The road was quiet for the moment, clear of all passersby but him. Scurrying into the woods, he headed directly toward Jetta and Louis. Louis, sharing sentiments with his dream self, felt like wetting his pants. As if he could read Louis's mind, the man came directly at their tree, looked around once more and pulled his sheet up over his pants, unzipped his fly and relieved his bladder right through the boughs of the evergreen they stood behind. Sprays of urine cascaded toward them.

Well, thought Jetta, *you can pee on me, but we're not talking to you,* because the vision clearly involved speaking to the man. But then Louis sneezed. *Fuck!* she thought.

"I'm allergic to pine," he whispered in apology.

"Who's there?" The peeing man doused his own feet in his hurry to put his robes back on. "Who's in the woods?" He walked around the tree and ran head-on into Jetta and Louis, who were trying to make a hasty retreat. Haste was no longer in Jetta's ankle's vocabulary.

"What are you two doing behind this tree?" the man demanded.

Jetta opened her mouth to order Louis not to respond, to absolutely not speak to the man under any condition, to just walk away and pretend they'd never heard him. Better yet, she wanted to scream to not even look at the man, to not make eye contact and under no circumstances to touch him!

"We were just going," Louis said quietly, and turned them away as quickly as he could.

Jetta put her face in her hands and cried. Her shoulders shook and she could feel the tears slipping through her fingers onto the ferns they would later crush when they walked on. All it did was bring the man back to them. He put his arm around Jetta.

"I'm sorry, Sister. I must have frightened you. I apolo—"

"Get away! Get away!" Jetta screamed, as she wished she had done before Louis had responded to the man, making their contact a conversation, albeit brief.

"For the love of the Mother Healer, get away from us! You are ruining everything!"

The man ran, sure that the woman was completely mad and praying that the Mother Healer would be able to restore the woman's senses. He had complete faith that she would.

Wailing, Jetta sank to the floor of the forest, studying the rainbow of stars that rose up in her sight at the pain in her leg. The ankle was broken, she decided.

"Well, it was somewhat different than your vision," Louis said. Jetta just cried.

"We didn't speak to the man on the road. Your vision, your memory of this event, is speaking to him on the road. That's something, isn't it?"

"It's nothing." Jetta was making no attempt to get up or get on with things.

"It's a departure from the plot," he insisted.

"It's nothing." And indeed, though he tried to convince her otherwise, Louis could also feel the weight of what was to come like a sack of bricks on his back.

"There must be something we can still do. We'll avoid the next vision."

Jetta thought for a moment, feeling the last grains of time as they were passing. The memory visions kept coming at her.

"All I see is you and me walking—or, rather, hobbling—up to the cottage. What is there to change about that?"

Louis couldn't fathom how they would make things different. He supposed they could turn around and go back down to the camp, but he had a feeling they'd end up at the cottage all the same. Louis decided that fate was a dirty player lobbing the ball over their heads when they came too close to the net. He helped Jetta stand and they made their way up the mountain as fast as they could.

Chapter Thirty-one

Penny stepped forward out of the protective line and into the crowd. People were running around her, frantically touching one person in white, then another and another, looking for that burst of electrical something that healed. They had felt it in their very cells, even if it hadn't helped them, even if they'd missed the moment. Reflexively they pushed the hair on their arms back down as they ran on around the circle of bodies trying to find her. She just stood, looking at the movement, feeling like a reporter who waits amid the fire as soldiers and civilians scurry about. Turning 360 degrees, she surveyed her situation. The human fence was proving to be a fickle border. The pressure of the crowd had it whipping back and forth in recurring S and C shapes that tried unsuccessfully to reform themselves into a strong O. Hands reaching across its vast gaps opened and closed, seeking out other links. The crowd poured in through the holes, injecting its sick and dying into the hygienic white of the encampment.

Penny stepped over duffel bags and around tents as she walked the perimeter of the hill. The shouting of the followers and the pleas of individuals seemed oddly far away to her, the way a boxing match might sound on a small television in some adjacent room. Individual human figures swarmed, unable to reunite as one body, and entire families held on to the sturdy pines, refusing to be plucked off and thrown out of the followers' camp. The phrase *sacred ground* floated along the air above the screams and begging, only to land on the discarded Styrofoam cups and tousled blankets. There was a blue camping chair, the collapsible kind with a cup holder on each arm that Penny had seen at her niece's soccer game. She'd desperately wanted two to keep in their trunk. The thought seemed foreign now, and she reached down to set the chair upright before moving on.

Amid the chaos of people, the lines of coffins stood out, stretched across the landscape in tight, quiet rows. Between the individual boxes was just enough space for someone to fit through, and indeed she saw the relative of each standing guard, encircling them or waiting beside them, a hand resting on the gleaming wood. Filth encrusted the sleeves and bottoms of their shirts, and even a hundred yards off she could see them absentmindedly brush off the crumbs of dirt that were no longer there. Mostly they were parents, and they treated the coffins as if they were the children themselves. For the first time Penny understood the whole idea of a coffin. She'd often wondered why people didn't bury their dead wrapped up in blankets or plain pinewood boxes. It went into the ground. It was covered in dirt and wasn't seen again. What was the point? It had always seemed like a colossal waste of money and a scam, with funeral directors playing the heartstrings of victims. The dead didn't know they were being laid out on ten thousand dollars the living didn't even have. Did they? There's Uncle Henry still on the credit card, fondly remembered through minimum monthly payments.

But Penny saw their hands now, brushing the lacquered tops and holding the brass handles, feeling the beveled corners rounded to an artistic perfection. If they could no longer hold their precious child, they would lay them out on silk, they would place their beautiful heads on soft pillows and cover their sweet bodies with the blankies they could not part with in life. Nothing could make closing the box any easier. It could only be made so that they didn't kill themselves in the process of saying good-bye to their child. Many still did anyway.

Penny was almost afraid to approach them. They were such a miserable lot. If everyone else projected their pains to her in loud highway signs of neon greens and yellows, these people's hurts were more akin to a tsunami in towering heights of skyscraper proportions. At fifty yards Penny fell to her knees and had to sit next to a tree to gather herself up against their despair. It could pull her under, and she cried for them, weeping into the sheets out loud until she could get ahold of herself. She wasn't even at all sure if that was possible. How in the hell did these people slug through their lives with such sadness? she wondered. And she wasn't even there to help them. She was ashamed before she even started.

First in line Penny could see Nathan Dobbs, a timid little man blinking out at the scene of confusion from behind a thick set of glasses that won the Coke bottle award if any pair ever did. His face was dirty, cleaned in streaks from tears that had come and gone almost unnoticed and unpredictable since he'd dug up his daughter's grave with the same shovel he and his ex-wife had used to plant their azaleas. Dead children were apparently a do-not-pass go, do-not-collect-$200, Go-directly-to-divorce situation. Her coffin was first in line, and that was probably the extent of poor Mr. Dobbs's luck. It was the smallest box on the mountain. Little Ashley was four when she died. Her father now raised an eyebrow, an involuntary response to the madness in the not-so-far distance. At the sound of the name Mother Healer, Penny could feel his hopefulness rise up, his heartbeat quicken.

"She's here! She's here!" they screamed up at the camp.

Nathan Dobbs flinched in spite of his increasing thirst for this dream to come true. The sound Nathan heard that morning, that morning to end all mornings, was also screaming. He wondered even now how he could have missed that it was the last morning he'd have with his daughter. Alexi, his ex-wife, his I-can-do-it-all, I'm-on-my-way-to-a-partnership-position-there-aren't-enough-high-powered-women-lawyers-you-know ex-wife, had already been at the office for hours when he woke up Ashley. As always, they were late. Ashley wanted to tell him a "Knock, knock" joke and he'd told her to be quiet and eat or she wouldn't be able to watch *CatDog* before they left for day care. Alexi had urged him to be a stay-at-home dad. "I am, after all, the primary breadwinner," she seemed to love to say. The idea alone made Nathan Dobbs feel as though he'd had a penisectomy with a castration chaser.

Ashley, with her four-year-old sense of humor, felt that Nathan was really missing out on something too hysterical to keep in. "Knock, knock, Daddy!"

"Ashley, please, we have to get moving."

"You're supposed to say 'Who's there?', silly!" she chastised, cornflakes leaking out onto her pink teddy T-shirt.

"Please eat, Ashley."

Nathan Dobbs had gotten a warning at All Ryder Insurance that if he continued to be so consistently late, he would find someone else at his desk one morning, someone of the security-guard type on a Here's-your-personal-effects-there's-the-door mission.

"I love you, Daddy." Ashley knew enough to know when Daddy was starting to look stressed, but four was four, after all. "It's orange!" she continued gleefully, ignoring the idea that a regulation "Knock, knock" joke needs two willing participants.

Nathan was washing out his breakfast dishes and trying to get their belongings somewhere close to the front door so that he'd only be fifteen minutes late as opposed to half an hour, and that was when the gremlin inside of him blinked on like that annoying flashing E-mail light that scared him every time it popped its annoying self onto his computer screen. "Meeting!" the little miscreant said in his head. "Meeting!" And Nathan Dobbs knew even fifteen minutes late was too late already. His boss and the boss's boss would be looking at his empty chair in the not-too-distant future.

"Shit!" he muttered, just as Ashley, still in the throes of her joke, proclaimed, "Orange you glad I didn't say *strawberry?*" and threw up her hands in happiness, giggling like an elf who'd had one too many and spilling her glass of milk in the process.

"Goddamn it, Ashley Marie!" he screamed. "Can't we ever get out of this fucking house on time!"

Ashley was crying, the joke forgotten and the milk embedded in the interstices of the cracked Mexican tile that was all the new rage and Alexi had just had to have. By the time they squealed out of the driveway, milk drying and smelling up the kitchen, Nathan's lunch forgotten on the counter, Ashley as red and puffy as an overripe tomato, Nathan thought he might just explode with anger. An old man was doing twenty-five in the forty-mile-an-hour zone on the one-lane road out to the highway, and when he turned at the light, Nathan saw his opportunity to make up some lost time. At the next red light he watched the opposing signal turn yellow and shot ahead, jumping the light, anticipating the green and fully expecting the oncoming SUV to yield to the yellow and slow to a halt. Nathan's car made it into the box of the intersection and just past the walkway. In the middle of the seconds it took for him to arrive there, Ashley, in the rear passenger side seat, was lined up perfectly to take on the grille of the SUV coming toward her at forty-five miles an hour. Not a stupid child, Ashley started screaming before the truck hit her and continued as her lower extremities were crushed and ripped off. She bled out as Nathan was trying to unbuckle what was left of her car seat. The car was sliced into two gaping sections.

"Knock, knock," she whispered as she went.

"Who's there?" he returned, and found only himself left. It was Nathan Dobbs's turn to scream.

If he could only have her back. If he could only try again. They'd only been able to bury half of her. That thought alone pushed all of the nerves in his body and felt as though an electric shock were running through his heart. He would make it up to her. He would be a stay-at-home Dad. It was all he wanted now. How could he have wanted that shameful job? If Ashley were back, he could do anything and with joy, and even the slightest chance that she could be back made his body shake. He wanted to tell her he loved her. He wanted to hold her.

Penny came toward him the way a veteran firefighter approaches a four-alarmer that has already been burning for hours. Louis had just been gone, not dead for months. There was something of a life force around him at the time, something she could grab on to. His body had been intact. This girl, this half a girl, had been dead long enough for her body to begin to decompose. She'd had to hold on to Louis. Would she be able to open a coffin and hold on to a bone or a piece of rotting flesh and bring it back as a whole? She'd gone after Louis in the place he'd sunk into and it had seemed a forever distance away. Of course, all of that didn't matter. If she could just get onto the bridge at all, she'd be accomplishing her goal. She had no hope of bringing anyone back with her. It had to be a child. Going to where Louis had ended up would be no help to her at all. She was betting that only an innocent life would be the closest guarantee of getting onto the bridge.

She was the only one in white this far away from the confusion. The area had cleared considerably with all able bodies rushing up to the place where others had received their healing. Only the most infirm were still planted where they'd been placed by relatives who'd run off without them. It was quiet here in the shadow of the greater activity up the mountain. They saw Penny approach from many yards away. Those who were sitting stood up. Some came around to the back of the coffin they'd brought so as not to be between her and it. Most stopped breathing. The line led down the mountain, and Penny saw that she couldn't count them. There were just too many, but their guardians were at attention, their sadness put tentatively in the wings, on hold for the briefest moment of anticipation. A slight wind picked up the ends of her robes and she let herself imagine it was propelling her forward into action.

Nathan Dobbs found he could not speak to her. He saw her steady walk and knew she was coming to him. And he was sure that if he moved even an inch, it would alter her course. He'd killed his own daughter and was so afraid of distracting the Mother Healer's attention from her casket, he was as frozen as if he'd been turned to stone on the spot. When she got close to the small coffin, she lifted her eyes and seemed to look through him, though she did not touch the box.

"It's okay," she whispered. "Breathe."

He choked in the air and for a second he felt sure he would collapse. Just when he thought the moment had passed, he was in her arms on the grass and he couldn't see anything, but his body tingled.

"You fainted," she explained.

"I can't see," he said, and added as an afterthought, "Everything is blurry."

He tried to look at her, but her face was just a swirl of indistinct peach with dark holes that he assumed were eyes. He began feeling around him for his glasses, which he figured must have fallen off when he hit the ground.

"No, no," the woman was saying—the woman he couldn't bring himself to call the Mother Healer because it would bring his hope to a dangerously high precipice. Surely he would fall off and shatter into a thousand pieces. It was what he expected. What she was saying made no sense at all.

"Take off your glasses," she said, and repeated it when he kept feeling around for them in the dirt. Finally she just reached out and plucked them off his face. The coffin bearers watched from their spots, always with a hand on their precious one's resting place as if it was a personal home base in a phenomenally morbid game of tag. Penny came into focus in front of Nathan Dobbs. He put his glasses back on out of sheer confusion. She was blurry again. The whole world seemed to be working in reverse.

"Your eyes are healed," she said to him, and put his glasses in a pocket hidden under a fold of her robes so he would stop putting them on.

"I don't know if I can help your daughter," she said, apologizing in advance for what she assumed would be a failure from his perspective.

Nathan Dobbs, blinking at her from perfect twenty-twenty vision, was still immobilized. He stood when she stood, but she expected she would get little else from the man. Should she open the coffin? she wondered again. Nathan had it resting on top of a child's cart, a sturdy updated model of the little red wagon Penny had pulled around herself as a kid. Barely bending, she was able to extend a hand and touch the top of the casket they'd told

Mr. Dobbs was called the Little Angel model. The edge was gilded in a soft gold, and Penny curled her fingers gently beneath it. It was all that was needed.

Pictures of Ashley exploded into Penny's mind, her short four years, her beautiful yellow hair and the one curl that graced her forehead. A home danced in front of her eyes, the small bed that had been the little girl's and the dolls that were at the tea party that now had no end. Fluffy the Bear would be there in the coffin, moldy and decaying right along with the body of the girl who was flashing like a star in Penny's thoughts. And then Penny felt herself gone. Rising above it all, she saw herself bent at the waist, face to the sky, hand clutching the shiny box. The mountain looked like an anthill with some very angry inhabitants. That was all irrelevant now; it was all fading.

The bridge was as supple as it had been when she first walked across it. It stayed in its forever foggy state and the lights seemed to be playing the same odd games. A haunting quietness continued to linger along its edges, but Penny was unmoved; this time, instead of heading back toward her loved ones and the life she knew, she took to the bridge and walked forward with a steady, heavy march. It was still a long-ass bridge, but Penny was a bigger person now. It hadn't taken her by surprise. She'd planned to take it by storm.

"Where are you now?" she yelled out, after walking what felt like the length of three football fields. She knew it was out there.

"I said, where are you?" Penny plodded forward, hoping to get to the bridge's end before she used up all of her energy. Everything looked exactly like the place on the bridge where she'd started out. Yes, she remembered its tricks. Formations of clouds drifted under her.

"I want to discuss the deal we made," she said, turning around, looking for signs of life. No response.

"I'm here to take it all back." She thought she heard a bird. It could have been in her own mind. "Nothing is coming of any of it."

The bridge, finally, seemed to widen and the clouds seemed less ominous, somehow lighter, and she kept moving, feeling as though she were walking up the down escalator or going the wrong way on a conveyor belt.

"Take me now." Penny was ready to stay and play out the end she thought she was originally meant for those few short days ago.

The bridge narrowed again as if running in some sort of linear loop. They would have to take her now. She could never make it back the way she had come. The bridge was too long. The timing of the trip seemed pressed and finite.

"I'm going to just keep on walking!" she shouted. "I'm not going back. I am not going to stop." The bridge seemed to care very little about her proclamations.

After what seemed to be miles and miles, Penny finally stopped and sat down on its receptive sponginess. She'd been so sure someone would respond and take her or answer her questions. A desire to end the whole experience was overwhelming, and she couldn't be sure if that was just the environment or an understanding that without her whatever plan was in place would fizzle. If she was the catalyst, then without her there'd be no reaction. Obviously, though, the powers that be would rather let her walk this bridge for eternity than let her rest in peace. She pulled upright again. An image of Nathan Dobbs's little girl came into her thoughts.

"Ashley Marie Dobbs!" and this time she positively screamed instead of politely yelling. She would literally wake the dead if she had to in order to break this deal. Up ahead, something looked different, and she went toward it.

"*Ashley Marie Dobbs!*" Penny's voice box projected across the vastness of the place where she stood, and she could finally see the first step off of the mammoth stretch of bridge and the crowd that stood there. They waited patiently as if they were expecting her.

Penny ran the last few yards, sure now that her plan was the right one. She would be absorbed into the hereafter and the craziness would end on earth. Perhaps she would become some sort of legend and they would create holidays for her. The humor in that was astounding. It would be a long time before she saw her children again, but they could live long, healthy, normal lives. They could have lives that involved Girl Scouts and soccer, bake sales and proms. Hal would remarry. Hell, he'd practically left her already. This was best for everyone. The key to finding the door was Ashley, but now Penny would just join her. Three more steps and she could almost touch the little girl in the crowd. A twinge of sorrow passed through her for Nathan Dobbs, and she thought of him as she put one foot up and forward to step into the crowd on the other side of the bridge.

Chapter Thirty-two

Penny felt the figure standing with her on the bridge before she saw it, the same one who'd bargained her out of everything the first time she was there. Hal had asked if it was God. What Penny hadn't said was she hoped it wasn't God. Now it stood between her and the incline leading to the other side, to whatever was beyond the bridge.

Her physical body tugged at her the way it had before. Concentration was needed to stay so far across this distance from it, and she tried to mentally dig in her heels. The figure waited for her. She studied it this time, her final footstep into the beyond thwarted and her mind turned toward it, trying to get a reading, a feel for what it was.

"You are blocking my bridge again," it said, just a mass of light, an unformed shape with no face.

In trying to read it with that extra sense, she could feel only herself, her own insides. Reaching out to it, she got an odd image of an earring. It was an earring she knew very well, one she'd lost a very long time ago. The teardrop shape was outlined in her mind, beautiful tiny dried flowers encased within it. She still had it in her jewelry box somewhere. It was one of a pair that she'd usually worn when spending time with one of her oldest friends, Flori, whom she'd grown up and gone all through school with. Penny often melded into the people around her, picking up accents an easy five minutes after talking with them. Hal always knew who she was talking to on the phone. She mimicked their speech patterns, unconsciously becoming them when they spoke. The earrings with their flowers reminded her of nature and were a little louder with their long, dangling bright yellow background than Penny was accustomed to. But she always picked them to wear when she saw Flori, a vegetarian with an interest in nature and a bubbling wild side wrapped in a peasant skirt. Hal teased her, "When in Rome . . ." as she left to meet Flori at this alternative bookstore or that meditation center. Flori breathed life into Penny with her colorful ideas and her intense style of listening. When Flori's husband Mike felt her ideas had become just a bit too out there for his taste, they split, and Penny and Hal got Mike in the divorce. Penny lost Flori. There were days she'd hunt through the jewelry box and pull out the earrings, looking for some trace of Flori she could still hold. On one of those occasions she'd only found a single earring and was stricken over the loss of its mate. The whole family had searched the house, but it was gone. Here she was, like some sort of paranormal psychic being given visions of a symbol she'd seen on late-night TV when she was up feeding the babies. "I see a gray fedora," the psychic would say, hand planted against his forehead. "Yes! Yes! That was my father's hat," the audience member would scream.

The remaining earring symbolized a piece of her heart that was gone, one of the best friends she'd ever had and the hole that would always be there without her. Penny thought that her vision reflected the tone of the bridge. The bridge, instead of being guarded by wild dogs, was protected by this overwhelming feeling of what was lost by those who walked over it and on to whatever came next. It held them in check, a powerful unseen string jerking them back toward the living.

"I've already lost much more than that," she told the figure. "Do you think the idea of that one earring is going to convince me to return and play out this horror story?"

The figure stood silent, and Penny couldn't tell if she'd won any ground.

"I'm ending things here. I'm bowing out. I've given all I'm willing to give."

"Do you think you have any say in the order of things?"

"I know you can't finish this up without me."

Penny noticed that the group on the ground beyond the bridge was getting larger. They were silent and she couldn't feel any part of them at all. It was as though she were looking at a billboard rather than real people.

"The first time I was here I should have gone forward and on to wherever I was meant to go. I should have accepted that it was my time to die instead of agreeing to go back."

The group in front of her pressed forward, but Penny saw that they could not advance beyond a certain point. They had their hands up, ready to touch her.

The figure shimmered and stretched, looking as though it were trying to digest Penny's ideas and having some trouble.

"Things are in motion."

"Are you saying I can't change what's happening? I was shown different scenarios. That means it all could go different ways."

"Things are in motion," it repeated, as if she hadn't heard.

"It has to stop," Penny insisted.

"It's for the good of the many," the figure said, looking up and past her.

Penny felt weak enough to be pulled backward. Her strength and hold on the bridge were slipping. Stubbornly she held on to the idea that nothing could be completed without her. Even as the thought passed through her mind, it felt wrong. People began to be healed before she was conscious. And now it was almost physically impossible for her not to heal someone. The gift had grown into a need frighteningly close to an addiction of some sort. As long as she could feel their pain, she would have to help, and it was becoming as second nature to her as the need to breathe. Her final plan was a good one: It was clear and felt right.

Before she could be dragged backward even one more inch, Penny collected her strength and ran. She was up to and around the figure faster than she ever could have imagined, hurling herself forward with her arms flailing around with the fury of her resolve. The group watched as she hit whatever separated them and slipped onto the floor of the bridge. Standing up, she reached out to touch the barrier and found it to be a clear membrane, supple but strong. Pushing against it created a small wake of motion but little else. The group all had their palms resting on the wall, fingers splayed, waiting for her. A last-ditch effort to get another running start by stepping back a few paces was also a failure. The group didn't flinch when she slammed into the barrier and fell backward again. The figure seemed unconcerned and had even stepped aside to make way for her. This time Penny stayed down and wept, facing the idea that she would not be allowed to rest in that place. It had been her last plan, her final idea.

Perhaps she could achieve it differently. She now thought of returning back down to the mountain and stepping in front of a bus. Why hadn't she done that in the first place? Of course, part of her held out the hope that she could somehow renegotiate things and get her life back. She turned to go and found the figure in front of her again, this time blocking her retreat. It sent her a recurring image of herself at the bottom of her mountain, stepping out onto the highway in front of an eighteen-wheeler going seventy. The driver, three months away from retirement, his eight grandchildren's pictures taped to his sun visor, pulled the wheel with a hard left and hopped the divider into oncoming traffic to avoid hitting her. Six cars would flatten themselves into his cab, and everyone involved would die. Penny would be the only one unscathed, left standing in the road to watch. Guns would jam. Pills would be thrown up. Everything she could imagine was unsuccessful, including a vision of jumping off a cliff where she would get her shirt stuck on a jutting limb and eventually be rescued. Building windows would be stuck, roof doors locked. The only idiot, she thought, who can't kill herself. Wasn't that one of the constitutional rights? The right to off yourself? The figure threw her the results of each of her scenarios. This was *his* bridge. Penny was tiring. Her body could no longer endure the stress of being separated from its essence and tugged at her to return. She turned to go, defeated.

The figure again blocked her way, and for a moment Penny thought he would let her pass on, count her losses and move forward. For a second she thought she'd won. He was letting her through after all. She thought that the world had learned enough in the last twenty-four hours to move itself onto whatever right track was necessary, that her own unfortunate circumstances had been the pebble under its wheel and that it would veer in the best possible direction. She held out a hope that her own small family, insignificant in terms of the population of the world, might somehow be spared. Why did there always have to be a sacrifice?

The figure made the light and shadows of its outline create an arm pointing her back to the crowd beyond the barrier, and Penny happily marched over, letting her hopes have their way with her. Again, though, she could not make her way through. Now she knew what it wanted from her, and selfishly she did not want to grant it. Why should she save these people? Their families would be so happy to see them emerge. They could regain their lives and what had been lost to them. They could rebuild and re-create. Their sorrow, so brutally intense, would multiply their joy exponentially. The idea of it all dragged on her, like a woman who'd miscarried sitting at her best friend's baby shower.

She would take them back, of course. She almost had to now, with this hardwired need to heal pulsing through her, looking for a fix. Now it would take some kind of intestinal fortitude to turn away from giving out the gift she had, and the energy she was expending to hold herself there was almost gone. She just couldn't resist. It was as easy as any of it had been. Their hands, splayed like so many starfish against the clear membrane, met her own, matching them finger for finger on her side. Instead of letting her in, it brought them out one by one until she could hear them with that funny ear inside of her.

Soon they were all there on her side of the bridge, and the place beyond the bridge had become an empty walkway. Penny was surprised that there weren't more coming. Didn't more want to come back? It took her a moment to realize that these would be only the ones whose coffins were on the hill. She stopped and gazed down the pathway, wondering what lay beyond it and feeling cheated out of the ultimate escape. And although Penny accepted that things were in motion, as the figure said—perhaps one distinct forward motion—she held out a hope that within that framework she might still find some happiness for her family.

The bridge was rolling under Penny's feet, an ocean picking up a passing wave, and when she turned around she saw Ashley jumping up and down.

"Can we go now?" she asked Penny, an impatient four-year-old even in the hereafter.

The group set forth, following Penny, who held the little girl's hand. "What was it like in heaven?" Penny asked her.

"Heaven?" Ashley asked.

"The place where you just were. What was it like?" Penny felt almost desperate to know.

Ashley scrunched up her face in thought and looked warily at Penny as if she doubted Penny's ability to understand.

One of the group, a young man, came close to Penny. "It's fading now, my memory of it."

Penny stopped. "Please think: What was there?"

The man hemmed and hawed as Ashley had done, his head bending from side to side. "It's gone now. I'm sorry."

"But it must be a good place to be," Penny said, almost to herself. The others around her nodded.

"So then why would you want to go back with me? That doesn't make any sense."

"Unfinished business?" volunteered one woman. "That just seems to make sense to me."

"What kind of unfinished business?"

"I'm not at all sure," the woman replied, and it was all Penny could get out of her.

They started forward again and Penny felt terribly dissatisfied with what she'd learned, which was just about nothing. She'd changed nothing as well.

"Were all of you religious?" she asked as they walked, more quickly now as they got closer to the beginning again.

"*I* was," a few of them answered.

"Not especially," said a couple of others.

"You must all have done something good to have gotten into heaven," Penny insisted.

They looked at her as if they couldn't for the life of them pinpoint what that could possibly have been. It was all extremely unhelpful. If Penny couldn't cut her own life short to end the madness, she was hoping at least to learn something to pass on. If people listened to her message, maybe that would be a positive way to make things calm down. Perhaps she could give them what they needed and be done. John Q. Public seemed to be listening to everything that had her name attached to it. If it came directly from her lips, maybe it would be enough. But what would she tell them?

They continued to walk, and the farther along they went, the more Penny could feel their confusion. "Where are we?" asked the same man who'd tried to recall heaven.

"Where's Daddy?" Ashley wanted to know. "Where's the big car that wanted to run us over?"

"It's okay," Penny assured her. "We're going to meet Daddy now."

And then they were back on the threshold, Penny feeling not at all the wiser for the trip. The crowd that had gathered competed well with the one that had met her there the first time. This time, though, she recognized some of the faces as the unfortunates gathered around the mountain. Some were dying; others were injured in one way or another, a piece of themselves somehow up here waiting for her. Penny laughed at herself for trying to make sense of any of it. They parted to make a path for her, as she expected they would. "Hold hands, everyone," she told her little group. "Stay together or I'll lose you."

Holding one hand out, she brushed up against each of the waiting bodies as she moved forward, as much like the little girl with a stick on the picket fence as she'd been the week before. The crowd collapsed in on itself behind her.

The entire crowd followed, a celestial parade marching back toward the living, and they were all whole in every conceivable way. In the next instant she felt herself horizontal, her eyes snapping open, a patch of blue sky winking through an old maple tree. A root lay under her and her back felt as though it had nearly been broken. Gingerly she lifted herself up onto her elbows and tried to get her tired eyes to focus. It seemed as though nothing had happened. Nathan Dobbs was staring at her, and his compatriots still looked as if their hands had been Krazy Glued to the coffins. They all stared at her. Obviously she'd failed. How long had she been on the floor? Where were they? Under her breath, so that only poor Mr. Dobbs could hear, she breathed the words "Come out."

Almost with the practiced timing of Olympic synchronized swimmers, the lids opened, beginning with Ashley's, and down the line around the mountain and through the makeshift town that now surrounded it. Those who watched Penny go into what they would later describe as a trance hoped for something to happen, even if they didn't quite believe it would. Others, miles down the road, may have been talking to a neighbor or helping out an injured party next to them. Some had even fallen asleep. There were more fainting spells and exclamations, happy though they were, of "Shit!" at the bottom of the mountain than at the top, but all were shocked.

Nathan Dobbs lifted his newly whole daughter out of that confining box, the silk and ten layers of lacquer now seen for the horror they were. He touched her as though he might break her into a thousand pieces if he moved the wrong way. He sobbed loudly, the way men are not supposed to, and his daughter said, "It's okay, Daddy."

"I'm so, so sorry, Ash. Daddy is so sorry. I'm gonna make it up to you, honey. Daddy is going to love you up."

Ashley was hugging her father and laughing. "Hey, Daddy!" She patted his wet cheek. "Knock, knock, Daddy." But Nathan Dobbs was crying too hard to answer.

Ashley Marie Dobbs forged ahead anyway: "Orange you glad I didn't say *banana?*" She was still laughing when her father reached past her and pushed the tiny coffin off of the little red wagon. He seemed to consider for a moment putting his daughter in the wagon to pull her, but decided instead to hold her with one arm that now seemed so incredibly strong. The wagon trailed after them as they made their way through the reunions. People were crying and some even threw up in the emotional upheaval of the moment. Nathan and Ashley didn't notice. They were telling each other "Knock, knock" jokes all the way down the mountain. Nathan turned briefly a few feet down the path, looked around for Penny to say thank you and felt a twinge of guilt for not thinking of it earlier.

Penny was already gone, searching for the media and comparing them in her mind to red lights when you're trying to eat breakfast while driving your car. There are never any around when you need them—except, of course, when you're late. She figured they couldn't be far off, especially now with all hell having broken loose. The sheets, as Penny thought of them, had lost control: Their barriers were now breached and their encampment swarming with invaders. There was no sign of the human fence, though the plants they'd trampled made clear lines in the earth, showing where it had once stood. Fewer people were crossing that line to go up the mountain than were stepping across it to come down. There were no more groups of the waiting sick. A mulberry bush stood off to one side, protected by a thicket of trees people had to go around instead of through. Penny settled herself there in front of it to watch the newly healed walk beside their families and to see the risen dead resume their place in life. It was small comfort, but it was something, and it was easy to linger there for one brief moment before everything rolled forward.

Chapter Thirty-three

Daisy's goal was to suffocate Isaac's plans. She imagined herself a large wool blanket like the one that hung in a steel cylinder inside her grandmother's kitchen so many years ago, stolen from some old tenement building and designed to snuff out fires. In her anger it had slipped her mind that she'd opened that cylinder when her grandmother had finally passed away. Having dwelled on it for close to a decade, it had become in her imagination almost too heavy to carry, probably gray and a sure bet on putting out a small blaze. Yet, when she opened it to finally match the reality with the image in her mind, she'd been taken aback to find a thin polyester square lined around the perimeter with a cheap satin and plagued with large holes. Moths had apparently dwelled on the blanket as well.

Daisy felt herself becoming that blanket—not the strong efficient one she dreamt about but the real one that was no help to anyone, frayed and eaten from the inside out. It was maddening. First, she had blundered allowing herself to feel secure in her role as Isaac's partner. Truly she'd believed they were full cohorts in the scams. He'd gotten her but good. It had taken him twenty years but the results were the same, and among the list of stolen property were all those years of her life.

She'd had to steal the gun, and it had turned out to be

no easy matter. Daisy was used to stealing from someone who was handing his property over on a silver platter. Stores liked to keep things locked up, and she'd earned a few gray hairs extracting the piece and its proper ammunition. That small operation was a success, and it gave her the adrenaline she'd needed to go at the bigger sting of isolating Isaac in a wall of people. It was her idea of a humorous, ironic twist to hold him fenced in with his favorite marks: ordinary gullible people.

Persuading the members of their little group that Penny was "the One" was relatively easy. The calls she had made to the groups they'd formed and still kept afloat were equally as successful. Daisy had her own small army, and their funds were at her disposal so fast, she thought for a moment that her head was actually spinning. Moving all of her people to box him in felt positively exhilarating, the way a dog must feel when he finally gets to take a big, satisfying chunk out of the mailman's ass.

She'd allowed Isaac—or whatever the hell he was calling himself now—no leeway in using Penny for any personal gain. He couldn't make any money holed up there; more than that, he couldn't have any say if she was controlling his environment. Daisy wanted the whole Mother Healer entourage to just fester up there until the world forgot about her and wrote off the whole mountain as some sort of crazy commune. The media would be sent away and no healing would occur, through mass hysteria or otherwise. Isolation would smother Isaac's newest meal ticket. It was a halfway decent plan as schemes go. It never even crossed Daisy's mind for a nanosecond that Penny could actually heal anyone. She wouldn't even consider the idea of a real healing a remote possibility. That gift was the wild card.

Daisy had had her hands on the gun when Jetta was in her tent, a shiny model designed to put holes in people big enough to fit an elephant's foot. A pillow would make an excellent silencer, considering how intense everyone had gotten around the camp. Dumping the body would have been child's play. The people in sheets—Daisy had to stifle a laugh—listened to everything she said. She'd found the one woman everyone on the planet had been looking for and delivered her to them. She'd tell the guards Jetta had shot herself in reverence to the Healer as a sort of sacrifice. It was shaky but she wasn't worried. They'd weigh her down and throw her in the lake, calling it a sacrificial water burial. The only thing that concerned her was that other sheets would get in the spirit of things and follow suit. She didn't want to start a trend. A high follower count—alive—kept things in motion, after all.

The pillow had been in her hand and she'd been backing up toward the gun's hiding place when Louis arrived. The dominoes fell quickly. Even as she was thinking how easy it would be to get rid of him and finish her business with this annoying Jetta, her people were bowing to him and refusing to follow orders. She was still reaching for the gun when the two impediments in her plan disappeared up the mountain. Daisy's mouth barely had time to fall open. When she did finally get her hands on the gun, she had no plan but to somehow quench the thirst of her anger for Isaac, and if Jetta and Louis went down with him, all the better.

Isaac had been isolated and kept at bay up until then, and if that situation was disintegrating, Daisy thought, then plan B would definitely have to involve something a little more drastic. The flap of her tent was open and she walked through it like a woman on her way to work, all focus and resolve. It was a quick ten-minute walk up to the Mother Healer's cottage—not enough time to cool Daisy off but just enough time for her to shoot the three of them very dead. Perhaps it would have been better if things fell out that way. Penny was already working her way through the encampment. Hal was up on the second floor of the cottage, packing all of their things to go, and Midge was tending to the children in the back living room. Jetta and Louis were lurking in the woods and just beginning to monkey with fate. Everyone was out of firing range. Isaac, on the steps, discussing with James whether to go hunt for Penny, would have been out in the open by the time she arrived. Daisy could have shot him dead right there and he could have been the only casualty.

But Daisy had only made it a few short strides forward when the cry of alarm rang out: "Guards! Reporter!" And Daisy thought, *This can't be happening.* They'd worked desperately all day extracting the media the way an owner pulls ticks out of his dog. If the entire event was going to fade anytime soon, the media had to get bored sitting around the periphery with nothing to report. Keeping out the camera crews had turned into a daylong job that required its own team and was the necessity that gave birth to the idea of the human fence. The newspeople had proven to be a formidable challenge, however. One man, from quite a high-profile broadcasting station, had been so persistent, he accidentally got himself killed in a struggle to keep him out. He was now hugging his camera at the bottom of the lake, reporting on the underwater life there, where Jetta should already have joined him, Daisy thought wryly. She wanted to just finish things with Isaac and leave this situation to play itself out. Perhaps she'd charge admission and build up her capital before retiring. Things could go wrong quickly with a reporter around, though, and she'd have to attend to that first.

Daisy oriented herself toward the commotion, tucking her revolver into her waistband and cursing her timing. The mess tent was just now being rushed. She came in the same side as the guards and, like them, found nothing.

"Where's the reporter?" Daisy asked.

"She got away," a woman answered.

"She?"

"Yes. It was a woman asking all sorts of questions. I assumed she was a reporter."

"Good job." She turned to the guards. "Make sure you get her."

The guards rushed out of the large tent and the follower turned to Daisy. "She obviously hadn't read *The White Book*. You'd think she'd have done some research."

Daisy was about to reply when she heard more screams, again off in the distance. "She's here! The Mother Healer is here!" On top of the incline she had a clear view of the medical tent, which was like a pregnant woman's swollen belly, her baby kicking a foot here, punching a fist there. The tent looked as though it might fall over with the pandemonium going on inside of it.

Getting a reporter out of camp was one thing, but what the hell was that woman doing down here? Daisy was infuriated with everyone's incompetence. Hundreds of people in this operation and they couldn't keep one middle-aged mother in one spot. This was no good at all. The more riled up everyone got, the more the staying power of this story. They had to get her back up to that decrepit little cottage. And how in God's name did they know it was her? It was probably some woman of the same age and build. *The White Book* clearly stated that the Mother Healer was to be left alone. Here they were all screaming. She waited for the tent to collapse. Idiots.

Penny had already made her exit when Daisy came down to the back of the tent with the intent of calming everyone down. The medical tent had been a stupid idea, she decided now. The sick could wait in line with everyone else. She would tell them the tent went against the teachings of the Mother Healer. They would dismantle it and carry the patients out to the other side of the fence. The movement inside was every bit as excited as it appeared from the outside. People were jumping up and down and holding each other. One older woman cried and repeated over and over, "She's healed me. I've been touched. She's healed me. I've been touched." A man held out a leg, and five or six of their "medics" ran their hands up and down it.

At first Daisy was inclined to think the whole section had gone hysterical. These were gullible, emotional people, after all. She rolled her eyes and figured they'd calm down eventually. What could she possibly say to their idea that they'd been healed? It was ridiculous and there was little to combat that line of thinking. She checked her gun, squeezing it in its hiding place, snug against her hip. This group will settle down. And what does it matter anyway, she figured. In a few minutes things would be over. Isaac, who'd clearly underestimated who he'd messed with this time, would be dead. It was the only thought that made her smile.

She turned for a second time to the path up the mountain, calm and sure of her next steps. It was still a good time, with a clear open shot at Isaac's heart. Out of the corner of her eye, though, Daisy saw the far-off inner layer of the "fence," and instead of standing still and solid, it appeared to be waving. It was so slight at this distance that she had to narrow her eyes to make it out. Something wasn't right. Their feet, hidden under the recesses of fabric, were peddling forward and backward, and the closer she got, the more she could see the strain on their faces as they tried to keep themselves hooked together.

Daisy was screaming for the guards when she detected an odd smell settling about the camp—a familiar smell. Her mind grappled in its cataloging system trying to give it a name. It wasn't fire, though her brain kept sending her that word. *Chemical spill* seemed to want to stay in her mind, and she guessed it was because the smell was so different, so new somehow. The closest she could come was lightning strike and the heavy ozone smell that followed it. The hair on her arms stood up straight and she figured she'd never gotten over her childhood fear of storms. But the sky when she looked up was a crystal-clear blue, and she threw that thought out her mental window. She didn't have time for this guessing-game crap. Probably someone had burned something in a fire at one of the camps below. That explained that.

Below, the fence had broken open. Daisy watched with horror as the guards tried to physically piece people back together. She saw them try to keep hold of the connection and lose terribly. The sick were pouring in toward her, the scene an oil-and-vinegar mixture of pure white and muddled colors. Rushing forward, Daisy hoped to do something to restore the order of things—though by what means exactly, she wasn't sure. She ran through the line, perhaps to yell at the sick to stay where they were, and somehow found a disturbing lack of waiting sick. Had they all rushed past her? Some were heading back down to the base of the mountain. What the hell was going on? Daisy stood watching, unable to piece any of it together within the framework of her belief system. Daisy could almost hear the fragile pieces of her mind taking on stress fractures, splintering up the middle in jagged lines.

The opening of the coffins was especially damaging. She could feel herself coming undone, and that was when she decided she'd been tricked at her own game. How else could each of the boxes have opened with such perfect timing as in some morose Broadway show? That was why all of the sick could walk away: They were actors. Isaac had beaten her at this. He'd used their hard-earned money to hire people to trick her. How many were in on it? Her whole encampment? Had he designed the Mother

Healer even while they were still together, behind her back? Yes, it was all making sense now. She watched the "families" next to the coffins and thought she could clearly tell who were the more seasoned actors. Daisy could almost admire Isaac for the grandness of his scheme, his ability to control thousands of people and take the media along for the ride. There should at least be some small acknowledgment that it was all for her, that it took such measures to bring her down.

But that, of course, was where the great Isaac was wrong. This whole situation may have gone afoul for her, but she had a small steel birdie in her pocket that told her it only took one pull of the trigger to pluck Isaac out of the sky. She sat down, leaning against a tree of her own, and watched the show. If it was all for her, she might as well enjoy it. She stroked the gun and breathed deeply, savoring this final act before she brought the curtains down. It was all going to be a joy. He'd wasted all of his energies for nothing. She would be the big winner.

Chapter Thirty-four

It had been a confusing day in the media. Make that a confusing week—from the first oddball reports of mass healings at the hospital, which were picked up by disreputable muckraking rags under the larger headings of Elvis sightings and UFO infiltrations, to a few short hours later, when an individual name emerged and editors of more mainstream news sources started weighing their reputations against what would surely end up as hollow sensationalism. A woman who can heal? A housewife? Oh, please. An easy call to ignore the thing, and certainly a comfortable fit in the boots of the notion that the media does make the news by deciding what is and what is not important. In the wee hours the bigwigs had decided, with great self-congratulation, not to add to the mass hysteria.

The whole thing was so persistent, though, and even multibillion-dollar industries have limits on what they can squash as not newsworthy. You can't have tens of thousands of people surround a hospital and leave as a group proclaiming to have been healed of every malady and write about the county fair instead. The little guys of the industry had taken up the slack quickly and run with the ball before the biggies could blink. There was less concern over having egg on their face. They had less to lose. So the major networks began to cover it, reluctantly, and weren't happy about it. Everybody likes a straightforward story swimming in verifiable facts. Photos are good. How do you record someone being healed? There had been lots of this sort of thing in the religious sector, and just as many follow-up investigations showing that Joe Blow in the wheelchair who walked after being touched on the forehead had no problem with his legs to begin with. *Scam, scam, scam* pulsed through the throbbing cranial arteries of the big boys who made the news. But it was not easily ignored. Every doctor and nurse went on record attesting to what had happened at Southlawn. They were giving out patient charts like candy at Halloween, and those documents were hard to refute. Everyone in the industry was swallowing a lot of coffee and antacids.

And then they were at the base of the mountain, a little late but definitely in the running. Their trucks and generous camera crews with their eighty miles of cable line displaced the local stations like whales in shallow water. Equipment- and exposure-wise, the four major networks and bigger cable stations outranked everyone, but getting up the mountain still turned out to be anybody's game. Tons of speculative reporting was already going on across the board, but mostly everyone wanted a piece of the Mother Healer herself. The followers, called by the news "sheets," had made that virtually impossible. Helicopters circled the mountaintop but had no landing sites. Visual coverage from an aerial perspective was all but completely blocked, thanks to the thick pines. The few who made it up before the human fence was erected were physically escorted out of the area, ending back at the base of the mountain on their asses. A buzz was going around about a midlevel guy who was actually missing. His bosses were questioning everyone, mostly looking for the $25,000 portable camera that had walked away with him.

In terms of actual news meat, it had been slim pickings

all morning. Not that the public wasn't glued to the live footage of the crowd camped at the base of Mt. Pleasant or the endless rows of coffins. If something is shown on television, it means something is probably going to happen, they reasoned, and the range of ideas of what could happen with those coffins was thrilling. They loved it, and all regular daytime shows were preempted with nary a complaint from any viewer. People in Australia were staying up all night watching the same tie-dyed Mother Healer shirt concession stand and array of trees defining the path up to her cottage. The people of Vatican City were behind closed doors with the sound turned down, but they were watching it just the same.

In this way the world had the opportunity to wet its pants collectively when the coffins began to open on live TV. "Shit!" was exclaimed in twenty-eight languages with a generous blend of "Oh, my God!" and "Come quickly!" to anyone unlucky enough to have averted their eyes to the action. After the original shock, much like Daisy, many people felt they must have been taken in. They watched with their mouths open and their brains scrambling to make it make sense. All they could see were the line of open boxes, and all they could hear was the families screaming and crying. A popular feed was one woman watching her husband climb out of the coffin in his nearly disintegrated pale blue Sunday suit (apparently the Mother Healer's abilities fell short with fabric). The world watched the blood run out of the wife's face and saw her throw up her breakfast. Those who were convinced it was all some sort of hoax admitted she was the best actress they had ever seen. How had she made herself turn pasty like that? That alone was worth an hour of talk radio speculation. The puking woman had her fifteen minutes of fame and a Hollywood contract offer by the end of the business day. Everyone wanted to talk to her.

This angle of dissecting the event, the way one would try to figure out how the magician had sawed and not sawed the woman in half, was simply more comfortable for people. It was certainly easier to digest, and it rolled forward as the theme not long after the last casket opened. Even in this light the handsome newscasters and nervous editors wanted the story, and when people began to stream down the mountain there was enough for all to feed on.

"Ma'am! Ma'am! Can I have a minute of your time?" Most people looked around as if no one could possibly be talking to them.

"Me?"

"Yes. Can you tell me why you're returning back down the mountain?"

Invariably there was a look of panic when the red recording light of a full-size television camera caught their eye. "I was healed."

The anchor would have to play dentist and pull some teeth. "What was wrong with you?"

After some squinting and a round of staring, one woman said, "I was blind."

"Come, now, you expect the world to believe you couldn't see and now you can?"

The woman handed the reporter a short walking stick. He looked at it, confused, and when he caught himself losing the upper hand, the woman pulled it away and extended it with three hard clicks heard even above the confusion. With the camera following her, she closed her eyes and skillfully walked among the crowd. Her other hand holding a neon-orange-collared and leather-harnessed German Shepherd by a metal halter added to her case. It was obvious the woman could maneuver her way to a lifeboat on the sinking *Titanic* without any visual cues. She opened her eyes, looked at the camera and smiled before giving the stick back to the reporter and walking away. They got a shot of her pausing to dismantle the steel handle from her dog. It then walked on a simple leash beside her, and they filmed them getting smaller and smaller in the distance until they were swallowed up by the crowd.

Some teams tried to make their way up the mountain, and while the followers were not physically preventing them, that particular direction was now also upstream, the tide of people walking down and against them. In the shuffle on the rough terrain, one cameraman ended up underneath his three hundred pounds of equipment. It was really no wonder, in the mixture of crowd and confusion and with the undertone of doubt at the roots of the story, that Penny's initial attempts to make contact with the media were unsuccessful. First she approached the network she watched most often just a week earlier but what seemed more like a lifetime ago.

"Excuse me," she said.

They were in the middle of talking to a man who insisted he'd regrown his leg, or had it healed, anyway.

"Either way you put it," the man was saying, "I came here with one leg and now I have two."

"Three, actually," his wife said from behind him, holding up a full-length prosthetic leg.

Instead of just straight interviewing, the reporter seemed to be arguing with the man. "That's just impossible. No one can grow back a limb. It's scientifically impossible."

"Apparently not," said the man, wiggling his naked toes. He had only one shoe but was wearing a three-martini-lunch kind of a smile.

"Shh!" an assistant told Penny. "Can't you see we're doing an interview?"

"Yes, but—"

"Look," said the assistant, "stick around and you can

tell us the story of your, um, experience. But it might be a while." He was ushering her over to a folding table manned by some other assistant apparently in charge of the paperwork. He took over where the first assistant left off. "You'll have to sign this disclosure form. It's a waiver of your right to privacy and enables us to show you or your likeness and whatever unfolds during the interview." He was reading from an index card.

"You don't understand," she began.

"I'm sorry, *you* don't understand. If you don't sign the form, we can't even breathe next to you with a camera."

"Okay," she said, picking up the paper and trying to read it and talk at the same time. "The thing is . . ." she tried.

"Just sign, ma'am. Do you want me to lose my job? I'm just an intern. I don't make the rules."

She signed Penny Chaney and handed the blasted thing back. "You see I'm the Mother Healer and I want—"

She was interrupted by the assistant's laughter. He actually snorted some of the coffee he'd been sipping out through his nose, which hurt, but didn't dampen his reaction. "That's a good one," he managed to get out before tearing her form in half and calling someone over to escort her away. With a large man on either side of her, she could hear the assistant, still chuckling and saying, "The Mother Healer. Ha. That's funny. Hey, Larry, I'm the pope! Want to interview me? I'm thinking up a new mortal sin!" The intern showed the paper around and got a lot of laughs about it. At the end of the day he would lose his job.

It went pretty much the same at the other major networks and a handful of cable news channels. Penny felt as if she were losing her time. She was anxious to get back up to the cottage. Her overwhelming need to heal was drained for now, but she could feel it trickling back like sand in an hourglass. Perhaps she would have to heal someone to get an interviewer to believe her. Nothing was easy. The smaller fish in the media ocean had been pushed off to the sides, and Penny went to work her way through those, hoping someone would put her on the air to say her piece. This time, though, she read them with that special sense during her approach, trying to feel them out to somehow determine who'd be most likely to believe her and want to help. Her face covering had come loose and she secured it again, trying to hold on to her anonymity.

A young looking man stood with a microphone in his hand, a camera trained on him like a hungry dog waiting for a treat. The reporter scanned the passersby, whose ranks were thinning. Some stations were packing to move up the hill. This particular team was trying to decide where it should go next. Penny waged a full frontal assault, getting right in the reporter's face.

"Please listen to me. I have tried all of the major networks and no one would believe me. I want to send a message out to the world. I am the Mother Healer, and if you don't believe me, some other sharp reporter will and you'll kick yourself for the rest of your natural life."

"Well, I . . ."

Penny held out her palm in a Stop-and-shut-up gesture. "Furthermore, I don't have a lot of time. I'll prove I am who I say I am if you want, but let's make it snappy."

Kevin Wood, indeed a very young reporter, closed his mouth and looked at the woman in front of him. He motioned with his index finger in small circles to his friend and cameraman, Bart Leezak, to roll the tape. The woman was probably just a crazy "sheet," but he could certainly do worse than a story about how this movement, possibly cult, throws people off the mental edge. Everyone was getting stories from the so-called healed. It would spice things up to do something different. It had been quite a long, boring wait with no fun powder to stick up his nose. His last hit had been four hours earlier and Kevin was starting to see some trembling in his hands. He'd been off in the truck, getting a little shot of some Jack D. to keep his head together, when the coffins opened up, and now he would be interviewing a crazy woman. *It's no wonder I drink,* he thought. Maybe he would join the family RV sales business, as his father wanted him to. There was more booze stashed in his father's office than could choke a cow. Out here in the field it was harder for a guy to do what he needed to do to keep up his spirits. He turned to start with the crazy lady but had to almost physically push down an image in his mind of five beautiful lines of coke.

"How do we know you're the real McCoy?"

Penny rolled her eyes and felt his addiction as if it were her own. "Do you have a knife?" she asked him.

Kevin laughed. "You're wrapped completely in sheets." He pulled on a tag sticking out under her arm. "The JCPenney white collection, to be exact." He raised his eyebrows for the camera. "You claim to be the most popular figure on television today, which is pretty unbelievable, and you want me to hand you a knife?"

The woman in front of him looked unshaken. "I don't want you to hand it to me. I want you to hold onto it yourself."

"And? . . ." Kevin's sarcasm dripped through the one-word question, and Penny now understood a little of what mental health patients feel.

"And I want you to cut yourself."

"Okay," Kevin said quickly. "That's it for you, lady. Have you lost your mind? What do you think this is? *Ripley's Believe It or*—"

"Do it," said a deep voice behind the camera.

"Have you lost your own mind, Leezak? Cut your own damn finger."

"And who the hell is going to film it, moron?" He poked his head up from behind the equipment. "I know," he said, matching Kevin's sarcasm, "we'll draw pictures of it all later."

"I'm not cutting myself." His mouth felt dry and his voice sounded more like a squeak. "Let's go get some of these people coming off of the mountain." He turned to go, but the microphone cable pulled him back and his teammate stood firm.

"Who are you, Wood? My grandmother?" *This guy is an albatross,* Bart thought. He knew about Kevin's drinking and recreational preferences and cursed the higher-ups for sticking him with this dummy. He threw a pocketknife at him, the kind with a thousand parts that fold out of it and no one ever actually uses.

Penny stood waiting and finally, after watching him fumble around with the knife, grabbed it from his hand and pulled out the blade. Kevin gasped out a small scream but took the knife when she handed it back to him, handle side forward. He acted as though she were giving him a rattlesnake.

"Just a tiny cut on one finger. You don't have to sever an artery, for Pete's sake." Penny was losing her patience.

Of course, after he cut it and squeezed it for the camera to get a good view of the blood, Penny reached out and put her hand on his shoulder and he was healed. The cameraman, Bart, watched through the eye of his lens and was truly amazed. He couldn't wait to do a slowed-down version of the footage to see the cut healed in each of its stages. It was too good to be true. All of these top-notch guys around, and he and Kevin had nabbed the Healer. Bart was seeing dollar signs all around him when he noticed how odd Kevin's reaction was. Kevin had gotten weepy and started to say in a tone Bart didn't recognize, "She healed me. I'm all better." The story of the century and his reporter was crying. Shit on a stick.

"I have footage of your finger, Kevin. Interview her!"

"No," he said. "You don't understand."

"I understand we have the award-winning story in our laps and you're crying like a baby."

Kevin turned to Penny. "Something's missing. A weight is off me. What is it?" After a minute he was able to put his finger on it, what it was that didn't have a choke hold on him anymore. "I don't feel like having a drink," he said. "I didn't know how strong the pull was until the rope was gone."

Penny smiled and put her arms around him, but only briefly. "It's only a start. You'll have to work to keep that particular demon away. I'm sorry, but I don't have a lot of time."

Kevin tried to pull himself together, wiping his face and holding his microphone more firmly. They forged ahead.

"This is Kevin Wood of WBAL. We're here at the foot of Mt. Pleasant with the Mother Healer herself." The camera studied her. "Tell us, how did this begin?" he asked. "Have you always had the ability to heal?"

"I don't have time to go into much detail. This only started when I was in the hospital. I was completely ordinary when it all began."

"Are you verifying the claims that you can bring people back from the dead?"

"I have a message for the world. Perhaps I'll have time for a full-fledged interview some other time. Things are happening fast and I want to make sure I reach people before everything spins out of control."

The camera now held only Penny, a simple face-forward head-on shot ready for a monologue, and Kevin stepped quietly out of the way, feeling what it was like not to be addicted for the first time in years.

"I was a housewife and a mother when this all started. There was nothing particularly special about me. I'm just like you. My husband, Hal, and I had the same dreams you all probably do. We wanted our children to be safe and healthy. We wished we had a new car and pictured ourselves in a bigger house some day. We were saving coins in a jar to go to Disney World when everyone was out of diapers." Penny laughed a small laugh as if she herself couldn't even believe what she was saying. Waiting at home for Hal to get home from work with Benny crying for a bottle, the girls coloring at their beat-up kitchen table and *Oprah* on the television seemed like a small piece of heaven, an unattainable paradise that she'd had without knowing it and was gone now, forever.

"And now here I am with this ability, this gift of healing other people, which has turned out to not be much of a gift for me or my family."

Kevin, having gotten his senses back somewhat, was already on a cell phone making sure his station was broadcasting them live and selling it for reproduction—before the bigger dogs got wind of it—noticed them only a few hundred yards away, and starting doing their own taping. Bart continued to train his camera on Penny. The mountain didn't seem to notice.

"I don't understand any of this," Penny continued. "When I died and before the doctors brought me back, I was told I would use this gift to change the world, to make it a better place. I don't think I've been especially successful at this. I can heal people's bodies but I'm not sure I know how to make people change their perspective and love each other more. If people are healed, are they more inclined to be kinder to others? I'm sorry I wasn't given more specific directions."

Penny paused, looking around, seeming to search her mind for what to say.

"I do know that I'm not a religion. I don't know who put together *The White Book*. It wasn't me. Please don't worship me. If you feel the urge for that, go back and recommit yourself to your own religion and listen to what it says. Seems like there's already plenty of organized religions to go around. And they have a lot of things in common: Love your neighbor. Pray to God. Do good things. Forgive the people in your life, even the idiots. Speak kindly. Maybe I was just sent as a reminder to all of that and the only way people would listen would be to get an extraordinary gift or see others getting that gift.

"Apparently, we're not all doing what we're supposed to do, and what we've become isn't at all what's expected of us. Go out and do something good. Or stay where you are and do something good. Rediscover your religion."

She stopped. After a few seconds she said, "And just keep that up."

She turned to Kevin. "Um, that's all I have to say."

Kevin had his eyebrows way down. "That's it?"

"What else do you want?" she asked.

"Well," he said out of the corner of his mouth, the tape still rolling. "Seems a little short."

"Short?"

"You're a profoundly famous healer. You can bring people back from the dead. I think people are looking to you to give us the secret to the world. The answers to the eternal questions."

"I just did," she said, and turned to walk back up the mountain.

Chapter Thirty-five

The final scene was a well-choreographed dance with players entering and exiting the stage as if on cue. The audience was the world, glued to their television sets, their necks craning around corners should they need to leave their living rooms to get something to eat, the volume turned up to its top setting when they needed to use the bathroom. Those without sets at work simply called in sick. WBAL, the golden child of the industry for the moment, was the first to televise the Mother Healer's message live, but the major stations paid dearly for the footage and were looping the tape. They ran it in a split-screen format, her message on audio with whatever live action there was running next to it. The news business dominated the tube almost entirely and was having an orgasm with each wild development. No one imagined it could get any better than it was, short of someone blowing up the whole mountain.

Showing the coffins opening had turned the world on its ear and rocked everyone's sense of equilibrium. Miracles were fine as long as they could live comfortably in the realm of folklore. "It's a sign," they proclaimed, though of what they couldn't exactly say. People were listening now. The Mother Healer had everyone's attention. Her spoken message was another thing.

A bar in Seattle had all of its overhead sets playing the

ongoing Mt. Pleasant saga. The sound was up to an obnoxious decibel and the jukebox, an antique Wurlitzer, was unplugged for the day. Closed captioning whipped past along the bottom of the screen, relaying every word anyone said. A man on one of the high stools wore a shirt that said HEAL THIS with an arrow pointing south.

"Hey, bud," he said to the bartender, "another one," and pushed forward his empty mug.

The barkeep looked at the man's T-shirt while he pulled at the draft handle. He pointed with his chin. "You don't buy any of this, eh?"

The man, three beers into his heavy drinking schedule for the day, looked down. "Oh, well." He wagged his head from side to side. "You can do anything on television. They can make it look like a UFO landed on top of the White House with their special-effects crap." He thought for a minute and shrugged. "But I don't know."

"It's a weird time," the bartender admitted.

And then Penny was facing the camera with her message for the first time. It was so short, it played through twice before anyone in Al's Pub said a word. For the moment patrons with an empty glass were shit out of luck, as they say.

"What the hell was that," the man in the mocking T-shirt asked, "the goddamned Girl Scout creed? What a hoot!"

The bartender laughed and the man drained his suds. "They almost had me going, too." He smiled. "I guess you can turn it off now."

"Who knows what they'll do next. I like a good show myself," the bartender said.

"Ah, I know when my leg's being pulled." The man slid off the high stool and went out the door. People went back to their conversations and someone tried to put a quarter in the jukebox. The volume of the multiple televisions was turned down a hair. The chain reaction of disbelief mimicked the opening coffins but traveled from home to home throughout the world.

Return to your religion? Anyone could come up with that. They threw pillows at their sets. The message looped and looped. They waited for further developments while they made fun of the Mother Healer and of themselves for starting to believe.

Kevin Wood and Bart Leezak would make them believe again through the only words the modern world understood. They beat out their competition for this last sensational piece to this story mostly by knowing which woman in white was the Mother Healer. The foot traffic had slowed down and the trek upward wasn't as difficult to make for their small, two-man team. The major networks were wrapping up their interviews and gathering up their lines of cable. The big fish would all be about two minutes too late.

Penny could feel them following her. She walked quickly now, pausing only to gaze into the eyes of the healed and to reach out to feel the mountain. Branches broke under her feet, and the thick pines seemed to be squeezing out the sun. It was an odd brand of fear that made her want to run and slow down at the same time, and when Penny saw the cottage for the last time, she was both sweating and cold. The little vacation house appeared deserted, the sheet people scattered down below in small groups, in disarray and without assignments for the moment. The sick had come and gone. It almost looked as it had the night they'd driven here when she'd still had some hope of how things would go. The minicamera crew gained on her and in the final stretch up the path Penny picked up speed, surprising them. She took the steps two at a time and ran around the porch to the back door, her sheets flapping in the wind she created with her movement. The door came open easily and she threw herself against it, immediately locking herself in. Inside the house she now ran from window to window, latching them closed and yanking down each shade. The front door was locked and she bolted it for good measure. Each movement she made echoed up and down the halls, and although Penny could feel all of their life signs humming through the house, it sounded with her ears as though she were all alone. The heartbeats of her three children pumped behind the closed door to her in-laws' bedroom. Midge was also in her own bedroom, packing. Slivers of Hal passed back and forth behind another almost-closed door of the bedroom they'd shared. Drawers opened and slammed shut. Penny crept up and could hear a zipper.

She stood on the threshold, waiting for Hal to slow down. "Hal?"

Hal continued packing, whirling around the room at a feverish pace. An oversize plastic bag proclaiming SAVINGS! lay on its side at the foot of the bed, a small plastic doll having fallen out.

"Hal, please,"

He stopped in his tracks and looked up at her. His hair lay limp across his forehead and his face was unshaven. "What have you done?" he asked her.

"Hal, we have to stay here. It's safe here."

"Safe?" Penny felt reasonably sure that if Hal weren't so exhausted, he would have lunged across the bed separating them and torn her apart.

"Safe?" he repeated. "Your so-called guards are gone." And then he spat out "Mother Healer."

"Hal, I made a promise to—"

"I don't care if you promised to mine cheese from the moon." Hal's voice climbed in time with the redness of his face. "What have you done to us?"

Penny opened her mouth, looking for an answer to fall out of it, one that would make any sense at all.

"This isn't normal!" he screamed at her.

"I can't argue with that, Hal. But, honey, you have to listen to me."

"Why should I listen to you? You just leave on your own and create this circus. It's fucking pandemonium out there."

"Hal, I'm sor—"

"And then"—he gulped in some air—"then I see you on television. You confirm that we're here and practically invite the entire free world to come to you. You have lost your mind."

Penny tried to interject but was unsuccessful.

"You could've gotten killed down there." His face scrunched up and Penny thought he would start to cry, but he was putting together as disgusted a face as he could. "Oh, I'm sorry, you could have just brought yourself back to life!"

"Hal, I thought I could—"

"You thought *nothing*!" A piece of plaster came down and landed in front of Penny. "You're not thinking of our safety, of your children's safety, of the fact that your children need you."

"What would you have me do?"

"Come with us and end this."

Penny didn't answer.

"You've saved thousands. Enough! You made a commitment when you married me. I'm calling in the marker."

"Hal, we have to stay here."

He looked at her for a long time. His eyebrows ran up to the top of his forehead, looking as if they were trying to hide. "You're crazy," he said in a quiet voice. "My God, this thing has driven you crazy."

"Hal, just one more night. I promise I'll come with you tomorrow. I feel that something bad is going to happen, Hal." Penny spoke as fast as she was able, desperate and hoping he would listen to her. She thought she had one more shot at making things work out, at pulling them all through this and being all right. But now Hal doubted her sanity.

"Hal, please. Just one more night. We'll keep the doors locked. We'll keep the shades closed and go to bed early. Please, Hal, I think we're all in a lot of danger."

"That's the only sane thing you've said for a week." Hal snorted. "We could already be gone. And safe! You wouldn't listen to me!" He turned his back on her and resumed his packing. "But you're well beyond that, aren't you? Shit, you can heal the sick. Why listen to anything I have to say? Who the hell am I, right?"

"It's not like that, Hal!"

"The hell it's not!" he screamed, and Penny could hear Benny crying.

"Just one night, Hal and I'll listen to anything you say. We'll go anywhere you want. I'll do anything you want."

"You've already shown me how you listen to my counsel. I have no faith in you anymore. Go tell it to the television, where they care."

Penny was crying, choking on her own tears. "Please, Hal. I'll stop healing. I'll walk away."

He hesitated, and for a second she thought that was it, she thought she'd won. She thought she'd be able to keep her family.

"Prove it by coming with me now."

"Just one more night here, Hal."

"That's what I thought. Good-bye, Penny."

"No!" It was Penny's turn to scream. "I think it would be safer tomorrow, Hal. Please."

"One day is not going to make a difference. This is not a normal life. I'm done."

Hal picked up the suitcases and threw them one by one down the staircase. A spindle broke free with the impact of the girls' pink rabbit bag, the one that said SOME BUNNY LOVES YOU! across the side. The crash of the pieces gave Penny an almost physical pain in her ears. Before Penny could absorb the swiftness of Hal's intended departure, he had Harvey and Mary's door open and the crying Benjamin in his arms. Each of the twins was wrapped around one of her in-laws and they were hurrying past, following the luggage down the stairs.

"Mom," she appealed to her mother-in-law, "I'll go too. Let me just hold one of the girls." She felt Mary's soupy Valium spirit bob past, her feet moving too quickly to turn around and respond to Penny.

"Hal, look, I'll go too," she pleaded. "Let me just hold Benny. Please, he'll stop crying. He needs me."

"Oh, now he needs you? How good of you to notice." Hal picked up speed.

Harvey stopped to pull a bottle out of the refrigerator and swing the baby bag over his shoulder.

"I said I'll come. Please. Let me hold him."

Hal whirled around, Benny's head snapping backward, making him let out a howl of protest. "You're not touching even one of these children until you're buckled in the car and we're off this wretched mountain." He pulled his arm around Benny so she couldn't even see him as Hal unlocked the front door and took one step forward to the outside world. The girls were crying and struggling to reach out to her as they bobbed down the front porch stairs. Penny raced after them.

"Mommy!" Lydia was crying.

Their truck, the one that had driven through the rainstorm to deliver Penny to the hospital, was off to the right, a good soldier turned double agent. What had brought her back to life in time was threatening to pull it all away in the end.

Penny followed them, trying to wrench off the sheets around her, which had turned stubborn and refused to give. Her eyes were trained on her children, their eyes as wide and frightened as her own, and Penny was sure that with the hood over her head she couldn't see them as well. There was a loud ripping sound as she tore at the fabric, which wouldn't let her go. Her headpiece hung off to one side and she worked at a safety pin under her arm while hopping after them and trying to drink in the faces of her children. If she couldn't touch them, she would caress them with her eyes.

"I love you," she shouted at them again and again. "Mommy loves you, Benny. I love you, Lydia. I love you, Julie!

"Please, Hal. Slow down," she yelled when her feet got caught in the sheets and she fell across the slate walkway. "I said I was coming. Please wait for me!" she yelled to the rapidly departing feet. The cameras taped everything: Penny falling to the ground. Penny trying to get to her knees, her white robes tangled around her and her front sopping with blood from her split lip.

In this drama of the speedy exit and almost comical chase, the cameras nearly missed the figure already behind the wheel of the truck. All six foot four of Isaac stepped out of the driver's side, grinning the smile of the victorious. He'd gotten there in time and patted himself on the back for ditching James and sneaking back up. He knew she wouldn't leave her children. He'd just waited. They couldn't go far without the truck. Oh, he felt so smart, so ahead of even himself. The beauty of how things work out. He wouldn't even need the damned rent-an-army. They'd just drive away while the sheeted followers were regrouping. He had a hard-on, it was all so delicious. Of course, he wouldn't leave without Penny. She was the prize. They could all sort out the messy details with their family therapist. He'd seen that bitch Daisy and hoped to drive the Mother Healer right past her nose. He hoped he ran over her foot. Hal couldn't go anywhere without the keys anyway, which Isaac had conveniently grabbed. Oh, he kept thinking what a glorious day it was.

Hal was racing Isaac's way, leading the pack, his poor son wailing as though he'd been stung by a bee. Hal's two parents were traveling faster than your average senior citizens but were carrying much bigger children. They lagged behind Hal and had both turned around when they heard Penny's face hit the stone walk. Isaac had also served as a beacon on the highway of their escape.

The tape of the moment the girls saw their mother on her knees and bleeding was frightening. It was a live feed, and the audience was caught in the middle of their mockery at the Mother Healer's message. They stopped in midjoke and gasped at both the amount of blood pouring from her mouth and the revelation of her true identity, her face uncovered and exposed. They were watching her lose her children and under their breath began to say, "Get in the car. Get in the car. Hurry. Get up and get in the car."

Isaac was coming toward Penny to help her up, the keys twinkling in his hand as he advanced. He made it just past Hal when he spotted Daisy at the edge of the forest. The setting sun gleamed off of the shiny cold metal barrel of the Colt she held pointed out at him, and the reflection got caught in Penny's eyes. Every sense she had was held captive. Her body was rolled up in the sheet with her hands trying to pull and rip it free; her ears were filled with the sounds of her crying children and her own pleas. Her mouth tasted the coppery slickness of the blood as her nose drank in its smell. The most horrible of all was that sixth sense that could detect Daisy's pain from yards and yards away, the kind of torment that makes animals in traps gnaw off their own limbs. In her mind Penny could see Daisy slide the clip up into the butt of the gun and secure it. Lock, stock and barrel, everything about the situation fell together with a sickening click.

From behind them, at the top of the cottage, a window flew open. Penny heard Midge scream, "There's a shooter! She has a gun!"

Daisy, being no marksman, was given only one lucky shot in the entire sequence of events. That it was the first shot of many to follow made it statistically unbelievable. From her stance just in front of the woods, with an untrained hand, Daisy aimed and shot Midge dead on. Brad Leezak filmed her falling headfirst out of the window and hitting the pavement with a sickening crunch. Viewers everywhere went wild. The hole in Midge's chest was big enough to fit a fist through. The TV stations were so stunned, they didn't edit out the scene of Midge lying broken on the ground. Brad himself was unable to move and seemed not to notice that he was still holding the camera. The shots mimicked his panic as he first stared at the body and then panned the surrounding area jerkily, looking for the shooter. Yards away, the microphone in Kevin's hand picked up his heavy breathing.

If Daisy's first shot had been wild and unsuccessful, most likely it would have frightened everyone into action. Penny might have gotten untangled. Mary and Harvey might have turned back toward the truck and lunged through the doors. Perhaps Hal would have hit the ground and covered his son with his body. Midge's forward dive out of the window was just too incredible and Daisy's shot too exact. Like a herd of deer caught in oncoming headlights, they were frozen, and even the children didn't breathe. The time between the first shot and the slew of firing that ensued was almost an eternity, time that almost no one was able to make any use of.

Chapter Thirty-six

Jetta had spent right up to the end of her life wondering what the point of it all was. She'd raised children but struggled as a mother. Was that her calling, to bring up her sons and daughters to do something wonderful for the world? Would one of them discover the cure for cancer? Would one of them dig up the bones to fill in the missing link of evolution? Maybe one of her grandchildren would. That just felt so far off. How unsatisfying, she'd often thought, for your entire purpose to not unfold until you were cold in your grave. Having the reason for your existence be to produce some other outstanding person three or four generations later seemed unfair. Each person should have their own distinct moment when the mark they would make on the world would be indelible. And shouldn't we know when that moment occurred? To be able to say "This is it! Give it everything you have right now!" would be fulfilling, she thought.

But what if your moment happened when you were a child? Jetta had seen all of those Olympic gold medal winners washed up at twelve. It made the rest of their lives anticlimactic, and who needed that? When she'd revisited the moment in her life when she'd died at the hospital, she saw that she'd been too dramatic. Big scenes were for theaters and two-hour movies. Her life had been a gentle unfolding of many important times. The earth hadn't been shattered by her presence. Life as she knew it hadn't been radically altered by her actions. That had ended up being all right. She'd been important just the same.

All of those thoughts struck her as terribly ironic now. The flashes of what was to come and her powerlessness to change any of it had been maddening. The final vision of what would happen—the memory of what she'd seen as her final act on earth—hit her as she and Louis took their last step from the forest out to the grassy ground that rolled up to the cottage. And it was exactly what she was put on earth to do. It was as vibrantly clear to her as her own name. Yes, the work she'd done as a mother—especially the sacrifices—had been important in reaching this exact moment. Her exploration into that crazy messianic group—how compelled she was to be a part of it made perfect sense now. Having so many sons and even the significance of playing ball with them—particularly basketball, with its dodging and weaving—was clear in the scheme of things.

She'd wanted to know exactly what she'd been born to do, the moment she would make the biggest impact on the world, and here it was. It was also understandable why that knowledge was such a bad idea. She was hideously afraid. Testing her visions and trying to change them hadn't worked, so the inevitability of the next sequence of events was sure. If she'd just been thrown into the mix of the action it would be easier, because she wouldn't be so frightened.

"Knowing what is going to happen to you isn't a good thing," she said to Louis.

Louis looked at her, not understanding.

"It's easier to be brave when you think everything is going to be all right."

Louis reached out to hold her hand, to pat it and tell her that of course everything was going to be all right, when they heard the first shot. He never got to her hand. Jetta stepped out from the cover of the woods with Louis trailing. They saw the group in front of the cottage and heard Midge fall from the window. Into the silence that enshrouded them, Louis screamed, *"No!"*

Jetta wasn't wasting any energy yelling. She took off toward the house, running as fast as she could on her broken ankle. The pain was excruciating but Jetta let it complain. She ground the bones together to get the speed she needed. With a backward turn of her head she saw Louis behind her, trying to catch up, and Daisy coming at her from the other side of the clearing. It wasn't Jetta she was after, Jetta knew, but Daisy would shoot at her just the same to get to Isaac. From deep inside her she forced her broken foot to run just a little bit faster.

Brad Leezak kept his camera on the circle of the Mother Healer and those around her. His film was designed to cover ladies' auxiliary events, mayors cutting the ribbons of new supermarkets, local political rallies. It wasn't meant to record a barrage of bullets. It wasn't the time-elapsed film used to show the slowed-down journey of a single raindrop or its splatter pattern when it made impact. Instead, editors would later take a page from the National Hockey League: They slowed everything down as much as physically possible and gave each bullet the color blue so it could be followed like a hockey puck on its trajectory into the targets. Even with this visual cue, it was difficult to follow the chain of events as each bullet orchestrated them.

After her one lucky shot, Daisy was just as stunned as everyone in her line of fire. Getting over that quickly, she stepped forward, facing Isaac and holding her weapon out in front of her. She savored the moment and the outlandish look in his eyes, which came more and more into focus the closer she got to him. Wrapping her hands around his throat would have been infinitely more satisfying, but this didn't suck, either. His frightened face was made all the more wonderful because it included a generous helping of shock. Was it shock over her balls? Was it wonder at her matching his ability to kill? It was irrelevant. He thought he'd get away with it and he hadn't. He wouldn't. Unconsciously mirroring Isaac's very sentiments just seconds ago, she thought, *Glorious, glorious day,* then opened fire into the crowd.

While Daisy was savoring the moment, Jetta was running as she never had in her whole life. She ran toward Penny but scanned each person's position. As Penny finally untangled herself and was rising to a standing position, Mary and Harvey stood with the twins in their arms, blocking her path to the truck. Hal was at the head of the line, holding Benny, and Isaac was moving off the path and back toward Hal. He'd been trying to get around everyone to get to Penny.

Penny could see Daisy aiming her gun directly at Isaac. The hole in Midge flashed in her memory, big and open. The first spray of bullets hit no people but everything around them. A ground-level window exploded. The old wagon wheel leaning against the porch lost its spokes. One wooden step shot up and clocked Kevin Wood in the head but good. His remaining interviews would be bloody. A plastic piece of the camera handle cracked off and Bart Leezak counted and recounted his fingers to be sure all were present and accounted for. Daisy realized she wasn't close enough. The gun kept bucking up on her and she placed her arm over the top of the barrel to counteract its swing like she'd seen a woman do in an old Western. She started aiming at Penny, hoping some of her shots would also down Isaac.

The next spray largely hit the cottage, leaving oddly shaped punch holes through its brick and siding. *Isaac probably thought I couldn't hit the side of a barn,* Daisy thought wildly. And she opened fire again. There were no direct hits this time, either, but a few ricocheted into the most unfortunate places. The news would put this bullet in blue and show how it found an old abandoned metal planter on its side and bounced from the porch into the group. Mary took the bullet through the back, a hole in her to match the ones in the house. Killed instantly, she fell on top of her granddaughter, who'd seen the front of Mary open up.

"Lydia!" Penny screamed. Lydia had missed the bullet by a quarter of an inch but was now in danger of being crushed.

Harvey dropped Julie to attend to his wife. Julie began wandering through the fire like a duck in a shooting gallery.

Jetta continued to run toward them, as close now as Daisy was but fighting every step not to fall. She directed all of her intensity on Penny and ignored the rest of the group, concentrating only on her target, her ultimate job. She thought of dragging Penny to safety, of pulling her behind the truck, although the house, looming in the distance, would be the safest spot. But she truly doubted she could get her to either of those places. She knew she couldn't. Just putting herself in front of Penny would do no good. The bullets were meant to tear through walls and destroy what was behind them. Her strategies raced in her mind, ricocheting like the bullets that flew around her.

When the tape was reviewed later, many would speculate on how this little old lady knew exactly what way to protect the Mother Healer. Jetta knew Penny would spring toward the children, aiming for the one most in jeopardy. Lydia was under her grandmother and Hal had

Benny. With a sweep of her eyes, Jetta spotted Julie off to her left. Penny was directly in front of Jetta, but like her son Frankie's double-fade basketball move against his brother Vinny, Jetta threw her body not to where Penny was but where she expected she'd be in the next second, lunging toward Julie. Penny wouldn't think about the value of her own life. Like any mother, she'd protect her babies at all costs. Jetta sprang at the same time Penny did. Julie was knocked to the ground and Jetta pulled Penny into a ball and under her, trying to squeeze her into a mass with as little surface area and as close to the ground as possible.

Louis himself had changed the direction of his trajectory. He didn't bring himself into the line of fire. The presence of the camera crew struck him as he ran, and he found himself tempted to flee into the cover of the woods and record an eyewitness account in his brain as he watched the climax of the drama unfold. The Pulitzer danced in front of him one last time. The indecision in his legs lasted not even one full second. Louis did change his path but headed towards Daisy, the air filling his lungs and giving him speed. Six steps were between them, and he planned to jump on the seventh and tackle her with his body.

James arrived on the scene as Jetta was putting herself between Penny and the bullets, as Louis was trying to get to Daisy, as Mary was bleeding onto the path, very much dead. Harvey, the first husband to cry over his wife that day, was shot in the head just as James was stumbling across his own wife, so alive when he left her only a half hour earlier. James would join her when a stray shot found the back of his neck, clean and vulnerable with the policeman traditional short crew cut. He would only have to endure the idea of living without his partner for a brief twenty-five seconds. Five more steps and Louis would have Daisy.

Jetta jumped to the left and collided with Penny in midair. Ignoring the screams of her ankle, she yanked Penny beneath her, forcing her to the ground and under her, using the sheets against her to wrap her up, putting her out of the way of the bullets as best as she could. Little Julie, in shock, had found her way behind the truck. Penny was screaming, "My children! I need to get to my children!"

Jetta screamed to Julie, "Get behind the house! Get behind the house!"

Julie was wandering toward the forest as if she were on a family hike, oblivious to the bullets. Her shock was deep, and Jetta's warnings didn't register with her at all.

Pinned down, Penny struggled against Jetta and tried desperately to get Hal's attention. Hal had turned and was heading to the truck, finally out of his own momentary shock and trying to find shelter. Before he could even turn in that direction, Isaac grabbed Benjamin out of Hal's arms as easily as picking a ripe blueberry off a bush.

Penny went completely wild. She bucked and screamed, "Hal! Get Benny! Get Benny! Hal! Hal!" and turned to Jetta, demanding, "Get off of me! My son!" But she was unable to throw the older woman off: Even in the midst of the chaos, Jetta's ankle was repaired at her contact with the Mother Healer, giving her just enough strength to push Penny down and keep her where she was.

The final shots erupted from the last clip Daisy had hidden under her robes. There was just enough time for one last spray as Hal threw himself at Isaac, who held Benny's tiny body in front of his own. He used the baby as some sort of protection when he ran back to the truck, keys jingling, like a cowardly gladiator with a tissue for a shield. Hal was a half step behind him, arms outstretched and trying to grab. Jetta gave Penny a final push earthward and Penny screamed, one last time, *"My SON!"*

"I'll be with him," Jetta promised, and closed her eyes tightly, waiting for the blasts.

Jetta took her bullets through the back, a group in the shape of a circle. She was again on the bridge and waiting for her small companion while Penny still struggled to get out from under her body. Three shots missed Hal by hairs, and he could hear them ringing through his ears as he watched the last bullet pierce his only son's chest and travel through Isaac. The loss was emphasized by the sound of Louis slamming into Daisy and both of them hitting the ground, the gun flying into a rock some twenty yards away. As if sympathetically expressing Hal and Penny's horror, the truck exploded with the impact of the bullet that ripped through its gas tank.

Everyone was thrown backward. The world screamed collectively in the private spaces in front of their televisions. The Mother Healer's loss was their own. Brad Leezak hit the ground still holding his camera, and the last thing people everywhere saw of his transmission was the blue, cloudless sky before their screens went black.

Chapter Thirty-seven

Penny could wriggle out from under Jetta's lifeless body. She could finally throw off the binding sheets. Just barely, she could pull her son out from Isaac's dead grasp. But she could do nothing to save him. Bringing him to her, she wrapped her arms around his silent form and brought her legs up, encircling him in front of her belly. If only she could put him back up inside of her, where she could start all over again and keep him safe. Her limbs were locked together and she bent her head to rest against his so that no part of him was left untouched. No one else would be there for her. Whether the sun was setting or Louis was crying as he restrained a screaming Daisy, it was all gone for her. The only thing she would see was her son, pictured in her mind as the perfect little boy she had, his golden hairs framing his beautiful face, his one white edge of a tooth still not fully emerged. His crying played in the back of her mind like a song, and she couldn't understand at all what had ever bothered her about it. Crying was breathing. Crying was being alive. She would encircle him and hold that gift out to him, carrying him back from the bridge. She would go there and not take no for an answer.

Hal was screaming behind her, as hysterical as a person can get without imploding. The last thing Penny felt was one of the arteries in his head bubble and bulge, threatening to burst.

"Penny! You have to bring him back! Penny, please!" He had his hands on her shoulders and he shook her back and forth as if that would expedite things.

Penny could no longer hear Hal. Everything was the gift, the healing she needed to give Benjamin. Over and over she tried to dive onto that path to the bridge, to ride the trip he'd taken and force herself there so she could bring him back. It had become almost a familiar place, easily accessible.

Hal's screaming seemed to go on somewhere almost apart from him. Louis watched the man, aware that a part of Hal had snapped. But Louis was busy holding down the shooter and looking for the gun. She'd surely bolt if he stood up. Louis straddled her, his knees tucked around, holding her arms against her body. She flapped like a fish, also screaming, and there were moments Louis couldn't tell who had said what.

"Don't you help Isaac! Don't you dare!"

"Do something, Penny!" Hal yelled, still shaking her back and forth.

Penny could see the bridge but not as she had before. It came and went like a bad radio transmission when you're driving through a rainstorm. It was there in her sight, then it would be gone. The mist was still around it, though it was somehow thicker. For half a second Penny saw Mary step onto the threshold to the bridge, but before she could look around for Benny she was back, holding his small, still body. She dove back in again, a swimmer diving for lost treasure.

Hal had finally shaken her so violently that she fell over, holding her fetal position and clamping down harder on her son. "What are you doing? You're going to suffocate him!" Hal was pacing back and forth in front of Penny, pulling out his hair in fistfuls that rained down around him until he could secure another patch between his clawing fingers. He caught sight of his mother, and in between yelling at Penny and crying he tore out another chunk of hair, then rushed to get his Lydia out from under her grandmother.

Penny was approaching the bridge, then on it, then off, on and off again and again, an old television set with its picture rolling. There was nothing she could hold on to and she could not see Benny there at all. Her mind was nauseous with confusion. She moaned.

Hal had heard that moan once before. He could see a picture of Penny in her eighteenth hour of labor with the twins, asking "Hal, why aren't I dying? Why isn't this pain killing me?" Her face was clamped tight and the obstetrician announced that they'd have to cut the babies from her. In three and a half minutes, a thin red line followed the surgeon's scalpel, and Lydia and Julie were pulled into the world. Hal had been so joyous yet so oddly disturbed to see a large hole in the middle of his wife. He couldn't imagine any amount of surgery being able to put her completely back together.

This scene was like a slaughterhouse, and Hal slipped in the puddles of blood, crashing down on his mother's body. Everyone who'd been shot had been dead less than two minutes, yet Hal would have sworn they'd been on that slate walkway nearly a lifetime. Surely the film in the camera had run out five times over by now. What could he do? His mother's big accusing eyes stared through him, her red lips parted as if wanting to give him some forceful direction even after death. *What should I do?* he wanted to ask her. He could not gather up his daughter in his arms. He could not bear the thought of searching for her twin, only to possibly find her dead. If he held Lydia now it would be giving up, settling for the business of comforting. Shock settled in oddly for Hal. Most people walk around dazed and unresponsive. Lydia was fitting into that category in a textbook-perfect way, her knees drawn up close to her, her eyes unseeing as she rocked herself back and forth, sucking her thumb until it might've fallen right off for the demands placed on it.

Hal watched himself and the scene. His consciousness was in the wings, detached almost completely from his moving self. *Look at me moving my dead mother's body,* he thought. *I'm having such a time. She's heavier than I ever imagined. This is where the term* deadweight *comes from. I'm laughing at that thought. Now I'm crying. Look at my face. It doesn't know what to do. . . .*

Hal pulled Mary, mangled and bloody over to Penny so that her body lay spoonlike against her daughter-in-law's. Not waiting for results, Hal found his father, a man he'd only had one true week with, a gift-wrapped person only recently opened and barely enjoyed. Mourning him would be hideous, and Hal, from his offstage seating, wondered if it might have been easier if he'd never had a glimpse of Harvey at all. It was like winning the lottery and getting mugged on the way to the bank. Hal dragged him over to Penny also, making sure they touched. Somehow it didn't seem gruesome to make Penny a sandwich of his dead parents and expect they'd all get up and walk away from it. There was no mental gravity anymore. Hal's sanity threatened to fly away with all of his old rules and assumptions that made perfect sense a week ago.

Touching Mary and Harvey brought the bridge back into better focus and gave Penny a leverage she hadn't had. The view of the threshold stayed in place and her surroundings came into focus. Mary and Harvey were ahead in the distance, holding hands and walking slowly toward the other end.

"Mary!" Penny screamed. "Harvey!"

From the corner of her eye she could see the side of the bridge where Jetta stood holding her son, and Penny rushed ahead to get to them. In only two steps the figure stood before her, blocking her way.

"I want my son!"

The figure was silent and Penny could feel an apologetic air about it.

"I need him!"

The figure held its shadow arms out, blocking the bridge to her.

"He's mine!" Penny waited. "Please," she started to beg. "Please. I'll heal the whole world. I'll do anything. Just bring back my son!"

Penny could see Jetta turn away from her and head up the bridge toward Mary and Harvey.

"Mary!" Penny yelled. "Harvey! Benny! Bring him back! Please!"

Before Penny could see any of their faces to know whether they'd heard her and would scoop Benjamin up and bring him back to her, the fog closed around them.

"Benny! I love you, Benny! Mommy loves you! I'm sorry!" And then she whispered, "Mommy's sorry."

Penny sank to her knees, collapsing and screaming again and again for them to help her get back her son. The figure stood guard. She would not leave until she had him.

Hal watched and waited, expecting the healing that refused to come.

The policemen, not having a headstart but unencumbered by television cameras and lighting equipment, came in a close second in the race to the top of the mountain. They four-wheeled their way up, leading the ambulances and landing also by water plane on the high lake. There was a uniform effect on those who stepped into the clearing, a pull of their heads back and away from the blood that looked as though it had been dumped from the sky. They stepped gingerly over the shrapnel from the truck and stomped on the evidence of the scene in their utter disbelief.

Media crews watched the police and medics trying to disengage the dead baby from its mother. All attempts to pull them apart failed even after it was determined Penny was still living, if unresponsive, and might need medical treatment. She was thrown on a stretcher, still a ball of protective motherhood encircling her child, a stiff human cage. They were put on the tiny plane for the nearest hospital, and only a sliver of Penny's mind registered that her daughters, alive, were becoming smaller and smaller, farther away from her, as she was airlifted off the mountain.

Chapter Thirty-eight

The blue highlights the news gave the bullet arcs were mesmerizing. It was only a three-minute film segment, but—slowed down to pinpoint all of the action—it felt as if it went on forever. People were positively shattered, but it was like a roadside accident: too gory not to look at. It was shown over and over, until the average viewer could describe each second with precise accuracy. Somehow the sounds of the gunshots and the screams of the Mother Healer begging for the lives of her children were more horrifying than the sight of it. Some stations again employed the split screens, one side showing the Mother Healer delivering her brief message voiced over the other side's film of the carnage. The length of the message was exactly the same as the time it took to watch each bullet find its way around the top of the mountain. It couldn't have been timed more perfectly had it been shot and edited in a studio.

The trial of Daisy Rourke was watched with equal interest. She was convicted in record time, and the city hosting her trial was overrun: Collectively, it's businesses took in more money than they had for the last ten years put together. Adding to the award-winning numbers was the amount of time Daisy actually put in toward her two consecutive life sentences. Despite being put into a protective custody section, Daisy was knifed after a brief two-week stint as an inmate. Investigations found no evidence against anyone in particular, although some details of the crime actually pointed toward a ring of guards. Their connection with the Mother Healer movement did not go unnoticed, but with so little proof, the hoopla died down quickly. No one screamed over the injustice. After such a short time apart, Isaac and Daisy were reunited.

In the days that immediately followed the shootings on the mountain, people kept an eye out for Penny's son's funeral. When none was forthcoming, they had their own, a memorial service for all who had died, but especially for the boy. It was a ceremony that was entirely too large for Penny's small hometown. One hundred thousand came, and some had to hear the prayers from miles away through speakers or on portable television sets they brought along. Strangers held on to one another, openly mourning the loss of the Mother Healer's son with an undercurrent of great sadness at their own loss of the Mother Healer herself who, seven days later, was still missing.

By the first year after the famous Mountain Miracle, thousands made a pilgrimage to the tiny house where the Mother Healer used to live. They filled her flower boxes with her favorite petunias. Collectors put back the Chaneys' furniture and returned her kitchen spoons. They brought flowers in huge bunches and made walls of them along the front and around to the back, marking off her yard. A group was quickly created, a restoration committee that declared the small country-blue home a historical building and was trying to recreate the exact look it had when Penny had lived there. A plaque was erected in the shape of a woman in long, flowing robes, her message spelled out word for word across the front. Her grass was cut and her windows washed. A candle-lighting ceremony was held every evening at sunset. Despite the tremendous volume, it was always a very quiet affair. People sobbed.

Mt. Pleasant was also quickly designated an official historical site. It went from police tape keeping out the public to a work in progress, with ten teams preserving every possible scintilla of artifact that marked the passing of the event. The followers' camp was made permanent, with placards set both outside and inside, describing the sites and their purposes. Canvas was lifted above the earth to prevent rot; foodstuff was shellacked and left in its exact location for all to see. *The White Book* was laid out in the sleeping tents, open to the page the followers were reading at the time of the Mountain Miracle.

The caskets were kept where they'd fallen when the dead had risen, with concrete poured carefully under each to make it permanent. They were varnished against the rain, and each person's life story was laid out on large metal plaques. At the base of the mountain were numbered parking lots in various colors to match the open shuttle buses that drove visitors to the gated entranceway. People bought white paper sheets for ten dollars, which they fastened around their bodies with white stickers instead of pins. For five dollars you could purchase a set for your child. Bright ski tags showed if you'd paid for the all-day pass, which included every sight on the mountain as well as their corresponding tours. Buckets were placed beyond the ticket booths for extra donations. Entries could be bought for the Finding the Mother Healer Lottery. The prize money would be split between those who guessed where she would be found and those that guessed when she would be found. Every day had been gobbled up until the year 2030. Stone walkways led tourists through the media camp at the bottom of the mountain, up past the coffins and to the plastic model of the human fence that had stood there. A marble statue of the Mother Healer, looking as if she had just walked through an opening in the fence, reached a robed arm toward the line of coffins.

Twenty thousand visitors viewed Aunt Myrtle's cabin by the end of the second week it was opened to the public. A copy of the Chaneys' luggage was strewn across the walkway next to the plastic statues of each person in his or her last position when found by the mass media and as described by the police. Jetta's body would forever hover over the Mother Healer's. Louis would go on tackling Daisy Rourke for the next two thousand years. Jetta and Louis would begin to be called saints until it was vocabulary as common as the name Mother Healer had become. The Catholic Church continuously tried to explain the beatification process and why Jetta and Louis could not legally wear the term *saint*, to no avail.

While most walked the tour, many found an inspirational spot and got down on their knees in the manner of the statues of the original followers. They found rocks around the cabin and rubbed them along their bodies or specifically on their areas of affliction. The Mother Healer's bed was a popular spot, and they bent over the velvet rope cordoning off the private items in the room to touch it, hoping some essence of her healing power remained there. Parents brought their sick children. In warmer months they dipped them in the lake; in colder ones they ran their small hands along the tiny open coffins, hoping this would ward off their illnesses. Many claimed to be healed.

As the tour wound down on the opposite side of the mountain, a security team frisked leaving visitors. No purses or bags of any kind were permitted past the gates upon entry. The paper sheets had no pockets, and all items found on your person upon exiting would be confiscated, including rocks and plant life. Chunks of wood from the log cabin were regularly glued back by a busy restoration team. An entire security squad roamed the mountain, asking people not to pick anything up. Cameras spotted tourists whose hands were seen under their robes. It was very difficult to leave with so much as a fern. Ebay was stocked with the pieces retrieved by only the most diligent burglars. It was a profitable trade, and some took it on as a full-time business.

Seminars were held at the followers' camp, with lectures given around the rock where Penny had pleaded to God. Flashing computer signs rolled out sentence after sentence, telling visitors about scholarly lecture times and the locations of each event. Hundreds of these pilgrims would go back to their towns and erect giant log cabins honoring the Mother Healer. Meetings would follow their grand openings, and one or two people, usually women, would be assigned the role of leader of the fellowship. Denials that their meetings, prayer groups and emergent literature constituted a full-fledged new religion were vehement until the government offered them their rightful tax write-offs. Who could turn their back on help?

A variant group formed, breaking away from the Healers, as they were called in their log cabins. They were those who'd attended the memorial service for Benjamin Chaney and were distinctly unhappy about having no body to weep over. It struck them as odd that the baby was not buried anywhere identifiable. No one spoke of the family service for him. The people at the hospital who claimed to have pried Penny Chaney and her son apart were unconvincing in that they had no signed sheet from any undertaker accepting his body. Where was the death certificate? The world felt the news was too big for there to be no informant. That the biggest family in the world could have a private funeral was laughable. The group started a movement called Follow the Son. They were convinced that the boy was under wraps—figuratively speaking, of course—and would follow in his mother's footsteps, perhaps in a bolder way, with somewhat more clarity as to what his people should do. They prayed to him regularly and waited for his return, searching the globe for signs of him. They poured out their hearts and their funds. Waiting is a costly business.

All of these factions were studied in universities in basic comparative religion courses. Students on the cusp of their doctoral dissertations began the complicated work of pulling the threads together, connecting the ancient texts to what had been done and said by the Mother Healer. One famous scholar showed quite clearly how the numerology of her brief message coincided perfectly with that of five major prophetic works. A group of theologians of varied backgrounds locked themselves up together in a Harvard think tank for three solid weeks and emerged with the final refinement of *The White Book*. A conservative representative of the Healers declared it as blasphemous, which consequently sent it to *The New York Times* Best Seller List for forty weeks. It bobbled from number to number but refused to fall off entirely. The publishing company hired an additional four hundred temporary employees to handle the shipping alone.

Scores of related books were also published. Most of these claimed to be eyewitness accounts of what had transpired. Everyone from the Chaneys' neighbors to the nurses at Southlawn Hospital to a myriad of the healed wrote of the chain of events they experienced. A larger book bringing all of these pieces together as collected works was in the making. The world soaked it up like starving children at a feast. Even mere speculation sold, and two people in chairs debating points regarding any area of the Mother Healer topic was watched with a frantic intensity. Elvis was moved to a lower line with a smaller font on the fronts of supermarket checkout magazines.

A cable network sprang up called the Healer's Network Television, HNT for short. Its logo was a log cabin perched on a mountainside, and their 800 number put you through to a televangelist who would offer healing for a meager twenty-five-dollar donation. The permanence of the healing effect, they warned, was based greatly on the subject's dedication to the Mother Healer's cause and thus could not be one hundred percent guaranteed. The fifty-five-dollar deluxe package came with *The White Book* and a guide to keeping your particular ailment at bay. HNT televised from cities around the globe. All those twenties assured a studio set of heavenly proportions. They told their adoring fans they were just one step away from catching up to the Mother Healer herself. Promos for upcoming shows always promised near glimpses of her.

A more serious team comprised of rich thirty-somethings with no kids and a nose for adventure had made their life's work finding the Mother Healer. A whiff of scuffle in South America and they were parachuting into the jungle, interviewing witnesses and studying clues. Stories of lame children suddenly walking and they were off to the Andes with their Nike hiking boots and subzero mountain packs. They were positive they were the ones who were only one step behind her. Their favorite jaunt so far was to Rio de Janeiro, where the beer was cold and the women hot, even if any trace of the Mother Healer was nowhere to be found.

A fraction of a single percent of the world's population returned to the religion they were originally born into and rededicated their lives to living its values. This was just enough.

Chapter Thirty-nine

The sun tries to rise in a small South African village. The mist struggles to keep the dark of the night. Dew has settled on everything, and Louis Klotz, former reporter, feels the dampness in his feet. He follows a beaten path around a squatting tree and sees her tent in the distance. Behind him, he knows people will be waking, readying themselves to fight the problems of the day. Tall grass swishes around his feet and he stomps through it to get to her.

"Penny," he calls softly, tapping his fingers lightly on the thin canvas triangle that is her door. He gets no response.

"Penny," he tries again. "You know we have to hurry. The sun is almost up."

He knows she is in there. He can hear her breathing.

"Mother Healer."

"I told you not to call me that!" Her words echo across the plains around them and bounce through his ears.

"It's the only way I can get you to answer me," he says simply, a matter-of-fact piece of his day. He looks at his watch, which tells him it is almost five o'clock.

Louis can hear her sigh and he sits down in the wet grass, waiting patiently.

Penny lifts her face out of her pillow and pulls her arms from beneath it. In her right hand is a newspaper picture that she sleeps with of Hal with Lydia and Julie.

They are taller now, almost to his shoulders, and they cringe from the bright lights of the camera, which assault them from all sides. Hal's mouth is open and his teeth poke out as he is caught shouting at what must be paparazzi. It looks like he will bite them in the next frame. They are leaving through the back door of a Howard Johnson's in Kansas. The last picture she had was of the three of them in Wyoming, but it was only their backs and sides and each of them had on hats and sunglasses. The ink has blackened Penny's hands as well as her sleeping bag. She tries to hold it by its corners as it is already beginning to fade. Part of Lydia's nose appears to be missing, and she can hardly tell how long Julie keeps her hair or if those are pants or jeans they're wearing.

Penny can smell cow dung with the next breath she takes and hears the bell of the guilty party as it is led out to pasture. She does know she must hurry, and the urgency inside her has built up to an intolerable level. It has been three days since she's healed, which is two days too many. They travel in a random manner, avoiding linear geographical patterns and jumping from continent to continent. All her work is done before full sunup. Louis will have collapsed their tents and packed their light bags before she even reaches the town clinic. She will move among the customers waiting in long winding lines around whatever roach-infested, condemned building that particular third world village calls its hospital. Carelessly bumping into each, they will curse her and call her names and she'll be gone, running as they realize what has happened to them. Louis follows, often yelling behind him, "Don't tell!" in whatever language the citizens speak. It is as much as she allows. He knows how to say this phrase seventeen different ways. Some towns are better than others at keeping her secret.

She pulls on a T-shirt and a faded pair of jeans, wondering if this will be the town she gets trapped in, if this will be the morning the world yells, "Found you!" followed by a round of "Ally, ally oxen free!" like in her childhood games of ring-a-levio, the rules of which she has forgotten. The tremendous filing cabinet of her memories has a few drawers shut now, locked to even her own prying fingers. Some things are easier to let stay buried.

The tent zipper sticks and Louis helps her out. A dab of some sort of jelly from his hurried breakfast makes a partial mustache on his upper lip and Penny wipes it away, brushing it off on her jeans. Louis could eat anything anywhere they went. He is softer, rounder now. His cheeks have filled out and his eyes are a clearer blue. Life on the run seems to suit him. Penny has not eaten since the day of the shootings. She imagines her large and small intestines collapsing from lack of work, filling with a dusty quietness she cannot achieve in her mind, which works enough for ten other organs. It tries to trick her into believing that everything was for the best. It tells her she has made and continues to make a difference in the world. Every night it tries to soothe her with dreams of her old life.

When Louis roused her, she was dreaming she was in her old kitchen, making a dinner with the food she and Hal had to buy on their meager budget. Grilled cheese sandwiches sizzled in the pan her grandmother had handed down to her. She was attempting to make something exotic out of canned fruit cocktail. One of the girls was in the bathroom yelling for assistance. Benjamin's bottle had fallen to the floor and he was screaming indignantly. Hal would walk through the door any minute. The sandwiches were sending out a message of smoke signals. Someone had dumped the large green box of tiny building blocks in the doorway to the kitchen. A can of creamed corn was boiling over on the stove. Right after

Benjamin was born, this was her worst nightmare. Everyone would be crying and ten things needed her attention and the house was a mess, wall-to-wall toys littering every square inch of living space. These dreams, then classified as nightmares, would send her bolting upright in bed, the sweat pouring off her in buckets. Now she cherished them. They were the oases of a life she hadn't known how much she loved. Some nights, lying on the sleeping bag, the moisture from her breath condensing along the top of her tent, she'd dream she was doing the laundry. Piles and piles of it would be heaped around her, and she sat in the middle, just folding. She resisted waking up. She wept because the dream was not reality.

Penny walks a few steps up the dirt path, just a groove where the grass does not grow. The scenery changes every few days so no place is ever familiar. The only consistent thing is the space around her, often miles of it. There are no Dairy Queens where she and Louis travel, no malls or mini-marts. Years or even decades from now she imagines she will still feel like a speck of dust on a windy plain. It is a real fear that she might suddenly blow away, having to hold on to the top of a tree so as not to be thrown into space. Most days she is just grateful that each of her feet, once lifted up and placed forward, make it back to the ground. She tries not to look up.

In their halting, quiet conversations Louis and Penny have discussed returning to the mainstream of the modern world. The sentences of suggestion fade off into the three dots of unfinished ideas. There was one time they were almost forced back into the world's eye, a time when they'd just started out and were more feeling but also more careless. Penny would come to each hospital and touch the patients individually. She would receive their thanks and their blessings. Local papers would write of her passing through, describing her and building monuments with her likeness from memory. Sometimes they stayed and enjoyed the hospitality of the families of those she'd healed. One morning they awoke to cameras and nearly didn't escape.

Penny makes her way up to this next village hospital, most likely a two-room hut with no running water. Louis tells her that today is the day this month when the city doctor will be in. The lines will be long and patients will have been walking since the middle of the night to get a spot along the wall of the building. She realizes some things are becoming familiar after all. Just once she would like to be there when the educated man with the medical bag arrives to find he has no sick to treat.

She turns the last bend. Louis is behind her with their few things. A little boy stands on the side of the path and turns his head up to look at Penny. He comes up to her waist and holds out his hand. Penny takes it and they walk on to the village. It is just one stop on the road from this place to the next and the next and the next.

Visit
❖ Pocket Books ❖
online at

www.SimonSays.com

Keep up on the latest new releases from your favorite authors, as well as author appearances, news, chats, special offers and more.

Pocket Books

2381-01